Key Scenes

- On the scaffold (pt. 1, <s>Hester +</s> Pearl
- Hester + Chillingworth at Jail
- Chilling. + Dimmes. at dimmes. house
- On the scaffold (Pt. 2) Dimmesdale
- Hester + Chill. talk at river
- Hester + Dimmes. talk in forest
- Dimmesdale's forest walk
- On the scaffold (Pt. 3) Dimmesdale, Hester and Pearl

Test Friday 9-29-17

Key Scenes
themes
Characters
Symbols

The Scarlet Letter

Nathaniel Hawthorne

THE EMC MASTERPIECE SERIES

Access Editions

EMC/Paradigm Publishing
St. Paul, Minnesota

Staff Credits:

For **EMC/Paradigm Publishing**, St. Paul, Minnesota

Laurie Skiba
Editor

Eileen Slater
Editorial Consultant

Shannon O'Donnell Taylor
Associate Editor

For **Penobscot School Publishing, Inc.**, Danvers, Massachusetts

Editorial

Robert D. Shepherd
President, Executive Editor

Christina Kolb
Managing Editor

Kim Leahy Beaudet
Editor

Sara Hyry
Editor

Marilyn Murphy Shepherd
Editor

Sharon Salinger
Copyeditor

Design and Production

Charles Q. Bent
Production Manager

Sara Day
Art Director

Tatiana Cicuto
Compositor

ISBN 0–8219–1617–3

Published by EMC/Paradigm Publishing
875 Montreal Way
St. Paul, Minnesota 55102

Printed in the United States of America.
16 15 14 13   xxx   15 16 17 18 19

Table of Contents

The Life and Works of Nathaniel Hawthorne iv
Time Line of Hawthorne's Life vi
The Historical Context of *The Scarlet Letter* viii
Characters in *The Scarlet Letter* xii
Illustrations xiv

The Custom-House, Introductory to "The Scarlet Letter"   1
Chapter I, The Prison-Door 42
Chapter II, The Market-Place 44
Chapter III, The Recognition 56
Chapter IV, The Interview 65
Chapter V, Hester at Her Needle 74
Chapter VI, Pearl 83
Chapter VII, The Governor's Hall 93
Chapter VIII, The Elf-Child and the Minister 100
Chapter IX, The Leech 111
Chapter X, The Leech and His Patient 120
Chapter XI, The Interior of a Heart 131
Chapter XII, The Minister's Vigil 138
Chapter XIII, Another View of Hester 150
Chapter XIV, Hester and the Physician 158
Chapter XV, Hester and Pearl 166
Chapter XVI, A Forest Walk 172
Chapter XVII, The Pastor and His Parishioner 180
Chapter XVIII, A Flood of Sunshine 189
Chapter XIX, The Child at the Brook-Side 197
Chapter XX, The Minister in a Maze 203
Chapter XXI, The New England Holiday 215
Chapter XXII, The Procession 223
Chapter XXIII, The Revelation of the Scarlet Letter . . . 235
Chapter XXIV, Conclusion 243

Plot Analysis of *The Scarlet Letter* 250
Creative Writing Activities 252
Critical Writing Activities 254
Projects 256
Glossary 258
Handbook of Literary Terms 267

Nathaniel Hawthorne

Nathaniel Hawthorne.
Peabody Essex Museum

Nathaniel Hawthorne (1804–1864). Born on July 4 in Salem, Massachusetts, Nathaniel was the second child and the only son of Elizabeth and Nathaniel Hathorne. By the time Nathaniel was born, five generations of Hathornes had lived in Salem. Two of the most infamous of these ancestors were William Hathorne and his son, John. William was a Puritan leader and a fierce persecutor of the Quakers. He ordered that a Quaker named Ann Coleman receive a public whipping; she almost died during this harsh punishment. John was a judge who conducted hearings during the Salem Witchcraft Trials. As a young man, Nathaniel added a *w* to his last name. Some speculate that he made this change to distance himself from his intolerant Puritan ancestors.

Nathaniel's father was a seaman who caught yellow fever and died in Surinam (Dutch Guiana) in 1808, when Nathaniel was only four years old. The sea captain left his wife with little money, so Elizabeth sold the Hathorne house and moved her family into the home of her more wealthy brothers, the Mannings.

When Nathaniel was nine, he injured his leg and was unable to attend school for almost two years; however, he began reading widely on his own. Hawthorne was particularly influenced by the allegory and symbolism in works such as John Bunyan's *Pilgrim's Progress* and Edmund Spenser's *The Faerie Queene*, as well as by Sir Walter Scott's historical romances and by the works of eighteenth-century novelists such as Henry Fielding and Tobias Smollet.

In September of 1821, Hawthorne entered Bowdoin College, where he befriended Henry Wadsworth Longfellow, Franklin Pierce, and Horatio Bridge. In college, Hawthorne continued his extensive reading, enjoyed the Maine outdoors, and excelled in composition. Hawthorne graduated from Bowdoin in 1825 and returned to Salem. For the next twelve years, he wrote prodigiously, attempting to establish himself as a respected writer. He published his first romance, *Fanshawe,* at his own expense but later tried to retrieve all copies of the book and burn them. Similarly, Hawthorne burned his first collection of stories, *Seven Tales of My Native Land,* because he failed to find a publisher. Eventually, in 1830, he published five stories in *The Salem Gazette,* and in 1834, some of his stories appeared in *New*

England Magazine. In 1836, Hawthorne worked as an editor for the Boston-based *The American Magazine of Useful and Entertaining Knowledge.* In 1837, he published *Twice-Told Tales,* a collection of stories that finally brought him recognition. Hawthorne was unaware that his college friend Horatio Bridge had given the publisher financial guarantees against failure as an incentive to publish this work. The same year, Hawthorne met his future wife, Sophia Amelia Peabody, to whom he was engaged in 1838. To save money for his marriage, Hawthorne worked as a salt and coal measurer in the Boston Custom House, and planning for his future, bought shares in Brook Farm, a utopian Transcendentalist community, intending to live there with Sophia once they were married. However, communal living did not agree with Hawthorne, and he soon requested the return of his stock.

Hawthorne and Sophia married on July 9, 1842, and moved into the Old Manse, a house in Concord that they rented from Ralph Waldo Emerson. In Concord, Hawthorne formed friendships with Transcendentalist writers and thinkers such as Emerson, Henry David Thoreau, and Bronson Alcott. In 1845, the Hawthorne family returned to Salem, and in the following year, Hawthorne published *Mosses from an Old Manse,* a work that brought critical acclaim but little financial success. Hawthorne's financial woes were temporarily solved when President James K. Polk made him surveyor of the Salem Custom House. Hawthorne wrote little while working at the Custom House. In 1849, Zachary Taylor, a Whig, became president, and Hawthorne, a Democrat, lost his office. In September, Hawthorne began work on *The Scarlet Letter* and on "The Custom-House," which satirizes the Salem Custom-House and its officers, as well as the Whigs who deprived him of his office. Hawthorne originally planned to include "The Custom House," *The Scarlet Letter,* and other works in a collection called *Old Time Legends; Together with Sketches, Experimental and Ideal.* By 1850, Hawthorne had published *The Scarlet Letter,* and he published *The House of the Seven Gables* by 1851. By this time, he, his wife, and their children had moved from Lenox, Massachusetts, to West Newton, Massachusetts, where Hawthorne's second daughter was born. The Hawthorne family returned to Concord in 1852.

In 1853, President Franklin Pierce appointed Hawthorne to the post of American consul at Liverpool, England, and Hawthorne served in this position for four years before moving his family to Italy for a year. Hawthorne and his family returned to Concord in 1860, where he published a collection of English sketches under the title *Our Old Home* in 1863. Nathaniel Hawthorne died in 1864, leaving several unfinished works.

Hawthorne's friend Ralph Waldo Emerson was a leading Transcendentalist. The Transcendentalists believed in spiritual truths that lay beyond sense perceptions and material things. They also believed that one could glimpse these truths through communion with nature.

Time Line of Hawthorne's Life

July 4, 1804

Nathaniel Hathorne is born in Salem, Massachusetts, son of Elizabeth Clarke Manning Hathorne and Nathaniel Hathorne.

1808

Nathaniel Hathorne's father catches yellow fever and dies in Surinam (Dutch Guiana) while working as a sea captain. Elizabeth Hathorne moves Nathaniel and his two sisters into the Manning family's house.

April 1813

Nathaniel is injured when a ball hits his foot. Unable to attend school for almost two years after this injury, he begins reading widely on his own.

1818

Hathorne's family moves to Raymond, Maine, where Hathorne wanders, hunts, and fishes.

1819

Hathorne returns to Salem to prepare for college.

1821

Hathorne enters Bowdoin College in Brunswick, Maine, near Raymond. There he meets Henry Wadsworth Longfellow, Horatio Bridge, and Franklin Pierce. Shortly after this time, Hawthorne adds a *w* to his last name.

1825

Hawthorne graduates from college and returns to live with his family in Salem.

1828

Hawthorne publishes *Fanshawe*, a romance set in a college, at his own expense, but later tries to recover and burn all the copies he can find. After he fails to find a publisher, Hawthorne also burns *Seven Tales of My Native Land*, a collection of stories that he began to write while in college.

1830

Hawthorne publishes five stories in *The Salem Gazette*.

1832

Hawthorne plans a collection called *The Story Teller*.

1834

Some of the stories Hawthorne planned to include in *The Story Teller* are published in *New England Magazine*.

1836

Hawthorne moves to Boston to edit a short-lived magazine called *The American Magazine of Useful and Entertaining Knowledge*.

1837

Hawthorne's *Twice-Told Tales* is published. Hawthorne meets Sophia Amelia Peabody, his future wife.

1838

Hawthorne becomes engaged to Sophia Peabody.

1839–1840

Hawthorne works as a salt and coal measurer in the Boston Custom House to save money for his marriage.

1841

Hawthorne tries communal living in the experimental Brook Farm community.

Hawthorne and Sophia Peabody marry and move to the Old Manse, a house that they rent from Ralph Waldo Emerson, in Concord, Massachusetts. **1842**

Hawthorne's first daughter, Una, is born. **1844**

Hawthorne moves to Salem with his wife and daughter. **1845**

Hawthorne's *Mosses from an Old Manse* is published and receives critical acclaim. Hawthorne is appointed surveyor of customs in Salem by President James K. Polk. Julian, Hawthorne's first son, is born. **1846**

Hawthorne is removed from office after Zachary Taylor, a Whig, is elected President. He begins writing *The Scarlet Letter* and "The Custom-House." **1849**

The Scarlet Letter is published. Hawthorne moves to Lenox, Massachusetts, in the Berkshires, where he meets Herman Melville. **1850**

The House of the Seven Gables is published. The Hawthornes move to West Newton, Massachusetts. Rose, Hawthorne's second daughter and third child, is born. **1851**

The Blithedale Romance is published. Hawthorne buys a house in Concord, which he names The Wayside. He writes a campaign biography of Presidential candidate and former classmate Franklin Pierce. **1852**

President Pierce appoints Hawthorne American consul at Liverpool, England. Hawthorne and his family move to England. Hawthorne keeps notebooks dealing with his experiences abroad. **1853**

Hawthorne gives up his consulship. **1857**

Hawthorne and his family travel to Rome and take up residence there and, later, in Florence. He begins writing a romance based on his observations in Italy. **1858**

Hawthorne returns to England and continues writing his Italian romance. **1859**

The Marble Fawn is published. Hawthorne returns with his family to The Wayside in Concord. **1860**

Hawthorne's English sketches are published under the title *Our Old Home*. **1863**

Hawthorne dies in Plymouth, New Hampshire, while traveling with Pierce. **1864**

The Scarlet Letter

The Protestant Reformation and Puritanism

For approximately twelve hundred years, the major religion of Europe was **Catholicism.** In the sixteenth century, a German monk named **Martin Luther** started a movement that was to overthrow the power of the Catholic Church and split Christian Europe into two major groups—the Catholics and the Protestants. In 1517, Luther nailed to the door of a church in Wittenburg, Germany, a list of objections to central beliefs and practices of the Catholic Church. While preparing for his ordination as a priest, Luther had been struck by his own unworthiness to take the holy sacraments. He believed that because of the **original sin** of Adam in the Garden of Eden, people were basically sinful and could not, through their works, become worthy of taking such sacraments as Holy Communion and Holy Orders. Instead, according to Luther, people had to depend on the grace of God, extended to them despite their sinfulness. Luther also objected to practices of the church such as the sale of indulgences, or pardons for sins. He challenged the authority of the Pope and of the church in general, claiming that religion was a matter of individual conscience to be worked out between each person and God without a priest as intermediary. This belief led him to emphasize reading of the Holy Scriptures, which was made possible for ordinary men and women by the invention of printing and the translation of the Bible from Latin and Greek into everyday European languages.

Luther's ideas spread throughout Europe, leading to a widespread, often bloody revolt against Catholic authority known as the **Protestant Reformation.** In England, King Henry VIII broke with Catholicism and formed the Church of England, or Anglican Church, a Protestant denomination with himself at its head, because the Catholic Church would not allow him to divorce.

A central figure in the Protestant Reformation was **John Calvin** of Switzerland, who took Luther's ideas about original sin a step further, teaching that all events are preordained by God, that God chose at the beginning of time which people (the **elect**) would be saved, and which would be damned. This Calvinist doctrine, known as **predestination**, became the central belief of the **Puritan Movement** that was to flourish in England and in the English colonies.

Puritanism in New England

Some Protestants in England did not accept the Anglican Church but wished to "purify" it by simplifying services and by enforcing stricter moral codes. Facing persecution in England, some of these **Puritans**, as their opponents called them, fled to America, where they hoped to establish colonies based on religious principles. The **Plymouth Colony**, founded in 1620, and the **Massachusetts Bay Colony**, founded in 1630, were Puritan settlements, both in New England. The New England colonists endured great difficulties and depended on the assistance of Native Americans to survive. The core group of the Plymouth colonists, often referred to as the Pilgrims, were Separatist Puritans, so called because they had officially separated from the Anglican Church due to its "Popish," or Catholic, tendencies. After moving from England to Holland to escape religious persecution, the Pilgrims set sail for North America on the Mayflower in 1620. They landed on Cape Cod and established their colony by means of the Mayflower Compact in what is now the town of Plymouth, Massachusetts. After a difficult winter, the colonists learned from native peoples how to plant crops that would grow in the harsh climate. Under the direction of governor William Bradford, the colony flourished.

In 1691, Plymouth incorporated with a much larger settlement of Puritans, the Massachusetts Bay Colony. This group was made up of Congregationalist Puritans who did not separate entirely from the Anglican Church, believing it could be reformed from within. They found courage to face the hardships of their new lives in America by believing that their actions were divinely guided. Their governor, John Winthrop, would write in his work, *A Model of Christian Charity*, that they were in the business of building, as described in the New Testament, a "city upon a hill" in the new land. Hawthorne's *The Scarlet Letter* is set in the Massachusetts Bay Colony in the early 1640s.

Puritan Beliefs

The Puritans in New England shared several basic religious and social beliefs. First, they believed strongly in the importance of the community as a whole. The idea that they were on a grand historical and religious mission gave them a common purpose. The societies that they created were **theocracies**, ruled by strict religious principles. Second, because they had a firm belief in original sin, they accepted the idea that people were basically wicked and could only be saved through grace. This belief in the wickedness of people led the Puritans to enact strict laws and punishments. Third, although the Puritans as a whole believed themselves to be chosen by God for a special mission, they did not believe that all the people among them had been chosen. They adopted John Calvin's theory of **predestination**, which held that God had chosen some people to be saved and some to be damned. They understood this to mean that they could not change their individual fates directly, by force of will. Since none could be sure of having been saved, however, they maintained a steady and humble watch over their lives for proof that they were among the **elect**, those chosen for salvation by God at the beginning of time. Finally, the Puritans shared a belief in hard work, thinking that material and social success were signs of God's providence and that such work, though it could not win salvation, was nonetheless a sign of salvation. This complex belief in strict moral propriety and hard work is today referred to as the **Puritan ethic.**

Politics, Society, and Orthodoxy

Despite the shared beliefs of the Puritans, their society was not entirely free of conflict, or dissent. Early Puritan leaders were largely intolerant of any opposition, religious or political. When **Roger Williams** voiced his objections in 1635 to intolerance of diversity and mistreatment of Native Americans, he was banished from the Massachusetts Bay Colony. He went on to found the colony of Rhode Island and to call for religious freedom. In 1637, when **Anne Hutchinson** bypassed the official church and began teaching her own theories in home Bible classes with other women and their husbands, she was accused of threatening the established religion and of being more a "husband than a wife." She was banished from the Massachusetts Bay Colony as well. Other dissenters did not fare so well. Puritan punishments could be extremely harsh and included public ridicule, placement in stockades, imprisonment, flogging, drowning, hanging, and being crushed under stones.

Pressures from progressive elements in New England led in 1662 to the **Half-Way Covenant**, a new law that relaxed old rules and allowed more people direct membership in the church. However, tensions remained. Some saw the relaxing of orthodoxy as a sign of weakness, and their concerns surfaced dramatically in the belief that Satan had infiltrated the town of Salem and nearby communities. **The Salem Witch Trials**, begun in 1692, resulted in the execution of twenty people and the imprisonment and torture of many more. Nathaniel Hawthorne was keenly aware of and embarrassed by his own ancestor's participation in these trials. Hawthorne was able to express his concern in his great novel, *The Scarlet Letter,* which deals with issues of sin, punishment, and redemption.

Characters in *The Scarlet Letter*

Main Characters

Hester Prynne. Hester is an English woman who is sent to live in the American colonies by her husband, Roger Prynne, an aged scholar. Prynne plans to join her after he settles business matters in Amsterdam, where the couple has been living. When the novel begins, Hester has been living in Boston for two years without her husband, who has never arrived. Hester has given birth to a child by a father unknown to the community and has been found guilty of the sin of adultery. As punishment, she must always wear a scarlet *A* on her dress and stand for three hours on a public scaffold, exposed to the ridicule and rancor of the community.

Reverend Arthur Dimmesdale. Arthur Dimmesdale, an unmarried man, is the pastor of Hester's congregation and the father of Hester's baby, Pearl. Hester refuses to name him as the father of the child, but Dimmesdale's private guilt and anguish eat away at him throughout the novel.

Pearl. Pearl is the daughter of Hester Prynne and the Reverend Arthur Dimmesdale. She is the living symbol of Hester's sin and grows up fascinated by her mother's scarlet *A*. Pearl has a strong, unpredictable personality, and Hester worries that Pearl will be taken from her.

Roger Chillingworth. Roger Chillingworth is the name Hester's husband assumes after he finally arrives in America. Native Americans have captured him, delaying his arrival in the colony. At the beginning of the novel, Hester recognizes her husband from her place on the public scaffold. Later, he asks her not to dishonor his name by revealing that he is her lawful husband. Chillingworth becomes obsessed with seeking revenge against Dimmesdale.

Minor Characters

Governor Richard Bellingham. This character, an actual historical figure who served as governor in Boston in 1641, 1654, and 1665, witnesses Hester's punishment on the public scaffold. Later in the novel, Hester must visit him to ask that Pearl not be removed from her home.

Mistress Hibbins. This character, another actual historical figure, is the sister of Governor Bellingham and is supposedly in league with the devil. She tries to tempt Hester and Dimmesdale to sink further into sin. The real Mistress Hibbins was executed for witchcraft.

John Wilson. This character advises Dimmesdale to try to find out from Hester who the father of her child is. When Hester refuses to reveal this information, Wilson delivers a sermon about adultery to the crowd watching Hester on the scaffold.

Master Brackett. Master Brackett is the jailer who brings Chillingworth to Hester as she sits in prison.

The Sexton. Dimmesdale stands on the public scaffold with Hester and Pearl one night, and the sexton, an employee of the church, finds Reverend Dimmesdale's glove there and returns it to him. The sexton asks Dimmesdale about the red letter *A* that appeared in the sky that night. The sexton believes that the *A* stands for "angel." Dimmesdale denies having seen the sign in the sky.

The Shipmaster. This character is the captain of the ship on which Hester, Pearl, and Dimmesdale hope to leave Boston. The shipmaster tells them that Roger Chillingworth also plans to be on the ship.

The woman and her daughter pictured to the right are wearing long dresses and caps, typical Puritan garb such as Hester and Pearl might have worn. The basket carried by the woman might hold food she has gathered from the forest or her garden, a parcel from a shop, her sewing, or some food for a sick neighbor.

The man pictured to the left is wearing an outfit that would have been common to colonial Puritans—knee breeches, coat, cape, and hat.

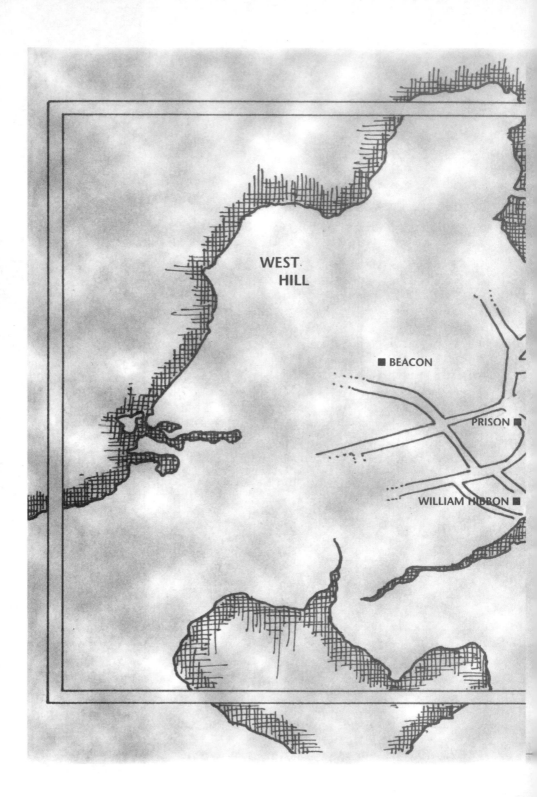

WEST
HILL

■ BEACON

PRISON ■

WILLIAM HIBBON ■

MILL
FIELD

■ REVEREND WILSON

N

FORT
HILL

BOSTON CIRCA 1645

Introductory to "The Scarlet Letter"

It is a little remarkable, that—though <u>disinclined</u> to talk overmuch of myself and my affairs at the fireside, and to my personal friends—an autobiographical impulse should twice in my life have taken possession of me, in addressing the public. The first time was three or four years since, when I favored the reader—inexcusably, and for no earthly reason, that either the indulgent reader or the intrusive author could imagine—with a description of my way of life in the deep quietude of an Old Manse. And now—because, beyond my deserts, I was happy enough to find a listener or two on the former occasion—I again seize the public by the button, and talk of my three years' experience in a Custom-House. The example of the famous "P. P., Clerk of this Parish,"[1] was never more faithfully followed. The truth seems to be, however, that, when he casts his leaves forth upon the wind, the author addresses, not the many who will fling aside his volume, or never take it up, but the few who will understand him, better than most of his schoolmates and lifemates. Some authors, indeed, do far more than this, and indulge themselves in such confidential depths of revelation as could fittingly be addressed, only and exclusively, to the one heart and mind of perfect sympathy; as if the printed book, thrown at large on the wide world, were certain to find out the divided segment of the writer's own nature, and complete his circle of existence by bringing him into communion with it. It is scarcely decorous, however, to speak all, even where we speak impersonally. But—as thoughts are frozen and utterance benumbed, unless the speaker stand in some true relation with his audience—it may be pardonable to imagine that a friend, a kind and apprehensive,[2] though not the closest friend, is listening to our talk; and then, a native reserve being

◄ *Who is speaking? What impulse has taken possession of this person?*

---

1. **"P. P., Clerk of this Parish."** Hawthorne is referring to a satirical biography he had read.
2. **apprehensive.** Quick to understand

Words For Everyday Use   **dis • in • clined** (dis´in klīnd´) *adj.*, unwilling, reluctant thawed by this <u>genial</u> consciousness, we may prate of the circumstances that lie around us, and even of ourself, but still keep the inmost Me behind its veil. To this extent and within these limits an author, methinks, may be autobiographical, without violating either the reader's rights or his own.

It will be seen, likewise, that this Custom-House sketch has a certain propriety, of a kind always recognized in literature, as explaining how a large portion of the following pages came into my possession, and as offering proofs of the authenticity of a narrative therein contained. This, in fact—a desire to put myself in my true position as editor, or very little more, of the most prolix among the tales that make up my volume[3]—this, and no other, is my true reason for assuming a personal relation with the public. In accomplishing the main purpose, it has appeared allowable, by a few extra touches, to give a faint representation of a mode of life not heretofore described, together with some of the characters that move in it, among whom the author happened to make one.

In my native town of Salem, at the head of what, half a century ago, in the days of old King Derby,[4] was a bustling wharf—but which is now burdened with decayed wooden warehouses, and exhibits few or no symptoms of commercial life; except, perhaps, a bark or brig,[5] half-way down its melancholy length, discharging hides; or, nearer at hand, a Nova Scotia schooner, pitching out her cargo of firewood—at the head, I say, of this <u>dilapidated</u> wharf, which the tide often overflows, and along which, at the base and in the rear of the row of buildings, the track of many <u>languid</u> years is seen in a border of unthrifty grass—here, with a view from its front windows adown this not very enlivening prospect, and thence across the harbor, stands a spacious edifice of brick. From the loftiest point of its roof, during precisely three and a half hours of each forenoon, floats or droops, in breeze or calm, the banner of the republic; but with the thirteen stripes turned vertically, instead of horizontally, and thus indicating that a civil, and not a military post of Uncle

► According to the narrator, what will the custom house sketch explain?

---

3. **my volume.** Hawthorne originally planned to publish "The Custom-House," *The Scarlet Letter,* and several other sketches and tales in one volume.
4. **King Derby.** Elias Hasket Derby (1739–1799), a merchant and ship owner
5. **bark or brig.** Types of boats

Words For Everyday Use

gen • i • al (jēn´yəl) *adj.,* friendly and sympathetic

di • lap • i • dat • ed (də lap´ə dāt´id) *adj.,* shabby, neglected, and broken down

lan • guid (laŋ´gwid) *adj.,* indifferent; dull

Sam's government, is here established. Its front is ornamented with a portico[6] of half a dozen wooden pillars, supporting a balcony, beneath which a flight of wide granite steps descends towards the street. Over the entrance hovers an enormous specimen of the American eagle, with outspread wings, a shield before her breast, and, if I recollect aright, a bunch of intermingled thunderbolts and barbed arrows in each claw. With the customary <u>infirmity</u> of temper that characterizes this unhappy fowl, she appears, by the fierceness of her beak and eye and the general <u>truculency</u> of her attitude, to threaten mischief to the inoffensive community; and especially to warn all citizens, careful of their safety, against intruding on the premises which she overshadows with her wings. Nevertheless, vixenly as she looks, many people are seeking, at this very moment, to shelter themselves under the wing of the federal eagle; imagining, I presume, that her bosom has all the softness and snugness of an eider-down pillow. But she has no great tenderness, even in her best of moods, and, sooner or later—oftener soon than late—is apt to fling off her nestlings with a scratch of her claw, a dab of her beak, or a rankling wound from her barbed arrows.

◄ *What does the narrator say about the nature of this eagle? How might the narrator's comments be related to Hawthorne's losing his job at the custom house? (See the biography on page iv.)*

The pavement round about the above-described edifice—which we may as well name at once as the Custom-House of the port—has grass enough growing in its chinks to show that it has not, of late days, been worn by any multitudinous resort of business. In some months of the year, however, there often chances a forenoon when affairs move onward with a livelier tread. Such occasions might remind the elderly citizen of that period, before the last war with England,[7] when Salem was a port by itself; not scorned, as she is now, by her own merchants and ship-owners, who permit her wharves to crumble to ruin, while their ventures go to swell, needlessly and imperceptibly, the mighty flood of commerce at New York or Boston. On some such morning, when three or four vessels happen to have arrived at once—usually from Africa or South America—or to be on the verge of their departure thitherward, there is a sound of frequent feet, passing briskly up and down the granite steps. Here, before his

---

6. **portico.** Porch or covered walk
7. **last war with England.** Refers to the War of 1812

Words For Everyday Use

in • fir • mi • ty (in fur´mə tē) *n.*, weakness

truc • u • len • cy (truk´yo͞o lən cē) *n.*, meanness, ferocity own wife has greeted him, you may greet the sea-flushed ship-master, just in port, with his vessel's papers under his arm in a tarnished tin box. Here, too, comes his owner, cheerful or somber, gracious or in the sulks, accordingly as his scheme of the now accomplished voyage has been realized in merchandise that will readily be turned to gold, or has buried him under a bulk of incommodities, such as nobody will care to rid him of. Here, likewise—the germ of the wrinkle-browed, grizzly-bearded, careworn merchant— we have the smart young clerk, who gets the taste of traffic as a wolf-cub does of blood, and already sends adventures[8] in his master's ships, when he had better be sailing mimic boats upon a mill-pond. Another figure in the scene is the outward-bound sailor, in quest of a protection; or the recently arrived one, pale and feeble, seeking a passport to the hospital. Nor must we forget the captains of the rusty little schooners that bring firewood from the British provinces; a rough-looking set of tarpaulins, without the alertness of the Yankee aspect, but contributing an item of no slight importance to our decaying trade.

Cluster all these individuals together, as they sometimes were, with other miscellaneous ones to diversify the group, and, for the time being, it made the Custom-House a stirring scene. More frequently, however, on ascending the steps, you would discern—in the entry, if it were summer time, or in their appropriate rooms, if wintry or inclement weather— a row of venerable figures, sitting in old-fashioned chairs, which were tipped on their hind legs back against the wall. Oftentimes they were asleep, but occasionally might be heard talking together, in voices between a speech and a snore, and with that lack of energy that distinguishes the occupants of alms-houses,[9] and all other human beings who depend for subsistence on charity, on monopolized labor, or anything else but their own independent exertions. These old gentlemen—seated, like Matthew, at the receipt of custom,[10] but not very liable to be summoned thence, like him, for apostolic errands—were Custom-House officers.

▶ *What are the custom house officers like? Do the officers take their jobs seriously? How do you know this?*

---

8. **sends adventures.** Young men who worked in shipping houses often invested some of their money in trading ventures.
9. **alms-houses.** Homes for poor, often elderly, people
10. **Matthew . . . custom.** Allusion to Matthew 9:9: "And as Jesus passed forth from thence, he saw a man, named Matthew, sitting at the receipt of custom: and he saith into him, Follow me. And he arose, and followed him."

Furthermore, on the left hand as you enter the front door, is a certain room or office, about fifteen feet square, and of a lofty height; with two of its arched windows commanding a view of the aforesaid dilapidated wharf, and the third looking across a narrow lane, and along a portion of Derby Street. All three give glimpses of the shops of grocers, block-makers, slop-sellers,[11] and ship-chandlers; around the doors of which are generally to be seen, laughing and gossiping, clusters of old salts,[12] and such other wharf-rats as haunt the Wapping[13] of a seaport. The room itself is cobwebbed, and dingy with old paint; its floor is strewn with gray sand, in a fashion that has elsewhere fallen into long disuse; and it is easy to conclude, from the general slovenliness of the place, that this is a sanctuary into which womankind, with her tools of magic, the broom and mop, has very infrequent access. In the way of furniture, there is a stove with a <u>voluminous</u> funnel; an old pine desk, with a three-legged stool beside it; two or three wooden-bottom chairs, exceedingly decrepit and infirm; and—not to forget the library—on some shelves, a score or two of volumes of the Acts of Congress, and a bulky Digest of the Revenue Laws. A tin pipe ascends through the ceiling, and forms a medium of vocal communication with other parts of the edifice. And here, some six months ago— pacing from corner to corner, or lounging on the long-legged stool, with his elbow on the desk, and his eyes wandering up and down the columns of the morning newspaper—you might have recognized, honored reader, the same individual who welcomed you into his cheery little study, where the sunshine glimmered so pleasantly through the willow branches, on the western side of the Old Manse. But now, should you go thither to seek him, you would inquire in vain for the Locofoco[14] Surveyor. The besom[15] of reform has swept him out of office; and a worthier successor wears his dignity and pockets his emoluments.[16]

This old town of Salem—my native place, though I have dwelt much away from it, both in boyhood and maturer

◄ Who does the narrator say the reader might have found in the custom house six months before? Why doesn't the narrator work there any more?

◄ How does the narrator feel about his "native place" of Salem?

---

11. **slop-sellers.** Clothing sellers
12. **old salts.** Old sailors
13. **Wapping.** Dockside area, named after the Wapping docking area of London
14. **Loco-foco.** Disparaging term once used for members of the Democratic party
15. **besom.** Broom
16. **emoluments.** Wages

Words
For
Everyday
Use

vo • lu • mi • nous (və lōōm´ə nəs) *adj.*, having a large capacity or interior area years—possesses, or did possess, a hold on my affections, the force of which I have never realized during my seasons of actual residence here. Indeed, so far as its physical aspect is concerned, with its flat, unvaried surface, covered chiefly with wooden houses, few or none of which pretend to architectural beauty—its irregularity, which is neither picturesque nor quaint, but only tame—its long and lazy street, lounging wearisomely through the whole extent of the peninsula, with Gallows Hill and New Guinea[17] at one end, and a view of the alms-house at the other—such being the features of my native town, it would be quite as reasonable to form a sentimental attachment to a disarranged checkerboard. And yet, though invariably happiest elsewhere, there is within me a feeling for old Salem, which, in lack of a better phrase, I must be content to call affection. The sentiment is probably assignable to the deep and aged roots which my family has struck into the soil. It is now nearly two centuries and a quarter since the original Briton, the earliest emigrant of my name, made his appearance in the wild and forest-bordered settlement, which has since become a city. And here his descendants have been born and died, and have mingled their earthly substance with the soil; until no small portion of it must necessarily be akin to the mortal frame wherewith, for a little while, I walk the streets. In part, therefore, the attachment which I speak of is the mere sensuous sympathy of dust for dust. Few of my countrymen can know what it is; nor, as frequent transplantation is perhaps better for the stock, need they consider it desirable to know.

But the sentiment has likewise its moral quality. The figure of that first ancestor, invested by family tradition with a dim and dusky grandeur, was present to my boyish imagination, as far back as I can remember. It still haunts me, and induces a sort of home-feeling with the past, which I scarcely claim in reference to the present phase of the town. I seem to have a stronger claim to a residence here on account of this grave, bearded, sable-cloaked, and steeple-crowned progenitor[18]— who came so early, with his Bible and his sword, and trode the unworn street with such a stately port, and made so large a figure, as a man of war and peace—a stronger claim than for myself, whose name is seldom heard and my face hardly known. He was a soldier, legislator, judge; he was a ruler in the Church; he had all the Puritanic traits, both good and

▶ *What sentiment, or feeling, connects the narrator to the town of Salem?*

---

17. **Gallows Hill and New Guinea.** Gallows Hill was the site of the hangings during the Salem witchcraft hysteria. New Guinea was the part of Salem where immigrants from southern Europe first settled.
18. **progenitor.** Ancestor

evil. He was likewise a bitter persecutor; as witness the Quakers, who have remembered him in their histories, and relate an incident of his hard severity towards a woman of their sect, which will last longer, it is to be feared, than any record of his better deeds, although these were many. His son,[19] too, inherited the persecuting spirit, and made himself so <u>conspicuous</u> in the martyrdom of the witches,[20] that their blood may fairly be said to have left a stain upon him. So deep a stain, indeed, that his dry old bones, in the Charter Street burial-ground, must still retain it, if they have not crumbled utterly to dust! I know not whether these ancestors of mine bethought themselves to repent, and ask pardon of Heaven for their cruelties; or whether they are now groaning under the heavy consequences of them, in another state of being. At all events, I, the present writer, as their representative, hereby take shame upon myself for their sakes, and pray that any curse incurred by them—as I have heard, and as the dreary and unprosperous condition of the race, for many a long year back, would argue to exist—may be now and henceforth removed.

Doubtless, however, either of these stern and black-browed Puritans would have thought it quite a sufficient retribution for his sins, that, after so long a lapse of years, the old trunk of the family tree, with so much venerable moss upon it, should have borne, as its topmost bough, an idler like myself. No aim, that I have ever cherished, would they recognize as laudable; no success of mine—if my life, beyond its domestic scope, had ever been brightened by success—would they deem otherwise than worthless, if not positively disgraceful. "What is he?" murmurs one grey shadow of my forefathers to the other. "A writer of story-books! What kind of business in life—what mode of glorifying God, or being serviceable to mankind in his day and generation—may that be? Why, the degenerate fellow might as well have been a fiddler!" Such are the compliments bandied between my great grandsires and myself, across the gulf of time! And yet, let them scorn me as they will, strong

◀ According to the narrator, what would his Puritan ancestors have thought of the narrator's devoting himself to writing?

---

19. **His son.** John Hathorne (1641–1717), who persecuted the Quakers
20. **martyrdom of the witches.** Salem Witch Trials of 1692, in which 150 people were imprisoned and 20 people were executed

Words For Everyday Use

con • spic • u • ous (kən spik´yo͞o əs) *adj.,* noticeable

traits of their nature have intertwined themselves with mine.

Planted deep, in the town's earliest infancy and childhood, by these two earnest and energetic men, the race has ever since subsisted here; always, too, in respectability; never, so far as I have known, disgraced by a single unworthy member; but seldom or never, on the other hand, after the first two generations, performing any memorable deed, or so much as putting forward a claim to public notice. Gradually, they have sunk almost out of sight; as old houses, here and there about the streets, get covered half-way to the eaves by the <u>accumulation</u> of new soil. From father to son, for above a hundred years, they followed the sea; a gray-headed shipmaster, in each generation, retiring from the quarter-deck to the homestead, while a boy of fourteen took the hereditary place before the mast, confronting the salt spray and the gale, which had blustered against his sire and grandsire. The boy, also, in due time, passed from the forecastle to the cabin, spent a <u>tempestuous</u> manhood, and returned from his world-wanderings, to grow old, and die, and mingle his dust with the natal earth. This long connection of a family with one spot, as its place of birth and burial, creates a kindred between the human being and the locality, quite independent of any charm in the scenery or moral circumstances that surround him. It is not love, but instinct. The new inhabitant—who came himself from a foreign land, or whose father or grandfather came—has little claim to be called a Salemite; he has no conception of the oyster-like <u>tenacity</u> with which an old settler, over whom his third century is creeping, clings to the spot where his successive generations have been imbedded. It is no matter that the place is joyless for him; that he is weary of the old wooden houses, the mud and dust, the dead level of site and sentiment, the chill east wind, and the chillest of social atmospheres;—all these, and whatever faults besides he may see or imagine, are nothing to the purpose. The spell survives, and just as powerfully as if the natal spot were an earthly paradise. So has it been in my case. I felt it almost as a destiny to make Salem my home; so that the

► *Does the narrator believe his family resided in Salem for so many years because they loved the town? Explain.*

Words For Everyday Use	**ac • cu • mu • la • tion** (ə kyo͞om′yo͞o lā′shən) *n.*, collection or pile that has increased over time
	tem • pes • tu • ous (tem pes′cho͞o əs) *adj.*, violent, turbulent
	te • nac • i • ty (tə nas′ə tē) *n.*, stubborn persistance

mold of features and cast of character which had all along been familiar here—ever, as one representative of the race lay down in his grave, another assuming, as it were, his sentry-march along the Main Street—might still in my little day be seen and recognized in the old town. Nevertheless, this very sentiment is an evidence that the connection, which has become an unhealthy one, should at last be severed. Human nature will not flourish, any more than a potato, if it be planted and replanted, for too long a series of generations, in the same worn-out soil. My children have had other birth-places, and, so far as their fortunes may be within my control, shall strike their roots into unaccustomed earth.

◄ According to the narrator, under what circumstances will human nature fail to flourish?

On emerging from the Old Manse, it was chiefly this strange, <u>indolent</u>, unjoyous attachment for my native town, that brought me to fill a place in Uncle Sam's brick edifice, when I might as well, or better, have gone somewhere else. My doom was on me. It was not the first time, nor the second, that I had gone away—as it seemed, permanently—but yet returned, like the bad half-penny; or as if Salem were for me the inevitable center of the universe. So, one fine morning, I ascended the flight of granite steps, with the President's commission[21] in my pocket, and was introduced to the corps of gentlemen who were to aid me in my weighty responsibility, as chief executive officer of the Custom-House.

I doubt greatly—or rather, I do not doubt at all—whether any public functionary of the United States, either in the civil or military line, has ever had such a patriarchal body of veterans under his orders as myself. The whereabouts of the Oldest Inhabitant was at once settled, when I looked at them. For upwards of twenty years before this epoch, the independent position of the Collector had kept the Salem Custom-House out of the whirlpool of political <u>vicissitude</u>, which makes the tenure of office generally so fragile. A soldier—New England's most distinguished soldier—he stood firmly on the pedestal of his gallant services; and, himself secure in the wise liberality of the successive administrations

---

21. **President's commission.** President James Polk appointed Hawthorne Surveyor.

| Words For Everyday Use | in • do • lent (in´də lənt) *adj.*, lazy; idle |
| | vi • cis • si • tude (vi sis´ə tōōd´) *n.*, change |

through which he had held office, he had been the safety of his subordinates in many an hour of danger and heart-quake. General Miller was radically conservative; a man over whose kindly nature habit had no slight influence; attaching himself strongly to familiar faces, and with difficulty moved to change, even when change might have brought unquestionable improvement. Thus, on taking charge of my department, I found few but aged men. They were ancient sea-captains, for the most part, who, after being tost on every sea, and standing up sturdily against life's tempestuous blast, had finally drifted into this quiet nook; where, with little to disturb them, except the periodical terrors of a Presidential election, they one and all acquired a new lease of existence. Though by no means less liable than their fellow-men to age and infirmity, they had evidently some talisman or other that kept death at bay. Two or three of their number, as I was assured, being gouty and rheumatic, or perhaps bed-ridden, never dreamed of making their appearance at the Custom-House, during a large part of the year; but, after a torpid winter, would creep out into the warm sunshine of May or June, go lazily about what they termed duty, and, at their own leisure and convenience, betake themselves to bed again. I must plead guilty to the charge of abbreviating the official breath of more than one of these venerable servants of the republic. They were allowed, on my representation, to rest from their arduous labors, and soon afterwards—as if their sole principle of life had been zeal for their country's service; as I verily believe it was—withdrew to a better world. It is a pious consolation to me, that, through my interference, a sufficient space was allowed them for repentance of the evil and corrupt practices, into which, as a matter of course, every Custom-House officer must be supposed to fall. Neither the front nor the back entrance of the Custom-House opens on the road to Paradise.

The greater part of my officers were Whigs. It was well for their venerable brotherhood, that the new Surveyor was not a politician, and, though a faithful Democrat in principle, neither received nor held his office with any reference to political services. Had it been otherwise—had an active

▶ *Why did the narrator fire the two customs officers?*

▶ *Some civil service jobs, in Hawthorne's day and in our own, are political appointments. Does the narrator approve of this method of filling government positions? Why, or why not?*

Words For Everyday Use

tor • pid (tôr′pid) *adj.*, dormant, sluggish

politician been put into this influential post, to assume the easy task of making head against a Whig Collector, whose infirmities withheld him from the personal administration of his office—hardly a man of the old corps would have drawn the breath of official life, within a month after the exterminating angel had come up the Custom-House steps. According to the received code in such matters, it would have been nothing short of duty, in a politician, to bring every one of those white heads under the ax of the guillotine.[22] It was plain enough to discern, that the old fellows dreaded some such discourtesy at my hands. It pained, and at the same time amused me, to behold the terrors that attended my advent, to see a furrowed cheek, weather-beaten by half a century of storm, turn ashy pale at the glance of so harmless an individual as myself; to detect, as one or another addressed me, the tremor of a voice, which, in long-past days, had been wont to bellow through a speaking-trumpet,[23] hoarsely enough to frighten Boreas[24] himself to silence. They knew, these excellent old persons, that, by all established rule—and, as regarded some of them, weighed by their own lack of efficiency for business—they ought to have given place to younger men, more orthodox in politics, and altogether fitter than themselves to serve our common Uncle. I knew it too, but could never quite find in my heart to act upon the knowledge. Much and deservedly to my own discredit, therefore, and considerably to the detriment of my official conscience, they continued, during my <u>incumbency</u>, to creep about the wharves, and loiter up and down the Custom-House steps. They spent a good deal of time, also, asleep in their accustomed corners, with their chairs tilted back against the wall; awaking, however, once or twice in a forenoon, to bore one another with the several thousandth repetition of old sea-stories and moldy jokes, that had grown to be pass-words and countersigns among them.

The discovery was soon made, I imagine, that the new Surveyor had no great harm in him. So, with lightsome hearts

◄ *What is the "received code" among political appointees?*

◄ *What kept the narrator from acting according to the "received code"?*

---

22. **guillotine.** Device used to behead persons convicted of capital offenses
23. **speaking trumpet.** Horn-shaped device used to magnify sound
24. **Boreas.** Greek god, a personification of the North Wind

Words For Everyday Use

in • cum • ben • cy (in kum´bən sē) *n.,* term of office and the happy consciousness of being usefully employed—in their own behalf, at least, if not for our beloved country—these good old gentlemen went through the various formalities of office. <u>Sagaciously</u>, under their spectacles, did they peep into the holds of vessels! Mighty was their fuss about little matters, and marvelous, sometimes, the <u>obtuseness</u> that allowed greater ones to slip between their fingers! Whenever such a mischance occurred—when a wagon-load of valuable merchandise had been smuggled ashore, at noonday, perhaps, and directly beneath their unsuspicious noses—nothing could exceed the vigilance and <u>alacrity</u> with which they proceeded to lock, and double-lock, and secure with tape and sealing-wax, all the avenues of the delinquent vessel. Instead of a reprimand for their previous negligence, the case seemed rather to require an eulogium on their praiseworthy caution, after the mischief had happened; a grateful recognition of the promptitude of their zeal, the moment that there was no longer any remedy!

Unless people are more than commonly disagreeable, it is my foolish habit to contract a kindness for them. The better part of my companion's character, if it have a better part, is that which usually comes uppermost in my regard, and forms the type whereby I recognize the man. As most of these old Custom-House officers had good traits, and as my position in reference to them, being paternal and protective, was favorable to the growth of friendly sentiments, I soon grew to like them all. It was pleasant, in the summer forenoons—when the fervent heat, that almost liquefied the rest of the human family, merely communicated a genial warmth to their half-torpid systems—it was pleasant to hear them chatting in the back entry, a row of them all tipped against the wall, as usual; while the frozen witticisms of past generations were thawed out, and came bubbling with laughter from their lips. Externally, the jollity of aged men has much in common with the mirth of children; the intellect, any more than a deep sense of humor, has little to do with the matter; it is, with both, a gleam that plays upon the surface, and imparts a sunny and cheery aspect alike to the green branch, and gray, moldering trunk. In one case, however, it is real sunshine; in the other, it more resembles the

▶ *Do you agree that the narrator primarily considers "the better part" of the customs officers' personalities? Why, or why not?*

Words For Everyday Use	sa • ga • cious • ly (sə gā′shəs lē) *adv.*, in a manner that shows keen perception or sound judgment
	ob • tuse • ness (äb to͞os′nəs) *n.*, slowness of understanding
	a • lac • ri • ty (ə lak′rə tē) *n.*, eager willingess or readiness

phosphorescent glow of decaying wood.

It would be sad injustice, the reader must understand, to represent all my excellent old friends as in their dotage.[25] In the first place, my coadjutors[26] were not invariably old; there were men among them in their strength and prime, of marked ability and energy, and altogether superior to the sluggish and dependent mode of life on which their evil stars had cast them. Then, moreover, the white locks of age were sometimes found to be the thatch of an intellectual tenement in good repair. But, as respects the majority of my corps of veterans, there will be no wrong done, if I characterize them generally as a set of wearisome old souls, who had gathered nothing worth preservation from their varied experience of life. They seemed to have flung away all the golden grain of practical wisdom, which they had enjoyed so many opportunities of harvesting, and most carefully to have stored their memories with the husks. They spoke with far more interest and <u>unction</u> of their morning's breakfast, or yesterday's, to-day's, or to-morrow's dinner, than of the shipwreck of forty or fifty years ago, and all the world's wonders which they had witnessed with their youthful eyes.

The father of the Custom-House—the patriarch, not only of this little squad of officials, but, I am bold to say, of the respectable body of tide-waiters all over the United States— was a certain permanent Inspector. He might truly be termed a legitimate son of the revenue system, dyed in the wool, or rather, born in the purple; since his sire, a Revolutionary colonel, and formerly collector of the port, had created an office for him, and appointed him to fill it, at a period of the early ages which few living men can now remember. This Inspector, when I first knew him, was a man of fourscore[27] years, or thereabouts, and certainly one of the most wonderful specimens of winter-green that you would be likely to discover in a lifetime's search. With his <u>florid</u> cheek, his compact figure, smartly arrayed in a bright-buttoned blue coat, his brisk and vigorous step, and his hale and hearty aspect, altogether, he seemed—not young,

---

25. **dotage.** Senility
26. **coadjutors.** Assistants or coworkers
27. **fourscore.** Eighty, a score equaling twenty years

Words
For
Everyday
Use

unc • tion (uŋk´shən) *n.*, earnestness

flor • id (flôr´id) *adj.*, ruddy, red

indeed—but a kind of new contrivance of Mother Nature in the shape of man, whom age and infirmity had no business to touch. His voice and laugh, which perpetually reëchoed through the Custom-House, had nothing of the <u>tremulous</u> quaver and cackle of an old man's utterance; they came strutting out of his lungs, like the crow of a cock, or the blast of a clarion. Looking at him merely as an animal—and there was very little else to look at—he was a most satisfactory object, from the thorough healthfulness and wholesomeness of his system, and his capacity, at that extreme age, to enjoy all, or nearly all, the delights which he had ever aimed at, or conceived of. The careless security of his life in the Custom-House, on a regular income, and with but slight and infrequent apprehensions of removal, had no doubt contributed to make time pass lightly over him. The original and more potent causes, however, lay in the rare perfection of his animal nature, the moderate proportion of intellect, and the very trifling admixture of moral and spiritual ingredients; these latter qualities, indeed, being in barely enough measure to keep the old gentleman from walking on all-fours. He possessed no power of thought, no depth of feeling, no troublesome sensibilities; nothing, in short, but a few commonplace instincts, which, aided by the cheerful temper which grew inevitably out of his physical well-being, did duty very respectably, and to general acceptance, in lieu of a heart. He had been the husband of three wives, all long since dead; the father of twenty children, most of whom, at every age of childhood or maturity, had likewise returned to dust. Here, one would suppose, might have been sorrow enough to imbue the sunniest disposition, through and through, with a sable tinge. Not so with our old Inspector! One brief sigh sufficed to carry off the entire burden of these dismal reminiscences. The next moment, he was as ready for sport as any unbreeched infant; far readier than the Collector's junior clerk, who, at nineteen years, was much the elder and graver man of the two.

▶ What tragedies have occurred in the inspector's life? How does the inspector respond to thoughts of these tragedies? What does his response reveal about him?

I used to watch and study this patriarchal personage with, I think, livelier curiosity than any other form of humanity there presented to my notice. He was, in truth, a rare phenomenon; so perfect in one point of view; so shallow, so

Words For Everyday Use

trem • u • lous (trem′yo͞o ləs) *adj.*, trembling, quivering delusive, so impalpable, such an absolute <u>nonentity,</u> in every other. My conclusion was that he had no soul, no heart, no mind; nothing, as I have already said, but instincts; and yet, withal, so cunningly had the few materials of his character been put together, that there was no painful perception of deficiency, but, on my part, an entire contentment with what I found in him. It might be difficult—and it was so—to conceive how he should exist hereafter, so earthy and sensuous did he seem; but surely his existence here, admitting that it was to terminate with his last breath, had been not unkindly given; with no higher moral responsibilities than the beasts of the field, but with a larger scope of enjoyment than theirs, and with all their blessed immunity from the dreariness and duskiness of age.

One point in which he had vastly the advantage over his four-footed brethren, was his ability to recollect the good dinners which it had made no small portion of the happiness of his life to eat. His gourmandism[28] was a highly agreeable trait; and to hear him talk of roast-meat was as appetizing as a pickle or an oyster. As he possessed no higher attribute, and neither sacrificed nor vitiated[29] any spiritual endowment by devoting all his energies and ingenuities to subserve the delight and profit of his maw, it always pleased and satisfied me to hear him expatiate on fish, poultry, and butcher's meat, and the most eligible methods of preparing them for the table. His reminiscences of good cheer, however ancient the date of the actual banquet, seemed to bring the savor of pig or turkey under one's very nostrils. There were flavors on his palate, that had lingered there not less than sixty or seventy years, and were still apparently as fresh as that of the mutton-chop which he had just devoured for his breakfast. I have heard him smack his lips over dinners, every guest at which, except himself, had long been food for worms. It was marvelous to observe how the ghosts of bygone meals were continually rising up before him; not in anger or retribution, but as if grateful for his former appreciation, and seeking to <u>reduplicate</u> an endless series of enjoyment, at once shadowy

---

28. **gourmandism.** Excessive love of food
29. **vitiated.** Weakened or corrupted

Words For Everyday Use

non • en • ti • ty (nän´en´tə tē) *n.*, person of little or no importance

re • du • pli • cate (ri dōō´plə kāt) *vt.*, to double, or repeat and sensual. A tenderloin of beef, a hind-quarter of veal, a spare-rib of pork, a particular chicken, or a remarkably praiseworthy turkey, which had perhaps adorned his board in the days of the elder Adams, would be remembered; while all the subsequent experience of our race, and all the events that brightened or darkened his individual career, had gone over him with as little permanent effect as the passing breeze. The chief tragic event of the old man's life, so far as I could judge, was his mishap with a certain goose, which lived and died some twenty or forty years ago; a goose of most promising figure, but which, at table, proved so <u>inveterately</u> tough that the carving-knife would make no impression on its carcass; and it could only be divided with an axe and handsaw.

But it is time to quit this sketch; on which, however, I should be glad to dwell at considerably more length, because, of all men whom I have ever known, this individual was fittest to be a Custom-House officer. Most persons, owing to causes which I may not have space to hint at, suffer moral <u>detriment</u> from this peculiar mode of life. The old Inspector was incapable of it, and, were he to continue in office to the end of time, would be just as good as he was then, and sit down to dinner with just as good an appetite.

There is one likeness, without which my gallery of Custom-House portraits would be strangely incomplete; but which my comparatively few opportunities for observation enable me to sketch only in the merest outline. It is that of the Collector, our gallant old General, who, after his brilliant military service, subsequently to which he had ruled over a wild Western territory, had come hither, twenty years before, to spend the decline of his varied and honorable life.

The brave soldier had already numbered, nearly or quite, his threescore years and ten, and was pursuing the remainder of his earthly march, burdened with infirmities which even the martial music of his own spirit-stirring recollections could do little towards lightening. The step was palsied now, that had been foremost in the charge. It was only with the assistance of a servant, and by leaning his hand heavily on the iron balustrade, that he could slowly and painfully ascend the Custom-House steps, and, with a toilsome

► According to the narrator, what is the "tragedy" of the old inspector's life? Given the actual events of the inspector's life, what does the man's concern about the tough goose reveal about him?

► What makes the inspector incapable of suffering "moral detriment"?

Words For Everyday Use

in • vet • er • ate • ly (in vet′ər it lē) *adv.*, firmly, habitually

det • ri • ment (de′trə mənt) *n.*, damage, injury, harm

progress across the floor, attain his customary chair beside the fireplace. There he used to sit, gazing with a somewhat dim serenity of aspect at the figures that came and went; amid the rustle of papers, the administering of oaths, the discussion of business, and the casual talk of the office; all which sounds and circumstances seemed but indistinctly to impress his senses, and hardly to make their way into his inner sphere of contemplation. His <u>countenance</u>, in this repose, was mild and kindly. If his notice was sought, an expression of courtesy and interest gleamed out upon his features; proving that there was light within him, and that it was only the outward medium of the intellectual lamp that obstructed the rays in their passage. The closer you penetrated to the substance of his mind, the sounder it appeared. When no longer called upon to speak, or listen, either of which operations cost him an evident effort, his face would briefly subside into its former not uncheerful quietude. It was not painful to behold this look; for, though dim, it had not the imbecility of decaying age. The framework of his nature, originally strong and massive, was not yet crumbled into ruin.

To observe and define his character, however, under such disadvantages, was as difficult a task as to trace out and build up anew, in imagination, an old fortress, like Ticonderoga,[30] from a view of its gray and broken ruins. Here and there, perchance, the walls may remain almost complete; but elsewhere may be only a shapeless mound, cumbrous[31] with its very strength, and overgrown, through long years of peace and neglect, with grass and alien weeds.

◀ To what does the narrator compare the general's character? What makes this characterization particularly appropriate?

Nevertheless, looking at the old warrior with affection—for, slight as was the communication between us, my feeling towards him, like that of all bipeds and quadrupeds who knew him, might not improperly be termed so—I could discern the main points of his portrait. It was marked with the noble and heroic qualities which showed it to be not by a mere accident, but of good right, that he had won a distinguished name. His spirit could never, I conceive, have been

---

30. **Ticonderoga.** Fort in New York, captured by the British in 1759 and by the Americans in 1775
31. **cumbrous.** Unwieldy; hard to handle

Words
For
Everyday
Use

coun • te • nance (koun´tə nəns) n., face

characterized by an uneasy activity; it must, at any period of his life, have required an impulse to set him in motion; but, once stirred up, with obstacles to overcome, and an adequate object to be attained, it was not in the man to give out or fail. The heat that had formerly pervaded his nature, and which was not yet extinct, was never of the kind that flashes and flickers in a blaze, but, rather, a deep, red glow, as of iron in a furnace. Weight, solidity, firmness; this was the expression of his repose, even in such decay as had crept untimely over him at the period of which I speak. But I could imagine, even then, that, under some excitement which should go deeply into his consciousness—roused by a trumpet-peal, loud enough to awaken all of his energies that were not dead, but only slumbering—he was yet capable of flinging off his infirmities like a sick man's gown, dropping the staff of age to seize a battle-sword, and starting up once more a warrior. And, in so intense a moment, his demeanor would have still been calm. Such an exhibition, however, was but to be pictured in fancy; not to be anticipated, nor desired. What I saw in him—as evidently as the indestructible ramparts of Old Ticonderoga, already cited as the most appropriate simile—were the features of stubborn and <u>ponderous</u> endurance, which might well have amounted to <u>obstinacy</u> in his earlier days; of integrity, that, like most of his other endowments, lay in a somewhat heavy mass, and was just as <u>unmalleable</u> and unmanageable as a ton of iron ore; and of benevolence, which, fiercely as he led the bayonets on at Chippewa or Fort Erie, I take to be of quite as genuine a stamp as what actuates any or all the polemical philanthropists of the age. He had slain men with his own hand, for aught I know;—certainly, they had fallen, like blades of grass at the sweep of the scythe, before the charge to which his spirit imparted its triumphant energy;—but, be that as it might, there was never in his heart so much cruelty as would have brushed the down off a butterfly's wing. I have not known the man, to whose innate kindliness I would more confidently make an appeal.

Many characteristics—and those, too, which contribute not the least forcibly to impart resemblance in a sketch—must have vanished, or been obscured, before I met the General. All merely graceful attributes are usually the most

► *In what way is the general like Fort Ticonderoga?*

Words For Everyday Use	**pon • der • ous** (pän´dər əs) *adj.*, labored
	ob • sti • na • cy (äb´stə nə sē) *n.*, stubbornness
	un • mal • le • a • ble (un mal´ē ə bəl) *adj.*, not pliable, not adaptable

evanescent; nor does Nature adorn the human ruin with blossoms of new beauty, that have their roots and proper nutriment only in the chinks and crevices of decay, as she sows wall-flowers over the ruined fortress of Ticonderoga. Still, even in respect of grace and beauty, there were points well worth noting. A ray of humor, now and then, would make its way through the veil of dim obstruction, and glimmer pleasantly upon our faces. A trait of native elegance, seldom seen in the masculine character after childhood or early youth, was shown in the General's fondness for the sight and fragrance of flowers. An old soldier might be supposed to prize only the bloody laurel[32] on his brow; but here was one, who seemed to have a young girl's appreciation of the floral tribe.

◀ *What surprising trait does the general reveal?*

There, beside the fireplace, the brave old General used to sit; while the Surveyor—though seldom, when it could be avoided, taking upon himself the difficult task of engaging him in conversation—was fond of standing at a distance, and watching his quiet and almost slumberous countenance. He seemed away from us, although we saw him but a few yards off; remote, though we passed close beside his chair; unattainable, though we might have stretched forth our hands and touched his own. It might be, that he lived a more real life within his thoughts, than amid the unappropriate environment of the Collector's office. The evolutions of the parade; the <u>tumult</u> of the battle; the flourish of old, heroic music, heard thirty years before—such scenes and sounds, perhaps, were all alive before his intellectual sense. Meanwhile, the merchants and ship-masters, the spruce clerks, and uncouth sailors, entered and departed; the bustle of this commercial and Custom-House life kept up its little murmur roundabout him; and neither with the men nor their affairs did the General appear to sustain the most distant relation. He was as much out of place as an old sword— now rusty, but which had flashed once in the battle's front, and showed still a bright gleam along its blade—would have been, among the inkstands, paper-folders, and mahogany rulers, on the Deputy Collector's desk.

---

32. **laurel.** Plant from which, in ancient Greece and Rome, ceremonial crowns were woven for victors or champions

Words For Everyday Use

tu • mult (too´mult´) *n.*, commotion, confusion

There was one thing that much aided me in renewing and re-creating the stalwart soldier of the Niagara frontier—the man of true and simple energy. It was the recollection of those memorable words of his—"I'll try, Sir!"—spoken on the very verge of a desperate and heroic enterprise, and breathing the soul and spirit of New England hardihood, comprehending all perils, and encountering all. If, in our country, valour were rewarded by heraldic honor, this phrase—which it seems so easy to speak, but which only he, with such a task of danger and glory before him, has ever spoken—would be the best and fittest of all mottoes for the General's shield of arms.

► According to the narrator, what helps a person to grow morally and intellectually? Do you agree with him?

It contributes greatly towards a man's moral and intellectual health, to be brought into habits of companionship with individuals unlike himself, who care little for his pursuits, and whose sphere and abilities he must go out of himself to appreciate. The accidents of my life have often afforded me this advantage, but never with more fullness and variety than during my continuance in office. There was one man, especially, the observation of whose character gave me a new idea of talent. His gifts were emphatically those of a man of business; prompt, acute, clear-minded; with an eye that saw

► What gifts suit this "man of business" to his job?

through all perplexities, and a faculty of arrangement that made them vanish, as by the waving of an enchanter's wand. Bred up from boyhood in the Custom-House, it was his proper field of activity; and the many intricacies of business, so harassing to the interloper, presented themselves before him with the regularity of a perfectly comprehended system. In my contemplation, he stood as the ideal of his class. He was, indeed, the Custom-House in himself; or, at all events, the main-spring that kept its variously revolving wheels in motion; for, in an institution like this, where its officers are appointed to subserve their own profit and convenience, and seldom with a leading reference to their fitness for the duty to be performed, they must perforce seek elsewhere the dexterity which is not in them. Thus, by an inevitable necessity, as a magnet attracts steel-filings, so did our man of business draw to himself the difficulties which everybody met with. With an easy <u>condescension</u>, and kind forbearance towards our stupidity—which, to his order of mind, must have seemed little short of crime—would he

Words For Everyday Use	con • de • scen • sion (kän´di sen´shən) *n.*, act of descending voluntarily to the level of another

forthwith, by the merest touch of his finger, make the incomprehensible as clear as daylight. The merchants valued him not less than we, his esoteric friends. His integrity was perfect; it was a law of nature with him, rather than a choice or a principle; nor can it be otherwise than the main condition of an intellect so remarkably clear and accurate as his, to be honest and regular in the administration of affairs. A stain on his conscience, as to anything that came within the range of his vocation, would trouble such a man very much in the same way, though to a far greater degree, than an error in the balance of an account, or an ink-blot on the fair page of a book of record. Here, in a word—and it is a rare instance in my life—I had met with a person thoroughly adapted to the situation which he held.

Such were some of the people with whom I now found myself connected. I took it in good part at the hands of Providence, that I was thrown into a position so little akin to my past habits; and set myself seriously to gather from it whatever profit was to be had. After my fellowship of toil and impracticable schemes, with the dreamy brethren of Brook Farm;[33] after living for three years within the subtle influence of an intellect like Emerson's;[34] after those wild, free days on the Assabeth, indulging fantastic speculations beside our fire of fallen boughs, with Ellery Channing;[35] after talking with Thoreau about pine-trees and Indian relics, in his hermitage at Walden;[36] after growing fastidious by sympathy with the classic refinement of Hillard's[37] culture; after becoming imbued with poetic sentiment at Longfellow's[38] hearth-stone—it was time, at length, that I should exercise other faculties of my nature, and nourish myself with food for which I had hitherto had little appetite. Even the old Inspector was desirable, as a change of diet, to a man who had known Alcott.[39] I looked upon it as an evidence, in some measure, of a system naturally well balanced, and lacking no essential part of a thorough organization, that, with such associates to remember, I could mingle at once with men of

33. **Brook Farm.** Idealistic experiment in communal living in which Hawthorne took part
34. **Emerson's.** Of Ralph Waldo Emerson (1803–1882), well-known American essayist and poet admired by Hawthorne
35. **Ellery Channing.** William Ellery Channing (1780–1842), American clergyman who was widely influential on social issues
36. **Thoreau . . . Walden.** Henry David Thoreau (1817–1862), American essayist who lived for a short while in a hut at Walden Pond
37. **Hillard's.** George Stillman Hillard (1808–1879), Boston lawyer who aided Thoreau
38. **Longfellow.** Henry Wadsworth Longfellow (1807–1882), writer, Hawthorne's friend and classmate at Bowdoin College
39. **Alcott.** Amos Bronson Alcott (1799–1888), idealistic Transcendentalist who lived in Concord during Hawthorne's stay there

altogether different qualities, and never murmur at the change.

Literature, its exertions and objects, were now of little moment in my regard. I cared not, at this period, for books; they were apart from me. Nature—except it were human nature—the nature that is developed in earth and sky, was, in one sense, hidden from me; and all the imaginative delight, wherewith it had been spiritualized, passed away out of my mind. A gift, a faculty, if it had not been departed, was suspended and inanimate within me. There would have been something sad, unutterably dreary, in all this, had I not been conscious that it lay at my own option to recall whatever was valuable in the past. It might be true, indeed, that this was a life which could not, with <u>impunity</u>, be lived too long; else, it might make me permanently other than I had been, without transforming me into any shape which it would be worth my while to take. But I never considered it as other than a <u>transitory</u> life. There was always a prophetic instinct, a low whisper in my ear, that, within no long period, and whenever a new change of custom should be essential to my good, change would come.

Meanwhile, there I was, a Surveyor of the Revenue, and, so far as I have been able to understand, as good a Surveyor as need be. A man of thought, fancy, and sensibility, (had he ten times the Surveyor's proportion of those qualities,) may, at any time, be a man of affairs, if he will only choose to give himself the trouble. My fellow-officers, and the merchants and sea-captains with whom my official duties brought me into any manner of connection, viewed me in no other light, and probably knew me in no other character. None of them, I presume, had ever read a page of my inditing, or would have cared a fig the more for me, if they had read them all; nor would it have mended the matter, in the least, had those same unprofitable pages been written with a pen like that of Burns[40] or of Chaucer,[41] each of whom was a Custom-House officer in his day, as well as I. It is a good lesson—though it may often be a hard one—for a man who has dreamed of

40. **Burns.** Robert Burns (1759–1796), Scottish poet and songwriter, appointed officer in the excise at Dumfries in 1791
41. **Chaucer.** Geoffrey Chaucer (c. 1342–1400), English narrative poet, appointed Controller of the Customs in London in 1374

▶ *In what way does working at the custom house change the narrator?*

Words For Everyday Use

im • pu • ni • ty (im pyōō´ni tē) *n.,* exemption
tran • si • to • ry (tran´sə tôr´ē) *adj.,* temporary, fleeting

literary fame, and of making for himself a rank among the world's dignitaries by such means, to step aside out of the narrow circle in which his claims are recognized, and to find how utterly <u>devoid</u> of significance, beyond that circle, is all that he achieves, and all he aims at. I know not that I especially needed the lesson, either in the way of warning or <u>rebuke</u>; but, at any rate, I learned it thoroughly; nor, it gives me pleasure to reflect, did the truth, as it came home to my perception, ever cost me a pang, or require to be thrown off in a sigh. In the way of literary talk, it is true, the Naval Officer—an excellent fellow, who came into office with me, and went out only a little later—would often engage me in a discussion about one or the other of his favorite topics, Napoleon[42] or Shakespeare.[43] The Collector's junior clerk, too, a young gentleman who, it was whispered, occasionally covered a sheet of Uncle Sam's letter-paper with what, (at the distance of a few yards,) looked very much like poetry—used now and then to speak to me of books, as matters with which I might possibly be conversant. This was my all of lettered intercourse; and it was quite sufficient for my necessities.

◀ What does the narrator learn, at the custom house, about literary fame?

No longer seeking or caring that my name should be blazoned abroad on title-pages, I smiled to think that it had now another kind of <u>vogue</u>. The Custom-House marker imprinted it, with a stencil and black paint, on pepper-bags, and baskets of anatto, and cigar-boxes, and bales of all kinds of dutiable merchandise, in testimony that these commodities had paid the impost, and gone regularly through the office. Borne on such queer vehicle of fame, a knowledge of my existence, so far as a name conveys it, was carried where it had never been before, and, I hope, will never go again.

◀ Where did the narrator's name formerly appear? Where does it appear while he is working at the custom house?

But the past was not dead. Once in a great while, the thoughts, that had seemed so vital and so active, yet had been put to rest so quietly, revived again. One of the most remarkable occasions, when the habit of bygone days awoke in me, was that which brings it within the law of literary propriety to offer the public the sketch which I am now writing.

In the second story of the Custom-House, there is a large

---

42. **Napoleon.** Napoleon Bonaparte (1769–1784), French military leader and emperor
43. **Shakespeare.** William Shakespeare (1564–1616), great English dramatist, actor, and poet

Words For Everyday Use

de • void (di void´) *adj.*, completely without
re • buke (ri byo͞ok´) *n.*, sharp reprimand
vogue (vōg) *n.*, popularity

room, in which the brick-work and naked rafters have never been covered with paneling and plaster. The edifice—originally projected on a scale adapted to the old commercial enterprise of the port, and with an idea of subsequent prosperity destined never to be realized—contains far more space than its occupants know what to do with. This airy hall, therefore, over the Collector's apartments, remains unfinished to this day, and, in spite of the aged cobwebs that festoon its dusky beams, appears still to await the labor of the carpenter and mason. At one end of the room, in a recess, were a number of barrels, piled one upon another, containing bundles of official documents. Large quantities of similar rubbish lay lumbering the floor. It was sorrowful to think how many days, and weeks, and months, and years of toil, had been wasted on these musty papers, which were now only an <u>encumbrance</u> on earth, and were hidden away in this forgotten corner, never more to be glanced at by human eyes. But, then, what reams of other manuscripts—filled, not with the dullness of official formalities, but with the thought of inventive brains and the rich <u>effusion</u> of deep hearts—had gone equally to oblivion; and that, moreover, without serving a purpose in their day, as these heaped-up papers had, and—saddest of all—without purchasing for their writers the comfortable livelihood which the clerks of the Custom-House had gained by these worthless scratchings of the pen. Yet not altogether worthless, perhaps, as materials of local history. Here, no doubt, statistics of the former commerce of Salem might be discovered, and memorials of her princely merchants—old King Derby—old Billy Gray—old Simon Forrester—and many another magnate in his day; whose powdered head, however, was scarcely in the tomb, before his mountain-pile of wealth began to dwindle. The founders of the greater part of the families which now compose the aristocracy of Salem might here be traced, from the petty and obscure beginnings of their traffic, at periods generally much posterior to the Revolution, upward to what their children look upon as long-established rank.

Prior to the Revolution, there is a dearth of records; the earlier documents and archives of the Custom-House having, probably, been carried off to Halifax, when all the king's officials

▶ Why do the "musty papers" sadden the narrator? Why do forgotten creative works sadden the narrator even more?

Words For Everyday Use	en • cum • brance (en kum´brəns) n., hindrance, burden ef • fu • sion (e fyo͞o´zhən) n., emotional expression

accompanied the British army in its flight from Boston.[44] It has often been a matter of regret with me; for, going back, perhaps, to the days of the Protectorate, those papers must have contained many references to forgotten or remembered men, and to antique customs, which would have affected me with the same pleasure as when I used to pick up Indian arrow-heads in the field near the Old Manse.

But, one idle and rainy day, it was my fortune to make a discovery of some little interest. Poking and burrowing into the heaped-up rubbish in the corner; unfolding one and another document, and reading the names of vessels that had long ago foundered at sea or rotted at the wharves, and those of merchants, never heard of now on 'Change,[45] nor very readily decipherable on their mossy tombstones; glancing at such matters with the saddened, weary, half-reluctant interest which we bestow on the corpse of dead activity—and exerting my fancy, sluggish with little use, to raise up from these dry bones an image of the old town's brighter aspect, when India was a new region, and only Salem knew the way thither—I chanced to lay my hand on a small package, carefully done up in a piece of ancient yellow parchment. This envelope had the air of an official record of some period long past, when clerks <u>engrossed</u> their stiff and formal chirography[46] on more substantial materials than at present. There was something about it that quickened an instinctive curiosity, and made me undo the faded red tape, that tied up the package, with the sense that a treasure would here be brought to light. Unbending the rigid folds of the parchment cover, I found it to be a commission, under the hand and seal of Governor Shirley, in favor of one Jonathan Pue,[47] as Surveyor of his Majesty's Customs for the port of Salem, in the Province of Massachusetts Bay. I remembered to have read (probably in Felt's Annals) a notice of the decease of Mr. Surveyor Pue, about fourscore years ago; and likewise, in a newspaper of recent times, an account of the digging up of his remains in the little grave-yard of St. Peter's Church, during the renewal of that edifice. Nothing, if I rightly call to mind, was

◄ Where does the narrator claim to make his "discovery of some little interest"?

---

44. **Halifax . . . flight from Boston.** In 1776, British troops, besieged by General George Washington, withdrew from Boston and moved to Halifax, Nova Scotia.
45. **'Change.** Boston Merchant's Exchange
46. **chirography.** Penmanship
47. **Jonathan Pue.** Hawthorne would most likely be familiar with Pue from Joseph Felt's *Annals of Salem*, from which he would have learned that Pue took office in 1752 and died in 1760.

Words
For
Everyday
Use

en • gross (en grōs) *vt.*, express formally

left of my respected predecessor, save an imperfect skeleton, and some fragments of apparel, and a wig of majestic frizzle; which, unlike the head that it once adorned, was in very satisfactory preservation. But, on examining the papers which the parchment commission served to envelop, I found more traces of Mr. Pue's mental part, and the internal operations of his head, than the frizzled wig had contained of the venerable skull itself.

. They were documents, in short, not official, but of a private nature, or, at least, written in his private capacity, and apparently with his own hand. I could account for their being included in the heap of Custom-House lumber only by the fact, that Mr. Pue's death had happened suddenly; and that these papers, which he probably kept in his official desk, had never come to the knowledge of his heirs, or were supposed to relate to the business of the revenue. On the transfer of the archives to Halifax, this package, proving to be of no public concern, was left behind, and had remained ever since unopened.

The ancient Surveyor—being little molested, I suppose, at that early day, with business pertaining to his office—seems to have devoted some of his many leisure hours to researches as a local antiquarian, and other inquisitions of a similar nature. These supplied material for petty activity to a mind that would otherwise have been eaten up with rust. A portion of his facts, by the by, did me good service in the preparation of the article entitled "MAIN STREET," included in the present volume. The remainder may perhaps be applied to purposes equally valuable, hereafter; or not impossibly may be worked up, so far as they go, into a regular history of Salem, should my <u>veneration</u> for the natal soil ever <u>impel</u> me to so pious a task. Meanwhile, they shall be at the command of any gentleman, inclined and competent, to take the unprofitable labor off my hands. As a final disposition, I contemplate depositing them with the Essex Historical Society.

But the object that most drew my attention to the mysterious package was a certain affair of fine red cloth, much worn and faded. There were traces about it of gold embroidery, which, however, was greatly frayed and defaced; so that none, or very little, of the glitter was left. It had been

▶ *What object in the package immediately catches the narrator's attention? What does the narrator believe this object was?*

| Words For Everyday Use | **ven • er • a • tion** (ven´ər ā´shən) *n.,* feeling of deep respect |
| | **im • pel** (im pel´) *vt.,* force, urge |

wrought,[48] as was easy to perceive, with wonderful skill of needlework; and the stitch (as I am assured by ladies conversant with such mysteries) gives evidence of a now forgotten art, not to be recovered even by the process of picking out the threads. This rag of scarlet cloth—for time, and wear, and a sacrilegious moth, had reduced it to little other than a rag— on careful examination, assumed the shape of a letter. It was the capital letter A. By an accurate measurement, each limb proved to be precisely three inches and a quarter in length. It had been intended, there could be no doubt, as an ornamental article of dress; but how it was to be worn, or what rank, honor, and dignity, in by-past times, were signified by it, was a riddle which (so <u>evanescent</u> are the fashions of the world in these particulars) I saw little hope of solving. And yet it strangely interested me. My eyes fastened themselves upon the old scarlet letter, and would not be turned aside. Certainly, there was some deep meaning in it, most worthy of interpretation, and which, as it were, streamed forth from the mystic symbol, subtly communicating itself to my sensibilities, but <u>evading</u> the analysis of my mind.

While thus perplexed—and cogitating,[49] among other hypotheses, whether the letter might not have been one of those decorations which the white men used to contrive, in order to take the eyes of Indians—I happened to place it on my breast. It seemed to me—the reader may smile, but must not doubt my word—it seemed to me, then, that I experienced a sensation not altogether physical, yet almost so, as of burning heat; and as if the letter were not of red cloth, but red-hot iron. I shuddered, and involuntarily let it fall upon the floor.

In the absorbing contemplation of the scarlet letter, I had hitherto neglected to examine a small roll of dingy paper, around which it had been twisted. This I now opened, and had the satisfaction to find, recorded by the old Surveyor's pen, a reasonably complete explanation of the whole affair. There were several foolscap[50] sheets, containing many particulars respecting the life and conversation of one Hester

◄ What does the narrator claim happened when he put the scarlet letter against his breast?

---

48. **wrought.** Made
49. **cogitating.** Thinking seriously about
50. **foolscap.** Writing paper

Words For Everyday Use

ev • a • nes • cent (ev´ə nes´ənt) *adj.*, ephemeral; short-lived; likely to vanish or disappear

e • vade (ē vād´) *vi.*, escape

Prynne, who appeared to have been rather a noteworthy personage in the view of our ancestors. She had flourished during the period between the early days of Massachusetts and the close of the seventeenth century. Aged persons, alive in the time of Mr. Surveyor Pue, and from whose oral testimony he had made up his narrative, remembered her, in their youth, as a very old, but not <u>decrepit</u> woman, of a stately and solemn aspect. It had been her habit, from an almost immemorial date, to go about the country as a kind of voluntary nurse, and doing whatever miscellaneous good she might; taking upon herself, likewise, to give advice in all matters, especially those of the heart; by which means, as a person of such <u>propensities</u> inevitably must, she gained from many people the reverence due to an angel, but, I should imagine, was looked upon by others as an intruder and a nuisance. Prying farther into the manuscript, I found the record of other doings and sufferings of this singular woman, for most of which the reader is referred to the story entitled "THE SCARLET LETTER"; and it should be borne carefully in mind that the main facts of that story are authorized and authenticated by the document of Mr. Surveyor Pue. The original papers, together with the scarlet letter itself—a most curious relic—are still in my possession, and shall be freely exhibited to whomsoever, induced by the great interest of the narrative, may desire a sight of them. I must not be understood as affirming that, in the dressing up of the tale, and imagining the motives and modes of passion that influenced the characters who figure in it, I have invariably confined myself within the limits of the old Surveyor's half a dozen sheets of foolscap. On the contrary, I have allowed myself, as to such points, nearly or altogether as much license as if the facts had been entirely of my own invention. What I contend for is the authenticity of the outline.

This incident recalled my mind, in some degree, to its old track. There seemed to be here the groundwork of a tale. It impressed me as if the ancient Surveyor, in his garb of a hundred years gone by, and wearing his immortal wig—which was buried with him, but did not perish in the grave—had met me in the deserted chamber of the Custom-House. In his port was the dignity of one who had borne his Majesty's

► *What does the narrator say about the story "The Scarlet Letter"? What does he say he has allowed himself to do? Has the narrator actually served only as an "editor" as he earlier claimed?*

Words For Everyday Use

de • crep • it (dē krep´it) *adj.*, broken down or worn out by age

pro • pen • si • ty (prə pen´sə tē) *n.*, inclination

commission, and who was therefore illuminated by a ray of the splendor that shone so dazzlingly about the throne. How unlike, alas! the hang-dog look of a republican official, who, as the servant of the people, feels himself less than the least, and below the lowest, of his masters. With his own ghostly hand, the <u>obscurely</u> seen, but majestic, figure had imparted to me the scarlet symbol, and the little roll of explanatory manuscript. With his own ghostly voice, he had <u>exhorted</u> me, on the sacred consideration of my filial duty and reverence towards him—who might reasonably regard himself as my official ancestor—to bring his moldy and moth-eaten lucubrations[51] before the public. "Do this," said the ghost of Mr. Surveyor Pue, emphatically nodding the head that looked so imposing within its memorable wig, "do this, and the profit shall be all your own! You will shortly need it; for it is not in your days as it was in mine, when a man's office was a life-lease, and oftentimes an heirloom. But, I charge you, in this matter of old Mistress Prynne, give to your predecessor's memory the credit which will be rightfully its due!" And I said to the ghost of Mr. Surveyor Pue—"I will!"

◄ What reason does the ghost imagined by the narrator give for bringing "his moldy and moth-eaten lucubrations before the public"?

On Hester Prynne's story, therefore, I bestowed much thought. It was the subject of my meditations for many an hour, while pacing to and fro across my room, or traversing, with a hundredfold repetition, the long extent from the front-door of the Custom-House to the side-entrance, and back again. Great were the weariness and annoyance of the old Inspector and the Weighers and Gaugers, whose slumbers were disturbed by the unmercifully lengthened tramp of my passing and returning footsteps. Remembering their own former habits, they used to say that the Surveyor was walking the quarter-deck. They probably fancied that my sole object—and, indeed, the sole object for which a sane man could ever put himself into voluntary motion—was, to get an appetite for dinner. And to say the truth, an appetite, sharpened by the east-wind that generally blew along the passage, was the only valuable result of so much <u>indefatigable</u> exercise. So little adapted is the atmosphere of a Custom-

◄ What difficulty does the narrator experience in trying to tell the tale of the "Scarlet Letter"? What causes this difficulty?

---

51. **lucubrations.** Pedantic literary writings, or narrow-minded scholarly works that adhere to certain arbitrary rules and forms

Words For Everyday Use	
ob • scure • ly (əb skyo͞or´lē) *adv.,* indistinctly	
ex • hort (eg zôrt) *vt.,* urge strongly	
in • de • fat • i • ga • ble (in´di fat´i gə bəl) *adj.,* untiring; not yielding to fatigue	

House to the delicate harvest of fancy and sensibility, that, had I remained there through ten Presidencies yet to come, I doubt whether the tale of "The Scarlet Letter" would ever have been brought before the public eye. My imagination was a tarnished mirror. It would not reflect, or only with miserable dimness, the figures with which I did my best to people it. The characters of the narrative would not be warmed and rendered malleable, by any heat that I could kindle at my intellectual forge. They would take neither the glow of passion nor the tenderness of sentiment, but retained all the rigidity of dead corpses, and stared me in the face with a fixed and ghastly grin of <u>contemptuous</u> defiance. "What have you to do with us?" that expression seemed to say. "The little power you might have once possessed over the tribe of unrealities is gone! You have bartered it for a pittance of the public gold. Go, then, and earn your wages!" In short, the almost torpid creatures of my own fancy twitted me with imbecility, and not without fair occasion.

It was not merely during the three hours and a half which Uncle Sam claimed as his share of my daily life, that this wretched numbness held possession of me. It went with me on my sea-shore walks and rambles into the country, whenever—which was seldom and reluctantly—I bestirred myself to seek that invigorating charm of Nature, which used to give me such freshness and activity of thought, the moment that I stepped across the threshold of the Old Manse. The same torpor, as regarded the capacity for intellectual effort, accompanied me home, and weighed upon me in the chamber which I most absurdly termed my study. Nor did it quit me, when, late at night, I sat in the deserted parlor, lighted only by the glimmering coal-fire and the moon, striving to picture forth imaginary scenes, which, the next day, might flow out on the brightening page in many-hued description.

If the imaginative faculty refused to act at such an hour, it might well be deemed a hopeless case. Moonlight, in a familiar room, falling so white upon the carpet, and showing all its figures so distinctly—making every object so minutely visible, yet so unlike a morning or noontide visibility—is a medium the most suitable for a romance-writer to get acquainted with his illusive guests. There is the little

▶ *In what way does the narrator claim to have been changed by working in the custom house?*

Words For Everyday Use

con • temp • tu • ous (kə temp´chōō əs) *adj.*, scornful, disdainful domestic scenery of the well-known apartment; the chairs, with each its separate individuality; the centre-table, sustaining a work-basket, a volume or two, and an extinguished lamp; the sofa; the book-case; the picture on the wall—all these details, so completely seen, are so spiritualized by the unusual light, that they seem to lose their actual substance, and become things of intellect. Nothing is too small or too <u>trifling</u> to undergo this change, and acquire dignity thereby. A child's shoe; the doll, seated in her little wicker carriage; the hobby-horse;—whatever, in a word, has been used or played with, during the day, is now invested with a quality of strangeness and remoteness, though still almost as vividly present as by daylight. Thus, therefore, the floor of our familiar room has become a neutral territory, somewhere between the real world and fairy-land, where the Actual and the Imaginary may meet, and each <u>imbue</u> itself with the nature of the other. Ghosts might enter here, without affrighting us. It would be too much in keeping with the scene to excite surprise, were we to look about us and discover a form, beloved, but gone hence, now sitting quietly in a streak of this magic moonshine, with an aspect that would make us doubt whether it had returned from afar, or had never once stirred from our fireside.

The somewhat dim coal-fire has an essential influence in producing the effect which I would describe. It throws its unobtrusive tinge throughout the room, with a faint ruddiness upon the walls and ceiling, and a reflected gleam from the polish of the furniture. This warmer light mingles itself with the cold spirituality of the moonbeams, and communicates, as it were, a heart and sensibilities of human tenderness to the forms which fancy summons up. It converts them from snow-images into men and women. Glancing at the looking-glass, we behold—deep within its haunted verge—the smoldering glow of the half-extinguished anthracite,[52] the white moon-beams on the floor, and a repetition of all the gleam and shadow of the picture, with one

---

52. **anthracite.** Type of coal

▶ According to the narrator, what does a person have to be able to do in order to write romances?

remove farther from the actual, and nearer to the imaginative. Then, at such an hour, and with this scene before him, if a man, sitting all alone, cannot dream strange things, and make them look like truth, he need never try to write romances.

But, for myself, during the whole of my Custom-House experience, moonlight and sunshine, and the glow of firelight, were just alike in my regard; and neither of them was of one whit more avail than the twinkle of a tallow-candle. An entire class of susceptibilities, and a gift connected with them—of no great richness or value, but the best I had—was gone from me.

It is my belief, however, that, had I attempted a different order of composition, my faculties would not have been found so pointless and inefficacious. I might, for instance, have contented myself with writing out the narratives of a veteran shipmaster, one of the Inspectors, whom I should be most ungrateful not to mention, since scarcely a day passed that he did not stir me to laughter and admiration by his marvellous gifts as a story-teller. Could I have preserved the picturesque force of his style, and the humorous coloring which nature taught him how to throw over his descriptions, the result, I honestly believe, would have been something new in literature. Or I might readily have found a more serious task. It was a folly, with the materiality of this daily life pressing so intrusively upon me, to attempt to fling myself back into another age; or to insist on creating the semblance of a world out of airy matter, when, at every moment, the <u>impalpable</u> beauty of my soap-bubble was broken by the rude contact of some actual circumstance. The wiser effort would have been, to diffuse thought and imagination through the opaque substance of to-day, and thus to make it a bright transparency; to spiritualize the burden that began to weigh so heavily; to seek, resolutely, the true and indestructible value that lay hidden in the petty and wearisome incidents, and ordinary characters, with which I was now conversant. The fault was mine. The page of life that was spread out before me seemed dull and commonplace, only because I had not fathomed its deeper import. A better book than I shall ever write was there; leaf after leaf

Words For Everyday Use

im • pal • pa • ble (im pal´pə bəl) *adj.*, lacking substance; not perceivable through touch presenting itself to me, just as it was written out by the reality of the flitting hour, and vanishing as fast as written, only because my brain wanted the insight and my hand the cunning to transcribe it. At some future day, it may be, I shall remember a few scattered fragments and broken paragraphs, and write them down, and find the letters turn to gold upon the page.

These perceptions had come too late. At the instant, I was only conscious that what would have been a pleasure once was now a hopeless toil. There was no occasion to make much moan about this state of affairs. I had ceased to be a writer of tolerably poor tales and essays, and had become a tolerably good Surveyor of the Customs. That was all. But, nevertheless, it is anything but agreeable to be haunted by a suspicion that one's intellect is dwindling away; or exhaling, without your consciousness, like ether out of a phial; so that, at every glance, you find a smaller and less volatile residuum. Of the fact, there could be no doubt; and, examining myself and others, I was led to conclusions in reference to the effect of public office on the character, not very favorable to the mode of life in question. In some other form, perhaps, I may hereafter develop these effects. Suffice it here to say, that a Custom-House officer, of long continuance, can hardly be a very praiseworthy or respectable personage, for many reasons; one of them, the tenure by which he holds his situation, and another, the very nature of his business, which—though, I trust, an honest one—is of such a sort that he does not share in the united effort of mankind.

◀ What effect does working at the custom house have on the narrator?

An effect—which I believe to be observable, more or less, in every individual who has occupied the position—is, that while he leans on the mighty arm of the Republic, his own proper strength departs from him. He loses, in an extent proportioned to the weakness or force of his original nature, the capability of self-support. If he possess an unusual share of native energy, or the <u>enervating</u> magic of place do not operate too long upon him, his forfeited powers may be redeemable. The ejected officer—fortunate in the unkindly shove that sends him forth betimes, to struggle amid a struggling world—may return to himself, and become all that he

---

Words For Everyday Use	**en • er • vat • ing** (en´ ər vāt´iŋ) *adj.*, debilitating, weakening

has ever been. But this seldom happens. He usually keeps his ground just long enough for his own ruin, and is then thrust out, with sinews all unstrung, to totter along the difficult footpath of life as he best may. Conscious of his own infirmity—that his tempered steel and elasticity are lost—he for ever afterwards looks wistfully about him in quest of support external to himself. His pervading and continual hope—a hallucination, which, in the face of all discouragement, and making light of impossibilities, haunts him while he lives, and, I fancy, like the convulsive throes of the cholera,[53] torments him for a brief space after death—is, that, finally, and in no long time, by some happy coincidence of circumstances, he shall be restored to office. This faith, more than anything else, steals the pith and availability out of whatever enterprise he may dream of undertaking. Why should he toil and moil, and be at so much trouble to pick himself up out of the mud, when, in a little while hence, the strong arm of his Uncle will raise and support him? Why should he work for his living here, or go to dig gold in California, when he is so soon to be made happy, at monthly intervals, with a little pile of glittering coin out of his Uncle's pocket? It is sadly curious to observe how slight a taste of office suffices to infect a poor fellow with this singular disease. Uncle Sam's gold—meaning no disrespect to the worthy old gentleman—has, in this respect, a quality of enchantment like that of the Devil's wages. Whoever touches it should look well to himself, or he may find the bargain to go hard against him, involving, if not his soul, yet many of its better <u>attributes</u>; its sturdy force, its courage and constancy, its truth, its self-reliance, and all that gives the emphasis to manly character.

Here was a fine prospect in the distance! Not that the Surveyor brought the lesson home to himself, or admitted that he could be so utterly undone, either by continuance in office or ejectment. Yet my reflections were not the most comfortable. I began to grow melancholy and restless; continually prying into my mind, to discover which of its poor properties were gone, and what degree of detriment had already <u>accrued</u> to the remainder. I endeavored to calculate how much longer I could stay in the Custom-House, and yet

▶ According to the narrator, what is the one hope of most custom house officers who lose their positions?

▶ To what does the narrator compare government pay?

---

53. **cholera.** Intestinal disease

> **Words For Everyday Use**
>
> **at • trib • ute** (ə trib′ yo͞ot) *n.*, characteristic or quality
> **ac • crue** (ə kro͞o′) *vi.*, come as a natural growth

go forth a man. To confess the truth, it was my greatest apprehension—as it would never be a measure of policy to turn out so quiet an individual as myself, and it being hardly in the nature of a public officer to resign—it was my chief trouble, therefore, that I was likely to grow gray and decrepit in the Surveyorship, and become much such another animal as the old Inspector. Might it not, in the <u>tedious</u> lapse of official life that lay before me, finally be with me as it was with this venerable friend—to make the dinner-hour the nucleus of the day, and to spend the rest of it, as an old dog spends it, asleep in the sunshine or in the shade? A dreary look-forward this, for a man who felt it to be the best definition of happiness to live throughout the whole range of his faculties and sensibilities! But, all this while, I was giving myself very unnecessary alarm. Providence had meditated better things for me than I could possibly imagine for myself.

A remarkable event of the third year of my Surveyorship—to adopt the tone of "P. P."—was the election of General Taylor[54] to the Presidency. It is essential, in order to form a complete estimate of the advantages of official life, to view the incumbent at the in-coming of a hostile administration. His position is then one of the most singularly <u>irksome</u>, and, in every contingency, disagreeable, that a wretched mortal can possibly occupy; with seldom an alternative of good, on either hand, although what presents itself to him as the worst event may very probably be the best. But it is a strange experience, to a man of pride and sensibility, to know that his interests are within the control of individuals who neither love nor understand him, and by whom, since one or the other must needs happen, he would rather be injured than obliged. Strange, too, for one who has kept his calmness throughout the contest, to observe the bloodthirstiness that is developed in the hour of triumph, and to be conscious that he is himself among its objects! There are few uglier traits of human nature than this tendency—which I now witnessed in men no worse than their neighbors—to grow cruel, merely because they possessed the power of inflicting harm. If the guillotine, as applied to office-holders,

◄ *How does the narrator feel about the way in which jobs are revoked and assigned depending on the political party in power? To what does he compare losing one's office?*

---

54. **Taylor.** Zachary Taylor (1784–1850) was elected president in 1848.

Words For Everyday Use	**te • di • ous** (tē′dē əs) *adj.*, tiresome, boring **irk • some** (ʉrk′səm) *adj.*, annoying

were a literal fact, instead of one of the most apt of metaphors, it is my sincere belief, that the active members of the victorious party were sufficiently excited to have chopped off all our heads, and have thanked Heaven for the opportunity! It appears to me—who have been a calm and curious observer, as well in victory as defeat—that this fierce and bitter spirit of malice and revenge has never distinguished the many triumphs of my own party as it now did that of the Whigs. The Democrats take the offices, as a general rule, because they need them, and because the practice of many years has made it the law of political warfare, which unless a different system be proclaimed, it was weakness and cowardice to murmur at. But the long habit of victory has made them generous. They know how to spare, when they see occasion; and when they strike, the axe may be sharp, indeed, but its edge is seldom poisoned with ill-will; nor is it their custom <u>ignominiously</u> to kick the head which they have just struck off.

In short, unpleasant as was my predicament, at best, I saw much reason to congratulate myself that I was on the losing side, rather than the triumphant one. If, heretofore, l had been none of the warmest of partisans, I began now, at this season of peril and adversity, to be pretty acutely sensible with which party my <u>predilections</u> lay; nor was it without something like regret and shame, that, according to a reasonable calculation of chances, I saw my own prospect of retaining office to be better than those of my democratic brethren. But who can see an inch into futurity, beyond his nose? My own head was the first that fell!

The moment when a man's head drops off is seldom or never, I am inclined to think, precisely the most agreeable of his life. Nevertheless, like the greater part of our misfortunes, even so serious a contingency brings its remedy and consolation with it, if the sufferer will but make the best, rather than the worst, of the accident which has befallen him. In my particular case, the consolatory topics were close at hand, and, indeed, had suggested themselves to my meditations a considerable time before it was requisite to use them. In view of my previous weariness of office, and vague thoughts of resignation, my fortune somewhat resembled that of a person

▶ *Does the narrator take a negative or a positive view of adversity? Explain.*

Words	ig • no • min • i • ous • ly (ig´nə min´ē əs lē) *adv.*, shame-
For	fully; despicably
Everyday	pred • i • lec • tion (pred˝l ek´shən) *n.*, preference;
Use	preconceived liking

who should entertain an idea of committing suicide, and, altogether beyond his hopes, meet with the good hap to be murdered. In the Custom-House, as before in the Old Manse, I had spent three years; a term long enough to rest a weary brain; long enough to break off old intellectual habits, and make room for new ones; long enough, and too long, to have lived in an unnatural state, doing what was really of no advantage nor delight to any human being, and withholding myself from toil that would, at least, have stilled an unquiet impulse in me. Then, moreover, as regarded his unceremonious ejectment, the late Surveyor was not altogether ill-pleased to be recognized by the Whigs as an enemy; since his inactivity in political affairs—his tendency to roam, at will, in that broad and quiet field where all mankind may meet, rather than confine himself to those narrow paths where brethren of the same household must <u>diverge</u> from one another—had sometimes made it questionable with his brother Democrats whether he was a friend. Now, after he had won the crown of martyrdom (though with no longer a head to wear it on,) the point might be looked upon as settled. Finally, little heroic as he was, it seemed more decorous to be overthrown in the downfall of the party with which he had been content to stand, than to remain a forlorn survivor, when so many worthier men were falling; and, at last, after subsisting for four years on the mercy of a hostile administration, to be <u>compelled</u> then to define his position anew, and claim the yet more humiliating mercy of a friendly one.

Meanwhile, the press had taken up my affair, and kept me for a week or two, careering through the public prints, in my decapitated state, like Irving's Headless Horseman,[55] ghastly and grim, and longing to be buried, as a politically dead man ought. So much for my figurative self. The real human being, all this time, with his head safely on his shoulders, had brought himself to the comfortable conclusion, that everything was for the best; and making an investment in ink, paper, and steel-pens, had opened his long-disused writing-desk, and was again a literary man.

◄ *What positive consequence did losing his job have for the narrator?*

---

55. **Irving's Headless Horseman.** Supernatural character in Washington Irving's "The Legend of Sleepy Hollow"

di • verge (dī vʉrj´) *vi.*, go or move in different directions
com • pel (kəm pel´) *vt.*, force

Now it was, that the lucubrations of my ancient predecessor, Mr. Surveyor Pue, came into play. Rusty through long idleness, some little space was requisite before my intellectual machinery could be brought to work upon the tale, with an effect in any degree satisfactory. Even yet, though my thoughts were ultimately much absorbed in the task, it wears, to my eye, a stern and somber aspect; too much ungladdened by genial sunshine; too little relieved by the tender and familiar influences which soften almost every scene of nature and real life, and, undoubtedly, should soften every picture of them. This uncaptivating effect is perhaps due to the period of hardly accomplished revolution, and still seething turmoil, in which the story shaped itself. It is no indication, however, of a lack of cheerfulness in the writer's mind; for he was happier, while straying through the gloom of these sunless fantasies, than at any time since he had quitted the Old Manse. Some of the briefer articles, which contribute to make up the volume, have likewise been written since my involuntary withdrawal from the toils and honors of public life, and the remainder are <u>gleaned</u> from annuals and magazines, of such antique date that they have gone round the circle, and come back to novelty again. Keeping up the metaphor of the political guillotine, the whole may be considered as the Posthumous Papers of a Decapitated Surveyor; and the sketch which I am now bringing to a close, if too autobiographical for a modest person to publish in his lifetime, will readily be excused in a gentleman who writes from beyond the grave. Peace be with all the world! My blessing on my friends! My forgiveness to my enemies! For I am in the realm of quiet!

The life of the Custom-House lies like a dream behind me. The old Inspector—who, by-the-bye, l regret to say, was overthrown and killed by a horse, some time ago; else he would certainly have lived for ever—he, and all those other venerable personages who sat with him at the receipt of custom, are but shadows in my view; white-headed and wrinkled images, which my fancy used to sport with, and has now flung aside for ever. The merchants—Pingree, Phillips, Shepard, Upton, Kimball, Bertram, Hunt—these and many other names, which had such classic familiarity for my ear six months

Words For Everyday Use

glean (glēn) *vi.*, collect or gather

ago—these men of traffic, who seemed to occupy so important a position in the world—how little time has it required to disconnect me from them all, not merely in act, but recollection! It is with an effort that I recall the figures and appellations[56] of these few. Soon, likewise, my old native town will loom upon me through the haze of memory, a mist brooding over and around it; as if it were no portion of the real earth, but an overgrown village in cloud-land, with only imaginary inhabitants to people its wooden houses, and walk its homely lanes, and the unpicturesque prolixity of its main street. Henceforth, it ceases to be a reality of my life. I am a citizen of somewhere else. My good townspeople will not much regret me; for—though it has been as dear an object as any, in my literary efforts, to be of some importance in their eyes, and to win myself a pleasant memory in this <u>abode</u> and burial-place of so many of my forefathers—there has never been, for me, the genial atmosphere which a literary man requires, in order to ripen the best harvest of his mind. I shall do better amongst other faces; and these familiar ones, it need hardly be said, will do just as well without me.

It may be, however—O, transporting and triumphant thought!—that the great-grandchildren of the present race may sometimes think kindly of the scribbler of bygone days, when the antiquary of days to come, among the sites memorable in the town's history, shall point out the locality of THE TOWN PUMP.[57]

◄ *For what does the speaker hope?*

---

56. **appellations.** Names or titles
57. THE TOWN PUMP. In 1835, Hawthorne published a sketch entitled, "A Rill from the Town-Pump," which presented impressions of Salem.

Words For Everyday Use

a • bode (ə bōd´) n., home

Responding to the Selection

Would you have found work at the custom house interesting, or would it have dulled your spirits as it did those of the narrator? What kind of work would you find engaging and empowering? Why is it important for a person to find such work? Write about these questions in your journal.

Reviewing the Selection

Recalling and Interpreting

1. **R:** Why is the narrator drawn to the town of Salem? Who are some of the narrator's most well-known ancestors?

2. **I:** How important is history to this narrator? How does the narrator differ from his ancestors? In what way does the narrator feel a connection to his ancestors?

3. **R:** What people from the custom house does the narrator describe in great detail?

4. **I:** According to the narrator, what type of person is most likely to be found working at the custom house? What are his feelings toward the other custom house officials?

5. **R:** What items does the narrator find in a rubbish heap at the custom house? Who was Jonathan Pue?

6. **I:** What does the narrator learn about Jonathan Pue? What meaning does he find in the rag of scarlet cloth in the shape of an *A*. What does the narrator say about the origin of *The Scarlet Letter*?

7. **R:** What becomes of the narrator's job at the custom house?

8. **I:** Why does the narrator feel that what happens to his job at the custom house is probably for the best?

Synthesizing

9. Why does Hawthorne want to tell the story of the custom house? What does the place mean to him, and what does his essay tell you about his character?

10. What does this essay teach about the importance, to a creative person, of finding the right surroundings?

Understanding Literature

1. Satire. Satire is humorous writing or speech intended to point out errors, falsehoods, foibles, or failings. It is written for the purpose of reforming human behavior or human institutions. In what way is "The Custom-House" an example of satire? Name your favorite passages of satire in "The Custom-House." What errors or falsehoods does Hawthorne describe?

2. Tone. Tone is the emotional attitude toward the reader or toward the subject implied by a literary work. Examples of the different tones that a work might have include familiar, ironic, playful, sarcastic, serious, and sincere. What is the tone of "The Custom-House"? Does the tone change as the author discusses different subjects? Explain.

The Prison-Door

A throng of bearded men, in sad-colored garments and gray steeple-crowned hats, intermixed with women, some wearing hoods, and others bareheaded, was assembled in front of a wooden <u>edifice</u>, the door of which was heavily timbered with oak, and studded with iron spikes.

The founders of a new colony, whatever Utopia[1] of human virtue and happiness they might originally project, have invariably recognized it among their earliest practical necessities to allot a portion of the virgin soil as a cemetery, and another portion as the site of a prison. In accordance with this rule, it may safely be assumed that the forefathers of Boston had built the first prison-house, somewhere in the vicinity of Cornhill, almost as seasonably as they marked out the first burial-ground, on Isaac Johnson's lot,[2] and round about his grave, which subsequently became the <u>nucleus</u> of all the congregated sepulchers in the old churchyard of King's Chapel. Certain it is, that, some fifteen or twenty years after the settlement of the town,[3] the wooden jail was already marked with weather-stains and other indications of age, which gave a yet darker aspect to its beetle-browed and gloomy front. The rust on the <u>ponderous</u> iron-work of its oaken door looked more antique than anything else in the new world. Like all that pertains to crime, it seemed never to have known a youthful era. Before this ugly edifice, and between it and the wheel-track of the street, was a grass-plot, much overgrown with burdock, pig-weed, apple-peru, and such unsightly vegetation, which evidently found something <u>congenial</u> in the soil that had so early borne the black flower of civilized society, a prison. But on one side of the

▶ *What two places, found in any colony, provide evidence that there is no such thing as a utopia?*

▶ *What metaphor does the narrator use to describe the prison?*

---

1. **Utopia.** Ideal place
2. **Isaac Johnson's lot.** Isaac Johnson (1601–1630) was a colonist who died within months of arriving in New England.
3. **fifteen or twenty years. . . town.** Fifteen or twenty years after the settlement of Boston in 1630. Other allusions in the novel set the opening of the story twelve years later, in 1642.

Words
For
Everyday
Use

ed • i • fice (ed´i fis) *n.,* large, imposing building
nuc • le • us (nōō´ klē əs) *n.,* center
pon • der • ous (pän dər əs) *adj.,* heavy
con • ge • nial (kən jēn´yəl) *adj.,* compatible

portal,[4] and rooted almost at the threshold,[5] was a wild rose-bush, covered, in this month of June, with its delicate gems, which might be imagined to offer their fragrance and fragile beauty to the prisoner as he went in, and to the condemned criminal as he came forth to his doom, in token that the deep heart of Nature could pity and be kind to him.

This rose-bush, by a strange chance, has been kept alive in history; but whether it had merely survived out of the stern old wilderness, so long after the fall of the gigantic pines and oaks that originally overshadowed it—or whether, as there is fair authority for believing, it had sprung up under the foot-steps of the sainted Ann Hutchinson,[6] as she entered the prison-door—we shall not take upon us to determine. Finding it so directly on the threshold of our narrative, which is now about to issue from that <u>inauspicious</u> portal, we could hardly do otherwise than pluck one of its flowers and present it to the reader. It may serve, let us hope, to symbolize some sweet moral blossom, that may be found along the track, or relieve the darkening close of a tale of human frailty and sorrow.

◄ *What plant surprisingly grows outside the prison? Why does it grow there, according to the narrator?*

4. **portal.** Doorway
5. **threshold.** Entrance or doorsill
6. **Ann Hutchinson.** Hutchinson (1591–1643) was a religious leader banished from the Massachusetts Bay Colony because of her beliefs. See The Historical Context of *The Scarlet Letter* on page x.

Words For Everyday Use

in • aus • pi • cious (in´ô spish´əs) *adj.,* unfavorable, unlucky

II

The Market-Place

The grass-plot before the jail, in Prison Lane, on a certain summer morning, not less than two centuries ago, was occupied by a pretty large number of the inhabitants of Boston; all with their eyes intently fastened on the iron-clamped oaken door. Amongst any other population, or at a later period in the history of New England, the grim rigidity that petrified the bearded physiognomies[1] of these good people would have <u>augured</u> some awful business in hand. It could have betokened nothing short of the anticipated execution of some noted culprit, on whom the sentence of a legal tribunal had but confirmed the verdict of public sentiment. But, in that early <u>severity</u> of the Puritan character, an <u>inference</u> of this kind could not so <u>indubitably</u> be drawn. It might be that a sluggish bond-servant, or an undutiful child, whom his parents had given over to the civil authority, was to be corrected at the whipping-post. It might be, that an Antinomian, a Quaker, or other heterodox religionist,[2] was to be scourged[3] out of the town, or an idle or vagrant Indian, whom the white man's fire-water had made riotous about the streets, was to be driven with stripes into the shadow of the forest. It might be, too, that a witch, like old Mistress Hibbins,[4] the bitter-tempered widow of the magistrate,[5] was to die upon the gallows. In either case, there was very much the same solemnity of <u>demeanor</u> on the part of the spectators; as befitted a people amongst whom religion and law were almost identical, and in whose character both were so thoroughly interfused, that the mildest and the severest acts of public discipline were alike made <u>venerable</u> and awful. Meagre, indeed, and cold, was the sympathy that a

▶ How do the Puritans feel and act toward "trangressors," or people who break the law?

---

1. **physiognomies.** Faces or figures
2. **Antinomian . . . religionist.** People who did not follow Puritan moral or religious law
3. **scourged.** Whipped in punishment
4. **Mistress Hibbins.** Widow of a prominent Boston merchant, she was tried as a witch, condemned, and hanged in 1656.
5. **magistrate.** Person in civil office with the power to enforce the law

---

Words For Everyday Use

au • gur (ôˊger) vt., foretell, prophesize
se • ver • i • ty (sə verˊə tē) n., strictness
in • fer • ence (inˊfər əns) n., conclusion
in • du • bi • ta • bly (in do͞oˊbi tə blē) adv., unquestionably
de • mean • or (di mēnˊər) n., conduct
ven • er • a • ble (venˊər ə bəl) adj., impressive; worthy of respect

transgressor might look for, from such bystanders at the scaffold. On the other hand, a penalty which, in our days, would infer a degree of mocking <u>infamy</u> and ridicule, might then be invested with almost as stern a dignity as the punishment of death itself.

It was a circumstance to be noted, on the summer morning when our story begins its course, that the women, of whom there were several in the crowd, appeared to take a peculiar interest in whatever penal infliction might be expected to ensue. The age had not so much refinement, that any sense of impropriety restrained the wearers of petticoat and farthingale[6] from stepping forth into the public ways, and wedging their not unsubstantial persons, if occasion were, into the throng nearest to the scaffold at an execution. Morally, as well as materially, there was a coarser fibre in those wives and maidens of old English birth and breeding, than in their fair descendants, separated from them by a series of six or seven generations; for, throughout that chain of ancestry, every successive mother has transmitted to her child a fainter bloom, a more delicate and briefer beauty, and a slighter physical frame, if not character of less force and solidity than her own. The women, who were now standing about the prison-door, stood within less than half a century of the period when the man-like Elizabeth[7] had been the not altogether unsuitable representative of the sex. They were her countrywomen; and the beef and ale of their native land, with a moral diet not a whit more refined, entered largely into their composition. The bright morning sun, therefore, shone on broad shoulders and well-developed busts, and on round and ruddy cheeks, that had ripened in the far-off island, and had hardly yet grown paler or thinner in the atmosphere of New England. There was, moreover, a boldness and rotundity of speech among these matrons, as most of them seemed to be, that would startle us at the present day, whether in respect to its purport or its volume of tone.

"Goodwives," said a hard-featured dame of fifty, "I'll tell ye a piece of my mind. It would be greatly for the public behoof

◄ Who takes the most interest in the punishment that the offender will receive?

◄ How does the narrator characterize the women of "old English birth"?

------

6. **farthingale.** Hoops worn under skirts
7. **Elizabeth.** Queen of England from 1558 to 1603

Words
For
Everyday
Use

in • fa • my (in´ fə mē) *n.*, dishonor, disgrace

► Who is the criminal who will be punished? What does the "hard-featured dame" think would be good for their town?

► How will Hester Prynne be punished? How does the third matron think she should be punished?

► What does the young wife say about the mark that Hester will be forced to wear?

if we women, being of mature age and church-members in good repute, should have the handling of such malefactresses[8] as this Hester Prynne. What think ye, gossips? If the hussy stood up for judgment before us five, that are now here in a knot together, would she come off with such a sentence as the worshipful magistrates have awarded? Marry, I trow not!"

"People say," said another, "that the Reverend Master Dimmesdale, her godly pastor, takes it very grievously to heart that such a scandal should have come upon his congregation."

"The magistrates are God-fearing gentlemen, but merciful overmuch—that is a truth," added a third autumnal matron. "At the very least, they should have put the brand of a hot iron on Hester Prynne's forehead. Madame Hester would have winced at that, I warrant me. But she—the naughty baggage—little will she care what they put upon the bodice of her gown.[9] Why, look you, she may cover it with a brooch, or such like heathenish adornment, and so walk the streets as brave as ever."

"Ah, but," interposed, more softly, a young wife, holding a child by the hand, "let her cover the mark as she will, the pang of it will be always in her heart."

"What do we talk of marks and brands, whether on the bodice of her gown or the flesh of her forehead?" cried another female, the ugliest as well as the most pitiless of these self-constituted judges. "This woman has brought shame upon us all, and ought to die. Is there not law for it? Truly there is, both in the Scripture[10] and the statute-book. Then let the magistrates, who have made it of no effect, thank themselves if their own wives and daughters go astray!"

"Mercy on us, goodwife," exclaimed a man in the crowd, "is there no virtue in woman, save what springs from a wholesome fear of the gallows? That is the hardest word yet! Hush, now, gossips; for the lock is turning in the prison-door, and here comes Mistress Prynne herself."

The door of the jail being flung open from within, there appeared, in the first place, like a black shadow emerging into sunshine, the grim and grisly presence of the town-beadle,[11] with a sword by his side, and his staff of office in his hand. This personage prefigured and represented in his aspect the whole dismal severity of the Puritanic code of law,

---

8. **malefactresses.** Female criminals or evildoers
9. **upon the bodice . . . gown.** Hester has been condemned to wear a scarlet letter *A* on the bodice, or upper part, of her dress.
10. **Scripture.** The Bible
11. **town-beadle.** Messenger of a court of law

which it was his business to administer in its final and closest application to the offender. Stretching forth the official staff in his left hand, he laid his right upon the shoulder of a young woman, whom he thus drew forward; until, on the threshold of the prison-door, she repelled him, by an action marked with natural dignity and force of character, and stepped into the open air, as if by her own free-will. She bore in her arms a child, a baby of some three months old, who winked and turned aside its little face from the too vivid light of day; because its existence, heretofore, had brought it acquainted only with the gray twilight of a dungeon, or other darksome apartment of the prison.

◄ What character traits are revealed by Hester's action?

When the young woman—the mother of this child—stood fully revealed before the crowd, it seemed to be her first impulse to clasp the infant closely to her bosom; not so much by an impulse of motherly affection, as that she might thereby conceal a certain token, which was wrought or fastened into her dress. In a moment, however, wisely judging that one token of her shame would but poorly serve to hide another, she took the baby on her arm, and, with a burning blush, and yet a <u>haughty</u> smile, and a glance that would not be abashed, looked around at her townspeople and neighbors. On the breast of her gown, in fine red cloth, surrounded with an elaborate embroidery and fantastic flourishes of gold thread, appeared the letter A. It was so artistically done, and with so much fertility and gorgeous luxuriance of fancy, that it had all the effect of a last and fitting decoration to the apparel which she wore; and which was of a splendor in accordance with the taste of the age, but greatly beyond what was allowed by the sumptuary[12] regulations of the colony.

◄ What symbol does Hester have to wear?

The young woman was tall, with a figure of perfect elegance, on a large scale. She had dark and abundant hair, so glossy that it threw off the sunshine with a gleam, and a face which, besides being beautiful from regularity of feature and richness of complexion, had the impressiveness belonging to a marked brow and deep black eyes. She was lady-like, too, after the manner of the feminine gentility of those days; characterized by a certain state and dignity, rather than by the delicate, evanescent, and indescribable grace, which is now recognized as its indication. And never had Hester

◄ What is surprising about Hester's appearance? What inner qualities does her appearance reveal?

---

12. **sumptuary.** Regulating extravagance on religious grounds

Words For Everyday Use	**haugh • ty** (hôt´ ē) *adj.*, proud, scornful

Prynne appeared more lady-like, in the antique interpretation of the term, than as she issued from the prison. Those who had before known her, and had expected to behold her dimmed and obscured by a disastrous cloud, were astonished, and even startled, to perceive how her beauty shone out, and made a halo of the misfortune and <u>ignominy</u> in which she was enveloped. It may be true, that, to a sensitive observer, there was something exquisitely painful in it. Her attire, which, indeed, she had wrought for the occasion, in prison, and had modeled much after her own fancy, seemed to express the attitude of her spirit, the desperate recklessness of her mood, by its wild and picturesque peculiarity. But the point which drew all eyes, and, as it were, transfigured the wearer—so that both men and women, who had been familiarly acquainted with Hester Prynne, were now impressed as if they beheld her for the first time—was that Scarlet Letter, so fantastically embroidered and illuminated upon her bosom. It had the effect of a spell, taking her out of the ordinary relations with humanity, and inclosing her in a sphere by herself.

"She hath good skill at her needle, that's certain," remarked one of her female spectators; "but did ever a woman, before this brazen hussy, contrive such a way of showing it! Why, gossips, what is it but to laugh in the faces of our godly magistrates, and make a pride out of what they, worthy gentlemen, meant for a punishment?"

"It were well," muttered the most iron-visaged of the old dames, "if we stripped Madame Hester's rich gown off her dainty shoulders; and as for the red letter, which she hath stitched so curiously, I'll bestow a rag of mine own rheumatic flannel, to make a fitter one!"

"Oh, peace, neighbors—peace!" whispered their youngest companion. "Do not let her hear you! Not a stitch in that embroidered letter, but she has felt it in her heart."

The grim beadle now made a gesture with his staff. "Make way, good people, make way, in the King's name," cried he. "Open a passage; and I promise ye, Mistress Prynne shall be set where man, woman, and child may have a fair sight of her brave apparel, from this time till an hour past meridian.[13]

---

13. **meridian.** Noon

Words For Everyday Use

ig • no • min • y (ig´nə min´ē) *n.*, shame, dishonor

► *What effect does the scarlet letter have on Hester Prynne?*

► *What do some of the female spectators think about the way in which Hester has embroidered the letter?*

A blessing on the righteous Colony of the Massachusetts, where <u>iniquity</u> is dragged out into the sunshine! Come along, Madame Hester, and show your scarlet letter in the market-place!"

A lane was forthwith opened through the crowd of spectators. Preceded by the beadle, and attended by an irregular procession of stern-browed men and unkindly-visaged women, Hester Prynne set forth towards the place appointed for her punishment. A crowd of eager and curious schoolboys, understanding little of the matter in hand, except that it gave them a half-holiday, ran before her progress, turning their heads continually to stare into her face, and at the winking baby in her arms, and at the ignominious letter on her breast. It was no great distance, in those days, from the prison-door to the market-place. Measured by the prisoner's experience, however, it might be reckoned a journey of some length; for, haughty as her demeanor was, she perchance underwent an agony from every footstep of those that thronged to see her, as if her heart had been flung into the street for them all to spurn and trample upon. In our nature, however, there is a provision, alike marvelous and merciful, that the sufferer should never know the intensity of what he endures by its present torture, but chiefly by the pang that rankles after it. With almost a serene deportment, therefore, Hester Prynne passed through this portion of her ordeal, and came to a sort of scaffold, at the western extremity of the market-place. It stood nearly beneath the eaves of Boston's earliest church, and appeared to be a fixture there.

◄ *Why does the journey to the market place seem longer than usual to Hester? Why is Hester able to remain serene despite her agony?*

In fact, this scaffold constituted a portion of a penal machine, which now, for two or three generations past, has been merely historical and traditionary among us, but was held, in the old time, to be as effectual an agent in the promotion of good citizenship, as ever was the guillotine among the terrorists of France. It was, in short, the platform of the pillory;[14] and above it rose the framework of that instrument of discipline, so fashioned as to confine the human head in its tight grasp, and thus hold it up to the public gaze. The very ideal of ignominy was embodied and made <u>manifest</u> in this contrivance of wood and iron. There can be no outrage,

◄ *Why do you think the Puritans found public humiliation to be such an effective punishment?*

---

14. **pillory.** Wooden device with openings for the hands and the head, used to confine minor offenders and to display them for public scorn and ridicule

Words For Everyday Use

in • iq • ui • ty (i nik´wi tē) *n.,* wickedness
man • i • fest (man´ə fest) *adj.,* apparent to the senses

methinks, against our common nature—whatever be the delinquencies of the individual—no outrage more <u>flagrant</u> than to forbid the culprit to hide his face for shame; as it was the essence of this punishment to do. In Hester Prynne's instance, however, as not unfrequently in other cases, her sentence bore, that she should stand a certain time upon the platform, but without undergoing that gripe about the neck and confinement of the head, the proneness to which was the most devilish characteristic of this ugly engine. Knowing well her part, she ascended a flight of wooden steps, and was thus displayed to the surrounding multitude, at about the height of a man's shoulders above the street.

▶ With whom does the narrator contrast Hester Prynne?

Had there been a Papist[15] among the crowd of Puritans, he might have seen in this beautiful woman, so picturesque in her attire and <u>mien</u>, and with the infant at her bosom, an object to remind him of the image of Divine Maternity, which so many illustrious painters have <u>vied</u> with one another to represent; something which should remind him, indeed, but only by contrast, of that sacred image of sinless motherhood, whose infant was to redeem the world. Here, there was the <u>taint</u> of deepest sin in the most sacred quality of human life, working such effect, that the world was only the darker for this woman's beauty, and the more lost for the infant that she had borne.

The scene was not without a mixture of awe, such as must always invest the spectacle of guilt and shame in a fellow-creature, before society shall have grown corrupt enough to smile, instead of shuddering, at it. The witnesses of Hester Prynne's disgrace had not yet passed beyond their simplicity. They were stern enough to look upon her death, had that been the sentence, without a murmur at its severity, but had none of the heartlessness of another social state, which would find only a theme for jest in an exhibition like the present. Even had there been a disposition to turn the matter into ridicule, it must have been repressed and overpowered by the solemn presence of men no less dignified than the governor, and several of his counselors, a judge, a general, and

▶ What important figures witness Hester's punishment? What effect does the presence of these figures have on the spectacle?

---

15. **Papist.** Roman Catholic

Words For Everyday Use

fla • grant (flā´grəny) *adj.*, outrageous
mien (mēn) *n.*, manner, bearing
vie (vī) *vi.*, compete
taint (tānt) *n.*, corruption or evil; a moral defect considered as a stain or spot

the ministers of the town; all of whom sat or stood in a balcony of the meeting-house, looking down upon the platform. When such personages could <u>constitute</u> a part of the spectacle, without risking the majesty or reverence of rank and office, it was safely to be inferred that the infliction of a legal sentence would have an earnest and effectual meaning. Accordingly, the crowd was somber and grave. The unhappy culprit <u>sustained</u> herself as best a woman might, under the heavy weight of a thousand unrelenting eyes, all fastened upon her, and concentrated at her bosom. It was almost intolerable to be borne. Of an impulsive and passionate nature, she had fortified herself to encounter the stings and venomous stabs of public contumely,[16] wreaking itself in every variety of insult; but there was a quality so much more terrible in the solemn mood of the popular mind, that she longed rather to behold all those rigid countenances contorted with scornful merriment, and herself the object. Had a roar of laughter burst from the multitude—each man, each woman, each little shrill-voiced child, contributing their individual parts—Hester Prynne might have repaid them all with a bitter and disdainful smile. But, under the leaden infliction which it was her doom to endure, she felt, at moments, as if she must needs shriek out with the full power of her lungs, and cast herself from the scaffold down upon the ground, or else go mad at once.

◄ *What quality among the spectators does Hester find almost intolerable to endure? What different reaction from the crowd might have allowed her to cope more easily?*

Yet there were intervals when the whole scene, in which she was the most conspicuous object, seemed to vanish from her eyes, or, at least, glimmered indistinctly before them, like a mass of imperfectly shaped and spectral images. Her mind, and especially her memory, was <u>preternaturally</u> active, and kept bringing up other scenes than this roughly hewn street of a little town, on the edge of the Western wilderness;[17] other faces than were lowering upon her from beneath the brims of those steeple-crowned hats. <u>Reminiscences</u>, the most trifling and immaterial, passages of infancy and school-days, sports, childish quarrels, and the little domestic traits of her maiden years, came swarming back upon her,

---

16. **contumely.** Humiliating treatment
17. **Western wilderness.** The lands west of the coastal settlements in New England were largely unsettled by Europeans

Words
For
Everyday
Use

con • sti • tute (kän´stə tōōt´) *vt.*, form
sus • tain (sə stān) *vt.*, support, buoy up
pre • ter • nat • u • ral • ly (prē´tər nach´ər əl lē) *adv.*, abnormally, supernaturally

rem • i • nis • cence (rem´ə nis´ əns) *n.*, memory, recollection intermingled with recollections of whatever was <u>gravest</u> in her subsequent life; one picture precisely as vivid as another; as if all were of similar importance, or all alike a play. Possibly, it was an instinctive device of her spirit, to relieve itself, by the exhibition of these phantasmagoric[18] forms, from the cruel weight and hardness of the reality.

Be that as it might, the scaffold of the pillory was a point of view that revealed to Hester Prynne the entire track along which she had been treading, since her happy infancy. Standing on that miserable <u>eminence</u>, she saw again her native village, in Old England, and her paternal home; a decayed house of gray stone, with a poverty-stricken aspect, but retaining a half obliterated shield of arms over the portal, in token of antique gentility. She saw her father's face, with its bald brow, and reverend white beard, that flowed over the old-fashioned Elizabethan ruff; her mother's, too, with the look of <u>heedful</u> and anxious love which it always wore in her remembrance, and which, even since her death, had so often laid the <u>impediment</u> of a gentle <u>remonstrance</u> in her daughter's pathway. She saw her own face, glowing with girlish beauty, and illuminating all the interior of the dusky mirror in which she had been wont to gaze at it. There she beheld another countenance, of a man well stricken in years, a pale, thin, scholar-like visage, with eyes dim and bleared by the lamp-light that had served them to pore over many ponderous books. Yet those same bleared optics had a strange, penetrating power, when it was their owner's purpose to read the human soul. This figure of the study and the cloister,[19] as Hester Prynne's womanly fancy failed not to recall, was slightly deformed, with the left shoulder a trifle higher than the right. Next rose before her, in memory's picture-gallery, the intricate and narrow thoroughfares, the tall, gray houses, the huge cathedrals, and the public edifices, ancient in date and quaint in architecture, of a Continental city;[20] where new life had awaited her, still in connection

► *What power does the scholar have?*

---

18. **phantasmagoric.** Sequence of haphazard or fantastic images, as seen in dreams or fever
19. **cloister.** Place, especially a monastery or convent, devoted to religious seclusion
20. **Continental city.** Many colonists had emigrated from Britain to the Dutch city of Amsterdam before coming to the New World.

Words For Everyday Use

grave (grāv) *adj.,* serious; grievous
em • i • nence (em´i nəns) *n.,* high place
heed • ful (hēd´ fəl) *adj.,* careful

im • ped • i • ment (im ped´ə mənt) *n.,* obstacle
re • mon • strance (ri män´strəns) *n.,* act of protesting or objecting

with the misshapen scholar: a new life, but feeding itself on time-worn materials, like a tuft of green moss on a crumbling wall. Lastly, in lieu of [21] these shifting scenes, came back the rude market-place of the Puritan settlement, with all the townspeople assembled and leveling their stern regards at Hester Prynne—yes, at herself—who stood on the scaffold of the pillory, an infant on her arm, and the letter A, in scarlet, fantastically embroidered with gold thread, upon her bosom!

Could it be true? She clutched the child so fiercely to her breast, that it sent forth a cry; she turned her eyes downward at the scarlet letter, and even touched it with her finger, to assure herself that the infant and the shame were real. Yes! these were her realities—all else had vanished!

◄ *What are Hester's two realities? How might she be feeling at this moment?*

---

21. **in lieu of.** In place of

Responding to the Selection

Describe what you think of Hester Prynne as she stands with her child before her community. Describe what you think of the members of Hester's community as they watch her.

Reviewing the Selection

Recalling and Interpreting

1. **R:** In chapter 1, in what condition is Boston's old wooden jail and the plot of land outside the jail?

2. **I:** According to the narrator, in what way is the condition of the jail related to its function in the community? What unusual plant has grown outside the jail, and what do people say in an attempt to explain it?

3. **R:** What is Hester Prynne's crime, and what is her punishment? According to the women, in what way has the crime affected Hester's pastor, the Reverend Dimmesdale?

4. **I:** What do most of Boston's women think of Hester and her punishment? Why does one young woman disagree with the others?

5. **R:** What do people say when they see the elaborate scarlet *A* that Hester has stitched?

6. **I:** Is Hester prideful as she walks through the crowd and stands on the scaffold, as some in the crowd say? Why does Hester feel that the crowd's solemn mood is worse than scornful laughter?

7. **R:** Of what does Hester dream as she stands on the scaffold? What events led her to be in America alone?

8. **I:** While she stands on the scaffold, what realization interrupts Hester's thoughts and causes her suddenly to clutch her child and to look down?

Synthesizing

9. What about Hester's appearance and her crime seems to bother the community, particularly the other women, the most?

10. What do the attitudes of the crowd say about early Puritan society?

Understanding Literature

1. Mood and Setting. Mood, or **atmosphere,** is the emotion created in the reader by part or all of a literary work. The **setting** of a literary work is the time and place in which it occurs, together with all the details used to create a sense of a particular time and place. In the opening chapter of the novel, Hawthorne calls *The Scarlet Letter* "a tale of human frailty and sorrow." What is the mood of the opening of this novel? Name the concrete details that work together to create the mood. What is the setting of *The Scarlet Letter?* Does this setting add to the mood of the piece? If so, in what way?

2. Symbol. A **symbol** is a thing that stands for or represents both itself and something else. *The Scarlet Letter* is a novel rich with symbolism. In the opening chapters, Hawthorne presents several important symbols—the prison, the grass plot overgrown with "unsightly vegetation," a wild rosebush, and the beadle who leads Hester to the scaffold. Hawthorne also presents the first appearance of what will be a recurring symbol—Hester's embroidered scarlet *A.* What do you think each of these things symbolizes?

III

The Recognition

From this intense consciousness of being the object of severe and universal observation, the wearer of the scarlet letter was at length relieved by <u>discerning</u>, on the outskirts of the crowd, a figure which irresistibly took possession of her thoughts. An Indian, in his native garb, was standing there; but the red men were not so infrequent visitors of the English settlements, that one of them would have attracted any notice from Hester Prynne, at such a time; much less would he have excluded all other objects and ideas from her mind. By the Indian's side, and evidently sustaining a companionship with him, stood a white man, clad in a strange disarray of civilized and savage costume.

He was small in stature, with a furrowed visage, which, as yet, could hardly be termed aged. There was a remarkable intelligence in his features, as of a person who had so cultivated his mental part that it could not fail to mold the physical to itself, and become manifest by unmistakable tokens. Although, by a seemingly careless arrangement of his <u>heterogeneous</u> garb, he had endeavored to conceal or <u>abate</u> the peculiarity, it was sufficiently evident to Hester Prynne, that one of this man's shoulders rose higher than the other. Again, at the first instant of perceiving that thin visage, and the slight deformity of the figure, she pressed her infant to her bosom with so <u>convulsive</u> a force that the poor babe uttered another cry of pain. But the mother did not seem to hear it.

At his arrival in the market-place, and some time before she saw him, the stranger had bent his eyes on Hester Prynne. It was carelessly, at first, like a man chiefly accustomed to look inward, and to whom external matters are of little value and import, unless they bear relation to something within his mind. Very soon, however, his look became keen and penetrative. A <u>writhing</u> horror twisted itself across his features, like a snake gliding swiftly over them, and making

> ► What physical feature does Hester notice when looking at the strangely dressed man? How does she react? Why might she react in this way?

> ► How does the stranger react when he sees Hester on the scaffold? In what way are the reactions of the stranger and of Hester similar?

Words For Everyday Use

dis • cern (di zʉrn´) vt, recognize
het • er • o • ge • ne • ous (het´ər ō´jē´nē əs) adj., varied; made up of unlike parts
a • bate (ə bāt´) vt., lessen, diminish

con • vul • sive (kən vul´ siv) adj., having the nature of violent, involuntary spasms
writh • ing (rīth´ iŋ) adj., twisting, distressing

one little pause, with all its wreathed intervolutions in open sight. His face darkened with some powerful emotion, which, nevertheless, he so instantaneously controlled by an effort of his will, that, save at a single moment, its expression might have passed for calmness. After a brief space, the convulsion grew almost imperceptible, and finally subsided into the depths of his nature. When he found the eyes of Hester Prynne fastened on his own, and saw that she appeared to recognize him, he slowly and calmly raised his finger, made a gesture with it in the air, and laid it on his lips.

◄ *What gesture does the stranger make?*

Then touching the shoulder of a townsman who stood near to him, he addressed him in a formal and courteous manner.

"I pray you, good Sir," said he, "who is this woman?—and wherefore is she here set up to public shame?"

"You must needs be a stranger in this region, friend," answered the townsman, looking curiously at the questioner and his savage companion, "else you would surely have heard of Mistress Hester Prynne, and her evil doings. She hath raised a great scandal, I promise you, in godly Master Dimmesdale's church."

"You say truly," replied the other. "I am a stranger, and have been a wanderer, sorely against my will. I have met with grievous mishaps by sea and land, and have been long held in bonds among the heathen-folk, to the southward; and am now brought hither by this Indian, to be redeemed out of my captivity. Will it please you, therefore, to tell me of Hester Prynne's—have I her name rightly?—of this woman's offenses, and what has brought her to yonder scaffold?"

"Truly, friend, and methinks it must gladden your heart, after your troubles and <u>sojourn</u> in the wilderness," said the townsman, "to find yourself, at length, in a land where iniquity is searched out, and punished in the sight of rulers and people; as here in our godly New England. Yonder woman, Sir, you must know, was the wife of a certain learned man, English by birth, but who had long dwelt in Amsterdam, whence, some good time agone, he was minded to cross over and cast in his lot with us of the Massachusetts. To this purpose, he sent his wife before him, remaining himself to look

◄ *What does the townsman reveal about Hester's history?*

Words
For
Everyday
Use

so • journ (sō´ jurn) *n.*, brief or temporary stay

after some necessary affairs. Marry, good Sir, in some two years, or less, that the woman has been a dweller here in Boston, no tidings have come of this learned gentleman, Master Prynne; and his young wife, look you, being left to her own misguidance—"

"Ah!—aha!—I conceive you," said the stranger, with a bitter smile. "So learned a man as you speak of should have learned this too in his books. And who, by your favor, Sir, may be the father of yonder babe—it is some three or four months old, I should judge—which Mistress Prynne is holding in her arms?"

"Of a truth, friend, that matter remaineth a riddle; and the Daniel[1] who shall expound it is yet a-wanting," answered the townsman. "Madame Hester absolutely refuseth to speak, and the magistrates have laid their heads together in vain. Peradventure the guilty one stands looking on at this sad spectacle, unknown of man, and forgetting that God sees him."

"The learned man," observed the stranger with another smile, "should come himself to look into the mystery."

▶ Why didn't the magistrates condemn Hester to death? How have they shown their leniency?

"It behooves him well, if he be still in life," responded the townsman. "Now, good Sir, our Massachusetts magistracy, bethinking themselves that this woman is youthful and fair, and doubtless was strongly tempted to her fall—and that, moreover, as is most likely, her husband may be at the bottom of the sea, they have not been bold to put in force the extremity of our righteous law against her. The penalty thereof is death. But in their great mercy and tenderness of heart, they have doomed Mistress Prynne to stand only a space of three hours on the platform of the pillory, and then and thereafter, for the remainder of her natural life, to wear a mark of shame upon her bosom."

▶ How does the stranger feel about the punishment that Hester is receiving? Why do you think the stranger says "he will be known!" three times? Who might this stranger be?

"A wise sentence!" remarked the stranger, gravely bowing his head. "Thus she will be a living sermon against sin, until the ignominious letter be engraved upon her tombstone. It irks me, nevertheless, that the partner of her iniquity should not, at least, stand on the scaffold by her side. But he will be known!—he will be known!—he will be known!"

He bowed courteously to the communicative townsman, and whispering a few words to his Indian attendant, they both made their way through the crowd.

While this passed, Hester Prynne had been standing on her pedestal, still with a fixed gaze towards the stranger; so fixed a gaze, that, at moments of intense absorption, all other objects in the visible world seemed to vanish, leaving only him and her. Such an interview, perhaps, would have been

---

1. **Daniel.** Biblical prophet known for his powers of interpretation

more terrible than even to meet him as she now did, with the hot, mid-day sun burning down upon her face, and lighting up its shame; with the scarlet token of infamy on her breast; with the sin-born infant in her arms; with a whole people, drawn forth as to a festival, staring at the features that should have been seen only in the quiet gleam of the fireside, in the happy shadow of a home, or beneath a matronly veil, at church. Dreadful as it was, she was conscious of a shelter in the presence of these thousand witnesses. It was better to stand thus, with so many betwixt him and her, than to greet him, face to face, they two alone. She fled for refuge, as it were, to the public exposure, and dreaded the moment when its protection should be withdrawn from her. Involved in these thoughts, she scarcely heard a voice behind her, until it had repeated her name more than once, in a loud and solemn tone, audible to the whole multitude.

◄ *Why might Hester rather see the stranger in a crowd than alone?*

"Hearken unto me, Hester Prynne!" said the voice.

It has already been noticed, that directly over the platform on which Hester Prynne stood was a kind of balcony, or open gallery, appended to the meeting-house. It was the place whence proclamations were wont to be made, amidst an assemblage of the magistracy, with all the ceremonial that attended such public observances in those days. Here, to witness the scene which we are describing, sat Governor Bellingham[2] himself, with four sergeants about his chair, bearing halberds,[3] as a guard of honor. He wore a dark feather in his hat, a border of embroidery on his cloak, and a black velvet tunic beneath; a gentleman advanced in years, with a hard experience written in his wrinkles. He was not ill fitted to be the head and representative of a community, which owed its origin and progress, and its present state of development, not to the impulses of youth, but to the stern and tempered energies of manhood, and the sombre <u>sagacity</u> of age; accomplishing so much, precisely because it imagined and hoped so little. The other <u>eminent</u> characters, by whom the chief ruler was surrounded, were distinguished by a dignity of mien, belonging to a period when the forms of

---

2. **Governor Bellingham.** Richard Bellingham (c. 1592–1672) was elected governor in 1641 and again in 1654. He served as assistant governor between those terms.
3. **halberds.** Ceremonial weapons combining the attributes of spears and battle axes

---

| Words For Everyday Use | **sa • gac • i • ty** (sə gas´ə tē) *n.*, shrewdness; intelligence and sound judgment |
| | **em • i • nent** (em´ə nent) *adj.*, famous; distinguished |

▶ What does the
narrator say about
the judges? Why
might the judges be
unable to judge
Hester wisely?

authority were felt to possess the sacredness of divine institutions. They were, doubtless, good men, just, and sage. But,
out of the whole human family, it would not have been easy
to select the same number of wise and virtuous persons, who
should be less capable of sitting in judgment on an erring
woman's heart, and disentangling its mesh of good and evil,
than the sages of rigid aspect towards whom Hester Prynne
now turned her face. She seemed conscious, indeed, that
whatever sympathy she might expect lay in the larger and
warmer heart of the multitude; for, as she lifted her eyes
towards the balcony, the unhappy woman grew pale, and
trembled.

The voice which had called her attention was that of the
reverend and famous John Wilson,[4] the eldest clergyman of
Boston, a great scholar, like most of his contemporaries in
the profession, and withal[5] a man of kind and genial spirit.
This last attribute, however, had been less carefully developed than his intellectual gifts, and was, in truth, rather a
matter of shame than self-congratulation with him. There he
stood, with a border of grizzled locks beneath his skull-cap;[6]
while his gray eyes, accustomed to the shaded light of his
study, were winking, like those of Hester's infant, in the
unadulterated[7] sunshine. He looked like the darkly engraved
portraits which we see prefixed to old volumes of sermons;
and had no more right than one of those portraits would
have, to step forth, as he now did, and meddle with a question of human guilt, passion, and anguish.

"Hester Prynne," said the clergyman, "I have striven with
my young brother here, under whose preaching of the word
you have been privileged to sit"—here Mr. Wilson laid his
hand on the shoulder of a pale young man beside him—"I
have sought, I say, to persuade this godly youth, that he
should deal with you, here in the face of Heaven, and before
these wise and upright rulers, and in hearing of all the people, as touching the <u>vileness</u> and blackness of your sin.
Knowing your natural temper better than I, he could the better judge what arguments to use, whether of tenderness or

---

4. **John Wilson.** (1591–1667) Church teacher and opponent of Anne
Hutchinson
5. **withal.** In addition
6. **skull-cap.** Light, close-fitting, brimless hat
7. **unadulterated.** Pure

| Words For Everyday Use | **vile • ness** (vīl´nəs) *n.*, evilness, offensiveness |

terror, such as might <u>prevail</u> over your hardness and obstinacy; insomuch that you should no longer hide the name of him who tempted you to this grievous fall. But he opposes to me, (with a young man's oversoftness, albeit wise beyond his years,) that it were wronging the very nature of woman to force her to lay open her heart's secrets in such broad daylight, and in presence of so great a multitude. Truly, as I sought to convince him, the shame lay in the commission of the sin, and not in the showing of it forth. What say you to it, once again, brother Dimmesdale? Must it be thou, or I that shall deal with this poor sinner's soul?"

◄ According to Wilson, what reason did the young clergyman have for not questioning Hester about the father of her child?

There was a murmur among the dignified and reverend occupants of the balcony; and Governor Bellingham gave expression to its purport, speaking in an authoritative voice, although tempered with respect towards the youthful clergyman whom he addressed.

"Good Master Dimmesdale," said he, "the responsibility of this woman's soul lies greatly with you. It behooves you, therefore, to exhort her to repentance, and to confession, as a proof and consequence thereof."

The directness of this appeal drew the eyes of the whole crowd upon the Reverend Mr. Dimmesdale; a young clergyman, who had come from one of the great English universities, bringing all the learning of the age into our wild forest-land. His eloquence and religious <u>fervor</u> had already given the earnest of high eminence in his profession. He was a person of very striking aspect, with a white, lofty, and impending brow, large, brown, melancholy eyes, and a mouth which, unless when he forcibly compressed it, was apt to be tremulous, expressing both nervous sensibility and a vast power of self-restraint. Notwithstanding his high native gifts and scholar-like attainments, there was an air about this young minister—an <u>apprehensive</u>, a startled, a half-frightened look—as of a being who felt himself quite astray and at a loss in the pathway of human existence, and could only be at ease in some seclusion of his own. Therefore, so far as his duties would permit, he trode in the shadowy by-paths, and thus kept himself simple and childlike; coming forth, when occasion was, with a freshness, and fragrance, and dewy purity of thought, which, as many people said, affected them like the speech of an angel.

◄ In what way does the narrator describe Dimmesdale's manner?

◄ To whom is Dimmesdale compared?

Words For Everyday Use

pre • vail (prē vāl´) vi., triumph

fer • vor (fur´vər) n., zeal, passion

ap • pre • hen • sive (ap´rē hen´siv) adj., anxious or fearful

Such was the young man whom the Reverend Mr. Wilson and the Governor had introduced so openly to the public notice, bidding him speak, in the hearing of all men, to that mystery of a woman's soul, so sacred even in its pollution. The trying nature of his position drove the blood from his cheek, and made his lips tremulous.

"Speak to the woman, my brother," said Mr. Wilson. "It is of moment to her soul, and therefore, as the worshipful Governor says, momentous to thine own, in whose charge hers is. Exhort her to confess the truth!"

The Reverend Mr. Dimmesdale bent his head, in silent prayer, as it seemed, and then came forward.

► What is Dimmesdale asking Hester to do? Why?

"Hester Prynne," said he, leaning over the balcony, and looking down steadfastly into her eyes, "thou hearest what this good man says, and seest the accountability under which I labor. If thou feelest it to be for thy soul's peace, and that thy earthly punishment will thereby be made more effectual to salvation, I charge thee to speak out the name of thy fellow-sinner and fellow-sufferer! Be not silent from any mistaken pity and tenderness for him; for, believe me, Hester, though he were to step down from a high place, and stand there beside thee, on thy pedestal of shame, yet better were it so, than to hide a guilty heart through life. What can thy silence do for him, except it tempt him—yea, compel him, as it were—to add hypocrisy to sin? Heaven hath granted thee an open ignominy, that thereby thou mayest work out an open triumph over the evil within thee, and the sorrow without. Take heed how thou deniest to him—who, perchance, hath not the courage to grasp it for himself—the bitter, but wholesome, cup that is now presented to thy lips!"

► According to Dimmesdale, what type of sin is worse— an open one or a hidden one? For what does Dimmesdale blame Hester? What does he say about her partner in sin?

The young pastor's voice was tremulously sweet, rich, deep, and broken. The feeling that it so evidently manifested, rather than the direct purport of the words, caused it to vibrate within all hearts, and brought the listeners into one accord of sympathy. Even the poor baby, at Hester's bosom, was affected by the same influence; for it directed its hitherto vacant gaze towards Mr. Dimmesdale, and held up its little arms, with a half-pleased, half <u>plaintive</u> murmur. So powerful seemed the minister's appeal, that the people could not believe but that Hester Prynne would speak out the guilty

► What does Hester's baby do after hearing Dimmesdale's plea?

Words For Everyday Use

plain • tive (plān´ tiv) *adj.,* mournful; sad

name; or else that the guilty one himself, in whatever high or lowly place he stood, would be drawn forth by an inward and inevitable necessity, and compelled to ascend the scaffold.

Hester shook her head.

"Woman, <u>transgress</u> not beyond the limits of Heaven's mercy!" cried the Reverend Mr. Wilson, more harshly than before. "That little babe hath been gifted with a voice, to second and confirm the counsel which thou hast heard. Speak out the name! That, and thy repentance, may avail to take the scarlet letter off thy breast."

"Never!" replied Hester Prynne, looking, not at Mr. Wilson, but into the deep and troubled eyes of the younger clergyman. "It is too deeply branded. Ye cannot take it off. And would that I might endure his agony, as well as mine!"

"Speak, woman!" said another voice, coldly and sternly, proceeding from the crowd about the scaffold, "Speak; and give your child a father!"

"I will not speak!" answered Hester, turning pale as death, but responding to this voice, which she too surely recognized. "And my child must seek a heavenly Father; she shall never know an earthly one!"

"She will not speak!" murmured Mr. Dimmesdale, who, leaning over the balcony, with his hand upon his heart, had awaited the result of his appeal. He now drew back, with a long respiration. "Wondrous strength and generosity of a woman's heart! She will not speak!"

Discerning the impracticable state of the poor culprit's mind, the elder clergyman, who had carefully prepared himself for the occasion, addressed to the multitude a discourse on sin, in all its branches, but with continual reference to the ignominious letter. So forcibly did he dwell upon this symbol, for the hour or more during which his periods were rolling over the people's heads, that it assumed new terrors in their imagination, and seemed to derive its scarlet hue from the flames of the infernal pit. Hester Prynne, meanwhile, kept her place upon the pedestal of shame, with glazed eyes, and an air of weary indifference. She had borne, that morning, all that nature could endure; and as her temperament was not of the order that escapes from too intense suffering by a swoon, her spirit could only shelter itself

◄ *What does the Reverend Wilson say might happen if Hester reveals the name? In what way do you interpret Hester's response?*

◄ *What is Dimmesdale's reaction to Hester's decision?*

Words For Everyday Use	**trans • gress** (trans gres´) *vi.,* break a law or commandment; commit a sin

► What did the peo-
ple say that they saw
as Hester walked into
the prison?

beneath a stony crust of insensibility, while the faculties of animal life remained entire. In this state, the voice of the preacher thundered remorselessly, but unavailingly, upon her ears. The infant, during the latter portion of her ordeal, pierced the air with its wailings and screams; she strove to hush it mechanically, but seemed scarcely to sympathize with its trouble. With the same hard demeanor, she was led back to prison, and vanished from the public gaze within its iron-clamped portal. It was whispered, by those who peered after her, that the scarlet letter threw a lurid gleam along the dark passage-way of the interior.

IV

The Interview

After her return to the prison, Hester Prynne was found to be in a state of nervous excitement that demanded constant watchfulness, lest she should <u>perpetrate</u> violence on herself, or do some half-frenzied mischief to the poor babe. As night approached, it proving impossible to quell her <u>insubordination</u> by rebuke or threats of punishment, Master Brackett, the jailer, thought fit to introduce a physician. He described him as a man of skill in all Christian modes of physical science, and likewise familiar with whatever the savage people could teach, in respect to medicinal herbs and roots that grew in the forest. To say the truth, there was much need of professional assistance, not merely for Hester herself, but still more urgently for the child; who, drawing its sustenance from the maternal bosom, seemed to have drank in with it all the turmoil, the anguish, and despair, which <u>pervaded</u> the mother's system. It now writhed in convulsions of pain, and was a forcible type, in its little frame, of the moral agony which Hester Prynne had borne throughout the day.

◄ *Of what is the infant's sickness a "type," or symbol?*

Closely following the jailer into the dismal apartment, appeared that individual, of singular aspect, whose presence in the crowd had been of such deep interest to the wearer of the scarlet letter. He was lodged in the prison, not as suspected of any offense, but as the most convenient and suitable mode of disposing of him, until the magistrates should have conferred with the Indian sagamores[1] respecting his ransom. His name was announced as Roger Chillingworth. The jailer, after ushering him into the room, remained a moment, marvelling at the comparative quiet that followed his entrance; for Hester Prynne had immediately become as still as death, although the child continued to moan.

◄ *Who comes to visit Hester? What is Hester's reaction?*

---

1. **sagamores.** Chiefs

Words For Everyday Use

per • pe • trate (pʉr´pe trāt´) *vt.*, commit; do something wrong
in • sub • or • di • na • tion (in´ sə bor´də nā´shən) *n.*, disobedience
per • vade (pər vād´) *vt.*, be prevalent throughout

"Prithee, friend, leave me alone with my patient," said the practitioner. "Trust me, good jailer, you shall briefly have peace in your house; and, I promise you, Mistress Prynne shall hereafter be more <u>amenable</u> to just authority than you may have found her heretofore."

"Nay, if your worship can accomplish that," answered Master Brackett, "I shall own you for a man of skill, indeed! Verily, the woman hath been like a possessed one; and there lacks little that I should take in hand to drive Satan out of her with stripes."

The stranger had entered the room with the characteristic quietude of the profession to which he announced himself as belonging. Nor did his demeanor change, when the withdrawal of the prison-keeper left him face to face with the woman, whose absorbed notice of him, in the crowd, had intimated so close a relation between himself and her. His first care was given to the child; whose cries, indeed, as she lay writhing on the trundle-bed, made it of <u>peremptory</u> necessity to postpone all other business to the task of soothing her. He examined the infant carefully, and then proceeded to unclasp a leathern case, which he took from beneath his dress. It appeared to contain certain medical preparations, one of which he mingled with a cup of water.

▶ What has Roger Chillingworth studied?

"My old studies in alchemy,"[2] observed he, "and my sojourn, for above a year past, among a people well versed in the kindly properties of simples,[3] have made a better physician of me than many that claim the medical degree. Here, woman! The child is yours—she is none of mine—neither will she recognize my voice or aspect as a father's. Administer this draught, therefore, with thine own hand."

▶ Why does Hester refuse to give the baby the medicine prepared by Roger Chillingworth?

Hester repelled the offered medicine, at the same time gazing with strongly marked apprehension into his face.

"Wouldst thou <u>avenge</u> thyself on the innocent babe?" whispered she.

"Foolish woman!" responded the physician, half coldly, half soothingly. "What should ail me to harm this misbegotten and miserable babe? The medicine is potent for good;

---

2. **alchemy.** Early form of chemistry, with philosophic and magical associations
3. **simples.** Medicines made from one source, usually an herb or other plant

Words
For
Everyday
Use

a • me • na • ble (ə mē´nə bəl) *adj.,* obedient
per • emp • to • ry (pər emp´tə rē) *adj.,* unable to be delayed
a • venge (ə venj´) *vt.,* get revenge

and were it my child—yea, mine own, as well as thine!—I could do no better for it."

As she still hesitated, being, in fact, in no reasonable state of mind, he took the infant in his arms, and himself administered the draught. It soon proved its <u>efficacy</u>, and redeemed the leech's[4] pledge. The moans of the little patient subsided; its convulsive tossings gradually ceased; and in a few moments, as is the custom of young children after relief from pain, it sank into a <u>profound</u> and dewy slumber. The physician, as he had a fair right to be termed, next bestowed his attention on the mother. With calm and intent <u>scrutiny</u>, he felt her pulse, looked into her eyes—a gaze that made her heart shrink and shudder, because so familiar, and yet so strange and cold—and, finally, satisfied with his investigation, proceeded to mingle another draught.

"I know not Lethe nor Nepenthe,"[5] remarked he; "but I have learned many new secrets in the wilderness, and here is one of them—a recipe that an Indian taught me, in requital of some lessons of my own, that were as old as Paracelsus.[6] Drink it! It may be less soothing than a sinless conscience. That I cannot give thee. But it will calm the swell and heaving of thy passion, like oil thrown on the waves of a tempestuous sea."

He presented the cup to Hester, who received it with a slow, earnest look into his face; not precisely a look of fear, yet full of doubt and questioning, as to what his purposes might be. She looked also at her slumbering child.

"I have thought of death," said she—"have wished for it—would even have prayed for it, were it fit that such as I should pray for anything. Yet, if death be in this cup, I bid thee think again, ere thou beholdest me quaff it. See! It is even now at my lips."

"Drink, then," replied he, still with the same cold composure. "Dost thou know me so little, Hester Prynne? Are my purposes wont to be so shallow? Even if I imagine a scheme of vengeance, what could I do better for my object than to let thee live—than to give thee medicines against all harm

◄ *According to Roger Chillingworth, what is the best way for him to seek vengeance upon Hester?*

---

4. **leech.** Physician
5. **Lethe nor Nepenthe.** In Greek mythology, Lethe was a river in Hades that caused forgetfulness. Nepenthe was a substance that banished grief.
6. **Paracelsus.** Pseudonym of Theophrastus von Hohenheim (1493–1541), an alchemist

Words For Everyday Use

ef • fi • ca • cy (ef´i kə sē) *n.*, effectiveness
pro • found (prō found´) *adj.*, very deep
scru • ti • ny (skrōōt´ nē) *n.*, close examination

and peril of life—so that this burning shame may still blaze upon thy bosom?"—As he spoke, he laid his long forefinger on the scarlet letter, which forthwith seemed to scorch into Hester's breast, as if it had been red-hot. He noticed her involuntary gesture, and smiled. "Live, therefore, and bear about thy doom with thee, in the eyes of men and women— in the eyes of him whom thou didst call thy husband—in the eyes of yonder child! And, that thou mayest live, take off this draught."

Without further <u>expostulation</u> or delay, Hester Prynne drained the cup, and, at the motion of the man of skill, seated herself on the bed where the child was sleeping; while he drew the only chair which the room afforded, and took his own seat beside her. She could not but tremble at these preparations; for she felt that—having now done all that humanity, or principle, or, if so it were, a refined cruelty, impelled him to do, for the relief of physical suffering—he was next to treat with her as the man whom she had most deeply and irreparably injured.

► *According to Roger, what is the reason for Hester's fall?*

"Hester," said he, "I ask not wherefore, nor how, thou hast fallen into the pit, or say rather, thou hast ascended to the pedestal of infamy, on which I found thee. The reason is not far to seek. It was my folly, and thy weakness. I—a man of thought—the book-worm of great libraries—a man already in decay, having given my best years to feed the hungry dream of knowledge—what had I to do with youth and beauty like thine own! Misshapen from my birth-hour, how could I delude myself with the idea that intellectual gifts might veil physical deformity in a young girl's fantasy? Men call me wise. If sages were ever wise in their own behoof, I might have foreseen all this. I might have known that, as I came out of the vast and dismal forest, and entered this settlement of Christian men, the very first object to meet my eyes would be thyself, Hester Prynne, standing up, a statue of ignominy, before the people. Nay, from the moment when we came down the old church-steps together, a married pair, I might have beheld the bale-fire[7] of that scarlet letter blazing at the end of our path!"

► *What does Roger say he should have recognized as inevitable? When should he have recognized this?*

---

7. **bale-fire.** Funeral pyre

Words For Everyday Use

ex • pos • tu • la • tion (eks päś chə lā´ shən) *n.,* objection

"Thou knowest," said Hester—for, depressed as she was, she could not endure this last quiet stab at the token of her shame—"thou knowest that I was frank with thee. I felt no love, nor <u>feigned</u> any."

"True!" replied he. "It was my folly! I have said it. But, up to that epoch of my life, I had lived in vain. The world had been so cheerless! My heart was a habitation large enough for many guests, but lonely and chill, and without a household fire. I longed to kindle one! It seemed not so wild a dream—old as I was, and somber as I was, and misshapen as I was—that the simple bliss, which is scattered far and wide, for all mankind to gather up, might yet be mine. And so, Hester, I drew thee into my heart, into its innermost chamber, and sought to warm thee by the warmth which thy presence made there!"

"I have greatly wronged thee," murmured Hester.

"We have wronged each other," answered he. "Mine was the first wrong, when I betrayed thy budding youth into a false and unnatural relation with my decay. Therefore, as a man who has not thought and philosophized in vain, I seek no vengeance, plot no evil against thee. Between thee and me, the scale hangs fairly balanced. But, Hester, the man lives who has wronged us both! Who is he?"

◀ Why doesn't Hester's husband want to seek vengeance against her? What does he want from her?

"Ask me not!" replied Hester Prynne, looking firmly into his face. "That thou shalt never know!"

"Never, sayest thou?" rejoined he, with a smile of dark and self-relying intelligence. "Never know him! Believe me, Hester, there are few things—whether in the outward world, or, to a certain depth, in the invisible sphere of thought—few things hidden from the man, who devotes himself earnestly and unreservedly to the solution of a mystery. Thou mayest cover up thy secret from the prying multitude. Thou mayest conceal it, too, from the ministers and magistrates, even as thou didst this day, when they sought to wrench the name out of thy heart, and give thee a partner on thy pedestal. But, as for me, I come to the inquest with other senses than they possess. I shall seek this man, as I have sought truth in books; as I have sought gold in alchemy. There is a sympathy that will make me conscious of him. I shall see him tremble. I shall feel myself shudder, suddenly and unawares. Sooner or later, he must needs be mine!"

◀ What is Roger Chillingworth determined to do?

Words For Everyday Use

feign (fān) vt., make a false show of; pretend

The eyes of the wrinkled scholar glowed so intensely upon her, that Hester Prynne clasped her hand over her heart, dreading lest he should read the secret there at once.

"Thou wilt not reveal his name? Not the less he is mine," resumed he, with a look of confidence, as if destiny were at one with him. "He bears no letter of infamy wrought into his garment, as thou dost; but I shall read it on his heart. Yet fear not for him! Think not that I shall interfere with Heaven's own method of <u>retribution</u>, or, to my own loss, betray him to the gripe of human law. Neither do thou imagine that I shall <u>contrive</u> aught against his life; no, nor against his fame, if, as I judge, he be a man of fair repute. Let him live! Let him hide himself in outward honor, if he may! Not the less he shall be mine!"

"Thy acts are like mercy," said Hester, bewildered and <u>appalled</u>. "But thy words interpret thee as a terror!"

"One thing, thou that wast my wife, I would enjoin upon thee," continued the scholar. "Thou hast kept the secret of thy paramour. Keep, likewise, mine! There are none in this land that know me. Breathe not, to any human soul, that thou didst ever call me husband! Here, on this wild outskirt of the earth, I shall pitch my tent; for, elsewhere a wanderer, and isolated from human interests, I find here a woman, a man, a child, amongst whom and myself there exist the closest ligaments. No matter whether of love or hate; no matter whether of right or wrong! Thou and thine, Hester Prynne, belong to me. My home is where thou art, and where he is. But betray me not!"

"Wherefore dost thou desire it?" inquired Hester, shrinking, she hardly knew why, from this secret bond. "Why not announce thyself openly, and cast me off at once?"

"It may be," he replied, "because I will not encounter the dishonor that besmirches the husband of a faithless woman. It may be for other reasons. Enough, it is my purpose to live and die unknown. Let, therefore, thy husband be to the world as one already dead, and of whom no tidings shall ever come. Recognize me not, by word, by sign, by look! Breathe not the secret, above all, to the man thou wottest[8] of.

---

8. **wottest.** Know

Words For Everyday Use	ret • ri • bu • tion (re′trə byōō′shen) *n.*, punishment con • trive (kən trīv′) *vt.*, scheme, plan ap • palled (ə pôld′) *adj.*, filled with horror or dismay

Shouldst thou fail me in this, beware! His fame, his position, his life, will be in my hands. Beware!"

"I will keep thy secret, as I have his," said Hester.

"Swear it!" rejoined he. And she took the oath.

"And now, Mistress Prynne," said old Roger Chillingworth, as he was hereafter to be named, "I leave thee alone; alone with thy infant, and the scarlet letter! How is it, Hester? Doth thy sentence bind thee to wear the token in thy sleep? Art thou not afraid of nightmares and hideous dreams?"

"Why dost thou smile so at me?" inquired Hester, troubled at the expression of his eyes. "Art thou like the Black Man that haunts the forest[8] round about us? Hast thou <u>enticed</u> me into a bond that will prove the ruin of my soul?"

"Not thy soul," he answered, with another smile. "No, not thine!"

◄ *What does Hester swear that she will do?*

◄ *Whom does Hester think Roger is like? Whose soul does Roger intend to ruin?*

---

8. **Black . . . forest.** The Puritans associated the forest with Satan. Forests, or dark woods, are traditional symbols of moral confusion or of being lost.

Words For Everyday Use

en • tice (en tīs´) vt., tempt, lure

Responding to the Selection

Do you understand Hester's wish to keep the baby's father a secret? What are your feelings toward Roger Chillingworth? Explain your responses.

Reviewing the Selection

Recalling and Interpreting

1. **R:** At the beginning of chapter 3, who in the crowd captures Hester's attention?

2. **I:** Describe Hester's reaction to the stranger in the crowd. Describe the stranger's reaction to Hester's situation. Who might this stranger be?

3. **R:** In chapter 3, what does Mr. Wilson want Reverend Dimmesdale to ask Hester? What is Hester's response to Dimmesdale's speech?

4. **I:** What is the crowd's opinion of Dimmesdale? In what state of mind does Dimmesdale seem to be as he is called to address Hester? How do you know?

5. **R:** Who is Roger Chillingworth, and what are his reasons for visiting Hester and the baby in jail? What information does Chillingworth want from Hester?

6. **I:** Why does Chillingworth "seek no vengeance, plot no evil against" Hester? Who, according to Chillingworth, is most deserving of vengeance?

7. **R:** What does Chillingworth vow to spend his time doing? What is his goal? What information does he want Hester to conceal?

8. **I:** What are Hester's feelings toward Chillingworth's new goal? Does she feel comfortable keeping Chillingworth's secret? Why, or why not?

Synthesizing

9. By the end of chapter 4, what two important facts related to Hester's situation are being concealed? Whose ruin do you think Chillingworth is predicting at the end of chapter 4?

10. Why does Hester associate Chillingworth with the Black Man? What ominous character traits does Chillingworth have? What might be the significance of Chillingworth's name?

Understanding Literature (QUESTIONS FOR DISCUSSION)

1. Tone. Tone is the emotional attitude toward the reader or toward the subject implied by a literary work. Examples of tones that literary works may have include lighthearted, sarcastic, serious, gloomy, innocent, and playful. Reread the following passage from the end of chapter 3:

> The infant, during the latter portion of her ordeal, pierced the air with its wailings and screams; she strove to hush it mechanically, but seemed scarcely to sympathize with its trouble. With the same hard demeanor, she was led back to prison, and vanished from public gaze within its iron-clamped portal. It was whispered, by those who peered after her, that the scarlet letter threw a lurid gleam along the dark passage-way of the interior.

Describe the tone of this passage. What words and phrases contribute to this tone?

2. Dialogue. Dialogue is conversation involving two or more people or characters. As a reader, you can learn a great deal about characters and their relationships by paying attention to dialogue and to the ways in which characters interact. Hawthorne packs a great deal of information into the dialogue between Hester Prynne and Roger Chillingworth in chapter 4. What do you learn from this dialogue about their individual personalities and about how they are feeling? What do you learn about the history of their relationship?

V

Hester at Her Needle

Hester Prynne's term of confinement was now at an end. Her prison-door was thrown open, and she came forth into the sunshine, which, falling on all alike, seemed, to her sick and morbid heart, as if meant for no other purpose than to reveal the scarlet letter on her breast. Perhaps there was a more real torture in her first unattended footsteps from the threshold of the prison, than even in the procession and spectacle that have been described, where she was made the common infamy, at which all mankind was summoned to point its finger. Then, she was supported by an unnatural tension of the nerves, and by all the combative energy of her character, which enabled her to <u>convert</u> the scene into a kind of <u>lurid</u> triumph. It was, moreover, a separate and insulated event, to occur but once in her lifetime, and to meet which, therefore, reckless of economy, she might call up the vital strength that would have <u>sufficed</u> for many quiet years. The very law that condemned her—a giant of stern features, but with vigor to support, as well as to <u>annihilate</u>, in his iron arm—had held her up, through the terrible ordeal of her ignominy. But now, with this unattended walk from her prison-door, began the daily custom, and she must either sustain and carry it forward by the ordinary resources of her nature, or sink beneath it. She could no longer borrow from the future, to help her through the present grief. To-morrow would bring its own trial with it; so would the next day, and so would the next; each its own trial, and yet the very same that was now so unutterably grievous to be borne. The days of the far-off future would toil onward, still with the same burden for her to take up, and bear along with her, but never to fling down; for the accumulating days, and added years, would pile up their misery upon the heap of shame. Throughout them all, giving up her individuality, she would become the general symbol at which the preacher and moralist might point, and in which they might vivify and embody their images of woman's frailty and sinful passion. Thus the young and pure would be taught to look at

> ► Why is leaving the prison on her own harder for Hester than was the public procession from the prison?

> ► What does Hester fear will happen to her individuality?

Words For Everyday Use	
con • vert (kən vurt´) vt., transform	
lu • rid (loor´ id) adj., shocking, sensational	
suf • fice (sə fīs´) vi., be sufficient; be enough	
an • ni • hi • late (ə nī´ə lāt´) vt., destroy completely; kill	

her, with the scarlet letter flaming on her breast—at her, the child of honorable parents—at her, the mother of a babe, that would hereafter be a woman—at her, who had once been innocent—as the figure, the body, the reality of sin. And over her grave, the infamy that she must carry thither would be her only monument.

It may seem marvelous, that, with the world before her— kept by no restrictive clause of her <u>condemnation</u> within the limits of the Puritan settlement, so remote and so obscure— free to return to her birthplace, or to any other European land, and there hide her character and identity under a new exterior, as completely as if emerging into another state of being—and having also the passes of the dark, <u>inscrutable</u> forest open to her, where the wildness of her nature might <u>assimilate</u> itself with a people whose customs and life were alien from the law that had condemned her—it may seem marvelous, that this woman should still call that place her home, where, and where only, she must needs be the type of shame. But there is a fatality, a feeling so irresistible and <u>inevitable</u> that it has the force of doom, which almost invariably compels human beings to linger around and haunt, ghost-like, the spot where some great and marked event has given the color to their lifetime; and still the more irresistibly, the darker the tinge that saddens it. Her sin, her ignominy, were the roots which she had struck into the soil. It was as if a new birth, with stronger assimilations than the first, had converted the forest-land, still so uncongenial to every other pilgrim and wanderer, into Hester Prynne's wild and dreary, but life-long home. All other scenes of earth— even that village of rural England, where happy infancy and stainless maidenhood seemed yet to be in her mother's keeping, like garments put off long ago—were foreign to her, in comparison. The chain that bound her here was of iron links, and <u>galling</u> to her inmost soul, but could never be broken.

It might be, too—doubtless it was so, although she hid the secret from herself, and grew pale whenever it struggled out of her heart, like a serpent from its hole—it might be that another feeling kept her within the scene and pathway that had been so fatal. There dwelt, there trode the feet of one with whom she deemed herself connected in a union, that, unrecognized on earth, would bring them together before

◄ *What does the narrator say is "marvelous"? What prevents Hester from leaving the settlement?*

◄ *What other feeling keeps Hester from leaving the settlement?*

Words For Everyday Use

con • dem • na • tion (kän′dəm nā′shən) *n.*, severe reproof or censure

in • scru • ta • ble (in skrōō′tə bəl) *adj.*, mysterious

as • sim • i • late (ə sim′ə lāt) *vt.*, make like

in • ev • i • ta • ble (in ev′i tə bəl) *adj.*, unavoidable

gal • ling (gôl′ liŋ) *adj.*, annoying; bitter

the bar of final judgment, and make that their marriage-altar, for a joint futurity of endless <u>retribution</u>. Over and over again, the tempter of souls had thrust this idea upon Hester's contemplation, and laughed at the passionate and desperate joy with which she seized, and then strove to cast it from her. She barely looked the idea in the face, and hastened to bar it in its dungeon. What she compelled herself to believe—what, finally, she reasoned upon, as her motive for continuing a resident of New England—was half a truth, and half a self-delusion. Here, she said to herself, had been the scene of her guilt, and here should be the scene of her earthly punishment; and so, perchance, the torture of her daily shame would at length purge her soul, and work out another purity than that which she had lost; more saint-like, because the result of martyrdom.

Hester Prynne, therefore, did not flee. On the outskirts of the town, within the verge of the peninsula, but not in close vicinity to any other habitation, there was a small thatched cottage. It had been built by an earlier settler, and abandoned, because the soil about it was too sterile for cultivation, while its comparative remoteness put it out of the sphere of that social activity which already marked the habits of the emigrants. It stood on the shore, looking across a basin of the sea at the forest-covered hills, towards the west. A clump of scrubby trees, such as alone grew on the peninsula, did not so much conceal the cottage from view, as seem to denote that here was some object which would fain have been, or at least ought to be, concealed. In this little, lonesome dwelling, with some slender means that she possessed, and by the license of the magistrates, who still kept an <u>inquisitorial</u> watch over her, Hester established herself, with her infant child. A mystic shadow of suspicion immediately attached itself to the spot. Children, too young to comprehend wherefore this woman should be shut out from the sphere of human charities, would creep nigh enough to behold her plying her needle at the cottage-window, or standing in the door-way, or laboring in her little garden, or coming forth along the pathway that led townward; and, discerning the scarlet letter on her breast, would scamper off, with a strange, contagious fear.

Words For Everyday Use

ret • ri • bu • tion (rĕtrə byōō´shən) n., punishment
in • quis • i • to • ri • al (in kwiz´ə tôr´ē əl) adj., questioning; prying

Lonely as was Hester's situation, and without a friend on earth who dared to show himself, she, however, <u>incurred</u> no risk of want. She possessed an art that sufficed, even in a land that afforded comparatively little scope for its exercise, to supply food for her thriving infant and herself. It was the art—then, as now, almost the only one within a woman's grasp—of needle-work. She bore on her breast, in the curiously embroidered letter, a specimen of her delicate and imaginative skill, of which the dames of a court might gladly have availed themselves, to add the richer and more spiritual adornment of human <u>ingenuity</u> to their fabrics of silk and gold. Here, indeed, in the sable simplicity that generally characterized the Puritanic modes of dress, there might be an infrequent call for the finer productions of her handiwork. Yet the taste of the age, demanding whatever was elaborate in compositions of this kind, did not fail to extend its influence over our stern progenitors,[1] who had cast behind them so many fashions which it might seem harder to dispense with. Public ceremonies, such as ordinations, the installation of magistrates, and all that could give majesty to the forms in which a new government manifested itself to the people, were, as a matter of policy, marked by a stately and well-conducted ceremonial, and a somber, but yet a studied magnificence. Deep ruffs, painfully wrought bands, and gorgeously embroidered gloves, were all deemed necessary to the official state of men assuming the reins of power; and were readily allowed to individuals dignified by rank or wealth, even while sumptuary laws forbade these and similar extravagances to the plebeian[2] order. In the array of funerals, too—whether for the apparel of the dead body, or to typify, by manifold emblematic devices of sable cloth and snowy lawn, the sorrow of the survivors—there was a frequent and characteristic demand for such labor as Hester Prynne could supply. Baby-linen—for babies then wore robes of state—afforded still another possibility of toil and <u>emolument</u>.

By degrees, nor very slowly, her handiwork became what would now be termed the fashion. Whether from commiseration for a woman of so miserable a destiny; or from the morbid curiosity that gives a fictitious value even to common or worthless things; or by whatever other intangible circumstance was

---

1. **progenitors.** Ancestors
2. **plebeian.** Of the common people in a country

Words For Everyday Use	**in • cur** (in kʉr´) *vt.,* bring upon oneself
	in • ge • nu • i • ty (in´jə no͞o´ə tē) *adj.,* cleverness
	e • mol • u • ment (ē mäl´yo͞o ment) *n.,* payment for work

then, as now, sufficient to bestow, on some persons, what others might seek in vain; or because Hester really filled a gap which must otherwise have remained vacant; it is certain that she had ready and fairly requited employment for as many hours as she saw fit to occupy with her needle. Vanity, it may be, chose to mortify itself, by putting on, for ceremonials of pomp and state, the garments that had been wrought by her sinful hands. Her needle-work was seen on the ruff of the Governor; military men wore it on their scarfs, and the minister on his band; it decked the baby's little cap; it was shut up, to be mildewed and moulder away, in the coffins of the dead. But it is not recorded that, in a single instance, her skill was called in to embroider the white veil which was to cover the pure blushes of a bride. The exception indicated the ever relentless vigor with which society frowned upon her sin.

► What garments is Hester never asked to embroider? Why?

Hester sought not to acquire anything beyond a subsistence, of the plainest and most <u>ascetic</u> description, for herself, and a simple abundance for her child. Her own dress was of the coarsest materials and the most somber hue; with only that one ornament—the scarlet letter—which it was her doom to wear. The child's attire, on the other hand, was distinguished by a fanciful, or, we may rather say, a fantastic ingenuity, which served, indeed, to heighten the airy charm that early began to develop itself in the little girl, but which appeared to have also a deeper meaning. We may speak further of it hereafter. Except for that small expenditure in the decoration of her infant, Hester bestowed all her <u>superfluous</u> means in charity, on wretches less miserable than herself, and who not unfrequently insulted the hand that fed them. Much of the time, which she might readily have applied to the better efforts of her art, she employed in making coarse garments for the poor. It is probable that there was an idea of penance in this mode of occupation, and that she offered up a real sacrifice of enjoyment, in devoting so many hours to such rude handiwork. She had in her nature a rich, voluptuous, Oriental characteristic—a taste for the gorgeously beautiful, which, save in the exquisite productions of her needle, found nothing else, in all the possibilities of her life, to exercise itself upon. Women derive a pleasure, incomprehensible to the other sex, from the delicate toil of the needle.

► In what way does Hester try to help those who are less fortunate?

Words For Everyday Use

as • cet • ic (ə set´ik) *adj.,* severe; self-denying
su • per • flu • ous (sə pʉr´flo͞o əs) *adj.,* excessive; unnecessary

To Hester Prynne it might have been a mode of expressing, and therefore soothing, the passion of her life. Like all other joys, she rejected it as sin. This morbid meddling of conscience with an immaterial matter betokened, it is to be feared, no genuine and steadfast penitence, but something doubtful, something that might be deeply wrong, beneath.

◄ What does Hester express through her art?

In this matter, Hester Prynne came to have a part to perform in the world. With her native energy of character, and rare capacity, it could not entirely cast her off, although it had set a mark upon her, more intolerable to a woman's heart than that which branded the brow of Cain.[3] In all her intercourse with society, however, there was nothing that made her feel as if she belonged to it. Every gesture, every word, and even the silence of those with whom she came in contact, implied, and often expressed, that she was banished, and as much alone as if she inhabited another sphere, or communicated with the common nature by other organs and senses than the rest of human kind. She stood apart from mortal interests, yet close beside them, like a ghost that revisits the familiar fireside, and can no longer make itself seen or felt; no more smile with the household joy, nor mourn with the kindred sorrow; or, should it succeed in manifesting its forbidden sympathy, awakening only terror and horrible <u>repugnance</u>. These emotions, in fact, and its bitterest scorn besides, seemed to be the sole portion that she retained in the universal heart. It was not an age of delicacy; and her position, although she understood it well, and was in little danger of forgetting it, was often brought before her vivid self-perception, like a new anguish, by the rudest touch upon the tenderest spot. The poor, as we have already said, whom she sought out to be the objects of her bounty, often reviled the hand that was stretched forth to <u>succor</u> them. Dames of elevated rank, likewise, whose doors she entered in the way of her occupation, were accustomed to distill drops of bitterness into her heart; sometimes through that alchemy of quiet <u>malice</u>, by which women can concoct a subtle poison from ordinary trifles; and sometimes, also, by a coarser expression, that fell upon the sufferer's defenseless breast like

◄ To what other outcast is Hester compared? Who does the narrator say suffered more?

---

3. **set a mark . . . Cain.** In Genesis, the first book of the Bible, Cain kills his brother Abel, is marked by God, and becomes an outcast.

Words For Everyday Use	re • pug • nance (ri pug´nəns) n., extreme dislike; aversion suc • cor (suk´ər) vt., assist, help mal • ice (mal´is) n., ill will; spite

► In what way does Hester react to the cruel behavior of the townspeople? In what way is she unable to become a perfect martyr?

► What makes Hester's punishment a constant source of anguish?

a rough blow upon an ulcerated wound. Hester had schooled herself long and well; and she never responded to these attacks, save by a flush of crimson that rose <u>irrepressibly</u> over her pale cheek, and again subsided into the depths of her bosom. She was patient—a martyr, indeed—but she forbore to pray for enemies; lest, in spite of her forgiving aspirations, the words of the blessing should stubbornly twist themselves into a curse.

Continually, and in a thousand other ways, did she feel the innumerable throbs of anguish that had been so cunningly contrived for her by the undying, the ever-active sentence of the Puritan tribunal. Clergymen paused in the street to address words of <u>exhortation</u>, that brought a crowd, with its mingled grin and frown, around the poor, sinful woman. If she entered a church, trusting to share the Sabbath smile of the Universal Father, it was often her mishap to find herself the text of the discourse. She grew to have a dread of children; for they had <u>imbibed</u> from their parents a vague idea of something horrible in this dreary woman, gliding silently through the town, with never any companion but one only child. Therefore, first allowing her to pass, they pursued her at a distance with shrill cries, and the utterances of a word that had no distinct purport to their own minds, but was none the less terrible to her, as proceeding from lips that babbled it unconsciously. It seemed to argue so wide a diffusion of her shame, that all nature knew of it; it could have caused her no deeper pang had the leaves of the trees whispered the dark story among themselves—had the summer breeze murmured about it—had the wintry blast shrieked it aloud! Another peculiar torture was felt in the gaze of a new eye. When strangers looked curiously at the scarlet letter—and none ever failed to do so—they branded it afresh in Hester's soul; so that, oftentimes, she could scarcely refrain, yet always did refrain, from covering the symbol with her hand. But then, again, an accustomed eye had likewise its own anguish to inflict. Its cool stare of familiarity was intolerable. From first to last, in short, Hester Prynne had always this dreadful agony in feeling a human eye upon the token; the spot never grew callous; it seemed, on the contrary, to grow more sensitive with daily torture.

Words For Everyday Use

ir • re • press • i • bly (ir´ri pres´ə ble) *adv.*, unrestrainably
ex • hor • ta • tion (eg´zôr tā´shən) *n.*, plea; warning
im • bibe (im bīb´) *vi.*, drink

But sometimes, once in many days, or perchance in many months, she felt an eye—a human eye—upon the ignominious brand, that seemed to give a momentary relief, as if half of her agony were shared. The next instant, back it all rushed again, with still a deeper throb of pain; for, in that brief interval, she had sinned anew. Had Hester sinned alone?

◄ What gives Hester "momentary relief" from her agony?

Her imagination was somewhat affected, and, had she been of a softer moral and intellectual fiber, would have been still more so, by the strange and solitary anguish of her life. Walking to and fro, with those lonely footsteps, in the little world with which she was outwardly connected, it now and then appeared to Hester—if altogether fancy, it was nevertheless too <u>potent</u> to be resisted—she felt or fancied, then, that the scarlet letter had <u>endowed</u> her with a new sense. She shuddered to believe, yet could not help believing, that it gave her a sympathetic knowledge of the hidden sin in other hearts. She was terror-stricken by the revelations that were thus made. What were they? Could they be other than the <u>insidious</u> whispers of the bad angel, who would fain have persuaded the struggling woman, as yet only half his victim, that the outward guise of purity was but a lie, and that, if truth were everywhere to be shown, a scarlet letter would blaze forth on many a bosom besides Hester Prynne's? Or, must she receive those intimations—so obscure, yet so distinct—as truth? In all her miserable experience, there was nothing else so awful and so loathsome as this sense. It perplexed, as well as shocked her, by the <u>irreverent</u> <u>inopportuneness</u> of the occasions that brought it into vivid action. Sometimes, the red infamy upon her breast would give a sympathetic throb, as she passed near a venerable minister or magistrate, the model of piety and justice, to whom that age of antique reverence looked up, as to a mortal man in fellowship with angels. "What evil thing is at hand?" would Hester say to herself. Lifting her reluctant eyes, there would be nothing human within the scope of view, save the form of this earthly saint! Again a mystic sisterhood would <u>contumaciously</u> assert itself, as she met the sanctified frown of some matron, who, according to the rumor of all tongues, had kept cold snow within her bosom throughout life. That unsunned snow in the matron's bosom, and the burning shame on Hester Prynne's—what had the two in common?

◄ What "new sense" does Hester imagine the scarlet letter gives her?

Words For Everyday Use

po • tent (pōt´ 'nt) *adj.,* powerful
en • dow (en dou´) *vt.,* provide with a quality
in • sid • i • ous (in sid´ē əs) *adj.,* sly, crafty
ir • rev • er • ent (ir rev´ər ənt) *adj.,* disrespectful

in • op • por • tune • ness (in äp´ər toon nes) *n.,* inappropriateness; poor timing
con • tu • ma • cious • ly (kän´ tyoo mā´shəs lē) *adv.,* rebelliously

Or, once more, the electric thrill would give her warning—"Behold, Hester, here is a companion!"—and, looking up, she would detect the eyes of a young maiden glancing at the scarlet letter, shyly and aside, and quickly averted, with a faint, chill crimson in her cheeks; as if her purity were somewhat sullied by that momentary glance. O Fiend, whose talisman was that fatal symbol, wouldst thou leave nothing, whether in youth or age, for this poor sinner to revere?—Such loss of faith is ever one of the saddest results of sin. Be it accepted as a proof that all was not corrupt in this poor victim of her own frailty, and man's hard law, that Hester Prynne yet struggled to believe that no fellow-mortal was guilty like herself.

The vulgar, who, in those dreary old times, were always contributing a grotesque horror to what interested their imaginations, had a story about the scarlet letter which we might readily work up into a terrific legend. They <u>averred</u> that the symbol was not mere scarlet cloth, tinged in an earthly dye-pot, but was red-hot with infernal fire, and could be seen glowing all alight, whenever Hester Prynne walked abroad in the night-time. And we must needs say, it seared Hester's bosom so deeply, that perhaps there was more truth in the rumor than our modern <u>incredulity</u> may be inclined to admit.

▶ *What is "one of the saddest results of sin"? What is revealed about Hester by her struggle to believe that no one other than she is guilty?*

Words For Everyday Use

a • ver (ə vʉr´) vt., affirm; declare to be true
in • cre • du • li • ty (in´ krə dōō ´lə tē) n., unwillingness to believe; doubt

VI

Pearl

We have as yet hardly spoken of the infant; that little creature, whose innocent life had sprung, by the inscrutable
decree of Providence, a lovely and immortal flower, out of
the rank luxuriance of a guilty passion. How strange it
seemed to the sad woman, as she watched the growth, and
the beauty that became every day more brilliant, and the
intelligence that threw its quivering sunshine over the tiny
features of this child! Her Pearl!—For so had Hester called
her; not as a name expressive of her aspect, which had nothing of the calm, white, unimpassioned luster that would be
indicated by the comparison. But she named the infant
"Pearl," as being of great price,[1]—purchased with all she
had—her mother's only treasure! How strange, indeed! Man
had marked this woman's sin by a scarlet letter, which had
such potent and disastrous efficacy that no human sympathy
could reach her, save it were sinful like herself. God, as a
direct consequence of the sin which man thus punished, had
given her a lovely child, whose place was on that same dis-
honored bosom, to connect her parent for ever with the race
and descent of mortals, and to be finally a blessed soul in
heaven! Yet these thoughts affected Hester Prynne less with
hope than apprehension. She knew that her deed had been
evil; she could have no faith, therefore, that its result would
be good. Day after day, she looked fearfully into the child's
expanding nature; ever dreading to detect some dark and wild
peculiarity that should correspond with the guiltiness to
which she owed her being.

Certainly, there was no physical defect. By its perfect shape,
its vigor, and its natural dexterity in the use of all its untried
limbs, the infant was worthy to have been brought forth in
Eden; worthy to have been left there, to be the plaything of the
angels, after the world's first parents were driven out. The child
had a native grace which does not invariably coexist with fault-
less beauty; its attire, however simple, always impressed the
beholder as if it were the very garb that precisely became it best.
But little Pearl was not clad in rustic weeds. Her mother, with a
morbid purpose that may be better understood hereafter, had

◄ Why did Hester name her daughter Pearl?

◄ About what is Hester worried?

◄ In what way does Hester dress Pearl?

1. **of great price.** In Matthew 13:45–46, Christ relates the following parable:
"Again, the kingdom of heaven is like unto a merchant man, seeking goodly
pearls: who, when he has found one pearl of great price, went and sold all that
he had, and bought it."

bought the richest tissues that could be <u>procured,</u> and allowed her imaginative faculty its full play in the arrangement and decoration of the dresses which the child wore, before the public eye. So magnificent was the small figure, when thus arrayed, and such was the splendor of Pearl's own proper beauty, shining through the gorgeous robes which might have extinguished a paler loveliness, that there was an absolute circle of radiance around her, on the darksome cottage-floor. And yet a russet gown, torn and soiled with the child's rude play, made a picture of her just as perfect. Pearl's aspect was imbued with a spell of infinite variety; in this one child there were many children, comprehending the full scope between the wild-flower prettiness of a peasant-baby, and the pomp, in little, of an infant princess. Throughout all, however, there was a trait of passion, a certain depth of hue, which she never lost; and if in any of her changes, she had grown fainter or paler, she would have ceased to be herself;—it would have been no longer Pearl!

This outward <u>mutability</u> indicated, and did not more than fairly express, the various properties of her inner life. Her nature appeared to possess depth, too, as well as variety; but—or else Hester's fears deceived her—it lacked reference and adaptation to the world into which she was born. The child could not be made amenable to rules. In giving her existence, a great law had been broken; and the result was a being, whose elements were perhaps beautiful and brilliant, but all in disorder; or with an order peculiar to themselves, amidst which the point of variety and arrangement was difficult or impossible to be discovered. Hester could only account for the child's character—and even then, most vaguely and imperfectly—by recalling what she herself had been, during that momentous period while Pearl was imbibing her soul from the spiritual world, and her bodily frame from its material of earth. The mother's impassioned state had been the medium through which were transmitted to the unborn infant the rays of its moral life; and, however white and clear originally, they had taken the deep stains of crimson and gold, the fiery luster, the black shadow, and the untempered light, of the <u>intervening</u> substance. Above all, the warfare of Hester's spirit, at that epoch, was perpetuated in Pearl. She could recognize her wild, desperate, defiant

► *What quality marks Pearl?*

► *What is unusual about Pearl? To what does Hester attribute this quality?*

Words For Everyday Use

pro • cure (prō kyoor´) *vt.,* obtain
mu • ta • bil • i • ty (myōō´tə bil´i tē) *n.,* ability to change
in • ter • ven • ing (in´tər vēn´ iŋ) *adj.,* coming between

mood, the flightiness of her temper, and even some of the very cloud-shapes of gloom and despondency that had brooded in her heart. They were now illuminated by the morning radiance of a young child's disposition, but, later in the day of earthly existence, might be <u>prolific</u> of the storm and whirlwind.

The discipline of the family, in those days, was of a far more rigid kind than now. The frown, the harsh rebuke, the frequent application of the rod, enjoined by Scriptural authority, were used, not merely in the way of punishment for actual offenses, but as a wholesome regimen for the growth and promotion of all childish virtues. Hester Prynne, nevertheless, the lonely mother of this one child, ran little risk of erring on the side of undue severity. Mindful, however, of her own errors and misfortunes, she early sought to impose a tender, but strict, control over the infant immortality that was committed to her charge. But the task was beyond her skill. After testing both smiles and frowns, and proving that neither mode of treatment possessed any calculable influence, Hester was ultimately compelled to stand aside, and permit the child to be swayed by her own impulses. Physical <u>compulsion</u> or restraint was effectual, of course, while it lasted. As to any other kind of discipline, whether addressed to her mind or heart, little Pearl might or might not be within its reach, in accordance with the <u>caprice</u> that ruled the moment. Her mother, while Pearl was yet an infant, grew acquainted with a certain peculiar look, that warned her when it would be labor thrown away to insist, persuade, or plead. It was a look so intelligent, yet inexplicable, so <u>perverse</u>, sometimes so malicious, but generally accompanied by a wild flow of spirits, that Hester could not help questioning, at such moments, whether Pearl was a human child. She seemed rather an airy sprite, which, after playing its fantastic sports for a little while upon the cottage-floor, would flit away with a mocking smile. Whenever that look appeared in her wild, bright, deeply black eyes, it invested her with a strange remoteness and intangibility; it was as if she were hovering in the air and might vanish, like a glimmering light that comes we know not whence, and goes we know not whither. Beholding it, Hester was constrained to rush towards the child—to pursue the little elf in

◀ *How were Puritan children typically raised? How does Hester raise Pearl?*

◀ *What does Hester wonder about Pearl?*

Words For Everyday Use

pro • lif • ic (prō lif´ik) *adj.*, fertile; abounding
com • pul • sion (kəm pul´shən) *n.*, force, coercion
ca • price (kə prēs) *n.*, whim
per • verse (pər vʉrs) *adj.*, stubbornly contrary; wicked

the flight which she invariably began—to snatch her to her bosom, with a close pressure and earnest kisses—not so much from overflowing love, as to assure herself that Pearl was flesh and blood, and not utterly delusive. But Pearl's laugh, when she was caught, though full of merriment and music, made her mother more doubtful than before.

Heart-smitten at this bewildering and baffling spell, that so often came between herself and her sole treasure, whom she had bought so dear, and who was all her world, Hester sometimes burst into passionate tears. Then, perhaps—for there was no foreseeing how it might affect her—Pearl would frown, and clench her little fist, and harden her small features into a stern, unsympathizing look of discontent. Not seldom, she would laugh anew, and louder than before, like a thing incapable and unintelligent of human sorrow. Or—but this more rarely happened—she would be convulsed with a rage of grief, and sob out her love for her mother, in broken words, and seem intent on proving that she had a heart, by breaking it. Yet Hester was hardly safe in confiding herself to that gusty tenderness; it passed as suddenly as it came. Brooding over all these matters, the mother felt like one who has evoked a spirit, but, by some irregularity in the process of <u>conjuration</u>, has failed to win the master-word that should control this new and incomprehensible intelligence. Her only real comfort was when the child lay in the <u>placidity</u> of sleep. Then she was sure of her, and tasted hours of quiet, sad, delicious happiness; until—perhaps with that perverse expression glimmering from beneath her opening lids—little Pearl awoke!

How soon—with what strange rapidity, indeed!—did Pearl arrive at an age that was capable of social intercourse, beyond the mother's ever-ready smile and nonsense-words! And then what a happiness would it have been, could Hester Prynne have heard her clear, bird-like voice mingling with the uproar of other childish voices, and have distinguished and unraveled her own darling's tones, amid all the entangled outcry of a group of sportive children! But this could never be. Pearl was a born outcast of the infantile world. An imp of evil, emblem and product of sin, she had no right among christened infants. Nothing was more remarkable than the instinct, as it seemed, with which the child

> ▶ *Of what does Pearl sometimes seem incapable?*

> ▶ *Why can't Pearl play with the other children? Does this seem particularly cruel to you? Why, or why not?*

Words For Everyday Use

con • ju • ra • tion (kän´jo͞o ra´shən) *n.*, magic; sorcery
pla • cid • i • ty (plə sid´ə tē) *n.*, calmness, tranquility

comprehended her loneliness; the destiny that had drawn an inviolable circle round about her; the whole peculiarity, in short, of her position in respect to other children. Never, since her release from prison, had Hester met the public gaze without her. In all her walks about the town, Pearl, too, was there; first as the babe in arms, and afterwards as the little girl, small companion of her mother, holding a forefinger with her whole grasp, and tripping along at the rate of three or four footsteps to one of Hester's. She saw the children of the settlement, on the grassy margin of the street, or at the domestic thresholds, disporting themselves in such grim fashions as the Puritanic nurture would permit; playing at going to church, perchance; or at scourging Quakers; or taking scalps in a sham-fight with the Indians; or scaring one another with freaks of imitative witchcraft. Pearl saw, and gazed intently, but never sought to make acquaintance. If spoken to, she would not speak again. If the children gathered about her, as they sometimes did, Pearl would grow positively terrible in her puny wrath, snatching up stones to fling at them, with shrill, incoherent exclamations that made her mother tremble, because they had so much the sound of a witch's anathemas in some unknown tongue.

◄ How does Pearl react to the other children?

The truth was, that the little Puritans, being of the most intolerant brood that ever lived, had got a vague idea of something outlandish, unearthly, or at variance with ordinary fashions, in the mother and child; and therefore scorned them in their hearts, and not unfrequently reviled them with their tongues. Pearl felt the sentiment, and requited it with the bitterest hatred that can be supposed to rankle in a childish bosom. These outbreaks of a fierce temper had a kind of value, and even comfort, for the mother; because there was at least an intelligible earnestness in the mood, instead of the fitful caprice that so often thwarted her in the child's manifestations. It appalled her, nevertheless, to discern here, again, a shadowy reflection of the evil that had existed in herself. All this enmity and passion had Pearl inherited, by inalienable right, out of Hester's heart. Mother and daughter stood together in the same circle of seclusion from human society; and in the nature of the child seemed to be perpetuated those unquiet elements that had distracted Hester Prynne before Pearl's birth, but had since begun to be

◄ Why does Pearl react as she does to the other children?

Words For Everyday Use	
in • vi • o • la • ble (in vī´ō lə bəl) adj., safe or secure against envy or violation; sacred	a • nath • e • ma (ə nath´ə mə) n., curse
in • co • her • ent (in´kō hir´ənt) adj., not clearly articulated; not logically connected	out • land • ish (out´lan´dish) adj., very odd, bizarre
	en • mi • ty (en´mə tē) n., hostility

soothed away by the softening influences of maternity.

At home, within and around her mother's cottage, Pearl wanted not a wide and various circle of acquaintance. The spell of life went forth from her ever creative spirit, and communicated itself to a thousand objects, as a torch kindles a flame wherever it may be applied. The unlikeliest materials, a stick, a bunch of rags, a flower, were the puppets of Pearl's witchcraft, and, without undergoing any outward change, became spiritually adapted to whatever drama occupied the stage of her inner world. Her one baby-voice served a multitude of imaginary personages, old and young, to talk withal.

▶ What does Pearl imagine when she plays?

The pine-trees, aged, black, and solemn, and flinging groans and other melancholy utterances on the breeze, needed little transformation to figure as Puritan elders; the ugliest weeds of the garden were their children, whom Pearl smote down and uprooted most unmercifully. It was wonderful, the vast variety of forms into which she threw her intellect, with no continuity, indeed, but darting up and dancing, always in a state of preternatural activity—soon sinking down, as if exhausted by so rapid and feverish a tide of life—and succeeded by other shapes of a similar wild energy. It was like nothing so much as the phantasmagoric play of the northern lights. In the mere exercise of the fancy, however, and the sportiveness of a growing mind, there might be a little more than was observable in other children of bright faculties; except as Pearl, in the <u>dearth</u> of human playmates, was thrown more upon the visionary throng which she created. The singularity lay in the hostile feelings with which the child regarded all these offsprings of her own heart and mind. She never created a friend, but seemed always to be sowing broadcast the dragon's teeth, whence sprung a harvest of armed enemies, against whom she rushed to battle. It was inexpressibly sad—then what depth of sorrow to a mother, who felt in her own heart the cause!—to observe, in one so young, this constant recognition of an <u>adverse</u> world, and so fierce a training of the energies that were to make good her cause, in the contest that must ensue.

▶ Why does Pearl imagine only enemies, never friends?

Gazing at Pearl, Hester Prynne often dropped her work upon her knees, and cried out with an agony which she would fain have hidden, but which made utterance for itself, betwixt speech and a groan—"O Father in Heaven—if Thou

Words For Everyday Use	**dearth** (durth) *n.,* scarcity, lack **ad • verse** (ad vurs̆) *adj.,* unfavorable, harmful

art still my Father—what is this being which I have brought into the world!" And Pearl, overhearing the ejaculation, or aware, through some more subtle channel, of those throbs of anguish, would turn her vivid and beautiful little face upon her mother, smile with sprite-like intelligence, and resume her play.

One peculiarity of the child's deportment remains yet to be told. The very first thing which she had noticed, in her life, was—what?—not the mother's smile, responding to it, as other babies do, by that faint, embryo smile of the little mouth, remembered so doubtfully afterwards, and with such fond discussion whether it were indeed a smile. By no means! But that first object of which Pearl seemed to become aware was—shall we say it?—the scarlet letter on Hester's bosom! One day, as her mother stooped over the cradle, the infant's eyes had been caught by the glimmering of the gold embroidery about the letter; and, putting up her little hand, she grasped at it, smiling, not doubtfully, but with a decided gleam, that gave her face the look of a much older child. Then, gasping for breath, did Hester Prynne clutch the fatal token, instinctively endeavoring to tear it away; so infinite was the torture inflicted by the intelligent touch of Pearl's baby-hand. Again, as if her mother's agonized gesture were meant only to make sport for her, did little Pearl look into her eyes, and smile! From that epoch, except when the child was asleep, Hester had never felt a moment's safety; not a moment's calm enjoyment of her. Weeks, it is true, would sometimes elapse, during which Pearl's gaze might never once be fixed upon the scarlet letter; but then, again, it would come at unawares, like the stroke of sudden death, and always with that peculiar smile, and odd expression of the eyes.

Once this freakish, elfish cast came into the child's eyes while Hester was looking at her own image in them, as mothers are fond of doing; and, suddenly—for women in solitude, and with troubled hearts, are pestered with unaccountable delusions—she fancied that she beheld, not her own miniature portrait, but another face in the small black mirror of Pearl's eye. It was a face, fiend-like, full of smiling malice, yet bearing the semblance of features that she had known full well, though seldom with a smile, and never with malice, in them. It was as if an evil spirit possessed the child, and had just then peeped forth in mockery. Many a time afterwards had Hester been tortured, though less vividly, by the same illusion.

In the afternoon of a certain summer's day, after Pearl grew big enough to run about, she amused herself with gathering

◀ What was the first thing of which Pearl was aware?

◀ What does Hester imagine?

handfuls of wild-flowers, and flinging them, one by one, at her mother's bosom; dancing up and down, like a little elf, whenever she hit the scarlet letter. Hester's first motion had been to cover her bosom with her clasped hands. But whether from pride or <u>resignation</u>, or a feeling that her penance might best be wrought out by this unutterable pain, she resisted the impulse, and sat erect, pale as death, looking sadly into little Pearl's wild eyes. Still came the battery of flowers, almost invariably hitting the mark, and covering the mother's breast with hurts for which she could find no balm in this world, nor knew how to seek it in another. At last, her shot being all expended, the child stood still and gazed at Hester, with that little, laughing image of a fiend peeping out—or, whether it peeped or no, her mother so imagined it—from the unsearchable abyss of her black eyes.

"Child, what art thou?" cried the mother.

"O, I am your little Pearl!" answered the child.

But, while she said it, Pearl laughed, and began to dance up and down, with the humorsome <u>gesticulation</u> of a little imp, whose next freak[2] might be to fly up the chimney.

"Art thou my child, in very truth?" asked Hester.

Nor did she put the question altogether idly, but, for the moment, with a portion of genuine earnestness; for, such was Pearl's wonderful intelligence, that her mother half doubted whether she were not acquainted with the secret spell of her existence, and might not now reveal herself.

"Yes; I am little Pearl!" repeated the child, continuing her antics.

▶ What impulse often comes to Hester even when she is suffering?

"Thou art not my child! Thou art no Pearl of mine!" said the mother half playfully; for it was often the case that a sportive impulse came over her, in the midst of her deepest suffering. "Tell me, then, what thou art, and who sent thee hither?"

"Tell me, mother!" said the child, seriously, coming up to Hester, and pressing herself close to her knees. "Do thou tell me!"

▶ Whom does Hester say sent Pearl into this world? How does Hester say this? What message does she unwittingly communicate to Pearl? What is Pearl's reaction?

"Thy Heavenly Father sent thee!" answered Hester Prynne.

But she said it with a hesitation that did not escape the <u>acuteness</u> of the child. Whether moved only by her ordinary freakishness, or because an evil spirit prompted her, she put up her small forefinger, and touched the scarlet letter.

---

2. **freak.** Sudden fancy, odd notion

Words
For
Everyday
Use

res • ig • na • tion (rez´ig nā´shən) *n.*, passive acceptance
ges • tic • u • la • tion (jes tik´yōō lā´shən) *n.*, energetic motion
a • cute • ness (ə kyōōt´nəs) *n.*, quickness of mind; sensitivity to impressions

"He did not send me!" cried she, positively. "I have no Heavenly Father!"

"Hush, Pearl, hush! Thou must not talk so!" answered the mother, suppressing a groan. "He sent us all into the world. He sent even me, thy mother. Then, much more, thee! Or, if not, thou strange and elfish child, whence didst thou come?"

"Tell me! Tell me!" repeated Pearl, no longer seriously, but laughing, and capering about the floor. "It is thou that must tell me!"

But Hester could not resolve the query, being herself in a dismal labyrinth of doubt. She remembered—betwixt a smile and a shudder—the talk of the neighboring townspeople; who, seeking vainly elsewhere for the child's paternity, and observing some of her odd attributes, had given out that poor little Pearl was a demon offspring: such as, ever since old Catholic times, had occasionally been seen on earth, through the agency of their mother's sin, and to promote some foul and wicked purpose. Luther,[3] according to the scandal of his monkish enemies, was a brat of that hellish breed; nor was Pearl the only child to whom this inauspicious origin was assigned, among the New England Puritans.

◄ *What do the townspeople say about Pearl?*

---

3. **Luther.** Martin Luther (1483–1546), German religious leader and founder of Protestantism

Responding to the Selection

Imagine that you were present in Hester's community. How would you have treated Hester? What would you say to the townspeople about their treatment of Hester? What advice might you offer Hester?

Reviewing the Selection

Recalling and Interpreting

1. **R:** To what place does Hester move after she is released from prison?

2. **I:** Why does Hester chose to move back to a community that condemns her? What might be her reasons?

3. **R:** What do young women, children, and "women of elevated rank" do to make Hester feel like an outcast? Despite this treatment, who makes use of Hester's skilled needle work?

4. **I:** What are Hester's feelings about her continual persecution by the townspeople? Why might the Puritans be so attracted to Hester's designs?

5. **R:** What are some of Pearl's personality traits?

6. **I:** Why does Hester worry about Pearl's personality? In what way does Hester feel that the circumstances of Pearl's birth might have affected Pearl's personality?

7. **R:** What do people in town say about Pearl?

8. **I:** Why does Pearl lose her temper with other Puritan children? What reason does the narrator give for this behavior?

Synthesizing

9. What does the narrator mean when he says that "Mother and daughter stood together in the same circle of seclusion from human society"?

10. Do other townspeople judge Hester and Pearl too severely? Does Hester judge herself and her daughter too severely? Why, or why not?

Understanding Literature (QUESTIONS FOR DISCUSSION)

Symbol. A **symbol** is a thing that stands for or represents both itself and something else. What does the scarlet *A* constantly represent to Hester and to the other townspeople, even after she is released from prison? What does Pearl and her often unruly behavior represent to Hester on a daily basis?

VII

The Governor's Hall

Hester Prynne went, one day to the mansion of Governor Bellingham, with a pair of gloves, which she had fringed and embroidered to his order, and which were to be worn on some great occasion of state; for, though the chances of a popular election had caused this former ruler to descend a step or two from the highest rank, he still held an honorable and influential place among the colonial magistracy.

Another and far more important reason than the delivery of a pair of embroidered gloves impelled Hester, at this time, to seek an interview with a personage of so much power and activity in the affairs of the settlement. It had reached her ears, that there was a design on the part of some of the leading inhabitants, cherishing the more rigid order of principles in religion and government, to deprive her of her child. On the <u>supposition</u> that Pearl, as already hinted, was of demon origin, these good people not unreasonably argued that a Christian interest in the mother's soul required them to remove such a stumbling-block from her path. If the child, on the other hand, were really capable of moral and religious growth, and possessed the elements of ultimate salvation, then, surely, it would enjoy all the fairer prospect of these advantages by being transferred to wiser and better guardianship than Hester Prynne's. Among those who promoted the design, Governor Bellingham was said to be one of the most busy. It may appear singular, and, indeed, not a little <u>ludicrous,</u> that an affair of this kind, which, in later days would have been referred to no higher jurisdiction than that of the selectmen[1] of the town, should then have been a question publicly discussed, and on which statesmen of eminence took sides. At that epoch of <u>pristine</u> simplicity, however,

◄ *Why is Hester going to speak with Governor Bellingham?*

◄ *Why do the townspeople think that Pearl should be taken away?*

---

1. **selectmen.** Officials elected to manage town affairs

Words For Everyday Use	**sup • pos • i • tion** (sup'ə zish' ən) *n.*, assumption, hypothesis **lu • di • crous** (lōō'di krəs) *adj.*, absurd, ridiculous **pris • tine** (pris'tēn) *adj.*, pure, uncorrupted

matters of even slighter public interest, and of far less <u>intrinsic</u> weight than the welfare of Hester and her child, were strangely mixed up with the deliberations of legislators and acts of state. The period was hardly, if at all, earlier than that of our story, when a dispute concerning the right of property in a pig, not only caused a fierce and bitter contest in the legislative body of the colony, but resulted in an important modification of the framework itself of the legislature.

Full of concern, therefore—but so conscious of her own right, that it seemed scarcely an unequal match between the public, on the one side, and a lonely woman, backed by the sympathies of nature, on the other—Hester Prynne set forth from her solitary cottage. Little Pearl, of course, was her companion. She was now of an age to run lightly along by her mother's side, and, constantly in motion from morn till sunset, could have accomplished a much longer journey than that before her. Often, nevertheless, more from caprice than necessity, she demanded to be taken up in arms, but was soon as <u>imperious</u> to be let down again, and frisked onward before Hester on the grassy pathway, with many a harmless trip and tumble. We have spoken of Pearl's rich and luxuriant beauty; a beauty that shone with deep and vivid tints; a bright complexion, eyes possessing intensity both of depth and glow, and hair already of a deep, glossy brown, and which, in after years, would be nearly akin to black. There was fire in her and throughout her; she seemed the unpremeditated offshoot of a passionate moment. Her mother, in contriving the child's garb, had allowed the gorgeous tendencies of her imagination their full play; arraying her in a crimson velvet tunic, of a peculiar cut, abundantly embroidered with fantasies and flourishes of gold thread. So much strength of coloring, which must have given a wan and pallid aspect to cheeks of a fainter bloom, was admirably adapted to Pearl's beauty, and made her the very brightest little jet of flame that ever danced upon the earth.

But it was a remarkable attribute of this garb, and, indeed, of the child's whole appearance, that it irresistibly and inevitably reminded the beholder of the token which Hester Prynne was doomed to wear upon her bosom. It was the scarlet letter in another form: the scarlet letter endowed with

► *How has Hester dressed Pearl? What does she resemble?*

Words For Everyday Use	**in • trin • sic** (in trin'sik) *adj.,* not dependent on exterior forces; inherent **im • per • i • ous** (im pir'ē əs) *adj.,* commanding

life! The mother herself—as if the red ignominy were so deeply scorched into her brain, that all her conceptions assumed its form—had carefully wrought out the <u>similitude</u>; lavishing many hours of morbid ingenuity, to create an analogy between the object of her affection, and the emblem of her guilt and torture. But, in truth, Pearl was the one, as well as the other; and only in consequence of that identity had Hester contrived so perfectly to represent the scarlet letter in her appearance.

◄ In what way is Pearl like the scarlet letter?

As the two wayfarers came within the precincts of the town, the children of the Puritans looked up from their play,—or what passed for play with those somber little urchins,—and spake gravely one to another:—

"Behold, verily, there is the woman of the scarlet letter; and of a truth, moreover, there is the likeness of the scarlet letter running along by her side! Come, therefore, and let us fling mud at them!"

But Pearl, who was a <u>dauntless</u> child, after frowning, stamping her foot, and shaking her little hand with a variety of threatening gestures, suddenly made a rush at the knot of her enemies, and put them all to flight. She resembled, in her fierce pursuit of them, an infant <u>pestilence</u>,—the scarlet fever, or some such half-fledged angel of judgment,—whose mission was to punish the sins of the rising generation. She screamed and shouted, too, with a terrific volume of sound, which doubtless caused the hearts of the fugitives to quake within them. The victory accomplished, Pearl returned quietly to her mother, and looked up smiling, into her face.

Without further adventure, they reached the dwelling of Governor Bellingham. This was a large wooden house, built in a fashion of which there are specimens still <u>extant</u> in the streets of our older towns, now moss-grown, crumbling to decay, and <u>melancholy</u> at heart with the many sorrowful or joyful occurrences, remembered or forgotten, that have happened and passed away, within their dusky chambers. Then, however, there was the freshness of the passing year on its exterior, and the cheerfulness, gleaming forth from the sunny windows, of a human habitation, into which death had never entered. It had, indeed, a very cheery aspect; the walls being overspread with a kind of stucco, in which

◄ What seems unusual about Governor Bellingham's house?

Words For Everyday Use

si • mil • i • tude (sə mil′ə tōōd′) *n.*, likeness

daunt • less (dônt′ les) *adj.*, fearless

pes • ti • lence (pes′tə ləns) *n.*, fatal, contagious disease

ex • tant (eks′tənt) *adj.*, existing

mel • an • chol • y (mel′ən käl′ē) *adj.*, sad; gloomy

fragments of broken glass were plentifully intermixed; so that, when the sunshine fell aslant-wise over the front of the edifice, it glittered and sparkled as if diamonds had been flung against it by the double handful. The brilliancy might have befitted Aladdin's palace, rather than the mansion of a grave old Puritan ruler. It was further decorated with strange and seemingly <u>cabalistic</u> figures and diagrams, suitable to the quaint taste of the age, which had been drawn in the stucco when newly laid on, and had now grown hard and durable, for the admiration of after times.

Pearl, looking at this bright wonder of a house, began to caper and dance, and <u>imperatively</u> required that the whole breadth of sunshine should be stripped off its front, and given her to play with.

"No, my little Pearl!" said her mother; "Thou must gather thine own sunshine. I have none to give thee!"

They approached the door, which was of an arched form, and flanked on each side by a narrow tower or projection of the edifice, in both of which were lattice-windows, with wooden shutters to close over them at need. Lifting the iron hammer that hung at the portal, Hester Prynne gave a summons, which was answered by one of the Governor's bond-servants—a free-born Englishman, but now a seven years' slave.[2] During that term he was to be the property of his master, and as much a commodity of bargain and sale as an ox, or a joint-stool. The serf wore the blue coat, which was the customary garb of serving-men at that period, and long before, in the old hereditary halls of England.

"Is the worshipful Governor Bellingham within?" inquired Hester.

"Yea, forsooth," replied the bond-servant, staring with wide-open eyes at the scarlet letter, which, being a new-comer in the country, he had never before seen. "Yea, his honorable worship is within. But he hath a godly minister or two with him, and likewise a leech. Ye may not see his worship now."

"Nevertheless, I will enter," answered Hester Prynne; and the bond-servant, perhaps judging from the decision of her

► What does the bond-servant think that the scarlet letter means?

---

2. **seven years' slave.** Freeborn Englishman who indentured himself for seven years to a wealthy person in return for passage to the New World

Words For Everyday Use	ca • ba • lis • tic (kab´ə lis´tik) *adj.*, occult im • per • a • tive • ly (im per´ə tiv lē) *adv.*, commandingly; urgently

air and the glittering symbol in her bosom, that she was a great lady in the land, offered no opposition.

So the mother and little Pearl were admitted into the hall of entrance. With many variations, suggested by the nature of his building-materials, diversity of climate, and a different mode of social life, Governor Bellingham had planned his new habitation after the residences of gentlemen of fair estate in his native land. Here, then, was a wide and reasonably lofty hall, extending through the whole depth of the house, and forming a medium of general communication, more or less directly, with all the other apartments. At one extremity, this spacious room was lighted by the windows of the two towers, which formed a small recess on either side of the portal. At the other end, though partly muffled by a curtain, it was more powerfully illuminated by one of those embowed hall-windows which we read of in old books, and which was provided with a deep and cushioned seat. Here, on the cushion, lay a folio tome, probably of the Chronicles of England, or other such substantial literature; even as, in our own days, we scatter gilded volumes on the centre-table, to be turned over by the casual guest. The furniture of the hall consisted of some ponderous chairs, the backs of which were elaborately carved with wreaths of oaken flowers; and likewise a table in the same taste, the whole being of the Elizabethan age, or perhaps earlier, and heirlooms, transferred hither from the Governor's paternal home. On the table—in token that the sentiment of old English hospitality had not been left behind—stood a large pewter tankard, at the bottom of which, had Hester or Pearl peeped into it, they might have seen the frothy remnant of a recent draught of ale.

On the wall hung a row of portraits, representing the forefathers of the Bellingham lineage, some with armor on their breasts, and others with stately ruffs and robes of peace. All were characterized by the sternness and severity which old portraits so invariably put on; as if they were the ghosts, rather than the pictures, of departed worthies, and were gazing with harsh and intolerant criticism at the pursuits and enjoyments of living men.

◄ *What impression do the portraits of Bellingham's ancestors produce in the viewer?*

At about the centre of the oaken panels, that lined the hall, was suspended a suit of mail, not, like the pictures, an ancestral relic, but of the most modern date; for it had been manufactured by a skilful armorer in London, the same year in which Governor Bellingham came over to New England. There was a steel head-piece, a cuirass, a gorget and greaves, with a pair of gauntlets[3] and a sword hanging beneath; all, and especially the helmet and breastplate, so highly burnished as to glow with white radiance, and scatter an illumination everywhere about upon the floor. This bright panoply[4] was not meant for mere idle show, but had been worn by the Governor on many a solemn muster and training field, and had glittered, moreover, at the head of a regiment in the Pequod war.[5] For, though bred a lawyer, and accustomed to speak of Bacon, Coke, Noye, and Finch,[6] as his professional associates, the <u>exigencies</u> of this new country had transformed Governor Bellingham into a soldier, as well as a statesman and ruler.

Little Pearl—who was as greatly pleased with the gleaming armor as she had been with the glittering frontispiece[7] of the house—spent some time looking into the polished mirror of the breastplate.

"Mother," cried she, "I see you here. Look! look!"

▶ What does Pearl want Hester to see?

Hester looked, by way of humoring the child; and she saw that, owing to the peculiar effect of this convex mirror, the scarlet letter was represented in exaggerated and gigantic proportions, so as to be greatly the most prominent feature of her appearance. In truth, she seemed absolutely hidden behind it. Pearl pointed upward, also, at a similar picture in the head-piece; smiling at her mother, with the elfish intelligence that was so familiar an expression on her small physiognomy. That look of naughty merriment was likewise reflected in the mirror, with so much breadth and intensity of effect, that it made Hester Prynne feel as if it could not be the image of her own child, but of an imp who was seeking to mold itself into Pearl's shape.

"Come along, Pearl!" said she, drawing her away, "Come and look into this fair garden. It may be, we shall see flowers there; more beautiful ones than we find in the woods."

Pearl, accordingly, ran to the bow-window, at the farther

---

3. **cuirass . . . gauntlets.** Parts of a suit of armor
4. **panoply.** Full set of armor
5. **Pequod war.** Conflict between the native Pequod people of southeast Connecticut and English colonists that lasted from 1633 to 1637
6. **Bacon . . . Finch.** Sir Francis Bacon (1561–1626), Sir Edward Coke (1552–1634), Sir William Noye (1577–1634), and Sir John Finch (1584–1660) were all prominent lawyers in England.
7. **frontispice.** Main façade, or front part of a building

Words For Everyday Use

ex • i • gen • cy (eks´ə jən sē) *n*, pressing need; demand; requirement end of the hall, and looked along the vista of a garden-walk, carpeted with closely shaven grass, and bordered with some rude and immature attempt at shrubbery. But the proprietor appeared already to have <u>relinquished</u>, as hopeless, the effort to perpetuate on this side of the Atlantic, in a hard soil and amid the close struggle for subsistence, the native English taste for ornamental gardening. Cabbages grew in plain sight; and a pumpkin vine, rooted at some distance, had run across the intervening space, and deposited one of its gigantic products directly beneath the hall-window; as if to warn the Governor that this great lump of vegetable gold was as rich an ornament as New England earth would offer him. There were a few rose-bushes, however, and a number of apple-trees, probably the descendants of those planted by the Reverend Mr. Blackstone, the first settler of the peninsula; that half mythological personage who rides through our early annals,[8] seated on the back of a bull.

Pearl, seeing the rose-bushes, began to cry for a red rose, and would not be pacified.

"Hush, child, hush!" said her mother earnestly. "Do not cry, dear little Pearl! I hear voices in the garden. The Governor is coming, and gentlemen along with him."

In fact, adown the vista of the garden-avenue, a number of persons were seen approaching towards the house. Pearl, in utter scorn of her mother's attempt to quiet her, gave an eldritch[9] scream, and then became silent; not from any notion of obedience, but because the quick and mobile curiosity of her disposition was excited by the appearance of these new personages.

◄ *What does Pearl want from the governor's house? How does she react when she cannot have it?*

---

8. **annals.** Historical records
9. **eldritch.** Ghastly or eerie

| Words For Everyday Use | **re • lin • quish** (ri liŋ´kwish) *vt.*, give up; abandon |

VIII

The Elf-Child and the Minister

Governor Bellingham, in a loose gown and easy cap,—such as elderly gentlemen loved to indue[1] themselves with, in their domestic privacy,—walked foremost, and appeared to be showing off his estate, and <u>expatiating</u> on his projected improvements. The wide circumference of an elaborate ruff, beneath his gray beard, in the antiquated fashion of King James's reign,[2] caused his head to look not a little like that of John the Baptist in a charger. The impression made by his aspect, so rigid and severe, and frost-bitten with more than autumnal age, was hardly in keeping with the appliances of worldly enjoyment wherewith he had evidently done his utmost to surround himself. But it is an error to suppose that our great forefathers—though accustomed to speak and think of human existence as a state merely of trial and warfare, and though <u>unfeignedly</u> prepared to sacrifice goods and life at the behest of duty—made it a matter of conscience to reject such means of comfort, or even luxury, as lay fairly within their grasp. This creed was never taught, for instance, by the venerable pastor, John Wilson, whose beard, white as a snow-drift, was seen over Governor Bellingham's shoulder; while its wearer suggested that pears and peaches might yet be naturalized in the New England climate, and that purple grapes might possibly be compelled to flourish, against the sunny garden-wall. The old clergyman, nurtured at the rich bosom of the English Church, had a long established and legitimate taste for all good and comfortable things; and however stern he might show himself in the pulpit, or in his public reproof of such transgressions as that of Hester Prynne, still, the genial <u>benevolence</u> of his private life had

► *What surprising fact does the narrator reveal about the Puritans?*

---

1. **indue.** Dress
2. **King James's reign.** James Stuart, king of England from 1603 to 1625

Words For Everyday Use

ex • pa • ti • ate (eks pā´shē āt´) *vi.*, speak in great detail; elaborate
un • feign • ed • ly (un fān´id le) *adv.*, genuinely, sincerely
be • nev • o • lence (bə nev´ə ləns) *n.*, kindliness; tendency to be charitable

won him warmer affection than was accorded to any of his professional contemporaries.

Behind the Governor and Mr. Wilson came two other guests; one, the Reverend Arthur Dimmesdale, whom the reader may remember, as having taken a brief and reluctant part in the scene of Hester Prynne's disgrace; and, in close companionship with him, old Roger Chillingworth, a person of great skill in physic, who, for two or three years past, had been settled in the town. It was understood that this learned man was the physician as well as friend of the young minister, whose health had severely suffered, of late, by his too unreserved self-sacrifice to the labors and duties of the pastoral relation.

◀ To whom is the Governor showing his estate?

◀ What has happened to Dimmesdale recently? To what might this occurrence be attributed?

The Governor, in advance of his visitors, ascended one or two steps, and, throwing open the leaves of the great hall-window, found himself close to little Pearl. The shadow of the curtain fell on Hester Prynne, and partially concealed her.

"What have we here?" said Governor Bellingham, looking with surprise at the scarlet little figure before him. "I profess, I have never seen the like, since my days of vanity, in old King James's time, when I was wont to esteem it a high favor to be admitted to a court mask! There used to be a swarm of these small apparitions, in holiday time, and we called them children of the Lord of Misrule.[3] But how gat such a guest into my hall?"

"Ay, indeed!" cried good old Mr. Wilson. "What little bird of scarlet plumage may this be? Methinks I have seen just such figures, when the sun has been shining through a richly painted window, and tracing out the golden and crimson images across the floor. But that was in the old land. Prithee, young one, who art thou, and what has ailed thy mother to bedizen[4] thee in this strange fashion? Art thou a Christian child—ha? Dost know thy catechism? Or art thou one of those naughty elfs or fairies, whom we thought to have left behind us, with other relics of Papistry, in merry old England?"

"I am mother's child," answered the scarlet vision, "and my name is Pearl!"

"Pearl?—Ruby, rather!—or Coral!—or Red Rose, at the very least, judging from thy hue!" responded the old minister, putting forth his hand in a vain attempt to pat little Pearl on the cheek. "But where is this mother of thine? Ah! I see," he

---

3. **Lord of Misrule.** Figure said to rule through the Christmas holidays, and to be guilty of encouraging scandalous behavior
4. **bedizen.** Dress or decorate in a cheap, showy way

added; and, turning to Governor Bellingham, whispered, "This is the selfsame child of whom we have held speech together; and behold here the unhappy woman, Hester Prynne, her mother!"

"Sayest thou so?" cried the Governor. "Nay, we might have judged that such a child's mother must needs be a scarlet woman, and a worthy type of her of Babylon!⁵ But she comes at a good time; and we will look into this matter forthwith."

Governor Bellingham stepped through the window into the hall, followed by his three guests.

"Hester Prynne," said he, fixing his naturally stern regard on the wearer of the scarlet letter, "there hath been much question concerning thee, of late. The point hath been weightily discussed, whether we, that are of authority and influence, do well discharge our consciences by trusting an immortal soul, such as there is in yonder child, to the guidance of one who hath stumbled and fallen, amid the pitfalls of this world. Speak thou, the child's own mother! Were it not, thinkest thou, for thy little one's <u>temporal</u> and eternal welfare, that she be taken out of thy charge, and clad soberly, and disciplined strictly, and instructed in the truths of heaven and earth? What canst thou do for the child, in this kind?"

"I can teach my little Pearl what I have learned from this!" answered Hester Prynne, laying her finger on the red token.

"Woman, it is thy badge of shame!" replied the stern magistrate. "It is because of the stain which that letter indicates, that we would transfer thy child to other hands."

► *What does Hester say she can do for Pearl?*

"Nevertheless," said the mother calmly, though growing more pale, "this badge hath taught me,—it daily teaches me,—it is teaching me at this moment,—lessons whereof my child may be the wiser and better, albeit they can profit nothing to myself."

"We will judge warily," said Bellingham, "and look well what we are about to do. Good Master Wilson, I pray you, examine this Pearl,—since that is her name,—and see whether she hath had such Christian nurture as befits a child of her age."

---

5. **her of Babylon.** A character from Revelation 17:4–5, associated with misdeeds

---

Words For Everyday Use	**tem • po • ral** (tem′pə rəl) *adj.*, existing in time; worldly; not spiritual

The old minister seated himself in an arm-chair, and made an effort to draw Pearl betwixt his knees. But the child, unaccustomed to the touch or familiarity of any but her mother, escaped through the open window, and stood on the upper step, looking like a wild, tropical bird, of rich plumage, ready to take flight into the upper air. Mr. Wilson, not a little astonished at this outbreak—for he was a grandfatherly sort of personage, and usually a vast favorite with children—essayed, however, to proceed with the examination.

"Pearl," said he, with great solemnity, "thou must take heed to instruction, that so, in due season, thou mayest wear in thy bosom the pearl of great price. Canst thou tell me, my child, who made thee?"

◀ What might the "pearl" be that Pearl may wear in her bosom someday? What does Wilson ask of Pearl? Who previously asked Pearl this question?

Now Pearl knew well enough who made her, for Hester Prynne, the daughter of a pious home, very soon after her talk with the child about her Heavenly Father, had begun to inform her of those truths which the human spirit, at whatever stage of immaturity, imbibes with such eager interest. Pearl, therefore, so large were the attainments of her three years' lifetime, could have borne a fair examination in the New England Primer,[6] or the first column of the Westminster Catechism,[7] although unacquainted with the outward form of either of those celebrated works. But that perversity, which all children have more or less of, and of which little Pearl had a tenfold portion, now, at the most inopportune moment, took thorough possession of her, and closed her lips, or impelled her to speak words amiss. After putting her finger in her mouth, with many ungracious refusals to answer good Mr. Wilson's question, the child finally announced that she had not been made at all, but had been plucked by her mother off the bush of wild roses that grew by the prison-door.

◀ In what way does Pearl answer Wilson? What do you think the Puritans would think of such a response?

This fantasy was probably suggested by the near proximity of the Governor's red roses, as Pearl stood outside of the window; together with her recollection of the prison rose-bush, which she had passed in coming hither.

---

6. **New England Primer.** Early schoolbook used to teach both moral lessons and the alphabet
7. **Westminster Catechism.** Statement of Calvinist doctrine

Words For Everyday Use

per • vers • i • ty (pər vʉr´sə tē) n., wickedness; stubborn contrariness

prox • im • i • ty (präks im´ə tē) n., nearness

► In what way has Roger Chillingworth changed since Hester last saw him?

Old Roger Chillingworth, with a smile on his face, whispered something in the young clergyman's ear. Hester Prynne looked at the man of skill, and even then, with her fate hanging in the balance, was startled to perceive what a change had come over his features—how much uglier they were—how his dark complexion seemed to have grown duskier, and his figure more misshapen—since the days when she had familiarly known him. She met his eyes for an instant, but was immediately <u>constrained</u> to give all her attention to the scene now going forward.

"This is awful!" cried the Governor, slowly recovering from the astonishment into which Pearl's response had thrown him. "Here is a child of three years old, and she cannot tell who made her! Without question, she is equally in the dark as to her soul, its present <u>depravity</u>, and future destiny! Methinks, gentlemen, we need inquire no further."

Hester caught hold of Pearl, and drew her forcibly into her arms, confronting the old Puritan magistrate with almost a fierce expression. Alone in the world, cast off by it, and with this sole treasure to keep her heart alive, she felt that she possessed <u>indefeasible</u> rights against the world, and was ready to defend them to the death.

► According to Hester, why should she be allowed to keep Pearl? Why do you think Hester dressed Pearl as she did for this interview?

"God gave me the child!" cried she. "He gave her in requital of all things else, which ye had taken from me. She is my happiness!—she is my torture, none the less! Pearl keeps me here in life! Pearl punishes me too! See ye not, she is the scarlet letter, only capable of being loved, and so endowed with a million-fold the power of retribution for my sin? Ye shall not take her! I will die first!"

"My poor woman," said the not unkind old minister, "the child shall be well cared for!—far better than thou canst do it."

"God gave her into my keeping," repeated Hester Prynne, raising her voice almost to a shriek. "I will not give her up!"—And here, by a sudden impulse, she turned to the young clergyman, Mr. Dimmesdale, at whom, up to this moment, she had seemed hardly so much as once to direct her eyes.—

► To whom does Hester turn for help?

"Speak thou for me!" cried she. "Thou wast my pastor, and hadst charge of my soul, and knowest me better than these men can. I will not lose the child! Speak for me! Thou know-

Words For Everyday Use

con • strain (kən strān´) *vt.*, force, compel; restrain
de • prav • i • ty (dē prav´ə tē) *n.*, corruption, wickedness
in • de • fea • si • ble (in´dē fē´zə bəl) *adj.*, not capable of being undone

est—for thou hast sympathies which these men lack!—thou knowest what is in my heart, and what are a mother's rights, and how much the stronger they are, when that mother has but her child and the scarlet letter! Look thou to it! I will not lose the child! Look to it!"

At this wild and singular appeal, which indicated that Hester Prynne's situation had <u>provoked</u> her to little less than madness, the young minister at once came forward, pale, and holding his hand over his heart, as was his custom whenever his peculiarly nervous temperament was thrown into <u>agitation</u>. He looked now more careworn and <u>emaciated</u> than as we described him at the scene of Hester's public ignominy; and whether it were his failing health, or whatever the cause might be, his large dark eyes had a world of pain in their troubled and melancholy depth.

"There is truth in what she says," began the minister, with a voice sweet, tremulous, but powerful, insomuch that the hall reëchoed, and the hollow armor rang with it—"truth in what Hester says, and in the feeling which inspires her! God gave her the child, and gave her, too, an instinctive knowledge of its nature and requirements—both seemingly so peculiar—which no other mortal being can possess. And, moreover, is there not a quality of awful sacredness in the relation between this mother and this child?"

"Ay—how is that, good Master Dimmesdale?" interrupted the Governor. "Make that plain, I pray you!"

"It must be even so," resumed the minister. "For, if we deem it otherwise, do we not hereby say that the Heavenly Father, the Creator of all flesh, hath lightly recognized a deed of sin, and made of no account the distinction between unhallowed lust and holy love? This child of its father's guilt and its mother's shame has come from the hand of God, to work in many ways upon her heart, who pleads so earnestly, and with such bitterness of spirit, the right to keep her. It was meant for a blessing—for the one blessing of her life! It was meant, doubtless, the mother herself hath told us, for a retribution too; a torture, to be felt at many an unthought of moment; a pang, a sting, an ever-recurring agony, in the midst of a troubled joy! Hath she not expressed this thought in the garb of the poor child, so forcibly reminding us of that

◄ What gesture does the minister make? In what way has he changed since the day Hester was publicly humiliated?

[handwritten margin notes: paradox – celebrates Pearl / she will live with the guilt]

Words For Everyday Use		
pro • voke (prō vōk´) *vt.*, excite to some feeling	**e • ma • ci • at • ed** (ē mā´ shē āt´ əd) *adj.*, abnormally thin
a • g • i • ta • tion (aj´ə tā´shən) *n.*, emotional disturbance	**ear • nest • ly** (ʉr´ nist lē) *adv.*, seriously and sincerely

red symbol which sears her bosom?"

"Well said, again!" cried good Mr. Wilson. "I feared the woman had no better thought than to make a mountebank[8] of her child!" ~~this~~ symbolization

"Oh, not so!—not so!" continued Mr. Dimmesdale. "She recognizes, believe me, the solemn miracle which God hath wrought, in the existence of that child. And may she feel, too—what, methinks, is the very truth—that this boon was meant, above all things else, to keep the mother's soul alive, and to preserve her from blacker depths of sin into which Satan might else have sought to plunge her! Therefore it is good for this poor, sinful woman, that she hath an infant immortality, a being capable of eternal joy or sorrow, confided to her care—to be trained up by her to righteousness— to remind her, at every moment, of her fall—but yet to teach her, as it were by the Creator's sacred pledge, that, if she bring the child to heaven, the child also will bring its parents thither! Herein is the sinful mother happier than the sinful father. For Hester Prynne's sake, then, and no less for the poor child's sake, let us leave them as Providence hath seen fit to place them!"

"You speak, my friend, with a strange earnestness," said old Roger Chillingworth, smiling at him.

"And there is a weighty import in what my young brother hath spoken," added the Reverend Mr. Wilson.

"What say you, worshipful Master Bellingham? Hath he not pleaded well for the poor woman?"

"Indeed hath he," answered the magistrate; "and hath adduced such arguments, that we will even leave the matter as it now stands; so long, at least, as there shall be no further scandal in the woman. Care must be had, nevertheless, to put the child to due and stated examination in the catechism at thy hands or Master Dimmesdale's. Moreover, at a proper season, the tithing-men[9] must take heed that she go both to school and to meeting."

The young minister, on ceasing to speak, had withdrawn a few steps from the group, and stood with his face partially

Margin notes:

► What does Dimmesdale say Pearl is meant to do for Hester?

Give her an eternal punishment

► What does Dimmesdale say Pearl will "teach" Hester? Why is the sinful mother "happier" than the sinful father?

► What does Roger Chillingworth note about Dimmesdale's plea?

---

8. **mountebank.** Person who mounted a bench, or platform, in a public place and sold phony medicines, usually attracting an audience by tricks or stories
9. **tithing-men.** Elected officials charged with enforcing regulation of the colony

Words
For
Everyday
Use

ad • duce (ad′yōos) vt., give as reason or proof

concealed in the heavy folds of the window-curtain; while the shadow of his figure, which the sunlight cast upon the floor, was tremulous with the vehemence of his appeal. Pearl, that wild and flighty little elf, stole softly towards him, and, taking his hand in the grasp of both her own, laid her cheek against it; a caress so tender, and withal so unobtrusive, that her mother, who was looking on, asked herself,— "Is that my Pearl?" Yet she knew that there was love in the child's heart, although it mostly revealed itself in passion, and hardly twice in her lifetime had been softened by such gentleness as now. The minister,—for, save the long-sought regards of woman, nothing is sweeter than these marks of childish preference, accorded spontaneously by a spiritual instinct, and therefore seeming to imply in us something truly worthy to be loved,—the minister looked round, laid his hand on the child's head, hesitated an instant, and then kissed her brow. Little Pearl's unwonted mood of sentiment lasted no longer; she laughed, and went capering down the hall, so airily, that old Mr. Wilson raised a question whether even her tiptoes touched the floor.

◀ What does Pearl do to Dimmesdale?

"The little baggage hath witchcraft in her, I profess," said he to Mr. Dimmesdale. "She needs no old woman's broomstick to fly withal!"

"A strange child!" remarked old Roger Chillingworth. "It is easy to see the mother's part in her. Would it be beyond a philosopher's research, think ye, gentlemen, to analyze that child's nature, and, from its make and mold, to give a shrewd guess at the father?"

◀ What does Roger Chillingworth suggest?

"Nay; it would be sinful, in such a question, to follow the clue of profane philosophy," said Mr. Wilson. "Better to fast and pray upon it; and still better, it may be, to leave the mystery as we find it, unless Providence reveal it of its own accord. Thereby, every good Christian man hath a title to show a father's kindness towards the poor, deserted babe."

The affair being so satisfactorily concluded, Hester Prynne, with Pearl, departed from the house. As they descended the steps, it is averred that the lattice of a chamber-window was thrown open, and forth into the sunny day was thrust the face of Mistress Hibbins, Governor Bellingham's bitter-tempered sister, and the same who, a few years later, was executed as a witch.

◀ What later happens to Governor Bellingham's sister, Mistress Hibbins?

"Hist, hist!" said she, while her ill-omened physiognomy seemed to cast a shadow over the cheerful newness of the house. "Wilt thou go with us to-night? There will be a merry company in the forest; and I wellnigh promised the Black Man that comely Hester Prynne should make one."

▶ What does Hester says she would have done if Pearl had been taken from her?

"Make my excuse to him, so please you!" answered Hester, with a triumphant smile. "I must tarry at home, and keep watch over my little Pearl. Had they taken her from me, I would willingly have gone with thee into the forest, and signed my name in the Black Man's book too, and that with mine own blood!"

"We shall have thee there anon!" said the witch-lady, frowning, as she drew back her head.

But here—if we suppose this interview betwixt Mistress Hibbins and Hester Prynne to be authentic, and not a parable[10]—was already an illustration of the young minister's argument against <u>sundering</u> the relation of a fallen mother to the offspring of her frailty. Even thus early had the child saved her from Satan's snare.

▶ From what has Pearl saved Hester?

---

10. **parable.** Short, simple story designed to teach a moral or religious lesson

Words
For
Everyday
Use

sun • der (sun'dər) *vt.*, break apart, separate

Responding to the Selection

Do you believe that Hester is the best person to raise Pearl? Why, or why not? Do you agree with the decision made by Mr. Wilson and Governor Bellingham?

Reviewing the Selection

Recalling and Interpreting

1. **R:** Why does Hester visit the governor's mansion? What do the Puritan children say to Hester and Pearl as the two walk to the governor's house, and what does Pearl do in response?

2. **I:** What do Pearl's actions show about her personality? Why might this behavior, particularly if other Puritans see it, worry Hester?

3. **R:** What does Pearl see reflected in the armor breastplate? What is the most prominent feature of this reflection?

4. **I:** In what way does Hester's image in the breastplate reflect how Hester feels about herself? What does Hester find disturbing about Pearl's reaction to the reflection?

5. **R:** What does Pearl say when she is asked, "Who made thee?" What are Mr. Wilson and Governor Bellingham prepared to do upon hearing her answer to the question?

6. **I:** What do Mr. Wilson and Governor Bellingham assume, based on Pearl's answer to their question, about Hester's parenting ability? Why, according to the narrator, does Pearl not give the answer she knows that she is supposed to give?

7. **R:** According to the narrator, what does Reverend Dimmesdale look like when Hester begs him to speak in her defense? Does Dimmesdale's speech have an effect on Mr. Wilson and Governor Bellingham? Why, or why not?

8. **I:** What is unusual about Pearl's reaction to Dimmesdale when he finishes speaking? What does Roger Chillingworth notice about Dimmesdale's speech?

Synthesizing

9. Why, according to Dimmesdale, should Hester raise Pearl? In what way is Pearl both Hester's "happiness," and her "torture"?

10. What value does Pearl offer to Hester? How does the conclusion of this chapter confirm that value and the truth of Dimmesdale's argument?

Understanding Literature (QUESTIONS FOR DISCUSSION)

1. Characterization. Characterization is the use of literary techniques to create a character. A reader can learn about characters by paying close attention to what they say and do and to how they interact with others. In chapters 7 and 8, the reader learns more about the characters of Hester, Pearl, Governor Bellingham, Arthur Dimmesdale, and Roger Chillingworth. Based on what you learned from reading these two chapters, make a statement or two about the personality of each character. Back up your statements with examples or details.

2. Image. An **image** is a word or phrase that names something that can be seen, heard, touched, tasted, or smelled. Describe the image of Pearl in her dress made by Hester and the image of Hester's reflection in the armor breastplate. In what way are these images variations of the novel's most striking symbol—the scarlet *A*? To what image from chapter 1 does Pearl refer when she is asked who her maker is?

IX

The Leech[1]

Under the appellation of Roger Chillingworth, the reader
will remember, was hidden another name, which its former
wearer had resolved should never more be spoken. It has
been related, how, in the crowd that witnessed Hester
Prynne's ignominious exposure, stood a man, elderly, travel-
worn, who, just emerging from the perilous wilderness,
beheld the woman, in whom he hoped to find embodied the
warmth and cheerfulness of home, set up as a type of sin
before the people. Her matronly fame was trodden under all
men's feet. Infamy was babbling around her in the public
market-place. For her kindred, should the tidings ever reach
them, and for the companions of her unspotted life, there
remained nothing but the contagion of her dishonor; which
would not fail to be distributed in strict accordance and proportion with the intimacy and sacredness of their previous
relationship. Then why—since the choice was with himself—should the individual, whose connection with the
fallen woman had been the most intimate and sacred of
them all, come forward to vindicate his claim to an inheritance so little desirable? He resolved not to be pilloried beside
her on her pedestal of shame. Unknown to all but Hester
Prynne, and possessing the lock and key of her silence, he
chose to withdraw his name from the roll of mankind, and,
as regarded his former ties and interest, to vanish out of life
as completely as if he indeed lay at the bottom of the ocean,
whither rumor had long ago consigned him. This purpose
once effected, new interests would immediately spring up,
and likewise a new purpose; dark, it is true, if not guilty, but
of force enough to engage the full strength of his faculties.

◄ What does Roger
Chillingworth think
would happen to him
if he revealed his
identity as Hester's
husband?

In pursuance of this resolve, he took up his residence in
the Puritan town, as Roger Chillingworth, without other
introduction than the learning and intelligence of which he
possessed more than a common measure. As his studies, at a
previous period of his life, had made him extensively
acquainted with the medical science of the day, it was as a
physician that he presented himself, and as such was cor-
dially received. Skillful men, of the medical and chirurgical[2]
profession, were of rare occurrence in the colony. They seldom,

◄ Why is
Chillingworth wel-
comed so readily
into the Puritan
community?

---

1. **Leech.** Archaic term for a physician
2. **chirurgical.** Surgical

it would appear, partook of the religious zeal that brought other emigrants across the Atlantic. In their researches into the human frame, it may be that the higher and more subtile faculties of such men were materialized, and that they lost the spiritual view of existence amid the intricacies of that wondrous mechanism, which seemed to involve art enough to comprise all of life within itself. At all events, the health of the good town of Boston, so far as medicine had aught to do with it, had hitherto lain in the guardianship of an aged deacon and apothecary, whose piety and godly deportment were stronger testimonials in his favor, than any that he could have produced in the shape of a diploma. The only surgeon was one who combined the occasional exercise of that noble art with the daily and habitual flourish of a razor. To such a professional body Roger Chillingworth was a brilliant acquisition. He soon manifested his familiarity with the ponderous and imposing machinery of antique physic; in which every remedy contained a multitude of far-fetched and heterogeneous ingredients, as elaborately compounded as if the proposed result had been the Elixir of Life.[3] In his Indian captivity, moreover, he had gained much knowledge of the properties of native herbs and roots; nor did he conceal from his patients, that these simple medicines, Nature's boon to the untutored savage, had quite as large a share of his own confidence as the European pharmacopeia, which so many learned doctors had spent centuries in elaborating.

This learned stranger was <u>exemplary</u>, as regarded at least the outward forms of a religious life, and, early after his arrival, had chosen for his spiritual guide the Reverend Mr. Dimmesdale. The young divine, whose scholar-like renown still lived in Oxford, was considered by his more <u>fervent</u> admirers as little less than a heaven-ordained apostle, destined, should he live and labor for the ordinary term of life, to do as great deeds for the now feeble New England Church, as the early Fathers had achieved for the infancy of the Christian faith. About this period, however, the health of Mr. Dimmesdale had evidently begun to fail. By those best

---

3. **Elixir of Life.** Substance, sought by alchemists, that would prolong life indefinitely

---

Words For Everyday Use

ex • em • pla • ry (eg zem´plə rē) *adj.*, serving as a model or example; worth imitating

fer • vent (fur´vənt) *adj.*, passionate, emotional

acquainted with his habits, the paleness of the young minister's cheek was accounted for by his too earnest devotion to study, his <u>scrupulous</u> fulfillment of parochial duty, and, more than all, to the fasts and vigils of which he made a frequent practice, in order to keep the grossness of this earthly state from clogging and obscuring his spiritual lamp. Some declared, that, if Mr. Dimmesdale were really going to die, it was cause enough, that the world was not worthy to be any longer trodden by his feet. He himself, on the other hand, with characteristic humility, avowed his belief, that, if Providence should see fit to remove him, it would be because of his own unworthiness to perform its humblest mission here on earth. With all this difference of opinion as to the cause of his decline, there could be no question of the fact. His form grew emaciated; his voice, though still rich and sweet, had a certain melancholy prophecy of decay in it; he was often observed, on any slight alarm or other sudden accident, to put his hand over his heart, with first a flush and then a paleness, indicative of pain.

◄ Of what do Dimmesdale's parishioners believe Dimmesdale's death would be a sign? To what would Dimmesdale attribute his own death?

Such was the young clergyman's condition, and so imminent the prospect that his dawning light would be extinguished, all untimely, when Roger Chillingworth made his <u>advent</u> to the town. His first entry on the scene, few people could tell whence, dropping down, as it were, out of the sky, or starting from the nether earth, had an aspect of mystery, which was easily heightened to the miraculous. He was now known to be a man of skill; it was observed that he gathered herbs, and the blossoms of wild-flowers, and dug up roots and plucked off twigs from the forest-trees, like one acquainted with hidden virtues in what was valueless to common eyes. He was heard to speak of Sir Kenelm Digby, and other famous men—whose scientific attainments were <u>esteemed</u> hardly less than supernatural—as having been his correspondents or associates. Why, with such rank in the learned world, had he come hither? What could he, whose sphere was in great cities, be seeking in the wilderness? In answer to this query, a rumor gained ground—and however absurd, was entertained by some very sensible people—that Heaven had wrought an absolute miracle, by transporting an eminent Doctor of Physic, from a German university, bodily

◄ What "absurd" rumor is told about Roger Chillingworth?

Words For Everyday Use

scru • pu • lous (skrōō′pyə ləs) *adj.*, extremely careful

ad • vent (ad′vent′) *n.*, coming or arrival

es • teem (e stēm′) *vt.*, regard highly

through the air, and setting him down at the door of Mr. Dimmesdale's study! Individuals of wiser faith, indeed, who knew that Heaven promotes its purposes without aiming at the stage-effect of what is called miraculous <u>interposition</u>, were inclined to see a providential hand in Roger Chillingworth's so opportune arrival.

This idea was countenanced by the strong interest which the physician ever manifested in the young clergyman; he attached himself to him as a parishioner, and sought to win a friendly regard and confidence from his naturally reserved sensibility. He expressed great alarm at his pastor's state of health, but was anxious to attempt the cure, and, if early undertaken, seemed not despondent of a favorable result. The elders, the deacons, the motherly dames, and the young and fair maidens, of Mr. Dimmesdale's flock, were alike importunate that he should make trial of the physician's frankly offered skill. Mr. Dimmesdale gently repelled their entreaties.

"I need no medicine," said he.

But how could the young minister say so, when, with every successive Sabbath, his cheek was paler and thinner, and his voice more tremulous than before—when it had now become a constant habit, rather than a casual gesture, to press his hand over his heart? Was he weary of his labors? Did he wish to die? These questions were solemnly propounded to Mr. Dimmesdale by the elder ministers of Boston and the deacons of his church, who, to use their own phrase, "dealt with him," on the sin of rejecting the aid which Providence so manifestly held out. He listened in silence, and finally promised to confer with the physician.

"Were it God's will," said the Reverend Mr. Dimmesdale, when, in fulfillment of this pledge, he requested old Roger Chillingworth's professional advice, "I could be well content, that my labors, and my sorrows, and my sins, and my pains, should shortly end with me, and what is earthly of them be buried in my grave, and the spiritual go with me to my eternal state, rather than that you should put your skill to the proof in my behalf."

"Ah," replied Roger Chillingworth, with that quietness which, whether imposed or natural, marked all his deportment, "it is thus that a young clergyman is apt to speak.

► In whom does the doctor immediately take a strong interest?

► What does Dimmesdale say would make him content?

Words For Everyday Use

in • ter • po • si • tion (in´tər pə zish´ən) *n.*, interruption or intervention

Youthful men, not having taken a deep root, give up their hold of life so easily! And saintly men, who walk with God on earth, would fain be away, to walk with him on the golden pavements of the New Jerusalem."

"Nay," rejoined the young minister, putting his hand to his heart, with a flush of pain flitting over his brow, "were I worthier to walk there, I could be better content to toil here."

"Good men ever interpret themselves too meanly," said the physician.

In this manner, the mysterious old Roger Chillingworth became the medical adviser of the Reverend Mr. Dimmesdale. As not only the disease interested the physician, but he was strongly moved to look into the character and qualities of the patient, these two men, so different in age, came gradually to spend much time together. For the sake of the minister's health, and to enable the leech to gather plants with healing balm in them, they took long walks on the sea-shore, or in the forest; mingling various talk with the plash and murmur of the waves, and the solemn wind-anthem among the tree-tops. Often, likewise, one was the guest of the other, in his place of study and retirement. There was a fascination for the minister in the company of the man of science, in whom he recognized an intellectual cultivation of no moderate depth or scope; together with a range and freedom of ideas, that he would have vainly looked for among the members of his own profession. In truth, he was startled, if not shocked, to find this attribute in the physician. Mr. Dimmesdale was a true priest, a true religionist, with the reverential sentiment largely developed, and an order of mind that impelled itself powerfully along the track of a creed, and wore its passage continually deeper with the lapse of time. In no state of society would he have been what is called a man of liberal views; it would always be essential to his peace to feel the pressure of a faith about him, supporting, while it confined him within its iron framework. Not the less, however, though with a tremulous enjoyment, did he feel the occasional relief of looking at the universe through the medium of another kind of intellect than those with which he habitually held converse. It was as if a window were thrown open, admitting a freer atmosphere into the close and stifled study, where his life was wasting itself away, amid lamp-light, or obstructed day-beams, and the musty fragrance, be it sensual or moral, that exhales from books. But the air was too fresh and chill to be long breathed, with comfort. So the minister, and the physician with him, withdrew again within the limits of what their Church defined as orthodox.

◄ *To what does Chillingworth attribute Dimmesdale's eagerness to die? What does Dimmesdale say to contradict him?*

◄ *In what is Chillingworth interested?*

◄ *In what is Dimmesdale interested?*

Thus Roger Chillingworth scrutinized his patient carefully, both as he saw him in his ordinary life, keeping an accustomed pathway in the range of thoughts familiar to him, and as he appeared when thrown amidst other moral scenery, the novelty of which might call out something new to the surface of his character. He deemed it essential, it would seem, to know the man, before attempting to do him good. Wherever there is a heart and an intellect, the diseases of the physical frame are tinged with the peculiarities of these. In Arthur Dimmesdale, thought and imagination were so active, and sensibility so intense, that the bodily infirmity would be likely to have its groundwork there. So Roger Chillingworth—the man of skill, the kind and friendly physician—strove to go deep into his patient's bosom, delving among his principles, prying into his recollections, and probing everything with a cautious touch, like a treasure-seeker in a dark cavern. Few secrets can escape an investigator, who has opportunity and license to undertake such a quest, and skill to follow it up. A man burdened with a secret should especially avoid the intimacy of his physician. If the latter possess native sagacity, and a nameless something more—let us call it <u>intuition</u>; if he show no intrusive egotism, nor disagreeable prominent characteristics of his own; if he have the power, which must be born with him, to bring his mind into such <u>affinity</u> with his patient's, that this last shall unawares have spoken what he imagines himself only to have thought; if such revelations be received without tumult, and acknowledged not so often by an uttered sympathy, as by silence, an inarticulate breath, and here and there a word, to indicate that all is understood; if, to these qualifications of a confidant be joined the advantages afforded by his recognized character as a physician;—then, at some inevitable moment, will the soul of the sufferer be dissolved, and flow forth in a dark, but transparent stream, bringing all its mysteries into the daylight.

Roger Chillingworth possessed all, or most, of the attributes above enumerated. Nevertheless, time went on; a kind of intimacy, as we have said, grew up between these two cultivated minds, which had as wide a field as the whole sphere of human thought and study, to meet upon; they discussed every topic of ethics and religion, of public affairs, and

► *What does Roger Chillingworth try to probe? Why does he do this?*

| Words For Everyday Use | **in • tu • i • tion** (in tōō ish'ən) *n.,* ability to know without conscious reasoning |
| | **af • fin • i • ty** (ə fin'i tē) *n.,* close relationship; connection |

private character; they talked much, on both sides, of matters that seemed personal to themselves; and yet no secret, such as the physician fancied must exist there, ever stole out of the minister's consciousness into his companion's ear. The latter had his suspicions, indeed, that even the nature of Mr. Dimmesdale's bodily disease had never fairly been revealed to him. It was a strange reserve!

After a time, at a hint from Roger Chillingworth, the friends of Mr. Dimmesdale effected an arrangement by which the two were lodged in the same house; so that every ebb and flow of the minister's life-tide might pass under the eye of his anxious and attached physician. There was much joy throughout the town, when this greatly desirable object was attained. It was held to be the best possible measure for the young clergyman's welfare; unless, indeed, as often urged by such as felt authorized to do so, he had selected some one of the many blooming damsels, spiritually devoted to him, to become his devoted wife. This latter step, however, there was no present prospect that Arthur Dimmesdale would be prevailed upon to take; he rejected all suggestions of the kind, as if priestly celibacy were one of his articles of church-discipline. Doomed by his own choice, therefore, as Mr. Dimmesdale so evidently was, to eat his unsavory morsel always at another's board, and endure the life-long chill which must be his lot who seeks to warm himself only at another's fireside, it truly seemed that this sagacious, experienced, <u>benevolent</u> old physician, with his <u>concord</u> of paternal and reverential love for the young pastor, was the very man, of all mankind, to be constantly within reach of his voice.

◄ *What do the townspeople want Dimmesdale to do? In what way does Dimmesdale react to this suggestion?*

◄ *Do you agree with the townspeople that "this sagacious, experienced, benevolent, old physician" is the best person to be watching over Dimmesdale?*

The new abode of the two friends was with a pious widow, of good social rank, who dwelt in a house covering pretty nearly the site on which the venerable structure of King's Chapel has since been built. It had the grave-yard, originally Isaac Johnson's homefield, on one side, and so was well adapted to call up serious reflections, suited to their respective employments, in both minister and man of physic. The motherly care of the good widow assigned to Mr. Dimmesdale a front apartment, with a sunny exposure, and heavy window-curtains, to create a noontide shadow, when desirable. The walls were hung round with tapestry, said to be from the

Words
For
Everyday
Use

be • nev • o • lent (bə nevˊə lənt) *adj.*, kind
con • cord (känˊkôrdˊ) *n.*, harmony; agreement

▶ *What Biblical stories are depicted on the tapestries in Dimmesdale's room? Why are these images particularly appropriate for Dimmesdale?*

Gobelin looms,[4] and, at all events, representing the Scriptural story of David and Bathsheba,[5] and Nathan the Prophet,[6] in colors still unfaded, but which made the fair woman of the scene almost as grimly picturesque as the woe-denouncing seer. Here, the pale clergyman piled up his library, rich with parchment-bound folios of the Fathers, and the lore of Rabbis, and monkish <u>erudition</u>, of which the Protestant divines, even while they <u>vilified</u> and decried that class of writers, were yet constrained often to avail themselves. On the other side of the house, old Roger Chillingworth arranged his study and laboratory; not such as a modern man of science would reckon even tolerably complete, but provided with a distilling apparatus, and the means of compounding drugs and chemicals, which the practiced alchemist knew well how to turn to purpose. With such commodiousness of situation, these two learned persons sat themselves down, each in his own domain, yet familiarly passing from one apartment to the other, and bestowing a mutual and not incurious inspection into one another's business.

And the Reverend Arthur Dimmesdale's best discerning friends, as we have intimated, very reasonably imagined that the hand of Providence had done all this, for the purpose—besought in so many public, and domestic, and secret prayers—of restoring the young minister to health. But—it must now be said—another portion of the community had latterly begun to take its own view of the relation betwixt Mr. Dimmesdale and the mysterious old physician. When an uninstructed multitude attempts to see with its eyes, it is exceedingly apt to be deceived. When, however, it forms its judgment, as it usually does, on the intuitions of its great and warm heart, the conclusions thus attained are often so profound and so unerring, as to possess the character of truths supernaturally revealed. The people, in the case of which we speak, could justify its prejudice against Roger Chillingworth by no fact or argument worthy of serious <u>refutation</u>. There was an aged handicraftsman, it is true, who

---

4. **Gobelin looms.** The cloth produced by the Gobelin family in fifteenth century Paris was prized all over the world.

5. **David and Bathsheba.** In 2 Samuel 11, Bathsheba, wife of Uriah, becomes pregnant by David. David then sends Uriah into battle to be killed.

6. **Nathan the Prophet.** In 2 Samuel 12, Nathan traps David into condemning himself by telling a parable about the greed of a rich man who takes from his neighbor.

Words For Everyday Use

er • u • di • tion (er´yo͞o dish´ən) *n.*, learning acquired by study

vil • i • fy (vil´ə fī´) *vt.*, put down; slander

ref • u • ta • tion (ref´yə ta´shən) *n.*, disproof

had been a citizen of London at the period of Sir Thomas Overbury's murder, now some thirty years agone; he testified to having seen the physician, under some other name, which the narrator of the story had now forgotten, in company with Dr. Forman, the famous old conjurer, who was <u>implicated</u> in the affair of Overbury. Two or three individuals hinted, that the man of skill, during his Indian captivity, had enlarged his medical attainments by joining in the incantations of the savage priests; who were universally acknowledged to be powerful enchanters, often performing seemingly miraculous cures by their skill in the black art. A large number—and many of these were persons of such sober sense and practical observation, that their opinions would have been valuable, in other matters—affirmed that Roger Chillingworth's aspect had undergone a remarkable change while he had dwelt in town, and especially since his abode with Mr. Dimmesdale. At first, his expression had been calm, meditative, scholar-like. Now, there was something ugly and evil in his face, which they had not previously noticed, and which grew still the more obvious to sight, the oftener they looked upon him. According to the vulgar idea, the fire in his laboratory had been brought from the lower regions, and was fed with infernal fuel; and so, as might be expected, his visage was getting sooty with the smoke.

◀ *What have a number of people noted about Roger Chillingworth? To what do some people attribute this change?*

To sum up the matter, it grew to be a widely diffused opinion that the Reverend Arthur Dimmesdale, like many other personages of special sanctity, in all ages of the Christian world, was haunted either by Satan himself, or Satan's emissary, in the guise of old Roger Chillingworth. This diabolical agent had the Divine permission, for a season, to burrow into the clergyman's intimacy, and plot against his soul. No sensible man, it was confessed, could doubt on which side the victory would turn. The people looked, with an unshaken hope, to see the minister come forth out of the conflict, transfigured with the glory which he would unquestionably win. Meanwhile, nevertheless, it was sad to think of the perchance mortal agony through which he must struggle towards his triumph.

◀ *What do some people think is happening between Chillingworth and Dimmesdale? What do these people believe the outcome will be? Why?*

Alas, to judge from the gloom and terror in the depths of the poor minister's eyes, the battle was a sore one, and the victory anything but secure!

Words For Everyday Use	im • pli • cate (im′pli kāt) *vt.*, show to be connected to a crime

X

The Leech And His Patient

► What is Roger Chillingworth investigating? In what way did Roger change over the course of his investigation?

Old Roger Chillingworth, throughout life, had been calm in temperament, kindly, though not of warm affections, but ever, and in all his relations with the world, a pure and upright man. He had begun an investigation, as he imagined, with the severe and equal <u>integrity</u> of a judge, desirous only of truth, even as if the question involved no more than the air-drawn lines and figures of a geometrical problem, instead of human passions, and wrongs inflicted on himself. But, as he proceeded, a terrible fascination, a kind of fierce, though still calm, necessity, seized the old man within its gripe, and never set him free again, until he had done all its bidding. He now dug into the poor clergyman's heart, like a miner searching for gold; or, rather, like a sexton delving into a grave, possibly in quest of a jewel that had been buried on the dead man's bosom, but likely to find nothing save mortality and corruption. Alas, for his own soul, if these were what he sought!

► What does the narrator say about Roger's search?

Sometimes, a light glimmered out of the physician's eyes, burning blue and <u>ominous</u>, like the reflection of a furnace, or, let us say, like one of those gleams of ghastly fire that darted from Bunyan's[1] awful door-way in the hill-side, and quivered on the pilgrim's face. The soil where this dark miner was working had perchance shown indications that encouraged him.

"This man," said he, at one such moment, to himself, "pure as they deem him—all spiritual as he seems—hath inherited a strong animal nature from his father or his mother. Let us dig a little further in the direction of this vein!"

Then, after long search into the minister's dim interior, and turning over many precious materials, in the shape of high <u>aspirations</u> for the welfare of his race, warm love of souls, pure sentiments, natural piety, strengthened by thought and study, and illuminated by revelation—all of which invaluable gold was perhaps, no better than rubbish to the seeker—he would turn back, discouraged, and begin his quest towards

► To what is Roger compared?

another point. He groped along as <u>stealthily</u>, with as cautious

---

1. **Bunyan's.** Referring to John Bunyan (1628–1688), author of *The Pilgrim's Progress*, a popular religious allegory

Words For Everyday Use	in • teg • ri • ty (in teg´rə tē) n., wholeness; soundness characterized by adherence to moral principles	as • pi • ra • tion (as´pə rā´shən) n., desire, ambition
	om • i • nous (äm´ə nəs) adj., threatening	stealth • i • ly (stel´thə lē) adv., slyly; in a secretive manner

a tread, and as wary an outlook, as a thief entering a chamber where a man lies only half asleep—or, it may be, broad awake—with purpose to steal the very treasure which this man guards as the apple of his eye. In spite of his premeditated carefulness, the floor would now and then creak; his garments would rustle; the shadow of his presence, in a forbidden proximity, would be thrown across his victim. In other words, Mr. Dimmesdale, whose sensibility of nerve often produced the effect of spiritual intuition, would become vaguely aware that something <u>inimical</u> to his peace had thrust itself into relation with him. But Old Roger Chillingworth, too, had perceptions that were almost intuitive; and when the minister threw his startled eyes towards him, there the physician sat; his kind, watchful, sympathizing, but never intrusive friend.

Yet Mr. Dimmesdale would perhaps have seen this individual's character more perfectly, if a certain morbidness, to which sick hearts are liable, had not rendered him suspicious of all mankind. Trusting no man as his friend, he could not recognize his enemy when the latter actually appeared. He therefore still kept up a familiar intercourse with him, daily receiving the old physician in his study; or visiting the laboratory, and, for recreation's sake, watching the processes by which weeds were converted into drugs of potency.

◄ *Why can't Dimmesdale recognize the physician as his enemy?*

One day, leaning his forehead on his hand, and his elbow on the sill of the open window, that looked towards the grave-yard, he talked with Roger Chillingworth, while the old man was examining a bundle of unsightly plants.

"Where," asked he, with a look askance at them—for it was the clergyman's peculiarity that he seldom, now-a-days, looked straight forth at any object, whether human or inanimate—"where, my kind doctor, did you gather those herbs, with such a dark, flabby leaf?"

"Even in the grave-yard, here at hand," answered the physician, continuing his employment. "They are new to me. I found them growing on a grave, which bore no tombstone, nor other memorial of the dead man, save these ugly weeds that have taken upon themselves to keep him in remembrance. They grew out of his heart, and typify, it may be, some hideous secret that was buried with him, and which he had done better to confess during his lifetime."

◄ *What does the physician say about the weeds? Why do you think he says this?*

Words For Everyday Use

i • nim • i • cal (i nim´i kəl) *adj.,* in opposition; hostile

"Perchance," said Mr. Dimmesdale, "he earnestly desired it, but could not."

"And wherefore?" rejoined the physician. "Wherefore not; since all the powers of nature call so earnestly for the confession of sin, that these black weeds have sprung up out of a buried heart, to make manifest an outspoken crime?"

"That, good Sir, is but a fantasy of yours," replied the minister. "There can be, if I forbode aright, no power, short of the Divine mercy, to disclose, whether by uttered words, or by type or emblem, the secrets that may be buried with the human heart. The heart, making itself guilty of such secrets, must perforce hold them, until the day when all hidden things shall be revealed. Nor have I so read or interpreted Holy Writ,[2] as to understand that the disclosure of human thoughts and deeds, then to be made, is intended as a part of the retribution. That, surely, were a shallow view of it. No; these revelations, unless I greatly err, are meant merely to promote the intellectual satisfaction of all intelligent beings, who will stand waiting, on that day, to see the dark problem of this life made plain. A knowledge of men's hearts will be needful to the completest solution of that problem. And I conceive, moreover, that the hearts holding such miserable secrets as you speak of will yield them up, at that last day, not with reluctance, but with a joy unutterable."

"Then why not reveal it here?" asked Roger Chillingworth, glancing quietly aside at the minister. "Why should not the guilty ones sooner avail themselves of this unutterable solace?"

"They mostly do," said the clergyman, griping hard at his breast, as if afflicted with an importunate throb of pain. "Many, many a poor soul hath given its confidence to me, not only on the death-bed, but while strong in life, and fair in reputation. And ever, after such an outpouring, O, what a relief have I witnessed in those sinful brethren! even as in one who at last draws free air, after a long stifling with his own polluted breath. How can it be otherwise? Why should a wretched man, guilty, we will say, of murder, prefer to keep the dead corpse buried in his own heart, rather than fling it forth at once, and let the universe take care of it!"

"Yet some men bury their secrets thus," observed the calm physician.

> ► What does Dimmesdale say about confessing hidden crimes?

---

2. **Holy Writ.** The Bible

"True; there are such men," answered Mr. Dimmesdale. "But not to suggest more obvious reasons, it may be that they are kept silent by the very constitution of their nature. Or—can we not suppose it?—guilty as they may be, retaining, nevertheless, a zeal for God's glory and man's welfare, they shrink from displaying themselves black and filthy in the view of men; because, thenceforward, no good can be achieved by them; no evil of the past be redeemed by better service. So, to their own unutterable torment, they go about among their fellow-creatures, looking pure as new-fallen snow, while their hearts are all speckled and spotted with iniquity of which they cannot rid themselves."

◄ According to Dimmesdale, why do some men bury their secret crimes deep within their hearts?

"These men deceive themselves," said Roger Chillingworth, with somewhat more emphasis than usual, and making a slight gesture with his forefinger. "They fear to take up the shame that rightfully belongs to them. Their love for man, their zeal for God's service—these holy impulses may or may not coexist in their hearts with the evil inmates to which their guilt has unbarred the door, and which must needs <u>propagate</u> a hellish breed within them. But, if they seek to glorify God, let them not lift heavenward their unclean hands! If they would serve their fellow-men, let them do it by making manifest the power and reality of conscience, in constraining them to penitential self-abasement! Wouldst thou have me to believe, O wise and pious friend, that a false show can be better—can be more for God's glory, or man's welfare—than God's own truth? Trust me, such men deceive themselves!"

◄ What does Roger Chillingworth think of Dimmesdale's argument?

"It may be so," said the young clergyman, <u>indifferently</u>, as waiving a discussion that he considered irrelevant or unseasonable. He had a ready faculty, indeed, of escaping from any topic that <u>agitated</u> his too sensitive and nervous temperament.—"But, now, I would ask of my well-skilled physician, whether, in good sooth, he deems me to have profited by his kindly care of this weak frame of mine?"

Before Roger Chillingworth could answer, they heard the clear, wild laughter of a young child's voice, proceeding from the adjacent burial-ground. Looking instinctively from the open window—for it was summer-time—the minister beheld Hester Prynne and little Pearl passing along the footpath that

Words For Everyday Use	**prop • a • gate** (präp´ə gāt´) *vt.*, reproduce **in • dif • fer • ent • ly** (in dif´ər ənt lē) *adv.*, apathetically; without interest **a • g • i • tate** (aj´i tāt´) *vt.*, excite; stir up strong emotions

traversed the enclosure. Pearl looked as beautiful as the day, but was in one of those moods of perverse merriment which, whenever they occurred, seemed to remove her entirely out of the sphere of sympathy or human contact. She now skipped irreverently from one grave to another; until, coming to the broad, flat, armorial tombstone of a departed worthy—perhaps of Isaac Johnson himself—she began to dance upon it. In reply to her mother's command and entreaty that she would behave more <u>decorously</u>, little Pearl paused to gather the prickly burrs from a tall burdock, which grew beside the tomb. Taking a handful of these, she arranged them along the lines of the scarlet letter that decorated the maternal bosom, to which the burrs, as their nature was, <u>tenaciously</u> adhered. Hester did not pluck them off.

Roger Chillingworth had by this time approached the window and smiled grimly down.

▶ What do the physician and the clergyman say about Pearl's nature?

"There is no law, nor reverence for authority, no regard for human ordinances or opinions, right or wrong, mixed up with that child's composition," remarked he, as much to himself as to his companion. "I saw her, the other day, bespatter the Governor himself with water, at the cattle-trough in Spring Lane. What, in heaven's name, is she? Is the imp altogether evil? Hath she affections? Hath she any discoverable principle of being?"

"None—save the freedom of a broken law," answered Mr. Dimmesdale, in a quiet way, as if he had been discussing the point within himself. "Whether capable of good, I know not."

The child probably overheard their voices, for, looking up to the window, with a bright, but naughty smile of mirth and intelligence, she threw one of the prickly burrs at the Reverend Mr. Dimmesdale. The sensitive clergyman shrunk, with nervous dread, from the light missile. Detecting his emotion, Pearl clapped her little hands in the most extravagant ecstasy. Hester Prynne, likewise, had involuntarily looked up; and all these four persons, old and young, regarded one another in silence, till the child laughed aloud, and shouted—"Come away, mother! Come away, or yonder old Black Man will catch you! He hath got hold of the minister already. Come away, mother or he will catch you! But he cannot catch little Pearl!"

▶ What does Pearl say about the physician? What does the child sense that Dimmesdale, though older, does not?

Words For Everyday Use

dec • o • rous • ly (dek´ə rəs lē) *adv.*, showing good behavior
te • na • cious • ly (tə nā´shəs lē) *adv.*, stubbornly; persistently

So she drew her mother away, skipping, dancing, and frisking fantastically among the hillocks of the dead people, like a creature that had nothing in common with a bygone and buried generation, nor owned herself akin to it. It was as if she had been made afresh, out of new elements, and must perforce be permitted to live her own life, and be a law unto herself, without her eccentricities being reckoned to her for a crime.

"There goes a woman," resumed Roger Chillingworth, after a pause, "who, be her demerits what they may, hath none of that mystery of hidden sinfulness which you deem so grievous to be borne. Is Hester Prynne the less miserable, think you, for that scarlet letter on her breast?"

"I do verily believe it," answered the clergyman. "Nevertheless, I cannot answer for her. There was a look of pain in her face, which I would gladly have been spared the sight of. But still, methinks, it must needs be better for the sufferer to be free to show his pain, as this poor woman Hester is, than to cover it up in his heart."

◀ *According to Dimmesdale, which is more painful, to admit wrongdoing and to bear the shame of it openly or to hide it away?*

There was another pause, and the physician began anew to examine and arrange the plants which he had gathered.

"You inquired of me, a little time agone," said he, at length, "my judgment as touching your health."

"I did," answered the clergyman, "and would gladly learn it. Speak frankly, I pray you, be it for life or death."

"Freely, then, and plainly," said the physician, still busy with his plants, but keeping a wary eye on Mr. Dimmesdale, "the disorder is a strange one; not so much in itself, nor as outwardly manifested—in so far, at least as the symptoms have been laid open to my observation. Looking daily at you, my good Sir, and watching the tokens of your aspect, now for months gone by, I should deem you a man sore sick, it may be, yet not so sick but that an instructed and watchful physician might well hope to cure you. But—I know not what to say—the disease is what I seem to know, yet know it not."

"You speak in riddles, learned Sir," said the pale minister, glancing aside out of the window.

"Then, to speak more plainly," continued the physician, "and I crave pardon, Sir—should it seem to require pardon—for this needful plainness of my speech. Let me ask—as your friend—as one having charge, under Providence, of your life and physical well-being—hath all the operation of this disorder been fairly laid open and recounted to me?"

"How can you question it?" asked the minister. "Surely, it were child's play to call in a physician, and then hide the sore!"

"You would tell me, then, that I know all?" said Roger Chillingworth, deliberately, and fixing an eye, bright with intense and concentrated intelligence, on the minister's face. "Be it so! But, again! He to whom only the outward and physical evil is laid open knoweth, oftentimes, but half the evil which he is called upon to cure. A bodily disease, which we look upon as whole and entire within itself, may, after all, be but a symptom of some ailment in the spiritual part. Your pardon, once again, good Sir, if my speech give the shadow of offense. You, Sir, of all men whom I have known, are he whose body is the closest conjoined, and imbued, and identified, so to speak, with the spirit whereof it is the instrument."

"Then I need ask no further," said the clergyman, somewhat hastily rising from his chair. "You deal not, I take it, in medicine for the soul!"

"Thus, a sickness," continued Roger Chillingworth, going on, in an unaltered tone, without heeding the interruption—but standing up, and confronting the emaciated and white-cheeked minister, with his low, dark, and misshapen figure—"a sickness, a sore place, if we may so call it, in your spirit, hath immediately its appropriate manifestation in your bodily frame. Would you, therefore, that your physician heal the bodily evil? How may this be, unless you first lay open to him the wound or trouble in your soul?"

"No!—not to thee!—not to an earthly physician!" cried Mr. Dimmesdale, passionately, and turning his eyes, full and bright, and with a kind of fierceness, on old Roger Chillingworth. "Not to thee! But, if it be the soul's disease, then do I commit myself to the one Physician of the soul! He, if it stand with his good pleasure, can cure; or he can kill! Let him do with me as, in his justice and wisdom, he shall see good. But who art thou, that meddlest in this matter?—that dares thrust himself between the sufferer and his God?"

With a frantic gesture he rushed out of the room.

"It is as well to have made this step," said Roger Chillingworth to himself, looking after the minister, with a grave smile. "There is nothing lost. We shall be friends again anon. But see, now, how passion takes hold upon this man, and hurrieth him out of himself! As with one passion, so with another. He hath done a wild thing ere now, this pious Master Dimmesdale, in the hot passion of his heart."

It proved not difficult to reëstablish the intimacy of the two companions, on the same footing and in the same degree as heretofore. The young clergyman, after a few hours

▶ What does the physician suggest is causing Dimmesdale's physical sickness?

▶ What does Dimmesdale say about his sickness? What does he accuse Chillingworth of doing?

▶ What does Roger Chillingworth see revealed in the minister's outburst?

of privacy, was sensible that the disorder of his nerves had hurried him into an unseemly outbreak of temper, which there had been nothing in the physician's words to excuse or palliate. He marvelled, indeed, at the violence with which he had thrust back the kind old man, when merely proffering the advice which it was his duty to bestow, and which the minister himself had expressly sought. With these remorseful feelings, he lost no time in making the amplest apologies, and besought his friend still to continue the care, which, if not successful in restoring him to health, had, in all probability, been the means of prolonging his feeble existence to that hour. Roger Chillingworth readily assented, and went on with his medical supervision of the minister; doing his best for him, in all good faith, but always quitting the patient's apartment, at the close of the professional interview, with a mysterious and puzzled smile upon his lips. This expression was invisible in Mr. Dimmesdale's presence, but grew strongly evident as the physician crossed the threshold.

"A rare case," he muttered. "I must needs look deeper into it. A strange sympathy betwixt soul and body! Were it only for the art's sake, I must search this matter to the bottom."

It came to pass, not long after the scene above recorded, that the Reverend Mr. Dimmesdale, at noonday, and entirely unawares, fell into a deep, deep slumber, sitting in his chair, with a large black-letter volume open before him on the table. It must have been a work of vast ability in the <u>somniferous</u> school of literature. The profound depth of the minister's repose was the more remarkable; inasmuch as he was one of those persons whose sleep, ordinarily, is as light, as fitful, and as easily scared away, as a small bird hopping on a twig. To such an unwonted remoteness, however, had his spirit now withdrawn into itself, that he stirred not in his chair, when old Roger Chillingworth, without any extraordinary precaution, came into the room. The physician advanced directly in front of his patient, laid his hand upon his bosom, and thrust aside the vestment, that, hitherto, had always covered it even from the professional eye.

◄ *What does Chillingworth do while Dimmesdale sleeps?*

Then, indeed, Mr. Dimmesdale shuddered, and slightly stirred.

After a brief pause, the physician turned away.

Words For Everyday Use

som • nif • er • ous (säm nif´ər əs) *adj.,* inducing sleep

► *What do you think Chillingworth has seen? Why does he react in this way to the sight?*

But with what a wild look of wonder, joy, and horror! With what a ghastly rapture, as it were, too mighty to be expressed only by the eye and features, and therefore bursting forth through the whole ugliness of his figure, and making itself even riotously manifest by the extravagant gestures with which he threw up his arms towards the ceiling, and stamped his foot upon the floor! Had a man seen old Roger Chillingworth, at that moment of his ecstasy, he would have had no need to ask how Satan comports himself, when a precious human soul is lost to heaven, and won into his kingdom.

But what distinguished the physician's ecstasy from Satan's was the trait of wonder in it!

Responding to the Selection

What are your feelings toward the following characters at this point in the novel: Chillingworth, Dimmesdale, and Hester? For which characters do you feel sympathy? For which do you feel disdain or aversion? Why?

Reviewing the Selection

Recalling and Interpreting

1. **R:** Why are the townspeople at first pleased to see Chillingworth living with Dimmesdale? What do people eventually say about Chillingworth?

2. **I:** Why does Chillingworth begin to make people uncomfortable? Do people believe that Dimmesdale is in permanent danger? Why, or why not?

3. **R:** Where did Chillingworth find the bundle of dark, unsightly herbs?

4. **I:** What is Chillingworth's opinion of people who conceal, rather than confess, terrible sins? Does Dimmesdale agree with him? Explain. Why do you think Chillingworth shares with Dimmesdale the story of the man who took a "hideous secret" to his grave?

5. **R:** What do Dimmesdale and Chillingworth observe Pearl doing as she and Hester walk around the burial-ground? What do Dimmesdale and Chillingworth say about Pearl?

6. **I:** Why does Pearl's behavior seem to cause the men, particularly Dimmesdale, concern? According to the men, in what way is Hester better off because she wears the scarlet *A* rather than carry her sin secretly?

7. **R:** When Chillingworth asks Dimmesdale if he has been completely open with him about his illness and the possible causes of it, what is Dimmesdale's response? What does Chillingworth do when he finds Dimmesdale asleep?

8. **I:** What does Chillingworth believe is wrong with Dimmesdale? In what way might his suspicions have been confirmed at the end of the chapter? Why does he react with "wonder, joy, and horror" to his mysterious discovery?

Synthesizing

9. Is it a mistake for Dimmesdale to put his health in the hands of Chillingworth? Why, or why not?

10. What seems to be happening to Chillingworth and to Dimmesdale as a result of their relationship?

Understanding Literature (QUESTIONS FOR DISCUSSION)

1. **Motivation.** A **motivation** is a force that moves a character to think, feel, or behave in a certain way. As Roger Chillingworth persists in trying to reach his goal, his personality and his popularity among other townspeople both take a turn for the worse. What is motivating him in his behavior? Do you think that his motives are positive, or have they become negative? Explain your response, using examples from chapters 9 and 10.

2. **Symbol.** A **symbol** is a thing that stands for or represents both itself and something else. In chapter 10, Reverend Dimmesdale finds Roger Chillingworth examining "a bundle of unsightly plants," and the plants prompt an important discussion between Dimmesdale and Chillingworth. Describe the significance of the plants in relation to this discussion. What do the plants look like, and what do they symbolize? Think about the scene in which Pearl gathers prickly burrs, arranges them around her mother's scarlet *A*, and then throws one at Dimmesdale. What might the prickly burrs and Pearl's actions symbolize? (Hint: think about what burrs look and feel like and about the pain suffered by characters in the novel.)

3. **Suspense. Suspense** is a feeling of expectation, anxiousness, or curiosity created by questions raised in the mind of a reader or viewer. Chapter 10 contains many moments of suspense. These moments leave the reader wondering who will be affected by Chillingworth's search for truth. Identify three or four moments of suspense in chapter 10. What questions are raised in your mind by these passages?

XI

The Interior of a Heart

After the incident last described, the intercourse between the clergyman and the physician, though externally the same, was really of another character than it had previously been. The intellect of Roger Chillingworth had now a sufficiently plain path before it. It was not, indeed, precisely that which he had laid out for himself to tread. Calm, gentle, passionless, as he appeared, there was yet, we fear, a quiet depth of malice, hitherto <u>latent</u>, but active now, in this unfortunate old man, which led him to imagine a more intimate revenge than any mortal had ever wreaked upon an enemy. To make himself the one trusted friend, to whom should be confided all the fear, the remorse, the agony, the ineffectual repentance, the backward rush of sinful thoughts, expelled in vain! All that guilty sorrow, hidden from the world, whose great heart would have pitied and forgiven, to be revealed to him, the Pitiless, to him, the Unforgiving! All that dark treasure to be lavished on the very man, to whom nothing else could so adequately pay the debt of vengeance!

◄ *What quality is becoming active in Roger Chillingworth? What "intimate revenge" has Chillingworth decided upon?*

The clergyman's shy and sensitive reserve had balked this scheme. Roger Chillingworth, however, was inclined to be hardly, if at all, less satisfied with the aspect of affairs, which Providence—using the avenger and his victim for its own purposes, and, perchance, pardoning, where it seemed most to punish—had substituted for his black devices. A revelation, he could almost say, had been granted to him. It mattered little, for his object, whether celestial, or from what other region. By its aid, in all the subsequent relations betwixt him and Mr. Dimmesdale, not merely the external presence, but the very inmost soul of the latter, seemed to be brought out before his eyes, so that he could see and comprehend its every movement. He became, thenceforth, not a spectator only, but a chief actor, in the poor minister's interior world. He could play upon him as he chose. Would he arouse him with a throb of agony? The victim was for ever on the

◄ *In what way does the physician torture Dimmesdale? What kinds of feelings are aroused in Dimmesdale by Chillingworth's comments and actions?*

Words For Everyday Use

la • tent (lāt′nt) *adj.*, present but not visible

rack; it needed only to know the spring that controlled the engine;—and the physician knew it well! Would he startle him with sudden fear? As at the waving of a magician's wand, uprose a grisly phantom—uprose a thousand phantoms—in many shapes, of death, or more awful shame, all flocking round-about the clergyman, and pointing with their fingers at his breast!

All this was accomplished with a subtlety so perfect, that the minister, though he had constantly a dim perception of some evil influence watching over him, could never gain a knowledge of its actual nature. True, he looked doubtfully, fearfully—even, at times, with horror and the bitterness of hatred—at the deformed figure of the old physician. His gestures, his gait, his grizzled beard, his slightest and most indifferent acts, the very fashion of his garments, were <u>odious</u> in the clergyman's sight; a token, <u>implicitly</u> to be relied on, of a deeper <u>antipathy</u> in the breast of the latter than he was willing to acknowledge to himself. For, as it was impossible to assign a reason for such distrust and <u>abhorrence,</u> so Mr. Dimmesdale, conscious that the poison of one morbid spot was infecting his heart's entire substance, attributed all his presentiments to no other cause. He took himself to task for his bad sympathies in reference to Roger Chillingworth, disregarded the lesson that he should have drawn from them, and did his best to root them out. Unable to accomplish this, he nevertheless, as a matter of principle, continued his habits of social familiarity with the old man, and thus gave him constant opportunities for perfecting the purpose to which—poor <u>forlorn</u> creature that he was, and more wretched than his victim—the avenger had devoted himself.

While thus suffering under bodily disease, and gnawed and tortured by some black trouble of the soul, and given over to the <u>machinations</u> of his deadliest enemy, the Reverend Mr. Dimmesdale had achieved a brilliant popularity in his sacred office. He won it, indeed, in great part, by his sorrows. His intellectual gifts, his moral perceptions, his power of experiencing and communicating emotion, were kept in a state of preternatural activity by the prick and anguish of his daily life. His fame, though still on its upward

► *How is Dimmesdale beginning to feel about Roger Chillingworth?*

► *In what way have Dimmesdale's sorrows affected his career?*

slope, already overshadowed the soberer reputations of his fellow-clergymen, eminent as several of them were. There were scholars among them, who had spent more years in acquiring <u>abstruse</u> lore, connected with the divine profession, than Mr. Dimmesdale had lived; and who might well, therefore, be more profoundly versed in such solid and valuable attainments than their youthful brother. There were men, too, of a sturdier texture of mind than his, and endowed with a far greater share of shrewd, hard, iron or granite understanding; which, duly mingled with a fair proportion of doctrinal ingredient, constitutes a highly respectable, efficacious, and unamiable variety of the clerical species. There were others, again, true saintly fathers, whose faculties had been elaborated by weary toil among their books, and by patient thought, and etherealized, moreover, by spiritual communications with the better world, into which their purity of life had almost introduced these holy personages, with their garments of mortality still clinging to them. All that they lacked was the gift that descended upon the chosen disciples, at Pentecost,[1] in tongues of flame; symbolizing, it would seem, not the power of speech in foreign and unknown languages, but that of addressing the whole human brotherhood in the heart's native language. These fathers, otherwise so apostolic, lacked Heaven's last and rarest attestation of their office, the Tongue of Flame. They would have vainly sought—had they ever dreamed of seeking—to express the highest truths through the humblest medium of familiar words and images. Their voices came down, afar and indistinctly, from the upper heights where they habitually dwelt.

◀ *What is the narrator's interpretation of the gift of tongues? In other words, what, according to the narrator, is someone with this gift able to do?*

Not improbably, it was to this latter class of men that Mr. Dimmesdale, by many of his traits of character, naturally belonged. To the high mountain-peaks of faith and sanctity he would have climbed, had not the tendency been <u>thwarted</u> by the burden, whatever it might be, of crime or anguish, beneath which it was his doom to totter. It kept him down, on a level with the lowest; him, the man of ethereal attributes, whose voice the angels might else have listened to and

---

1. **Pentecost.** Christian festival that occurs on the seventh Sunday after Easter

Words For Everyday Use

ab • struse (ab strōōs´) *adj.*, hard to understand
thwart (thwôrt) *vt.*, hinder, obstruct

► With whom can Dimmesdale sympathize?

answered! But this very burden it was, that gave him sympathies so intimate with the sinful brotherhood of mankind; so that his heart vibrated in unison with theirs, and received their pain into itself, and sent its own throb of pain through a thousand other hearts, in gushes of sad, persuasive eloquence. Oftenest persuasive, but sometimes terrible! The people knew not the power that moved them thus. They deemed the young clergyman a miracle of holiness. They fancied him the mouth-piece of Heaven's messages of wisdom, and rebuke, and love. In their eyes, the very ground on which he trod was sanctified. The virgins of his church grew pale around him, victims of a passion so imbued with religious sentiment, that they imagined it to be all religion, and brought it openly, in their white bosoms, as their most acceptable sacrifice before the altar. The aged members of his flock, beholding Mr. Dimmesdale's frame so feeble, while they were themselves so rugged in their infirmity, believed that he would go heavenward before them, and enjoined it upon their children, that their old bones should be buried close to their young pastor's holy grave. And, all this time, perchance, when poor Mr. Dimmesdale was thinking of his grave, he questioned with himself whether the grass would ever grow on it, because an accursed thing must there be buried!

► How does Dimmesdale feel about his popularity? Why?

It is <u>inconceivable</u>, the agony with which this public veneration tortured him! It was his genuine impulse to adore the truth, and to reckon all things shadow-like, and utterly devoid of weight or value, that had not its divine essence as the life within their life. Then, what was he?—a substance?—or the dimmest of all shadows? He longed to speak out, from his own pulpit, at the full height of his voice, and tell the people what he was. "I, whom you behold in these black garments of the priesthood—I, who ascend the sacred desk, and turn my pale face heavenward, taking upon myself to hold communion in your behalf, with the Most High Omniscience—I, in whose daily life you discern the sanctity of Enoch,[2]—I, whose footsteps, as you suppose, leave a gleam

► What does Dimmesdale long to do?

---

2. **sanctity of Enoch.** Enoch had such a perfect relationship with God that he was taken to Heaven without experiencing death.

Words For Everyday Use

in • con • ceiv • a • ble (in′kən sēv′ə bəl) *adj.*, that cannot be thought of, understood, or believed along my earthly track, whereby the pilgrims that shall come after me may be guided to the regions of the blest—I, who have laid the hand of baptism upon your children—I, who have breathed the parting prayer over your dying friends, to whom the Amen sounded faintly from a world which they had quitted—I, your pastor, whom you so reverence and trust, am utterly a pollution and a lie!"

More than once, Mr. Dimmesdale had gone into the pulpit, with a purpose never to come down its steps, until he should have spoken words like the above. More than once, he had cleared his throat, and drawn in the long, deep, and tremulous breath, which, when sent forth again, would come burdened with the black secret of his soul. More than once—nay, more than a hundred times—he had actually spoken! Spoken! But how? He had told his hearers that he was altogether vile, a viler companion of the vilest, the worst of sinners, an <u>abomination</u>, a thing of unimaginable iniquity, and that the only wonder was, that they did not see his wretched body shriveled up before their eyes, by the burning wrath of the Almighty! Could there be plainer speech than this? Would not the people start up in their seats, by a simultaneous impulse, and tear him down out of the pulpit which he <u>defiled</u>? Not so, indeed! They heard it all, and did but reverence him the more. They little guessed what deadly purport lurked in those self-condemning words. "The godly youth!" said they among themselves. "The saint on earth! Alas, if he discern such sinfulness in his own white soul, what horrid spectacle would he behold in thine or mine!" The minister well knew—subtle, but remorseful hypocrite that he was!—the light in which his vague confession would be viewed. He had striven to put a cheat upon himself by making the avowal of a guilty conscience, but had gained only one other sin, and a self-acknowledged shame, without the momentary relief of being self-deceived. He had spoken the very truth, and transformed it into the veriest falsehood. And yet, by the constitution of his nature, he loved the truth, and loathed the lie, as few men ever did. Therefore, above all things else, he loathed his miserable self!

His inward trouble drove him to practices, more in accordance with the old, corrupted faith of Rome, than with the

◀ How do people react when Dimmesdale speaks of his sins?

◀ In what way are Dimmesdale's "confessions" hypocritical?

◀ In what ways does Dimmesdale try to punish himself for his sin?

Words For Everyday Use	**a • bom • i • na • tion** (ə bäm´ə nā´shən) *n.*, something hateful or disgusting **de • file** (dē fīl´) *vt.*, corrupt, make impure

better light of the church in which he had been born and bred. In Mr. Dimmesdale's secret closet, under lock and key, there was a bloody scourge.[3] Oftentimes, this Protestant and Puritan divine had plied it on his own shoulders; laughing bitterly at himself the while, and smiting so much the more pitilessly, because of that bitter laugh. It was his custom, too, as it has been that of many other pious Puritans, to fast—not, however, like them, in order to purify the body and render it the fitter medium of celestial illumination—but rigorously, and until his knees trembled beneath him, as an act of penance. He kept vigils, likewise, night after night, sometimes in utter darkness; sometimes with a glimmering lamp; and sometimes, viewing his own face in a looking-glass, by the most powerful light which he could throw upon it. He thus typified the constant introspection wherewith he tortured, but could not purify, himself. In these lengthened vigils, his brain often reeled, and visions seemed to flit before him; perhaps seen doubtfully, and by a faint light of their own, in the remote dimness of the chamber, or more vividly, and close beside him, within the looking-glass. Now it was a herd of diabolic shapes, that grinned and mocked at the pale minister, and beckoned him away with them; now a group of shining angels, who flew upward heavily, as sorrow-laden, but grew more ethereal as they rose. Now came the dead friends of his youth, and his white-bearded father, with a saint-like frown, and his mother, turning her face away as she passed by. Ghost of a mother—thinnest fantasy of a mother—methinks she might yet have thrown a pitying glance towards her son! And now, through the chamber which these spectral thoughts had made so ghastly, glided Hester Prynne, leading along little Pearl, in her scarlet garb, and pointing her forefinger, first at the scarlet letter on her bosom, and then at the clergyman's own breast.

▶ Whom does Dimmesdale see in his vision? What does this person do?

None of these visions ever quite deluded him. At any moment, by an effort of his will, he could discern substances through their misty lack of substance, and convince himself that they were not solid in their nature, like yonder table of carved oak, or that big, square, leather-bound and brazen-clasped volume of divinity. But, for all that, they were, in one sense, the truest and most substantial things which the poor minister now dealt with. It is the unspeakable misery of a life so false as his, that it steals the pith and substance out of whatever realities there are around us, and which were meant by Heaven to be the spirit's joy and nutriment. To the untrue man, the whole universe is false—it is impalpable—it

---

3. **scourge.** Whip or other instrument for flogging

shrinks to nothing within his grasp. And he himself, in so far as he shows himself in a false light, becomes a shadow, or, indeed, ceases to exist. The only truth, that continued to give Mr. Dimmesdale a real existence on this earth, was the anguish in his inmost soul, and the undissembled expression of it in his aspect. Had he once found power to smile, and wear a face of gaiety, there would have been no such man!

On one of those ugly nights, which we have faintly hinted at, but forborne to picture forth, the minister started from his chair. A new thought had struck him. There might be a moment's peace in it. Attiring himself with as much care as if it had been for public worship, and precisely in the same manner, he stole softly down the staircase, undid the door, and issued forth.

XII

The Minister's Vigil

► Where does Dimmesdale go? Why might he do this?

Walking in the shadow of a dream, as it were, and perhaps actually under the influence of a species of somnambulism,[1] Mr. Dimmesdale reached the spot, where, now so long since, Hester Prynne had lived through her first hours of public ignominy. The same platform or scaffold, black and weather-stained with the storm or sunshine of seven long years, and foot-worn, too, with the tread of many culprits who had since ascended it, remained standing beneath the balcony of the meeting-house. The minister went up the steps.

It was an obscure night in early May. An unwearied pall of cloud muffled the whole expanse of sky from zenith[2] to horizon. If the same multitude which had stood as eyewitnesses while Hester Prynne sustained her punishment could now have been summoned forth, they would have discerned no face above the platform, nor hardly the outline of a human shape, in the dark gray of the midnight. But the town was all asleep. There was no peril of discovery. The minister might stand there, if it so pleased him, until morning should redden in the east, without other risk than that the dank and chill night-air would creep into his frame, and stiffen his joints with rheumatism, and clog his throat with catarrh and cough; thereby defrauding the expectant audience of to-morrow's prayer and sermon. No eye could see him, save that ever-wakeful one which had seen him in his closet, wielding the bloody scourge. Why, then, had he come hither? Was it but the mockery of penitence? A mockery, indeed, but in which his soul trifled with itself! A mockery at which angels blushed and wept, while fiends rejoiced, with jeering laughter! He had been driven hither by the impulse of that Remorse which dogged him everywhere, and whose own sister and closely linked companion was that Cowardice which invariably drew him back, with her tremulous gripe, just when the other impulse had hurried him to the verge of a disclosure. Poor, miserable man! what right had infirmity like his to burden itself with crime? Crime is for the iron-nerved, who have their choice either to endure it, or, if it press too hard, to exert their fierce and savage strength for a good purpose, and fling it off at once! This feeble and most

► What feelings lead Dimmesdale to this place?

---

1. **somnambulism.** Sleepwalking
2. **zenith.** Peak, summit

sensitive of spirits could do neither, yet continually did one thing or another, which intertwined, in the same inextricable knot, the agony of heaven-defying guilt and vain repentance.

And thus, while standing on the scaffold, in this vain show of expiation, Mr. Dimmesdale was overcome with a great horror of mind, as if the universe were gazing at a scarlet token on his naked breast, right over his heart. On that spot, in very truth, there was, and there had long been, the gnawing and poisonous tooth of bodily pain. Without any effort of his will, or power to restrain himself, he shrieked aloud; an outcry that went pealing through the night, and was beaten back from one house to another, and reverberated from the hills in the background; as if a company of devils, detecting so much misery and terror in it, had made a plaything of the sound, and were bandying it to and fro.

◄ What does Dimmesdale imagine? Where has Dimmesdale long experienced pain?

"It is done!" muttered the minister, covering his face with his hands. "The whole town will awake, and hurry forth, and find me here!"

But it was not so. The shriek had perhaps sounded with a far greater power, to his own startled ears, than it actually possessed. The town did not awake; or, if it did, the drowsy slumberers mistook the cry either for something frightful in a dream, or for the noise of witches; whose voices, at that period, were often heard to pass over the settlements or lonely cottages, as they rode with Satan through the air. The clergyman, therefore, hearing no symptoms of disturbance, uncovered his eyes and looked about him. At one of the chamber-windows of Governor Bellingham's mansion, which stood at some distance, on the line of another street, he beheld the appearance of the old magistrate himself with a lamp in his hand, a white night-cap on his head, and a long white gown enveloping his figure. He looked like a ghost evoked unseasonably from the grave. The cry had evidently startled him. At another window of the same house, moreover, appeared old Mistress Hibbins, the Governor's sister, also with a lamp, which, even thus far off, revealed the expression of her sour and discontented face. She thrust forth her head from the lattice, and looked anxiously upward. Beyond the shadow of a doubt, this venerable witch-lady had heard

◄ For what do the townspeople mistake Dimmesdale's cry?

Words For Everyday Use

in • ex • tri • ca • ble (in eks´tri kə bəl) *adj.*, incapable of being untangled or untied

ex • pi • a • tion (eks´ pē ā´ shən) *n.*, act of making amends; reparation

re • ver • ber • ate (ri vʉr´bə rāt´) *vi.*, echo

► For what does Mistress Hibbins mistake Dimmesdale's cry?

Mr. Dimmesdale's outcry, and interpreted it, with its multitudinous echoes and reverberations, as the clamor of the fiends and night-hags, with whom she was well known to make excursions in the forest.

Detecting the gleam of Governor Bellingham's lamp, the old lady quickly extinguished her own, and vanished. Possibly, she went up among the clouds. The minister saw nothing further of her motions. The magistrate, after a wary observation of the darkness—into which, nevertheless, he could see but little farther than he might into a mill-stone[3]—retired from the window.

The minister grew comparatively calm. His eyes, however, were soon greeted by a little glimmering light, which, at first a long way off, was approaching up the street. It threw a gleam of recognition on here a post, and there a garden-fence, and here a latticed window-pane, and there a pump, with its full trough of water, and here again an arched door of oak, with an iron knocker, and a rough log for the door-step. The Reverend Mr. Dimmesdale noted all these minute particulars, even while firmly convinced that the doom of his existence was stealing onward, in the footsteps which he now heard; and that the gleam of the lantern would fall upon him, in a few moments more, and reveal his long-hidden secret. As the light drew nearer, he beheld, within its illuminated circle, his brother clergyman—or, to speak more accurately, his professional father, as well as highly valued friend—the Reverend Mr. Wilson; who, as Mr. Dimmesdale now <u>conjectured</u>, had been praying at the bedside of some dying man. And so he had. The good old minister came freshly from the death-chamber of Governor Winthrop, who had passed from earth to heaven within that very hour. And now, surrounded, like the saint-like personage of olden times, with a radiant halo, that glorified him amid this gloomy night of sin—as if the departed Governor had left him an inheritance of his glory, or as if he had caught upon himself the distant shine of the celestial city, while looking thitherward to see the triumphant pilgrim pass within its gates—now, in short, good Father Wilson was moving homeward, aiding his footsteps with a lighted lantern! The glimmer of this luminary suggested the above conceits to Mr.

---

3. **mill-stone.** Stone used to grind grain

Words For Everyday Use

con • jec • ture (kən jek´chər) vi., guess

Dimmesdale, who smiled—nay, almost laughed at them—and then wondered if he was going mad.

◄ What does Dimmesdale wonder?

As the Reverend Mr. Wilson passed beside the scaffold, closely muffling his Geneva cloak[4] about him with one arm, and holding the lantern before his breast with the other, the minister could hardly restrain himself from speaking.

"A good evening to you, venerable Father Wilson! Come up hither, I pray you, and pass a pleasant hour with me!"

Good Heavens! Had Mr. Dimmesdale actually spoken? For one instant he believed that these words had passed his lips. But they were uttered only within his imagination. The venerable Father Wilson continued to step slowly onward, looking carefully at the muddy pathway before his feet, and never once turning his head towards the guilty platform. When the light of the glimmering lantern had faded quite away, the minister discovered, by the faintness which came over him, that the last few moments had been a crisis of terrible anxiety; although his mind had made an involuntary effort to relieve itself by a kind of lurid playfulness.

Shortly afterwards, the like <u>grisly</u> sense of the humorous again stole in among the solemn phantoms of his thought. He felt his limbs growing stiff with the unaccustomed chilliness of the night, and doubted whether he should be able to descend the steps of the scaffold. Morning would break, and find him there. The neighborhood would begin to rouse itself. The earliest riser, coming forth in the dim twilight, would perceive a vaguely defined figure aloft on the place of shame; and, half crazed betwixt alarm and curiosity, would go, knocking from door to door, summoning all the people to behold the ghost—as he needs must think it—of some defunct transgressor. A dusky tumult would flap its wings from one house to another. Then—the morning light still waxing stronger—old patriarchs would rise up in great haste, each in his flannel gown, and matronly dames, without pausing to put off their night-gear. The whole tribe of decorous personages, who had never heretofore been seen with a single hair of their heads awry, would start into public view, with the disorder of a nightmare in their aspects. Old Governor Bellingham would come grimly forth, with his King James' ruff fastened askew; and Mistress Hibbins, with

◄ What does Dimmesdale imagine will happen?

---

4. **Geneva cloak.** Long, black gown worn by many Protestant clergymen

Words For Everyday Use	**gris • ly** (griz′lē) *adj.*, ghastly; terrifying

some twigs of the forest clinging to her skirts, and looking sourer than ever, as having hardly got a wink of sleep after her night ride; and good Father Wilson too, after spending half the night at a death-bed, and liking ill to be disturbed, thus early, out of his dreams about the glorified saints. Hither, likewise, would come the elders and deacons of Mr. Dimmesdale's church, and the young virgins who so idolized their minister, and had made a shrine for him in their white bosoms, which now, by the by, in their hurry and confusion, they would <u>scantly</u> have given themselves time to cover with their kerchiefs. All people, in a word, would come stumbling over their thresholds, and turning up their amazed and horror-stricken visages around the scaffold. Whom would they discern there, with the red eastern light upon his brow? Whom, but the Reverend Arthur Dimmesdale, half frozen to death, overwhelmed with shame, and standing where Hester Prynne had stood!

► *Who responds to Dimmesdale's laughter?*

Carried away by the grotesque horror of this picture, the minister, unawares, and to his own infinite alarm, burst into a great peal of laughter. It was immediately responded to by a light, airy, childish laugh, in which, with a thrill of the heart—but he knew not whether of exquisite pain, or pleasure as acute—he recognized the tones of little Pearl.

"Pearl! Little Pearl!" cried he, after a moment's pause; then, suppressing his voice—"Hester! Hester Prynne! Are you there?"

"Yes; it is Hester Prynne!" she replied, in a tone of surprise; and the minister heard her footsteps approaching from the sidewalk, along which she had been passing.—"It is I, and my little Pearl."

"Whence come you, Hester?" asked the minister. "What sent you hither?"

"I have been watching at a death-bed," answered Hester Prynne—"at Governor Winthrop's death-bed, and have taken his measure for a robe, and am now going homeward to my dwelling."

"Come up hither, Hester, thou and little Pearl," said the Reverend Mr. Dimmesdale. "Ye have both been here before, but I was not with you. Come up hither once again, and we will stand all three together!"

Words For Everyday Use	**scant • ly** (skant´lē) *adv.,* scarcely, barely

She silently ascended the steps, and stood on the platform, holding little Pearl by the hand. The minister felt for the child's other hand, and took it. The moment that he did so, there came what seemed a tumultuous rush of new life, other life than his own, pouring like a torrent into his heart, and hurrying through all his veins, as if the mother and the child were communicating their vital warmth to his half-torpid system. The three formed an electric chain.

"Minister!" whispered little Pearl.

"What wouldst thou say, child?" asked Mr. Dimmesdale.

"Wilt thou stand here with mother and me, to-morrow noontide?" inquired Pearl.

◄ What does Pearl ask the minister to do? Why does Dimmesdale deny her request?

"Nay; not so, my little Pearl!" answered the minister; for, with the new energy of the moment, all the dread of public exposure, that had so long been the anguish of his life, had returned upon him; and he was already trembling at the conjunction in which—with a strange joy, nevertheless—he now found himself—"Not so, my child. I shall, indeed, stand with thy mother and thee one other day, but not to-morrow!"

Pearl laughed, and attempted to pull away her hand. But the minister held it fast.

"A moment longer, my child!" said he.

"But wilt thou promise," asked Pearl, "to take my hand, and mother's hand, to-morrow noontide?"

"Not then, Pearl," said the minister; "but another time!"

◄ According to Dimmesdale, when will he hold Pearl and Hester's hands again? When won't he meet with them in this way?

"And what other time?" persisted the child.

"At the great judgment day!" whispered the minister—and, strangely enough, the sense that he was a professional teacher of the truth impelled him to answer the child so. "Then, and there, before the judgment-seat, thy mother, and thou, and I, must stand together. But the daylight of this world shall not see our meeting!"

Pearl laughed again.

But, before Mr. Dimmesdale had done speaking, a light gleamed far and wide over all the muffled sky. It was doubtless caused by one of those meteors, which the night-watcher may so often observe burning out to waste, in the vacant regions of the atmosphere. So powerful was its radiance, that it thoroughly illuminated the dense medium of cloud betwixt the sky and earth. The great vault brightened, like

Words For Everyday Use

con • junc • tion (kən juŋk´shən) n., combination

the dome of an immense lamp. It showed the familiar scene of the street, with the distinctness of mid-day, but also with the awfulness that is always imparted to familiar objects by an unaccustomed light. The wooden houses, with their jutting stories and quaint gable-peaks; the doorsteps and thresholds with the early grass springing up about them; the garden-plots, black with freshly turned earth; the wheel-track, little worn, and, even in the market-place margined with green on either side—all were visible, but with a singularity of aspect that seemed to give another moral interpretation to the things of this world than they had ever borne before. And there stood the minister, with his hand over his heart; and Hester Prynne, with the embroidered letter glimmering on her bosom; and little Pearl, herself a symbol, and the connecting link between those two. They stood in the noon of that strange and solemn splendor, as if it were the light that is to reveal all secrets, and the daybreak that shall unite all who belong to one another.

► *What symbols are revealed in the light of the meteor?*

There was witchcraft in little Pearl's eyes; and her face, as she glanced upward at the minister, wore that naughty smile which made its expression frequently so elfish. She withdrew her hand from Mr. Dimmesdale's, and pointed across the street. But he clasped both his hands over his breast, and cast his eyes towards the zenith.

Nothing was more common, in those days, than to interpret all meteoric appearances, and other natural phenomena, that occurred with less regularity than the rise and set of sun and moon, as so many revelations from a supernatural source. Thus, a blazing spear, a sword of flame, a bow, or a sheaf of arrows, seen in the midnight sky, prefigured Indian warfare. Pestilence was known to have been foreboded by a shower of crimson light. We doubt whether any marked event, for good or evil, ever befell New England, from its settlement down to Revolutionary times, of which the inhabitants had not been previously warned by some spectacle of this nature. Not seldom, it had been seen by multitudes. Oftener, however, its <u>credibility</u> rested on the faith of some lonely eyewitness, who beheld the wonder through the colored, magnifying, and <u>distorting</u> medium of his imagination, and shaped it more distinctly in his after-thought. It

Words For Everyday Use

cred • i • bil • i • ty (kred´ə bil´i tē) *n.*, believability
dis • tort • ing (di stôrt´iŋ) *adj.*, shape-changing; modifying

was, indeed, a majestic idea, that the destiny of nations should be revealed, in these awful hieroglyphics, on the cope[5] of heaven. A scroll so wide might not be deemed too expensive for Providence to write a people's doom upon. The belief was a favorite one with our forefathers, as betokening that their infant commonwealth was under a celestial guardianship of peculiar intimacy and strictness. But what shall we say, when an individual discovers a revelation, addressed to himself alone, on the same vast sheet of record! In such a case, it could only be the symptom of a highly disordered mental state, when a man, rendered morbidly self-contemplative by long, intense, and secret pain, had extended his egotism over the whole expanse of nature, until the firmament itself should appear no more than a fitting page for his soul's history and fate.

◄ What did people used to believe about meteors?

◄ What does the narrator believe to be a symptom of Dimmesdale's disordered mental state and of his egotism?

We impute it, therefore, solely to the disease in his own eye and heart, that the minister, looking upward to the zenith, beheld there the appearance of an immense letter—the letter A—marked out in lines of dull red light. Not but the meteor may have shown itself at that point, burning duskily through a veil of cloud; but with no such shape as his guilty imagination gave it; or, at least, with so little definiteness, that another's guilt might have seen another symbol in it.

◄ What does Dimmesdale see in the sky?

There was a singular circumstance that characterized Mr. Dimmesdale's psychological state, at this moment. All the time that he gazed upward to the zenith, he was, nevertheless, perfectly aware that little Pearl was pointing her finger towards old Roger Chillingworth, who stood at no great distance from the scaffold. The minister appeared to see him, with the same glance that discerned the miraculous letter. To his features, as to all other objects, the meteoric light imparted a new expression; or it might well be that the physician was not careful then, as at all other times, to hide the malevolence with which he looked upon his victim. Certainly, if the meteor kindled up the sky, and disclosed the earth, with an awfulness that admonished Hester Prynne and the clergyman of the day of judgment, then might Roger Chillingworth have passed with them for the arch-fiend, standing there, with a smile and scowl, to claim his own. So vivid was the expression, or so intense the minister's perception of it, that it seemed

◄ Who has been observing this scene?

---

5. **cope.** Anything that covers like a cape

Words For Everyday Use	im • pute (im pyo͞ot´) vt., attribute; charge with
	ma • lev • o • lence (mə lev´ə ləns) n., malice, ill will

still to remain painted on the darkness, after the meteor had vanished, with an effect as if the street and all things else were at once annihilated.

► How does Dimmesdale feel about Roger Chillingworth now?

"Who is that man, Hester?" gasped Mr. Dimmesdale, overcome with terror. "I shiver at him! Dost thou know the man? I hate him, Hester!"

She remembered her oath, and was silent.

"I tell thee, my soul shivers at him," muttered the minister again. "Who is he? Who is he? Canst thou do nothing for me? I have a nameless horror of the man!"

"Minister," said little Pearl, "I can tell thee who he is!"

"Quickly, then, child!" said the minister, bending his ear close to her lips. "Quickly!—and as low as thou canst whisper."

Pearl mumbled something into his ear, that sounded, indeed, like human language, but was only such gibberish as children may be heard amusing themselves with by the hour together. At all events, if it involved any secret information in regard to old Roger Chillingworth, it was in a tongue unknown to the <u>erudite</u> clergyman, and did but increase the bewilderment of his mind. The elfish child then laughed aloud.

"Dost thou mock me now?" said the minister.

► Why does Pearl mock Dimmesdale?

"Thou wast not bold!—thou wast not true!" answered the child. "Thou wouldst not promise to take my hand, and mother's hand, to-morrow noontide!"

"Worthy sir," answered the physician, who had now advanced to the foot of the platform—"Pious Master Dimmesdale! can this be you? Well, well, indeed! We men of study, whose heads are in our books, have need to be straitly looked after! We dream in our waking moments, and walk in our sleep. Come, good Sir, and my dear friend, I pray you, let me lead you home!"

"How knewest thou that I was here?" asked the minister, fearfully.

"Verily, and in good faith," answered Roger Chillingworth, "I knew nothing of the matter. I had spent the better part of the night at the bedside of the worshipful Governor Winthrop, doing what my poor skill might to give him ease. He going home to a better world, I, likewise, was on my way homeward, when this light shone out. Come

Words For Everyday Use

er • u • dite (er´yōō dīt´) *adj.*, scholarly; learned

with me, I beseech you, Reverend Sir; else you will be poorly able to do Sabbath duty to-morrow. Aha! see now, how they trouble the brain—these books!—these books! You should study less, good Sir, and take a little pastime, or these night-whimseys will grow upon you!"

"I will go home with you," said Mr. Dimmesdale.

With a chill <u>despondency</u>, like one awakening, all nerveless, from an ugly dream, he yielded himself to the physician, and was led away.

The next day, however, being the Sabbath, he preached a discourse which was held to be the richest and most powerful, and the most replete with heavenly influences, that had ever proceeded from his lips. Souls, it is said, more souls than one, were brought to the truth by the efficacy of that sermon, and vowed within themselves to cherish a holy gratitude towards Mr. Dimmesdale throughout the long hereafter. But as he came down the pulpit-steps, the gray-bearded sexton met him, holding up a black glove, which the minister recognized as his own.

◄ What did Dimmesdale leave behind on the scaffold? In what way does the sexton interpret its appearance there?

"It was found," said the sexton, "this morning, on the scaffold, where evil-doers are set up to public shame. Satan dropped it there, I take it, intending a <u>scurrilous</u> jest against your reverence. But, indeed, he was blind and foolish, as he ever and always is. A pure hand needs no glove to cover it!"

"Thank you, my good friend," said the minister, gravely, but startled at heart; for, so confused was his remembrance, that he had almost brought himself to look at the events of the past night as visionary.

"Yes, it seems to be my glove, indeed!"

"And, since Satan saw fit to steal it, your reverence must needs handle him without gloves, henceforward," remarked the old sexton, grimly smiling. "But did your reverence hear of the portent that was seen last night? A great red letter in the sky—the letter A—which we interpret to stand for Angel. For, as our good Governor Winthrop was made an angel this past night, it was doubtless held fit that there should be some notice thereof!"

◄ In what way do the townspeople interpret the letter A that appeared In the sky?

"No," answered the minister, "I had not heard of it."

Responding to the Selection

"At the great judgment day! . . .Then, and there, before the judgment-seat, thy mother, and thou, and I, must stand together. But the daylight of this world shall not see our meeting!" In your opinion, does each of these people deserve harsh judgment? Why, or why not?

Reviewing the Selection

Recalling and Interpreting

1. **R:** What incident changed the relationship between Dimmesdale and Chillingworth? Is Dimmesdale aware of Chillingworth's feelings toward him?

2. **I:** In what way does Chillingworth become a "chief actor in the poor minister's interior world"?

3. **R:** What happens to Dimmesdale's physical and emotional health? What is the public reaction to the changes in Dimmesdale?

4. **I:** What is unusual about the public reaction to the deterioration of Dimmesdale's physical and emotional health? In what way does public opinion affect Dimmesdale?

5. **R:** When does Dimmesdale go to the scaffold outside the meeting house? What scene does Dimmesdale play in his mind as he stands on the scaffold? Why do Hester and Pearl walk by, and what do the three do?

6. **I:** What drives Dimmesdale to the scaffold? Why does he deny Pearl's request that he stand with them the next day at noon?

7. **R:** What phenomenon do Hester, Dimmesdale, and Pearl observe as they stand together? Who first notices Chillingworth in the darkness?

8. **I:** The next day, why does Dimmesdale deny having seen the strange phenomenon in the sky? What is Dimmesdale's reaction to seeing Chillingworth from the scaffold?

Synthesizing

9. Why is Dimmesdale unwilling to admit his guilt publicly? Who suffers most from his silence?

10. What symbolizes the eternal bond between Hester and Dimmesdale as they stand on the scaffold? Do you agree with Pearl's judgment about the minister? Why, or why not?

Understanding Literature (QUESTIONS FOR DISCUSSION)

1. **Irony. Irony** is the difference between appearance and reality. In irony of situation, an event occurs that violates the expectations of the characters, the reader, or the audience. Reread the following sentence from chapter 11: "While thus suffering under bodily disease, and gnawed and tortured by some black trouble of the soul, and given over to the machinations of his deadliest enemy, the Reverend Mr. Dimmesdale had achieved a brilliant popularity in his sacred office." What is ironic about the public's reaction to Dimmesdale's condition? Describe what Dimmesdale feels due to his awareness of this irony.

2. **Repetition. Repetition** is the use, again, of a sound, word, phrase, sentence, or other element. Two important images from earlier chapters are repeated in chapter 12. Describe chapter 12's scaffold scene, comparing it to the first scaffold scene in chapters 2 and 3. What is the purpose of the repetition of the scaffold scene? Does the placement of this scene exactly halfway through the book help to give the book unity? Explain. Then describe the variations on the image of the letter *A* in chapter 12. Why might the letter *A* appear in the sky? Why might it appear on Dimmesdale's chest?

XIII

Another View of Hester

▶ What shocks
Hester about
Dimmesdale?

In her late singular interview with Mr. Dimmesdale, Hester Prynne was shocked at the condition to which she found the clergyman reduced. His nerve seemed absolutely destroyed. His moral force was abased into more than childish weakness. It groveled helpless on the ground, even while his intellectual faculties retained their pristine strength, or had perhaps acquired a morbid energy, which disease only could have given them. With her knowledge of a train of cir-

▶ What can Hester
readily infer?

cumstances hidden from all others, she could readily infer, that, besides the legitimate action of his own conscience, a terrible machinery had been brought to bear, and was still operating, on Mr. Dimmesdale's well-being and <u>repose</u>. Knowing what this poor, fallen man had once been, her whole soul was moved by the shuddering terror with which he had appealed to her—the outcast woman—for support against his instinctively discovered enemy. She decided, moreover, that he had a right to her utmost aid. Little accustomed, in her long seclusion from society, to measure her ideas of right and wrong by any standard external to herself,

▶ Why is Hester
determined to help
Dimmesdale?

Hester saw—or seemed to see—that there lay a responsibility upon her, in reference to the clergyman, which she owed to no other, nor to the whole world besides. The links that united her to the rest of human kind—links of flowers, or silk, or gold, or whatever the material—had all been broken. Here was the iron link of mutual crime, which neither he nor she could break. Like all other ties, it brought along with it its obligations.

Hester Prynne did not now occupy precisely the same position in which we beheld her during the earlier periods of her ignominy. Years had come, and gone. Pearl was now seven years old. Her mother, with the scarlet letter on her breast, glittering in its fantastic embroidery, had long been a

▶ In what way has
the townspeople's
attitude toward
Hester changed?

familiar object to the townspeople. As is apt to be the case when a person stands out in any <u>prominence</u> before the

---

Words For Everyday Use

re • pose (ri pōz´) *n.*, rest; peace of mind

prom • i • nence (präm´ə nəns) *n.*, conspicuous position or state community, and, at the same time, interferes neither with public nor individual interests and convenience, a species of general regard had ultimately grown up in reference to Hester Prynne. It is to the credit of human nature, that, except where its selfishness is brought into play, it loves more readily than it hates. Hatred, by a gradual and quiet process, will even be transformed to love, unless the change be <u>impeded</u> by a continually new irritation of the original feeling of hostility. In this matter of Hester Prynne, there was neither irritation nor irksomeness. She never battled with the public, but submitted uncomplainingly to its worst usage; she made no claim upon it, in requital for what she suffered; she did not weigh upon its sympathies. Then, also, the blameless purity of her life, during all these years in which she had been set apart to infamy, was reckoned largely in her favor. With nothing now to lose, in the sight of mankind, and with no hope, and seemingly no wish, of gaining anything, it could only be a genuine regard for virtue that had brought back the poor wanderer to its paths.

It was perceived, too, that, while Hester never put forward even the humblest title to share in the world's privileges—farther than to breathe the common air, and earn daily bread for little Pearl and herself by the faithful labor of her hands—she was quick to acknowledge her sisterhood with the race of man, whenever benefits were to be conferred. None so ready as she to give of her little substance to every demand of poverty; even though the bitter-hearted pauper threw back a gibe in requital of the food brought regularly to his door, or the garments wrought for him by the fingers that could have embroidered a monarch's robe. None so self-devoted as Hester, when pestilence stalked through the town. In all seasons of <u>calamity</u>, indeed, whether general or of individuals, the outcast of society at once found her place. She came, not as a guest, but as a rightful inmate, into the household that was darkened by trouble; as if its gloomy twilight were a medium in which she was entitled to hold intercourse with her fellow-creatures. There glimmered the embroidered letter, with comfort in its unearthly ray. Elsewhere the token of sin, it was the taper of the sick-chamber. It had even thrown its gleam, in the sufferer's hard extremity, across the verge of

◄ *What does Hester's letter mean to those who are in trouble?*

Words For Everyday Use	**im • pede** (im pēd´) *vt.,* hinder **ca • lam • i • ty** (kə lam´ə tē) *n.,* disaster

time. It had shown him where to set his foot, while the light of earth was fast becoming dim, and ere the light of futurity could reach him. In such emergencies, Hester's nature showed itself warm and rich; a well-spring of human tenderness, unfailing to every real demand, and inexhaustible by the largest. Her breast, with its badge of shame, was but the softer pillow for the head that needed one. She was self-ordained a Sister of Mercy, or, we may rather say, the world's heavy hand had so ordained her, when neither the world nor she looked forward to this result. The letter was the symbol of her calling. Such helpfulness was found in her—so much power to do, and power to sympathize—that many people refused to interpret the scarlet A by its original signification. They said that it meant Able; so strong was Hester Prynne, with a woman's strength.

► In what way have people changed this interpretation of the meaning of the scarlet A?

It was only the darkened house that could contain her. When sunshine came again, she was not there. Her shadow had faded across the threshold. The helpful inmate had departed, without one backward glance to gather up the meed of gratitude, if any were in the hearts of those whom she had served so <u>zealously</u>. Meeting them in the street, she never raised her head to receive their greeting. If they were resolute to accost her, she laid her finger on the scarlet letter, and passed on. This might be pride, but was so like humility, that it produced all the softening influence of the latter quality on the public mind. The public is <u>despotic</u> in its temper; it is capable of denying common justice, when too strenuously demanded as a right; but quite as frequently it awards more than justice, when the appeal is made, as despots love to have it made, entirely to its generosity. Interpreting Hester Prynne's deportment as an appeal of this nature, society was inclined to show its former victim a more <u>benign</u> countenance than she cared to be favored with, or, perchance, than she deserved.

► In what way do the townspeople interpret Hester's failing to greet them?

► In what way does the narrator seem to interpret Hester's actions?

The rulers, and the wise and learned men of the community, were longer in acknowledging the influence of Hester's good qualities than the people. The prejudices which they shared in common with the latter were fortified in themselves by an iron framework of reasoning, that made it a far tougher labor to expel them. Day by day, nevertheless, their

---

Words For Everyday Use

zeal • ous • ly (zelʹəs lē) *adv.*, enthusiastically, fervently
des • pot • ic (des pätʹik) *adj.*, autocratic, tyrannical
be • nign (bi nīnʹ) *adj.*, kind

sour and rigid wrinkles were relaxing into something which, in the due course of years, might grow to be an expression of almost benevolence. Thus it was with the men of rank, on whom their eminent position imposed the guardianship of the public morals. Individuals in private life, meanwhile, had quite forgiven Hester Prynne for her frailty; nay, more, they had begun to look upon the scarlet letter as the token, not of that one sin, for which she had borne so long and dreary a penance, but of her many good deeds since. "Do you see that woman with the embroidered badge?" they would say to strangers. "It is our Hester—the town's own Hester—who is so kind to the poor, so helpful to the sick, so comfortable to the afflicted!" Then, it is true, the propensity of human nature to tell the very worst of itself, when embodied in the person of another, would constrain them to whisper the black scandal of bygone years. It was none the less a fact, however, that in the eyes of the very men who spoke thus, the scarlet letter had the effect of the cross on a nun's bosom. It imparted to the wearer a kind of sacredness, which enabled her to walk securely amid all peril. Had she fallen among thieves, it would have kept her safe. It was reported, and believed by many, that an Indian had drawn his arrow against the badge, and that the missile struck it, and fell harmless to the ground.

◄ What effect does the scarlet letter now have on people who used to be scandalized by it?

The effect of the symbol—or rather, of the position in respect to society that was indicated by it—on the mind of Hester Prynne, herself was powerful and peculiar. All the light and graceful foliage of her character had been withered up by this red-hot brand, and had long ago fallen away, leaving a bare and harsh outline, which might have been repulsive, had she possessed friends or companions to be repelled by it. Even the attractiveness of her person had undergone a similar change. It might be partly owing to the studied <u>austerity</u> of her dress, and partly to the lack of demonstration in her manners. It was a sad transformation, too, that her rich and luxuriant hair had either been cut off, or was so completely hidden by a cap, that not a shining lock of it ever once gushed into the sunshine. It was due in part to all these causes, but still more to something else, that there seemed to be no longer anything in Hester's face for Love to dwell upon; nothing in

◄ In what way has Hester changed during the course of her punishment?

Words For Everyday Use	**aus • ter • i • ty** (ô ster´ə tē) *n.*, plainness

Hester's form, though majestic and statue-like, that Passion would ever dream of clasping in its embrace; nothing in Hester's bosom, to make it ever again the pillow of Affection. Some attribute had departed from her, the permanence of which had been essential to keep her a woman. Such is frequently the fate, and such the stern development, of the feminine character and person, when the woman has encountered, and lived through, an experience of peculiar severity. If she be all tenderness, she will die. If she survive, the tenderness will either be crushed out of her, or—and the outward semblance is the same—crushed so deeply into her heart that it can never show itself more. The latter is perhaps the truest theory. She who has once been a woman, and ceased to be so, might at any moment become a woman again, if there were only the magic touch to effect the transformation. We shall see whether Hester Prynne were ever afterwards so touched, and so transfigured.

Much of the marble coldness of Hester's impression was to be attributed to the circumstance that her life had turned, in a great measure, from passion and feeling, to thought. Standing alone in the world—alone, as to any dependence on society, and with little Pearl to be guided and protected— alone, and hopeless of retrieving her position, even had she not scorned to consider it desirable—she cast away the fragments of a broken chain. The world's law was no law for her mind. It was an age in which the human intellect, newly <u>emancipated</u>, had taken a more active and a wider range than for many centuries before. Men of the sword had overthrown nobles and kings. Men bolder than these had overthrown and rearranged—not actually, but within the sphere of theory, which was their most real abode—the whole system of ancient prejudice, wherewith was linked much of ancient principle. Hester Prynne imbibed this spirit. She assumed a freedom of speculation, then common enough on the other side of the Atlantic, but which our forefathers, had they known it, would have held to be a deadlier crime than that stigmatized by the scarlet letter. In her lonesome cottage, by the sea-shore, thoughts visited her, such as dared to enter no other dwelling in New England; shadowy guests, that would have been as perilous as demons to their

▶ *How has Hester changed intellectually? How would this change be viewed by her community?*

Words
For
Everyday
Use

e • man • ci • pate (ē man´sə pāt´) *vt.*, make free

entertainer, could they have been seen so much as knocking at her door.

It is remarkable, that persons who speculate the most boldly often conform with the most perfect quietude to the external regulations of society. The thought suffices them, without investing itself in the flesh and blood of action. So it seemed to be with Hester. Yet, had little Pearl never come to her from the spiritual world, it might have been far otherwise. Then, she might have come down to us in history, hand in hand with Ann Hutchinson, as the foundress of a religious sect. She might, in one of her phases, have been a prophetess. She might, and not improbably would, have suffered death from the stern tribunals of the period, for attempting to undermine the foundations of the Puritan establishment. But, in the education of her child, the mother's enthusiasm of thought had something to wreak itself upon. Providence, in the person of this little girl, had assigned to Hester's charge the germ and blossom of womanhood, to be cherished and developed amid a host of difficulties. Everything was against her. The world was hostile. The child's own nature had something wrong in it, which continually betokened that she had been born amiss—the effluence of her mother's lawless passion— and often impelled Hester to ask, in bitterness of heart, whether it were for ill or good that the poor little creature had been born at all.

◄ *According to the narrator, what would Hester have been like if Pearl had never been born?*

Indeed, the same dark question often rose into her mind, with reference to the whole race of womanhood. Was existence worth accepting, even to the happiest among them? As concerned her own individual existence, she had long ago decided in the negative, and dismissed the point as settled. A tendency to speculation, though it may keep women quiet, as it does man, yet makes her sad. She discerns, it may be, such a hopeless task before her. As a first step, the whole system of society is to be torn down, and built up anew. Then, the very nature of the opposite sex, or its long hereditary habit, which has become like nature, is to be essentially modified, before woman can be allowed to assume what seems a fair and suitable position. Finally, all other difficulties being obviated, woman cannot take advantage of these preliminary reforms, until she herself shall have undergone a still mightier change;

◄ *What sorts of questions does Hester ponder?*

Words
For
Everyday
Use

ef • flu • ence (ef′lōō əns) *n.*, flowing forth; emanation

in which, perhaps, the ethereal essence, wherein she has her truest life, will be found to have evaporated. A woman never overcomes these problems by any exercise of thought. They are not to be solved, or only in one way. If her heart chance to come uppermost, they vanish. Thus, Hester Prynne, whose heart had lost its regular and healthy throb, wandered without a clue in the dark labyrinth of mind; now turned aside by an insurmountable <u>precipice</u>; now starting back from a deep chasm. There was wild and ghastly scenery all around her, and a home and comfort nowhere. At times, a fearful doubt strove to possess her soul, whether it were not better to send Pearl at once to Heaven, and go herself to such futurity as Eternal Justice should provide.

The scarlet letter had not done its office.

▶ *What does the narrator mean by this statement? In what way has the scarlet letter failed?*

Now, however, her interview with the Reverend Mr. Dimmesdale, on the night of his vigil, had given her a new theme of reflection, and held up to her an object that appeared worthy of any exertion and sacrifice for its attainment. She had witnessed the intense misery beneath which the minister struggled, or, to speak more accurately, had ceased to struggle. She saw that he stood on the verge of lunacy, if he had not already stepped across it. It was impossible to doubt, that, whatever painful efficacy there might be in the secret sting of remorse, a deadlier venom had been infused into it by the hand that proffered relief. A secret enemy had been continually by his side, under the semblance of a friend and helper, and had availed himself of the opportunities thus afforded for tampering with the delicate springs of Mr. Dimmesdale's nature. Hester could not but ask herself, whether there had not originally been a defect of truth, courage, and loyalty, on her own part, in allowing the minister to be thrown into a position where so much evil was to be foreboded, and nothing auspicious to be hoped. Her only justification lay in the fact that she had been able to discern no method of rescuing him from a blacker ruin than had overwhelmed herself, except by <u>acquiescing</u> in Roger Chillingworth's scheme of disguise. Under that impulse, she had made her choice, and had chosen, as it now appeared, the more wretched alternative of the two. She determined to redeem her error, so far as it might yet be possible. Strengthened by years of hard and solemn

---

Words For Everyday Use

prec • i • pice (pres´i pis) *n.*, steep cliff
ac • qui • esce (ak´wē es´) *vi.*, consent

trial, she felt herself no longer so inadequate to cope with Roger Chillingworth as on that night, abased by sin, and half-maddened by the ignominy that was still new, when they had talked together in the prison-chamber. She had climbed her way, since then, to a higher point. The old man, on the other hand, had brought himself nearer to her level, or perhaps below it, by the revenge which he had stooped for.

In fine, Hester Prynne resolved to meet her former husband, and do what might be in her power for the rescue of the victim on whom he had so evidently set his grip. The occasion was not long to seek. One afternoon, walking with Pearl in a retired part of the peninsula, she beheld the old physician, with a basket on one arm, and a staff in the other hand, stooping along the ground, in quest of roots and herbs to concoct his medicine withal.

◄ *Why does Hester now feel better able to cope with Roger Chillingworth?*

XIV

Hester and the Physician

Hester bade little Pearl run down to the margin of the water, and play with the shells and tangled sea-weed, until she should have talked awhile with yonder gatherer of herbs. So the child flew away like a bird, and, making bare her small white feet, went pattering along the moist margin of the sea. Here and there, she came to a full stop, and peeped curiously into a pool, left by the retiring tide as a mirror for Pearl to see her face in. Forth peeped at her, out of the pool, with dark, glistening curls around her head, and an elf-smile in her eyes, the image of a little maid whom Pearl, having no other play-mate, invited to take her hand and run a race with her. But the visionary little maid, on her part, beckoned likewise, as if to say—"This is a better place! Come thou into the pool!" And Pearl, stepping in, mid-leg deep, beheld her own white feet at the bottom; while, out of a still lower depth, came the gleam of a kind of fragmentary smile, floating to and fro in the agitated water.

Meanwhile her mother had accosted the physician. "I would speak a word with you," said she—"a word that concerns us much."

"Aha! And is it Mistress Hester that has a word for old Roger Chillingworth?" answered he, raising himself from his stooping posture. "With all my heart! Why, Mistress, I hear good tidings of you on all hands! No longer ago than yester-eve, a magistrate, a wise and godly man, was discoursing of your affairs, Mistress Hester, and whispered me that there had been question concerning you in the council. It was debated whether or no, with safety to the common weal, yonder scarlet letter might be taken off your bosom. On my life, Hester, I made my <u>entreaty</u> to the worshipful magistrate that it might be done forthwith!"

"It lies not in the pleasure of the magistrates to take off the badge," calmly replied Hester. "Were I worthy to be quit of it, it would fall away of its own nature, or be transformed

▶ *What news does Roger Chillingworth reveal?*

▶ *Why isn't Hester excited by the news that her punishment may end soon?*

Words For Everyday Use	en • treat • y (en trēt´ē) *n.*, earnest request

into something that should speak a different purport."

"Nay, then, wear it, if it suit you better," rejoined he. "A woman must needs follow her own fancy, touching the adornment of her person. The letter is gayly embroidered, and shows right bravely on your bosom!"

All this while, Hester had been looking steadily at the old man, and was shocked, as well as wonder-smitten, to discern what a change had been wrought upon him within the past seven years. It was not so much that he had grown older; for though the traces of advancing life were visible, he bore his age well, and seemed to retain a wiry vigor and alertness. But the former aspect of an intellectual and studious man, calm and quiet, which was what she best remembered in him, had altogether vanished, and been succeeded by a eager, searching, almost fierce, yet carefully guarded look. It seemed to be his wish and purpose to mask this expression with a smile; but the latter played him false, and flickered over his visage so deri̇sively, that the spectator could see his blackness all the better for it. Ever and anon, too, there came a glare of red light out of his eyes, as if the old man's soul were on fire, and kept on smoldering duskily within his breast, until, by some casual puff of passion, it was blown into a momentary flame. This he repressed as speedily as possible, and strove to look as if nothing of the kind had happened.

◄ What shocks Hester about Chillingworth's appearance?

In a word, old Roger Chillingworth was a striking evidence of man's faculty of transforming himself into a devil, if he will only, for a reasonable space of time, undertake a devil's office. This unhappy person had effected such a transformation by devoting himself, for seven years, to the constant analysis of a heart full of torture, and deriving his enjoyment thence, and adding fuel to those fiery tortures which he analyzed and gloated over.

◄ Of what is Chillingworth evidence?

The scarlet letter burned on Hester Prynne's bosom. Here was another ruin, the responsibility of which came partly home to her.

"What see you in my face," asked the physician, "that you look at it so earnestly?"

"Something that would make me weep, if there were any tears bitter enough for it," answered she. "But let it pass! It is of yonder miserable man that I would speak."

Words For Everyday Use

de • ri • sive • ly (di rī́siv lē) *adv.*, in a ridiculing manner
de • rive (di rīv´) *vt.*, get or receive

"And what of him?" cried Roger Chillingworth, eagerly, as if he loved the topic, and were glad of an opportunity to discuss it with the only person of whom he could make a confidant. "Not to hide the truth, Mistress Hester, my thoughts happen just now to be busy with the gentleman. So speak freely; and I will make answer."

"When we last spake together," said Hester, "now seven years ago, it was your pleasure to <u>extort</u> a promise of secrecy, as touching the former relation betwixt yourself and me. As the life and good fame of yonder man were in your hands, there seemed no choice to me, save to be silent, in accordance with your behest. Yet it was not without heavy misgivings that I thus bound myself; for, having cast off all duty towards other human beings, there remained a duty towards him; and something whispered me that I was betraying it, in pledging myself to keep your counsel. Since that day, no man is so near to him as you. You tread behind his every footstep. You are beside him, sleeping and waking. You search his thoughts. You burrow and rankle in his heart! Your clutch is on his life, and you cause him to die daily a living death; and still he knows you not. In permitting this, I have surely acted a false part by the only man to whom the power was left me to be true!"

▶ What does Hester say she has done by keeping Chillingworth's true identity secret to protect Dimmesdale?

"What choice had you?" asked Roger Chillingworth. "My finger, pointed at this man, would have hurled him from his pulpit into a dungeon—thence, peradventure, to the gallows!"

"It had been better so!" said Hester Prynne.

"What evil have I done the man?" asked Roger Chillingworth again. "I tell thee, Hester Prynne, the richest fee that ever physician earned from monarch could not have bought such care as I have wasted on this miserable priest! But for my aid, his life would have burned away in torments, within the first two years after the perpetration of his crime and thine. For, Hester, his spirit lacked the strength that could have borne up, as thine has, beneath a burden like thy scarlet letter. O, I could reveal a goodly secret! But enough! What art can do, I have exhausted on him. That he now breathes, and creeps about on earth, is owing all to me!"

▶ According to Chillingworth, in what way are Hester and Dimmesdale different?

Words For Everyday Use

ex • tort (eks tôrt´) *vt.*, get something through violence or threats

"Better he had died at once!" said Hester Prynne. "Yea, woman, thou sayest truly!" cried old Roger Chillingworth, letting the lurid fire of his heart blaze out before her eyes. "Better had he died at once! Never did mortal suffer what this man has suffered. And all, all, in the sight of his worst enemy! He has been conscious of me. He has felt an influence dwelling always upon him like a curse. He knew, by some spiritual sense—for the Creator never made another being so sensitive as this—he knew that no friendly hand was pulling at his heart-strings, and that an eye was looking curiously into him, which sought only evil, and found it. But he knew not that the eye and hand were mine! With the superstition common to his brotherhood, he fancied himself given over to a fiend, to be tortured with frightful dreams, and desperate thoughts, the sting of remorse and despair of pardon; as a foretaste of what awaits him beyond the grave. But it was the constant shadow of my presence;—the closest propinquity of the man whom he had most vilely wronged!— and who had grown to exist only by this perpetual poison of the direst revenge! Yea, indeed;—he did not err!—there was a fiend at his elbow! A mortal man, with once a human heart, has become a fiend for his especial torment!"

The unfortunate physician, while uttering these words, lifted his hands with a look of horror, as if he had beheld some frightful shape, which he could not recognize, usurping the place of his own image in a glass. It was one of those moments—which sometimes occur only at the interval of years—when a man's moral aspect is faithfully revealed to his mind's eye. Not improbably, he had never before viewed himself as he did now.

"Hast thou not tortured him enough?" said Hester, noticing the old man's look. "Has he not paid thee all?"

"No! no!—He has but increased the debt!" answered the physician;—and, as he proceeded, his manner lost its fiercer characteristics, and subsided into gloom. "Dost thou remember me, Hester, as I was nine years agone? Even then, I was in the autumn of my days, nor was it the early autumn. But all my life had been made up of earnest, studious, thoughtful, quiet years, bestowed faithfully for the increase of mine own knowledge, and faithfully, too, though this latter object was but casual to the other—faithfully for the advancement

◄ *What does Chillingworth admit? Why has he been so interested in keeping the minister alive?*

◄ *What does Chillingworth say that he has become?*

◄ *Why won't Chillingworth stop torturing Dimmesdale? For what does he blame Dimmesdale, aside from the adultery?*

of human welfare. No life had been more peaceful and innocent than mine; few lives so rich with benefits conferred.
Dost thou remember me? Was I not, though you might deem
me cold, nevertheless a man thoughtful for others, craving
little for himself—kind, true, just, and of constant, if not
warm affections? Was I not all this?"

"All this, and more," said Hester.

"And what am I now?" demanded he, looking into her
face, and permitting the whole evil within him to be written
on his features. "I have already told thee what I am! A fiend!
Who made me so?"

"It was myself," cried Hester, shuddering. "It was I, not
less than he. Why hast thou not avenged thyself on me?"

"I have left thee to the scarlet letter," replied Roger
Chillingworth. "If that has not avenged me, I can do no more!"

He laid his finger on it, with a smile.

"It has avenged thee!" answered Hester Prynne.

"I judged no less," said the physician. "And now, what
wouldst thou with me, touching this man?"

"I must reveal the secret," answered Hester, firmly. "He
must discern thee in thy true character. What may be the
result, I know not. But this long debt of confidence, due
from me to him, whose <u>bane</u> and ruin I have been, shall at
length be paid. So far as concerns the overthrow or preservation of his fair fame and his earthly state, and perchance his
life, he is in my hands. Nor do I—whom the scarlet letter has
disciplined to truth, though it be the truth of red-hot iron,
entering into the soul—nor do I perceive such advantage in
his living any longer a life of ghastly emptiness, that I shall
stoop to implore thy mercy. Do with him as thou wilt! There
is no good for him—no good for me—no good for thee!
There is no good for little Pearl! There is no path to guide us
out of this dismal maze!"

"Woman, I could wellnigh pity thee!" said Roger
Chillingworth, unable to restrain a thrill of admiration too;
for there was a quality almost majestic in the despair which
she expressed. "Thou hadst great elements. Peradventure,
hadst thou met earlier with a better love than mine, this evil
had not been. I pity thee, for the good that has been wasted
in thy nature."

▶ *What does Hester
say the scarlet letter
has done for her?
Why does she tell
Chillingworth to do
what he wills with
Dimmesdale?*

Words
For
Everyday
Use

bane (bān) *n.,* cause of distress, death, or ruin

"And I thee," answered Hester Prynne, "for the hatred that has transformed a wise and just man to a fiend! Wilt thou yet purge it out of thee, and be once more human? If not for his sake, then doubly for thine own! Forgive, and leave his further retribution to the Power that claims it! I said, but now, that there could be no good event for him, or thee, or me, who are here wandering together in this gloomy maze of evil, and stumbling, at every step, over the guilt wherewith we have strewn our path. It is not so! There might be good for thee, and thee alone, since thou hast been deeply wronged, and hast it at thy will to pardon. Wilt thou give up that only privilege? Wilt thou reject that priceless benefit?"

◄ What does Hester ask Chillingworth to do?

"Peace, Hester, peace!" replied the old man, with gloomy sternness. "It is not granted me to pardon. I have no such power as thou tellest me of. My old faith, long forgotten, comes back to me, and explains all that we do, and all we suffer. By thy first step <u>awry</u>, thou didst plant the germ of evil; but, since that moment, it has all been a dark necessity. Ye that have wronged me are not sinful, save in a kind of typical illusion; neither am I fiend-like, who have snatched a fiend's office from his hands. It is our fate. Let the black flower blossom as it may! Now go thy ways, and deal as thou wilt with yonder man."

◄ To what does Chillingworth attribute all that has happened to them? What does the black flower symbolize?

He waved his hand, and betook himself again to his employment of gathering herbs.

Words For Everyday Use

a • wry (ə rī´) *adj.,* wrong; amiss

Responding to the Selection

For whom do you have the most respect so far—Hester, Dimmesdale, or Chillingworth? For whom do you have the most sympathy? Explain your responses.

Reviewing the Selection

Recalling and Interpreting

1. **R:** Seven years after the birth of Pearl, what does Hester spend time doing in the community? In what ways has Hester's physical appearance changed?

2. **I:** What is the community's general opinion of Hester? What is the reason for this change in public opinion? Why have Hester's appearance and her outlook on life changed?

3. **R:** What observations does Hester make about Dimmesdale's condition on the night of his vigil?

4. **I:** According to Hester, who or what has caused Dimmesdale's deteriorated condition? What does she think she needs to do to correct the situation?

5. **R:** What does Hester notice about the changes in Chillingworth's physical appearance?

6. **I:** What does Hester believe has happened to Chillingworth's personality? Into what does Hester believe Chillingworth has been transformed?

7. **R:** According to Chillingworth and Hester, what kind of man was Chillingworth in the past?

8. **I:** What does Chillingworth say in defense of his actions? Why, according to him, is he powerless in controlling his actions against Dimmesdale? Why doesn't he feel a need to seek revenge against Hester?

Synthesizing

9. Of the three main characters—Hester, Dimmesdale, and Chillingworth—who has been most willing to take responsibility for his or her actions?

10. What price for their sins have Hester, Dimmesdale, and Chillingworth paid?

Understanding Literature (QUESTIONS FOR DISCUSSION)

1. Characterization. Characterization is the use of literary techniques to create a character. In chapters 13 and 14, Hawthorne updates his readers on what has happened to his three main characters—Hester, Dimmesdale, and Chillingworth—since the birth of Pearl seven years earlier. In this time, each character has undergone change. Describe the changes each character has experienced. What significant events, relationships, or experiences prompted these changes? Does understanding each person's experience help you to sympathize with that character?

2. Imagery. An **image** is a word or phrase that names something that can be seen, heard, touched, tasted, or smelled. The images in a literary work are referred to, collectively, as the work's **imagery**. Roger Chillingworth spends a great deal of time taking care of his plants, which include medicinal herbs. Hawthorne repeatedly uses images of and references to plants in passages of the novel that focus on Chillingworth. Find the plant imagery and the references to herbs in chapter 13. In what way do these images help to characterize Chillingworth? What does his cultivation of plants reflect?

XV

Hester and Pearl

So Roger Chillingworth—a deformed old figure, with a face that haunted men's memories longer than they liked—took leave of Hester Prynne, and went stooping away along the earth. He gathered here and there a herb, or grubbed up a root, and put it into the basket on his arm. His gray beard almost touched the ground, as he crept onward. Hester gazed after him a little while, looking with a half-fantastic curiosity to see whether the tender grass of early spring would not be blighted beneath him, and show the wavering track of his footsteps, sere and brown, across its cheerful verdure. She wondered what sort of herbs they were, which the old man was so <u>sedulous</u> to gather. Would not the earth, quickened to an evil purpose by the sympathy of his eye, greet him with poisonous shrubs, of species hitherto unknown, that would start up under his fingers? Or might it suffice him, that every wholesome growth should be converted into something <u>deleterious</u> and <u>malignant</u> at his touch? Did the sun, which shone so brightly everywhere else, really fall upon him? Or was there, as it rather seemed, a circle of ominous shadow moving along with his deformity, whichever way he turned himself? And whither was he now going? Would he not suddenly sink into the earth, leaving a barren and blasted spot, where, in due course of time, would be seen deadly nightshade, dogwood, henbane,[1] and whatever else of vegetable wickedness the climate could produce, all flourishing with hideous luxuriance? Or would he spread bat's wings and flee away, looking so much the uglier, the higher he rose towards heaven?

"Be it sin or no," said Hester Prynne, bitterly, as still she gazed after him, "I hate the man!"

She upbraided herself for the sentiment, but could not overcome or lessen it. Attempting to do so, she thought of those long-past days, in a distant land, when he used to

▶ *What does Hester wonder about Roger? What does she think of him?*

---

1. **deadly nightshade, dogwood, henbane.** Plants associated with witchcraft

Words For Everyday Use	sed • u • lous (sejˊoo ləs) *adj.,* diligent; working hard and steadily
	del • e • te • ri • ous (delˊə tirˊē əs) *adj.,* harmful to health or well-being
	ma • lig • nant (mə ligˊnənt) *adj.,* harmful, dangerous

emerge at eventide from the seclusion of his study, and sit down in the fire-light of their home, and in the light of her nuptial smile. He needed to bask himself in that smile, he said, in order that the chill of so many lonely hours among his books might be taken off the scholar's heart. Such scenes had once appeared not otherwise than happy, but now, as viewed through the dismal medium of her subsequent life, they classed themselves among her ugliest remembrances. She marveled how such scenes could have been! She marveled how she could ever have been wrought upon to marry him! She deemed it her crime most to be repented of, that she had ever endured, and <u>reciprocated</u>, the lukewarm grasp of his hand, and had suffered the smile of her lips and eyes to mingle and melt into his own. And it seemed a fouler offense committed by Roger Chillingworth, than any which had since been done by him, that, in the time when her heart knew no better, he had persuaded her to fancy herself happy by his side.

◄ *What does Hester think her worst crime is? What does she think Roger's worst crime is?*

"Yes, I hate him!" repeated Hester, more bitterly than before. "He betrayed me! He has done me worse wrong than I did him!"

◄ *What does Hester say about her crime?*

Let men tremble to win the hand of woman, unless they win along with it the utmost passion of her heart! Else it may be their miserable fortune, as it was Roger Chillingworth's, when some mightier touch than their own may have awakened all her sensibilities, to be reproached even for the calm content, the marble image of happiness, which they will have imposed upon her as the warm reality. But Hester ought long ago to have done with this injustice. What did it betoken? Had seven long years, under the torture of the scarlet letter, inflicted so much of misery, and wrought out no repentance?

◄ *What does the narrator say Hester's feelings indicate?*

The emotions of that brief space, while she stood gazing after the crooked figure of old Roger Chillingworth, threw a dark light on Hester's state of mind, revealing much that she might not otherwise have acknowledged to herself.

He being gone, she summoned back her child.

"Pearl! Little Pearl! Where are you?"

Pearl, whose activity of spirit never flagged, had been at no loss for amusement while her mother talked with the old gatherer of herbs. At first, as already told, she had flirted

| Words For Everyday Use | **re • cip • ro • cate** (ri sip´rə kāt´) *vt.,* give or do in return |

fancifully with her own image in a pool of water, beckoning the phantom forth, and—as it declined to venture—seeking a passage for herself into its sphere of impalpable earth and unattainable sky. Soon finding, however, that either she or the image was unreal, she turned elsewhere for better pastime. She made little boats out of birch-bark, and freighted them with snail-shells, and sent out more ventures on the mighty deep than any merchant in New England; but the larger part of them foundered near the shore. She seized a live horse-shoe by the tail, and made prize of several five-fingers, and laid out a jelly-fish to melt in the warm sun. Then she took up the white foam, that streaked the line of the advancing tide, and threw it upon the breeze, scampering after it with winged footsteps, to catch the great snow-flakes ere they fell. Perceiving a flock of beach-birds, that fed and fluttered along the shore, the naughty child picked up her apron full of pebbles, and, creeping from rock to rock after these small sea-fowl, displayed remarkable <u>dexterity</u> in pelting them. One little gray bird, with a white breast, Pearl was almost sure, had been hit by a pebble, and fluttered away with a broken wing. But then the elf-child sighed, and gave up her sport; because it grieved her to have done harm to a little being that was as wild as the sea-breeze, or as wild as Pearl herself.

Her final employment was to gather sea-weed of various kinds, and make herself a scarf, or mantle, and a head-dress, and thus assume the aspect of a little mermaid. She inherited her mother's gift for devising drapery and costume. As the last touch to her mermaid's garb, Pearl took some eel-grass, and imitated, as best she could, on her own bosom, the decoration with which she was so familiar on her mother's. A letter—the letter A—but freshly green, instead of scarlet! The child bent her chin upon her breast, and contemplated this device with strange interest; even as if the one only thing for which she had been sent into the world was to make out its hidden import.

"I wonder if mother will ask me what it means!" thought Pearl.

Just then, she heard her mother's voice, and, flitting along as lightly as one of the little sea-birds, appeared before Hester

▶ *What does Pearl do to decorate herself?*

Words For Everyday Use

dex • ter • i • ty (deks ter´ə tē) *n.*, skill in using hands

Prynne dancing, laughing, and pointing her finger to the ornament upon her bosom.

"My little Pearl," said Hester, after a moment's silence, "the green letter, and on thy childish bosom, has no purport. But dost thou know, my child, what this letter means which thy mother is doomed to wear?"

"Yes, mother," said the child. "It is the great letter A. Thou hast taught it me in the horn-book."[2]

Hester looked steadily into her little face; but though there was that singular expression which she had so often remarked in her black eyes, she could not satisfy herself whether Pearl really attached any meaning to the symbol. She felt a morbid desire to ascertain the point.

"Dost thou know, child, wherefore thy mother wears this letter?"

"Truly do I!" answered Pearl, looking brightly into her mother's face. "It is for the same reason that the minister keeps his hand over his heart!"

"And what reason is that?" asked Hester, half smiling at the absurd <u>incongruity</u> of the child's observation; but, on second thoughts, turning pale. "What has the letter to do with any heart, save mine?"

"Nay, mother, I have told all I know," said Pearl, more seriously than she was wont to speak. "Ask yonder old man whom thou hast been talking with! It may be he can tell. But in good earnest now, mother dear, what does this scarlet letter mean?—and why dost thou wear it on thy bosom?—and why does the minister keep his hand over his heart?"

She took her mother's hand in both her own, and gazed into her eyes with an earnestness that was seldom seen in her wild and capricious character. The thought occurred to Hester, that the child might really be seeking to approach her with childlike confidence, and doing what she could, and as intelligently as she knew how, to establish a meeting-point of sympathy. It showed Pearl in an <u>unwonted</u> aspect. Heretofore, the mother, while loving her child with the intensity of a sole affection, had schooled herself to hope for

◄ What does Hester say about this symbol on Pearl? Do you agree with Hester? What might Pearl's green letter signify?

◄ What connection has Pearl made between Hester and Dimmesdale?

---

2. **horn-book.** Sheet of parchment printed with letters of the alphabet and covered with a transparent sheet made of horn

---

Words
For
Everyday
Use

in • con • gru • i • ty (in´kän grōō´i tē) *n.*, lack of agreement or appropriateness
un • wont • ed (un wön´tid) *adj.*, unusual; rare

little other return than the waywardness of an April breeze; which spends its time in airy sport, and has its gusts of inexplicable passion, and is <u>petulant</u> in its best of moods, and chills oftener than caresses you, when you take it to your bosom; in requital of which misdemeanors, it will sometimes, of its own vague purpose, kiss your cheek with a kind of doubtful tenderness, and play gently with your hair, and then begone about its other idle business, leaving a dreamy pleasure at your heart. And this, moreover, was a mother's

► What does Hester hope?

estimate of the child's disposition. Any other observer might have seen few but unamiable traits, and have given them a far darker coloring. But now the idea came strongly into Hester's mind, that Pearl, with her remarkable <u>precocity</u> and acuteness, might already have approached the age when she could be made a friend, and intrusted with as much of her mother's sorrows as could be imparted, without irreverence either to the parent or the child. In the little <u>chaos</u> of Pearl's character, there might be seen emerging—and could have been, from the very first—the steadfast principles of an unflinching courage—an uncontrollable will—sturdy pride,

► What does Pearl scorn?

which might be disciplined into self-respect—and a bitter scorn of many things, which, when examined, might be found to have the taint of falsehood in them. She possessed affections, too, though hitherto acrid and disagreeable, as are the richest flavors of unripe fruit. With all these sterling attributes, thought Hester, the evil which she inherited from her mother must be great indeed, if a noble woman do not grow out of this elfish child.

► In what way might Pearl's interest in the scarlet letter be helpful to her mother?

Pearl's inevitable tendency to hover about the <u>enigma</u> of the scarlet letter seemed an <u>innate</u> quality of her being. From the earliest epoch of her conscious life, she had entered upon this as her appointed mission. Hester had often fancied that Providence had a design of justice and retribution, in endowing the child with this marked propensity; but never, until now, had she bethought herself to ask, whether, linked with that design, there might not likewise be a purpose of mercy and beneficence. If little Pearl were entertained with faith and trust, as a spirit-messenger no less than an earthly child, might it not be her errand to soothe away the sorrow that lay cold in her mother's heart, and converted it into a tomb?—and to help her to overcome the passion, once so wild, and

Words For Everyday Use	**pet • u • lant** (pech´ə lənt) *adj.,* impatient or irritable **pre • coc • i • ty** (pri käs´ə tē) *n.,* premature development	**cha • os** (kā´äs´) *n.,* extreme disorder and confusion **e • nig • ma** (i nig´mə) *n.,* mystery **in • nate** (in´nāt´) *adj.,* naturally existing from birth

even yet neither dead nor asleep, but only imprisoned within the same tomb-like heart?

Such were some of the thoughts that now stirred in Hester's mind, with as much vivacity of impression as if they had actually been whispered into her ear. And there was little Pearl, all this while, holding her mother's hand in both her own, and turning her face upward, while she put these searching questions, once and again, and still a third time.

"What does the letter mean, mother?—and why dost thou wear it?—and why does the minister keep his hand over his heart?"

"What shall I say?" thought Hester to herself.—"No! If this be the price of the child's sympathy, I cannot pay it."

Then she spoke aloud.

"Silly Pearl," said she, "what questions are these? There are many things in this world that a child must not ask about. What know I of the minister's heart? And as for the scarlet letter, I wear it for the sake of its gold thread."

In all the seven bygone years, Hester Prynne had never before been false to the symbol on her bosom. It may be that it was the talisman of a stern and severe, but yet a guardian spirit, who now forsook her; as recognizing that, in spite of his strict watch over her heart, some new evil had crept into it, or some old one had never been expelled. As for little Pearl, the earnestness soon passed out of her face.

But the child did not see fit to let the matter drop. Two or three times, as her mother and she went homeward, and as often at supper-time, and while Hester was putting her to bed, and once after she seemed to be fairly asleep, Pearl looked up, with mischief gleaming in her black eyes.

"Mother," said she, "what does the scarlet letter mean?"

And the next morning, the first indication the child gave of being awake was by popping up her head from the pillow, and making that other inquiry, which she had so unaccountably connected with her investigations about the scarlet letter:—

"Mother!—Mother!—Why does the minister keep his hand over his heart?"

"Hold thy tongue, naughty child!" answered her mother, with an <u>asperity</u> that she had never permitted to herself before. "Do not tease me; else I shall put thee into the dark closet!"

◀ *Why do you think that Hester cannot confide in Pearl?*

◀ *What has Hester never done before?*

Words
For
Everyday
Use

as • per • i • ty (ə sper´ə tē) *n.,* harshness of temper

XVI

A Forest Walk

Hester Prynne remained constant in her resolve to make known to Mr. Dimmesdale, at whatever risk of present pain or <u>ulterior</u> consequences, the true character of the man who had crept into his intimacy. For several days, however, she vainly sought an opportunity of addressing him in some of the meditative walks which she knew him to be in the habit of taking, along the shores of the peninsula, or on the wooded hills of the neighboring country. There would have been no scandal, indeed, nor peril to the holy whiteness of the clergyman's good fame, had she visited him in his own study; where many a penitent, ere now, had confessed sins of perhaps as deep a dye as the one betokened by the scarlet letter. But, partly that she dreaded the secret or undisguised interference of old Roger Chillingworth, and partly that her conscious heart imputed suspicion where none could have been felt, and partly that both the minister and she would need the whole wide world to breathe in, while they talked together— for all these reasons, Hester never thought of meeting him in any narrower privacy than beneath the open sky.

At last, while attending in a sick-chamber, whither the Reverend Mr. Dimmesdale had been summoned to make a prayer, she learned that he had gone, the day before, to visit the Apostle Eliot,[1] among his Indian converts. He would probably return, by a certain hour, in the afternoon of the morrow. Betimes, therefore, the next day, Hester took little Pearl—who was necessarily the companion of all her mother's expeditions, however inconvenient her presence—and set forth.

The road, after the two wayfarers had crossed from the Peninsula to the mainland, was no other than a footpath. It straggled onward into the mystery of the primeval forest. This hemmed it in so narrowly, and stood so black and dense

▶ Why won't Hester go to meet Dimmesdale in his study?

▶ To what is the "primeval" forest compared?

---

1. **Apostle Eliot.** John Eliot (1604–1690) was a minister in Massachusetts from 1630 to 1690. He preached to Native Americans at Dorchester Mills and translated the Bible into their language.

Words For Everyday Use

ul • te • ri • or (ul tir´ē ər) *adj.,* undisclosed; lying beyond what is evident or of immediate interest on either side, and disclosed such imperfect glimpses of the sky above, that, to Hester's mind, it imaged not amiss the moral wilderness in which she had so long been wandering. The day was chill and somber. Overhead was a gray expanse of cloud, slightly stirred, however, by a breeze; so that a gleam of flickering sunshine might now and then be seen at its solitary play along the path. This flitting cheerfulness was always at the farther extremity of some long vista through the forest. The sportive sunlight—feebly sportive, at best, in the predominant pensiveness of the day and scene—withdrew itself as they came nigh, and left the spots where it had danced the drearier, because they had hoped to find them bright.

"Mother," said little Pearl, "the sunshine does not love you. It runs away and hides itself, because it is afraid of something on your bosom. Now, see! There it is, playing, a good way off. Stand you here, and let me run and catch it. I am but a child. It will not flee from me; for I wear nothing on my bosom yet!"

"Nor ever will, my child, I hope," said Hester.

"And why not, mother?" asked Pearl, stopping short, just at the beginning of her race. "Will not it come of its own accord, when I am a woman grown?"

"Run away, child," answered her mother, "and catch the sunshine! It will soon be gone."

Pearl set forth, at a great pace, and, as Hester smiled to perceive, did actually catch the sunshine, and stood laughing in the midst of it, all brightened by its splendor, and scintillating with the <u>vivacity</u> excited by rapid motion. The light lingered about the lonely child, as if glad of such a playmate, until her mother had drawn almost nigh enough to step into the magic circle too.

"It will go now!" said Pearl, shaking her head.

"See!" answered Hester, smiling. "Now I can stretch out my hand and grasp some of it."

As she attempted to do so, the sunshine vanished; or, to judge from the bright expression that was dancing on Pearl's features, her mother could have fancied that the child had absorbed it into herself, and would give it forth again, with a gleam about her path, as they should plunge into some

◄ *Why does Pearl say that she can catch the sunshine while her mother cannot? What does Pearl believe will happen when she becomes a woman?*

gloomier shade. There was no other attribute that so much impressed her with a sense of new and untransmitted vigor in Pearl's nature, as this never-failing vivacity of spirits; she had not the disease of sadness, which almost all children, in these latter days, inherit, with the scrofula,[2] from the troubles of their ancestors. Perhaps this too, was a disease, and but the reflex of the wild energy with which Hester had fought against her sorrows, before Pearl's birth. It was certainly a doubtful charm, imparting a hard, metallic luster to the child's character. She wanted—what some people want throughout life—a grief that should deeply touch her, and thus humanize and make her capable of sympathy. But there was time enough yet for little Pearl!

"Come, my child!" said Hester, looking about her from the spot where Pearl had stood still in the sunshine. "We will sit down a little way within the wood, and rest ourselves."

"I am not aweary, mother," replied the little girl. "But you may sit down, if you will tell me a story meanwhile."

"A story, child!" said Hester. "And about what?"

"Oh, a story about the Black Man!" answered Pearl, taking hold of her mother's gown, and looking up, half earnestly, half mischievously, into her face.

"How he haunts this forest, and carries a book with him—a big, heavy book, with iron clasps; and how this ugly Black Man offers his book and an iron pen to every body that meets him here among the trees; and they are to write their names with their own blood. And then he sets his mark on their bosoms. Didst thou ever meet the Black Man, mother?"

"And who told you this story, Pearl?" asked her mother, recognizing a common superstition of the period.

"It was the old dame in the chimney-corner, at the house where you watched last night," said the child. "But she fancied me asleep while she was talking of it. She said that a thousand and a thousand people had met him here, and had written in his book, and have his mark on them. And that ugly-tempered lady, old Mistress Hibbins, was one. And, mother, the old dame said that this scarlet letter was the Black Man's mark on thee, and that it glows like a red flame when thou meetest him at midnight, here in the dark wood. Is it true, mother? And dost thou go to meet him in the nighttime?"

"Didst thou ever awake and find thy mother gone?" asked Hester.

▶ What does the narrator say Pearl's character needs?

▶ Whom does Pearl believe lives in the forest?

▶ What rumors have people been spreading about Hester?

---

2. **scrofula.** Tuberculosis of the lymph glands, a condition characterized by swelling of the glands, abscesses, and scar formation

"Not that I remember," said the child. "If thou fearest to leave me in our cottage, thou mightest take me along with thee. I would very gladly go! But, mother, tell me now! Is there such a Black Man? And didst thou ever meet him? And is this his mark?"

"Wilt thou let me be at peace, if I once tell thee?" asked her mother.

"Yes, if thou tellest me all," answered Pearl.

"Once in my life I met the Black Man!" said her mother. "This scarlet letter is his mark!"

Thus conversing, they entered sufficiently deep into the wood to secure themselves from the observation of any casual passenger along the forest-track. Here they sat down on a luxuriant heap of moss; which, at some epoch of the preceding century, had been a gigantic pine, with its roots and trunk in the darksome shade, and its head aloft in the upper atmosphere. It was a little dell where they had seated themselves, with a leaf-strewn bank rising gently on either side, and a brook flowing through the midst, over a bed of fallen and drowned leaves. The trees impending over it had flung down great branches, from time to time, which choked up the current, and compelled it to form eddies and black depths at some points; while, in its swifter and livelier passages, there appeared a channel-way of pebbles, and brown, sparkling sand. Letting the eyes follow along the course of the stream, they could catch the reflected light from its water, at some short distance within the forest, but soon lost all traces of it amid the bewilderment of tree-trunks and underbrush, and here and there a huge rock, covered over with gray lichens. All these giant trees and boulders of granite seemed intent on making a mystery of the course of this small brook; fearing, perhaps, that, with its never ceasing <u>loquacity</u>, it should whisper tales out of the heart of the old forest whence it flowed, or mirror its revelations on the smooth surface of a pool. Continually, indeed, as it stole onward, the streamlet kept up a babble, kind, quiet, soothing, but melancholy, like the voice of a young child that was spending its infancy without playfulness, and knew not how to be merry among sad acquaintance and events of somber hue.

◀ *What type of noise does the brook make?*

Words For Everyday Use

lo • quac • i • ty (lō kwas′ə tē) *n.,* talkativeness

"O brook! O foolish and tiresome little brook!" cried Pearl, after listening awhile to its talk. "Why art thou so sad? Pluck up a spirit, and do not be all the time sighing and murmuring!"

But the brook, in the course of its little lifetime among the forest-trees, had gone through so solemn an experience that it could not help talking about it, and seemed to have nothing else to say. Pearl resembled the brook, inasmuch as the current of her life gushed from a well-spring as mysterious, and had flowed through scenes shadowed as heavily with gloom. But, unlike the little stream, she danced and sparkled, and prattled airily along her course.

"What does this sad little brook say, mother?" inquired she.

"If thou hadst a sorrow of thine own, the brook might tell thee of it," answered her mother, "even as it is telling me of mine. But now, Pearl, I hear a footstep along the path, and the noise of one putting aside the branches. I would have thee betake thyself to play, and leave me to speak with him that comes yonder."

"Is it the Black Man?" asked Pearl.

"Wilt thou go and play, child?" repeated her mother, "But, do not stray far into the wood. And take heed that thou come at my first call."

"Yes, mother," answered Pearl, "But, if it be the Black Man, wilt thou not let me stay a moment, and look at him, with his big book under his arm?"

"Go, silly child!" said her mother, impatiently. "It is no Black Man! Thou canst see him now through the trees. It is the minister!"

► What does Pearl say about the minister? What does she want to know?

"And so it is!" said the child. "And, mother, he has his hand over his heart! Is it because, when the minister wrote his name in the book, the Black Man set his mark in that place? But why does he not wear it outside his bosom, as thou dost, mother?"

"Go now, child, and thou shalt tease me as thou wilt another time!" cried Hester Prynne. "But do not stray far. Keep where thou canst hear the babble of the brook."

The child went singing away, following up the current of the brook, and striving to mingle a more lightsome <u>cadence</u> with its melancholy voice. But the little stream would not be

Words
For
Everyday
Use

ca • dence (kād''ns) n., rhythmic flow of sound

comforted, and still kept telling its unintelligible secret of some very mournful mystery that had happened—or making a prophetic <u>lamentation</u> about something that was yet to happen—within the verge of the dismal forest. So Pearl, who had enough of shadow in her own little life, chose to break off all acquaintance with this repining brook. She set herself, therefore, to gathering violets and wood-anemones, and some scarlet columbines that she found growing in the crevice of a high rock.

When her elf-child had departed, Hester Prynne made a step or two towards the track that led through the forest, but still remained under the deep shadow of the trees. She beheld the minister advancing along the path, entirely alone, and leaning on a staff which he had cut by the way-side. He looked <u>haggard</u> and feeble, and betrayed a nerveless despondency in his air, which had never so remarkably characterized him in his walks about the settlement, nor in any other situation where he deemed himself liable to notice. Here it was woefully visible, in this intense seclusion of the forest, which of itself would have been a heavy trial to the spirits. There was a listlessness in his gait; as if he saw no reason for taking one step farther, nor felt any desire to do so, but would have been glad, could he be glad of anything, to fling himself down at the root of the nearest tree, and lie there passive for evermore. The leaves might bestrew him, and the soil gradually accumulate and form a little hillock over his frame, no matter whether there were life in it or no. Death was too definite an object to be wished for, or avoided.

To Hester's eye, the Reverend Mr. Dimmesdale exhibited no symptom of positive and vivacious suffering, except that, as little Pearl had remarked, he kept his hand over his heart.

Words For Everyday Use

lam • en • ta • tion (lam´ən tā´shən) n., expression of grief

hag • gard (hag´ərd) adj., having a wild, worn look

Responding to the Selection

Describe the loneliness of Hester—both the loneliness she felt in her marriage and the loneliness she feels raising Pearl on her own. Do you feel sympathetic toward her? Why, or why not?

Reviewing the Selection

Recalling and Interpreting

1. **R:** What memory does Hester recall as she leaves Chillingworth to gather his herbs at the beginning of Chapter 15?

2. **I:** Why does Hester believe that her husband betrayed her? Why does she believe that he is in part responsible for the events of the last seven years?

3. **R:** When Pearl asks the question "What does the scarlet letter mean?" what is Hester's final response? What is she tempted to tell Pearl?

4. **I:** Why is Hester tempted to confide in Pearl? Why does she feel uncomfortable with the answer that she finally gives Pearl?

5. **R:** As Hester and Pearl walk through the woods, what does Pearl want to know about the Black Man? What does Hester say when Pearl asks her if she has ever met the Black Man?

6. **I:** Why does the story of the Black Man and his mark have a personal meaning for Hester and Pearl?

7. **R:** When Hester meets Reverend Dimmesdale in the forest, what is she hoping to tell him?

8. **I:** When Dimmesdale appears, what do both Hester and Pearl notice about his hand, and what significance does this gesture have for the three of them?

Synthesizing

9. On page 167, the narrator asks about Hester, "Had seven long years . . . wrought out no repentance?" Do you share the narrator's belief that Hester should repent of her actions, or do you find them understandable and forgivable? Explain.

10. Hawthorne writes that Pearl resembles a brook running through the dark forest in that "the current of her life gushed from a wellspring as mysterious, and had flowed through scenes shadowed as heavily with gloom." He also adds that, unlike the murmuring brook, she dances and sparkles along her course. Explain these ideas, keeping in mind your knowledge of Pearl's personality and the people and complicated situations that surround her.

Understanding Literature (QUESTIONS FOR DISCUSSION)

1. Mood. Mood, or atmosphere, is the emotion created in the reader by part or all of a literary work. A writer creates a mood by carefully using vivid details. Discuss the mood of the opening paragraphs of chapter 15, when the narrator describes Chillingworth; and the opening paragraphs of chapter 16, when Hester and Pearl walk down a narrow footpath toward the cold forest. What words and phrases contribute to creating these moods?

2. Personification. Personification is a figure of speech in which an idea, animal, or thing is described as if it were a person. Personification often makes a piece seem more vivid and genuine to a reader. Chapter 16 contains many examples of personification in passages describing nature. Locate two or three examples of personification in the chapter, and explain what quality is shared in each case by human beings and the aspect of nature being described.

XVII

The Pastor and His Parishioner

Slowly as the minister walked, he had almost gone by, before Hester Prynne could gather voice enough to attract his observation. At length, she succeeded.

"Arthur Dimmesdale!" she said, faintly at first; then louder, but hoarsely. "Arthur Dimmesdale!"

"Who speaks?" answered the minister. Gathering himself quickly up, he stood more erect, like a man taken by surprise in a mood to which he was reluctant to have witnesses. Throwing his eyes anxiously in the direction of the voice, he indistinctly beheld a form under the trees, clad in garments so somber, and so little relieved from the gray twilight into which the clouded sky and the heavy foliage had darkened the noontide, that he knew not whether it were a woman or a shadow. It may be, that his pathway through life was haunted thus, by a specter that had stolen out from among his thoughts.

▶ What does the minister see first?

He made a step nigher, and discovered the scarlet letter.

"Hester! Hester Prynne!," said he. "Is it thou? Art thou in life?"

"Even so!" she answered. "In such life as has been mine these seven years past! And thou, Arthur Dimmesdale, dost thou yet live?"

▶ To what is Hester and Dimmesdale's encounter compared? Why are they "awe-stricken . . . at themselves"?

It was no wonder that they thus questioned one another's actual and bodily existence, and even doubted of their own. So strangely did they meet, in the dim wood, that it was like the first encounter, in the world beyond the grave, of two spirits who had been intimately connected in their former life, but now stood coldly shuddering, in mutual dread; as not yet familiar with their state, nor wonted to the companionship of disembodied beings. Each a ghost, and awe-stricken at the other ghost! They were awe-stricken likewise at themselves; because the crisis flung back to them their consciousness, and revealed to each heart its history and experience, as life never does, except at such breathless epochs. The soul beheld its features in the mirror of the passing moment. It was with fear, and tremulously, and, as it were, by a slow, reluctant necessity, that Arthur Dimmesdale put forth his hand, chill as death, and touched the chill hand of Hester Prynne. The grasp, cold as it was, took away what was dreariest in the interview. They now felt themselves, at least, inhabitants of the same sphere.

Without a word more spoken—neither he nor she assuming the guidance, but with an unexpressed consent—they glided back into the shadow of the woods, whence Hester had emerged, and sat down on the heap of moss where she and Pearl had before been sitting. When they found voice to speak, it was at first, only to utter remarks and inquiries such as any two acquaintances might have made, about the gloomy sky, the threatening storm, and, next, the health of each. Thus they went onward, not boldly, but step by step, into the themes that were brooding deepest in their hearts. So long estranged by fate and circumstances, they needed something slight and casual to run before, and throw open the doors of intercourse, so that their real thoughts might be led across the threshold.

After a while, the minister fixed his eyes on Hester Prynne's.

"Hester," said he, "hast thou found peace?"

She smiled drearily, looking down upon her bosom.

"Hast thou?" she asked.

"None!—nothing but despair!" he answered. "What else could I look for, being what I am, and leading such a life as mine? Were I an atheist—a man devoid of conscience—a wretch with coarse and brutal instincts—I might have found peace, long ere now. Nay, I never should have lost it! But, as matters stand with my soul, whatever of good capacity there originally was in me, all of God's gifts that were the choicest have become the ministers of spiritual torment. Hester, I am most miserable!"

◄ Hester only smiles drearily when asked if she has found peace, but Dimmesdale speaks at length about his misery. Which of the two has experienced the greater sorrow and guilt? Why?

"The people reverence thee," said Hester. "And surely thou workest good among them! Doth this bring thee no comfort?"

"More misery, Hester!—only the more misery!" answered the clergyman, with a bitter smile. "As concerns the good which I may appear to do, I have no faith in it. It must needs be a delusion. What can a ruined soul, like mine, effect towards the redemption of other souls?—or a polluted soul, towards their purification? And as for the people's reverence, would that it were turned to scorn and hatred! Canst thou deem it, Hester, a consolation, that I must stand up in my pulpit, and meet so many eyes turned upward to my face, as if the light of heaven were beaming from it!—must see my flock hungry for the truth, and listening to my words as if a tongue of Pentecost were speaking!—and then look inward, and discern the black reality of what they idolize? I have

◄ Do you agree with Dimmesdale here? Why, or why not?

laughed, in bitterness and agony of heart, at the contrast between what I seem and what I am! And Satan laughs at it!"

"You wrong yourself in this," said Hester, gently. "You have deeply and sorely repented. Your sin is left behind you, in the days long past. Your present life is not less holy, in very truth, than it seems in people's eyes. Is there no reality in the penitence thus sealed and witnessed by good works? And wherefore should it not bring you peace?"

"No, Hester, no!" replied the clergyman. "There is no substance in it! It is cold and dead, and can do nothing for me! Of penance I have had enough! Of penitence there has been none! Else, I should long ago have thrown off these garments of mock holiness, and have shown myself to mankind as they will see me at the judgment-seat. Happy are you, Hester, that wear the scarlet letter openly upon your bosom! Mine burns in secret! Thou little knowest what a relief it is, after the torment of a seven years' cheat, to look into an eye that recognizes me for what I am! Had I one friend—or were it my worst enemy!—to whom, when sickened with the praises of all other men, I could daily betake myself, and be known as the vilest of all sinners, methinks my soul might keep itself alive thereby. Even thus much of truth would save me! But now, it is all falsehood!—all emptiness!—all death!"

Hester Prynne looked into his face, but hesitated to speak. Yet, uttering his long-restrained emotions so <u>vehemently</u> as he did, his words here offered her the very point of circumstances in which to interpose what she came to say. She conquered her fears, and spoke.

"Such a friend as thou hast even now wished for," said she, "with whom to weep over thy sin, thou hast in me, the partner of it!"—Again she hesitated, but brought out the words with an effort.—"Thou hast long had such an enemy, and dwellest with him under the same roof!"

The minister started to his feet, gasping for breath, and clutching at his heart as if he would have torn it out of his bosom.

"Ha! What sayest thou?" cried he. "An enemy! And under mine own roof! What mean you?"

Hester Prynne was now fully sensible of the deep injury for which she was responsible to this unhappy man, in

► *How does the minister assess his situation and Hester's? Do you think that he is right?*

► *For what does Dimmesdale wish?*

► *What does Hester say about Dimmesdale's wish?*

Words For Everyday Use

ve • he • ment • ly (vē´ə mənt lē) *adv.*, passionately; violently permitting him to lie for so many years, or, indeed, for a single moment, at the mercy of one, whose purposes could not be other than malevolent. The very <u>contiguity</u> of his enemy, beneath whatever mask the latter might conceal himself, was enough to disturb the magnetic sphere of a being so sensitive as Arthur Dimmesdale. There had been a period when Hester was less alive to this consideration; or, perhaps, in the <u>misanthropy</u> of her own trouble, she left the minister to bear what she might picture to herself as a more tolerable doom. But of late, since the night of his vigil, all her sympathies towards him had been both softened and invigorated. She now read his heart more accurately. She doubted not, that the continual presence of Roger Chillingworth—the secret poison of his malignity, infecting all the air about him—and his authorized interference, as a physician, with the minister's physical and spiritual infirmities—that these bad opportunities had been turned to a cruel purpose. By means of them, the sufferer's conscience had been kept in an irritated state, the tendency of which was, not to cure by wholesome pain, but to disorganize and corrupt his spiritual being. Its result, on earth, could hardly fail to be insanity, and hereafter, that eternal alienation from the Good and True, of which madness is perhaps the earthly type.

Such was the ruin to which she had brought the man, once—nay, why should we not speak it?—still so passionately loved! Hester felt that the sacrifice of the clergyman's good name, and death itself, as she had already told Roger Chillingworth, would have been infinitely preferable to the alternative which she had taken upon herself to choose. And now, rather than have had this grievous wrong to confess, she would gladly have laid down on the forest-leaves, and died there, at Arthur Dimmesdale's feet.

◄ *How does Hester still feel about Dimmesdale?*

"Oh, Arthur!" cried she, "forgive me! In all things else, I have striven to be true! Truth was the one virtue which I might have held fast, and did hold fast through all extremity; save when thy good—thy life—thy fame—were put in question! Then I consented to a deception. But a lie is never good, even though death threaten on the other side! Dost thou not see what I would say? That old man!—the physician!—he whom they call Roger Chillingworth!—he was my husband!"

Words For Everyday Use	**con • ti • gu • i • ty** (kän´tə gyōō´ə tē) *n.*, nearness or contact **mis • an • thro • py** (mis an´thrə pē) *n.*, hatred or distrust of all people

► What hidden
characteristic does
Dimmesdale reveal
when his enemy's
identity is revealed?

The minister looked at her, for an instant, with all that violence of passion, which—intermixed in more shapes than one, with his higher, purer, softer qualities—was, in fact, the portion of him which the devil claimed, and through which he sought to win the rest. Never was there a blacker or a fiercer frown, than Hester now encountered. For the brief space that it lasted, it was a dark transfiguration. But his character had been so much enfeebled by suffering, that even its lower energies were incapable of more than a temporary struggle. He sank down on the ground, and buried his face in his hands.

"I might have known it!" murmured he. "I did know it! Was not the secret told me in the natural recoil of my heart, at the first sight of him, and as often as I have seen him since? Why did I not understand? O Hester Prynne, thou little, little knowest all the horror of this thing! And the shame!—the indelicacy!—the horrible ugliness of this exposure of a sick and guilty heart to the very eye that would gloat over it! Woman, woman, thou art accountable for this! I cannot forgive thee!"

► How does
Dimmesdale feel
about what Hester
has done?

"Thou shalt forgive me!" cried Hester, flinging herself on the fallen leaves beside him. "Let God punish! Thou shalt forgive!"

With sudden and desperate tenderness, she threw her arms around him, and pressed his head against her bosom; little caring though his cheek rested on the scarlet letter. He would have released himself, but strove in vain to do so. Hester would not set him free, lest he should look her sternly in the face. All the world had frowned on her—for seven long years had it frowned upon this lonely woman—and still she bore it all, nor ever once turned away her firm, sad eyes. Heaven, likewise, had frowned upon her, and she had not died. But the frown of this pale, weak, sinful, and sorrow-stricken man was what Hester could not bear, and live!

► Why is Hester
afraid of letting go of
Dimmesdale?

"Wilt thou yet forgive me?" she repeated, over and over again. "Wilt thou not frown? Wilt thou forgive?"

"I do forgive you, Hester," replied the minister, at length, with a deep utterance out of an abyss of sadness, but no anger. "I freely forgive you now. May God forgive us both! We are not, Hester, the worst sinners in the world. There is

► According to
Dimmesdale, what is
the worst sin that
has been committed,
and who has com-
mitted it?

Words For Everyday Use

en • fee • ble (en fē´bəl) vt., make weak or frail

one worse than even the polluted priest! That old man's revenge has been blacker than my sin. He has violated, in cold blood, the <u>sanctity</u> of a human heart. Thou and I, Hester, never did so!"

"Never, never!" whispered she. "What we did had a consecration of its own. We felt it so! We said so to each other! Hast thou forgotten it?"

◄ How do both Hester and Arthur Dimmesdale feel about their past relationship?

"Hush, Hester!" said Arthur Dimmesdale, rising from the ground. "No; I have not forgotten!"

They sat down again, side by side, and hand clasped in hand, on the mossy trunk of the fallen tree. Life had never brought them a gloomier hour; it was the point whither their pathway had so long been tending, and darkening ever, as it stole along;—and yet it inclosed a charm that made them linger upon it, and claim another, and another, and, after all, another moment. The forest was obscure around them, and creaked with a blast that was passing through it. The boughs were tossing heavily above their heads; while one solemn old tree groaned <u>dolefully</u> to another, as if telling the sad story of the pair that sat beneath, or <u>constrained</u> to forbode evil to come.

And yet they lingered. How dreary looked the forest-track that led backward to the settlement, where Hester Prynne must take up again the burden of her ignominy, and the minister the hollow mockery of his good name! So they lingered an instant longer. No golden light had ever been so precious as the gloom of this dark forest. Here, seen only by his eyes, the scarlet letter need not burn into the bosom of the fallen woman! Here, seen only by her eyes, Arthur Dimmesdale, false to God and man, might be, for one moment, true!

◄ Why do the two linger in the forest?

He started at a thought that suddenly occurred to him.

"Hester!" cried he, "here is a new horror! Roger Chillingworth knows your purpose to reveal his true character. Will he continue, then, to keep our secret? What will now be the course of his revenge?"

"There is a strange secrecy in his nature," replied Hester, thoughtfully; "and it has grown upon him by the hidden practices of his revenge. I deem it not likely that he will betray the secret. He will doubtless seek other means of satiating his dark passion."

◄ What question is raised by Hester's observation? What course do you think Chillingworth might take in the future?

Words For Everyday Use	sanc • ti • ty (sank´tə tē) n., sacredness
	dole • ful • ly (dōl´fəl lē) adv., mournfully
	con • strained (kən strānd´) adj., forced

"And I!—how am I to live longer, breathing the same air with this deadly enemy?" exclaimed Arthur Dimmesdale, shrinking within himself, and pressing his hand nervously against his heart—a gesture that had grown involuntary with him. "Think for me, Hester! Thou art strong. Resolve for me!"

► Why does Arthur ask Hester to think for him?

"Thou must dwell no longer with this man," said Hester, slowly and firmly. "Thy heart must be no longer under his evil eye!"

"It were far worse than death!" replied the minister. "But how to avoid it? What choice remains to me? Shall I lie down again on these withered leaves, where I cast myself when thou didst tell me what he was? Must I sink down there, and die at once?"

► Of what does Hester say Arthur Dimmesdale is dying?

"Alas, what a ruin has befallen thee!" said Hester, with the tears gushing into her eyes. "Wilt thou die for very weakness? There is no other cause!"

"The judgment of God is on me," answered the conscience-stricken priest. "It is too mighty for me to struggle with!"

"Heaven would show mercy," rejoined Hester, "hadst thou but the strength to take advantage of it."

"Be thou strong for me!" answered he. "Advise me what to do."

► What is Hester suggesting that Dimmesdale do?

"Is the world then so narrow?" exclaimed Hester Prynne, fixing her deep eyes on the minister's, and instinctively exercising a magnetic power over a spirit so shattered and subdued, that it could hardly hold itself erect. "Doth the universe lie within the compass of yonder town, which only a little time ago was but a leaf-strewn desert, as lonely as this around us? Whither leads yonder forest-track? Backward to the settlement, thou sayest! Yes; but onward, too! Deeper it goes, and deeper, into the wilderness, less plainly to be seen at every step; until, some few miles hence, the yellow leaves will show no <u>vestige</u> of the white man's tread. There thou art free! So brief a journey would bring thee from a world where thou hast been most wretched, to one where thou mayest still be happy! Is there not shade enough in all this boundless forest to hide thy heart from the gaze of Roger Chillingworth?"

"Yes, Hester; but only under the fallen leaves!" replied the minister, with a sad smile.

"Then there is the broad pathway of the sea!" continued Hester. "It brought thee hither. If thou so choose, it will bear thee back again. In our native land, whether in some remote

---

Words For Everyday Use

ves • tige (ves′tij) *n.*, trace of something that once existed rural village or in vast London—or, surely, in Germany, in France, in pleasant Italy—thou wouldst be beyond his power and knowledge! And what hast thou to do with all these iron men, and their opinions? They have kept thy better part in bondage too long already!"

◄ How does Hester feel toward the Puritans among whom she lives? Do you agree with her? Why, or why not?

"It cannot be!" answered the minister, listening as if he were called upon to realize a dream. "I am powerless to go. Wretched and sinful as I am, I have had no other thought than to drag on my earthly existence in the sphere where Providence hath placed me. Lost as my own soul is, I would still do what I may for other human souls! I dare not quit my post, though an unfaithful sentinel, whose sure reward is death and dishonor, when his dreary watch shall come to an end!"

"Thou art crushed under this seven years' weight of misery," replied Hester, fervently resolved to buoy him up with her own energy. "But thou shalt leave it all behind thee! It shall not cumber thy steps, as thou treadest along the forest-path; neither shalt thou freight the ship with it, if thou prefer to cross the sea. Leave this wreck and ruin here where it hath happened. Meddle no more with it! Begin all anew! Hast thou exhausted possibility in the failure of this one trial? Not so! The future is yet full of trial and success. There is happiness to be enjoyed! There is good to be done! Exchange this false life of thine for a true one. Be, if thy spirit summon thee to such a mission, the teacher and apostle of the red men. Or—as is more thy nature—be a scholar and a sage among the wisest and the most renowned of the cultivated world. Preach! Write! Act! Do any thing, save to lie down and die! Give up this name of Arthur Dimmesdale, and make thyself another, and a high one, such as thou canst wear without fear or shame. Why shouldst thou tarry so much as one other day in the torments that have so gnawed into thy life?—that have made thee feeble to will and to do!—that will leave thee powerless even to repent! Up, and away!"

◄ What advice does Hester give? Do you think that this advice is sensible?

"O Hester!" cried Arthur Dimmesdale, in whose eyes a fitful light, kindled by her enthusiasm, flashed up and died away, "thou tellest of running a race to a man whose knees are tottering beneath him! I must die here! There is not the strength or courage left me to <u>venture</u> into the wide, strange, difficult world alone!"

Words For Everyday Use

ven • ture (ven´chər) vi., go or do at some risk

► *What is Dimmesdale afraid of doing? What does Hester suggest? What does the narrator mean by "Then, all was spoken!"?*

It was the last expression of the <u>despondency</u> of a broken spirit. He lacked energy to grasp the better fortune that seemed within his reach.

He repeated the word. "Alone, Hester!"

"Thou shall not go alone!" answered she, in a deep whisper. Then, all was spoken!

Words For Everyday Use

de • spond • en • cy (di spän'dən sē) *n.*, dejection; loss of hope

XVIII

A Flood of Sunshine

Arthur Dimmesdale gazed into Hester's face with a look in which hope and joy shone out, indeed, but with fear betwixt them, and a kind of horror at her boldness, who had spoken what he vaguely hinted at, but dared not speak.

◀ Why is Hester bolder than Dimmesdale? What has made Hester bold?

But Hester Prynne, with a mind of native courage and activity, and for so long a period not merely estranged, but outlawed, from society, had habituated herself to such <u>lati-tude</u> of speculation as was altogether foreign to the clergyman. She had wandered, without rule or guidance, in a moral wilderness; as vast, as <u>intricate</u>, and shadowy as the untamed forest, amid the gloom of which they were now holding a <u>colloquy</u> that was to decide their fate. Her intellect and heart had their home, as it were, in desert places, where she roamed as freely as the wild Indian in his woods. For years past she had looked from this estranged point of view at human institutions, and whatever priests or legislators had established; criticizing all with hardly more reverence than the Indian would feel for the clerical band, the judicial robe, the pillory, the gallows, the fireside, or the church. The tendency of her fate and fortunes had been to set her free. The scarlet letter was her passport into regions where other women dared not tread. Shame, Despair, Solitude! These had been her teachers—stern and wild ones—and they had made her strong, but taught her much amiss.

◀ To what is the scarlet letter compared?

The minister, on the other hand, had never gone through an experience calculated to lead him beyond the scope of generally received laws; although, in a single instance, he had so fearfully transgressed one of the most sacred of them. But this had been a sin of passion, not of principle, nor even purpose. Since that wretched epoch, he had watched, with morbid zeal and minuteness, not his acts—for those it was easy to arrange—but each breath of emotion, and his every thought. At the head of the social system, as the clergymen of that day stood, he was only the more trammeled by its regulations, its principles, and

Words For Everyday Use	lat • i • tude (lat´ə tōōd´) n., freedom of opinion and action
	in • tri • cate (in´tri kit) adj., complex
	col • lo • quy (käl´ə kwē) n., formal discussion

even its prejudices. As a priest, the framework of his order inevitably hemmed him in. As a man who had once sinned, but who kept his conscience all alive and painfully sensitive by the fretting of an unhealed wound, he might have been supposed safer within the line of virtue, than if he had never sinned at all.

Thus we seem to see that, as regarded Hester Prynne, the whole seven years of outlaw and ignominy had been little other than a preparation for this very hour. But Arthur Dimmesdale! Were such a man once more to fall, what plea could be urged in <u>extenuation</u> of his crime? None; unless it avail him somewhat, that he was broken down by long and exquisite suffering; that his mind was darkened and confused by the very remorse which <u>harrowed</u> it; that, between fleeing as an avowed criminal, and remaining as a hypocrite, conscience might find it hard to strike the balance; that it was human to avoid the peril of death and infamy, and the inscrutable machinations of an enemy; that, finally, to this poor pilgrim, on his dreary and desert path, faint, sick, miserable, there appeared a glimpse of human affection and sympathy, a new life, and a true one, in exchange for the heavy doom which he was now expiating. And be the stern and sad truth spoken, that the breach which guilt has once made into the human soul is never, in this mortal state, repaired. It may be watched and guarded; so that the enemy shall not force his way again into the citadel, and might even, in his subsequent assaults, select some other avenue, in preference to that where he had formerly succeeded. But there is still the ruined wall, and, near it, the stealthy tread of the foe that would win over again his unforgotten triumph.

The struggle, if there were one, need not be described. Let it suffice that the clergyman resolved to flee, and not alone.

"If, in all these past seven years," thought he, "I could recall one instant of peace or hope, I would yet endure, for the sake of that earnest of Heaven's mercy. But now—since I am <u>irrevocably</u> doomed—wherefore should I not snatch the <u>solace</u> allowed to the condemned culprit before his execution? Or, if this be the path to a better life, as Hester would persuade me, I surely give up no fairer prospect by pursuing it! Neither can I any longer live without her companionship;

▶ To what is a person who has experienced terrible guilt compared?

▶ Why does Dimmesdale decide to go with Hester?

Words For Everyday Use	ex • ten • u • a • tion (ek sten′yŌŌ ā′shən) *n.*, partial excuse
	har • row (har′ō) *vt.*, cause mental distress
	ir • rev • o • ca • bly (ir′rəv′ə kə blē) *adv.*, unchangeably
	sol • ace (säl′is) *n.*, comfort; easing of sorrow

so powerful is she to sustain—so tender to soothe! O Thou to whom I dare not lift mine eyes, wilt Thou yet pardon me!"

"Thou wilt go!" said Hester calmly, as he met her glance.

The decision once made, a glow of strange enjoyment threw its flickering brightness over the trouble of his breast. It was the exhilarating effect—upon a prisoner just escaped from the dungeon of his own heart—of breathing the wild, free atmosphere of an unredeemed, unchristianized, lawless region. His spirit rose, as it were, with a bound, and attained a nearer prospect of the sky, than throughout all the misery which had kept him groveling on the earth. Of a deeply religious temperament, there was inevitably a tinge of the devotional in his mood.

◀ How does Dimmesdale feel once he has made his decision?

"Do I feel joy again?" cried he, wondering at himself. "Methought the germ of it was dead in me! O Hester, thou art my better angel! I seem to have flung myself—sick, sin-stained, and sorrow-blackened—down upon these forest-leaves, and to have risen up all made anew, and with new powers to glorify Him that hath been merciful! This is already the better life! Why did we not find it sooner?"

◀ To what does Dimmesdale compare Hester?

"Let us not look back," answered Hester Prynne. "The past is gone! Wherefore should we linger upon it now? See! With this symbol, I undo it all, and make it as if it had never been!"

◀ What does Hester do for the first time?

So speaking, she undid the clasp that fastened the scarlet letter, and, taking it from her bosom, threw it to a distance among the withered leaves. The mystic token alighted on the hither verge of the stream. With a hand's breadth further flight it would have fallen into the water, and have given the little brook another woe to carry onward, besides the <u>unintelligible</u> tale which it still kept murmuring about. But there lay the embroidered letter, glittering like a lost jewel, which some ill-fated wanderer might pick up, and thenceforth be haunted by strange phantoms of guilt, sinkings of the heart, and unaccountable misfortune.

The stigma gone, Hester heaved a long, deep sigh, in which the burden of shame and anguish departed from her spirit. O exquisite relief! She had not known the weight, until she felt the freedom! By another impulse, she took off the formal cap that confined her hair; and down it fell upon her shoulders, dark and rich, with at once a shadow and a light

◀ How does Hester feel without the scarlet letter?

Words For Everyday Use

un • in • tel • li • gi • ble (un´in tel´i jə bəl) *adj.*, incomprehensible; not understandable in its abundance, and imparting the charm of softness to her features. There played around her mouth, and beamed out of her eyes, a radiant and tender smile, that seemed gushing from the very heart of womanhood. A crimson flush was glowing on her cheek, that had been long so pale. Her sex, her youth, and the whole richness of her beauty, came back from what men call the irrevocable past, and clustered themselves, with her maiden hope, and a happiness before unknown, within the magic circle of this hour. And, as if the gloom of the earth and sky had been but the effluence of these two mortal hearts, it vanished with their sorrow. All at once, as with a sudden smile of heaven, forth burst the sunshine, pouring a very flood into the obscure forest, gladdening each green leaf, transmuting the yellow fallen ones to gold, and gleaming adown the gray trunks of the solemn trees. The objects that had made a shadow hitherto, embodied the brightness now. The course of the little brook might be traced by its merry gleam afar into the wood's heart of mystery, which had become a mystery of joy.

▶ In what way do the natural surroundings reflect Hester's and Dimmesdale's mood?

Such was the sympathy of Nature—that wild, heathen Nature of the forest, never <u>subjugated</u> by human law, nor illumined by higher truth—with the bliss of these two spirits! Love, whether newly born, or aroused from a deathlike slumber, must always create a sunshine, filling the heart so full of radiance, that it overflows upon the outward world. Had the forest still kept its gloom, it would have been bright in Hester's eyes, and bright in Arthur Dimmesdale's!

Hester looked at him with a thrill of another joy.

"Thou must know Pearl!" said she. "Our little Pearl! Thou hast seen her—yes, I know it!—but thou wilt see her now with other eyes. She is a strange child! I hardly comprehend her! But thou wilt love her dearly, as I do, and wilt advise me how to deal with her!"

▶ Whom does Hester want Dimmesdale to get to know?

"Dost thou think the child will be glad to know me?" asked the minister, somewhat uneasily. "I have long shrunk from children, because they often show a distrust—a backwardness to be familiar with me. I have even been afraid of little Pearl!"

"Ah, that was sad!" answered the mother. "But she will love thee dearly, and thou her. She is not far off. I will call her. Pearl! Pearl!"

Words For Everyday Use

sub • ju • gate (sub´jə gāt´) vt., make subservient

"I see the child," observed the minister. "Yonder she is, standing in a streak of sunshine, a good way off, on the other side of the brook. So thou thinkest the child will love me?"

Hester smiled, and again called to Pearl, who was visible, at some distance, as the minister had described her, like a bright-apparelled vision in a sunbeam, which fell down upon her through an arch of boughs. The ray quivered to and fro, making her figure dim or distinct—now like a real child, now like a child's spirit—as the splendor went and came again. She heard her mother's voice, and approached slowly through the forest.

Pearl had not found the hour pass wearisomely, while her mother sat talking with the clergyman. The great black forest—stern as it showed itself to those who brought the guilt and troubles of the world into its bosom—became the playmate of the lonely infant, as well as it knew how. Somber as it was, it put on the kindest of its moods to welcome her. It offered her the partridge-berries, the growth of the preceding autumn, but ripening only in the spring, and now red as drops of blood upon the withered leaves These Pearl gathered, and was pleased with their wild flavor. The small denizens[1] of the wilderness hardly took pains to move out of her path. A partridge, indeed, with a brood of ten behind her, ran forward threateningly, but soon repented of her fierceness, and clucked to her young ones not to be afraid. A pigeon, alone on a low branch, allowed Pearl to come beneath, and uttered a sound as much of greeting as alarm. A squirrel, from the lofty depths of his domestic tree, chattered either in anger or merriment—for the squirrel is such a choleric and humorous little personage, that it is hard to distinguish between his moods—so he chattered at the child, and flung down a nut upon her head. It was a last year's nut, and already gnawed by his sharp tooth. A fox, startled from his sleep by her light footstep on the leaves, looked inquisitively at Pearl, as doubting whether it were better to steal off, or renew his nap on the same spot. A wolf, it is said—but here the tale has surely lapsed into the improbable—came up, and smelt of Pearl's robe, and offered his savage head to be patted by her hand. The truth seems to be, however, that the mother-forest, and these wild things which it nourished, all recognized a kindred wildness in the human child.

◄ According to the narrator, what is the "truth" about Pearl?

And she was gentler here than in the grassy-margined streets of the settlement, or in her mother's cottage. The flowers appeared to know it; and one and another whispered, as she passed, "Adorn thyself with me, thou beautiful child,

---

1. **denizens**. Inhabitants

adorn thyself with me!"—and, to please them, Pearl gathered the violets, and anemones, and columbines, and some twigs of the freshest green, which the old trees held down before her eyes. With these she decorated her hair, and her young waist, and became a nymph-child, or an infant dryad,[2] or whatever else was in closest sympathy with the antique wood. In such guise had Pearl adorned herself, when she heard her mother's voice, and came slowly back.

Slowly; for she saw the clergyman!

▶ *Why is Pearl wary about returning to her mother?*

---

2. **dryad.** Nature goddess who lives in a wood

Responding to the Selection

"He (Chillingworth) has violated, in cold blood, the sanctity of a human heart! Thou and I, Hester, never did so!"

"Never, never," said she. "What we did had a consecration of its own. We felt it so!" Discuss this exchange between Hester and Dimmesdale. What do they mean? Do you agree with them? Why, or why not?

Reviewing the Selection

Recalling and Interpreting

1. **R:** About what do Hester and Dimmesdale first talk?

2. **I:** Why might the conversation between Dimmesdale and Hester at first be strained?

3. **R:** What does Dimmesdale say about Hester's scarlet letter? What does he believe might have saved him from the emotional anguish that he has been experiencing?

4. **I:** Why does Dimmesdale believe that his experience since the birth of Pearl has been in a way more torturous than Hester's experience?

5. **R:** What does Hester tell Dimmesdale about Chillingworth?

6. **I:** According to Dimmesdale, why is Chillingworth's sin blacker than his and Hester's?

7. **R:** What kind of life does Hester decide she wants for herself, for Dimmesdale, and for Pearl? Does Dimmesdale agree with her? What about Pearl worries Dimmesdale?

8. **I:** Why, alone in the forest, is it easy for Hester and Dimmesdale to renew their love and decide to escape from their troubles? Why might Pearl be uncomfortable with Dimmesdale?

Synthesizing

9. Why is Hester, who "for so long a period (was) not merely estranged, but outlawed, from society," more comfortable with the decision to leave than is Dimmesdale, who has remained at the "head of the social system"? Why does Hester seem to have been strengthened by her experiences since the birth of Pearl, while Dimmesdale seems to have been weakened by his experiences?

10. Do you support Hester and Dimmesdale's decision to escape together? What do you hope for them? Explain.

Understanding Literature

1. Dialogue. Dialogue is conversation involving two or more people or characters. Chapter 17 is important because, for the first time, the reader "overhears" an intimate conversation between Hester and Dimmesdale. In previous scenes, the two appeared together only briefly and in the company of other characters. For the first time in seven years, the two are able to discuss their situation freely. Why might there be tension in the beginning of the conversation? Does the relationship seem to warm as the dialogue progresses? Explain. Up until this point, has it been difficult for you as a reader to imagine the two as romantic partners? Why, or why not? In what ways does this chapter help you to understand this aspect of their relationship?

2. Transcendentalism. Transcendentalism was a literary movement in nineteenth-century New England characterized by belief in individualism and in the spiritual underpinnings of nature. Transcendentalists such as Ralph Waldo Emerson believed that spiritual truths could be revealed through close communion with and observation of nature. Think about what the forest symbolizes in chapter 18. How does the appearance of the forest change in the course of the chapter and why? Why are Hester and Dimmesdale comfortable expressing their love there and not elsewhere? With what activities is the forest associated elsewhere in the novel? In what ways does the forest symbolize the spiritual state of Hester and Dimmesdale in this chapter?

XIX

The Child at the Brook-Side

"Thou will love her dearly," repeated Hester Prynne, as she and the minister sat watching little Pearl. "Dost thou not think her beautiful? And see with what natural skill she has made those simple flowers adorn her! Had she gathered pearls, and diamonds, and rubies, in the wood, they could not have become her better. She is a splendid child! But I know whose brow she has!"

"Dost thou know, Hester," said Arthur Dimmesdale, with an unquiet smile, "that this dear child, tripping about always at thy side, hath caused me many an alarm? Methought—O Hester, what a thought is that, and how terrible to dread it!—that my own features were partly repeated in her face, and so strikingly that the world might see them! But she is mostly thine!"

◄ Why has Arthur Dimmesdale been worried about Pearl?

"No, no! Not mostly!" answered the mother, with a tender smile. "A little longer, and thou needest not to be afraid to trace whose child she is. But how strangely beautiful she looks, with those wild flowers in her hair! It is as if one of the fairies, whom we left in dear old England, had decked her out to meet us."

It was with a feeling which neither of them had ever before experienced, that they sat and watched Pearl's slow advance. In her was visible the tie that united them. She had been offered to the world, these seven past years, as the living hieroglyphic,[1] in which was revealed the secret they so darkly sought to hide—all written in this symbol—all plainly manifest—had there been a prophet or magician skilled to read the character of flame! And Pearl was the oneness of their being. Be the foregone evil what it might, how could they doubt that their earthly lives and future destinies were conjoined, when they beheld at once the material union, and the spiritual idea, in whom they met, and were to dwell immortally together? Thoughts like these—and perhaps other thoughts, which they did not acknowledge or define—threw an awe about the child, as she came onward.

◄ Of what is Pearl a living symbol?

"Let her see nothing strange—no passion or eagerness—in thy way of accosting her," whispered Hester. "Our Pearl is a fitful and fantastic little elf sometimes. Especially, she is seldom

---

1. **hieroglyphic.** Sacred carving; any symbol with obscure meaning

tolerant of emotion, when she does not fully comprehend the why and wherefore. But the child hath strong affections! She loves me, and will love thee!"

"Thou canst not think," said the minister, glancing aside at Hester Prynne, "how my heart dreads this interview, and yearns for it! But, in truth, as I already told thee, children are not readily won to be familiar with me. They will not climb my knee, nor prattle in my ear, nor answer to my smile; but stand apart, and eye me strangely. Even little babes, when I take them in my arms, weep bitterly. Yet Pearl, twice in her little lifetime, hath been kind to me! The first time—thou knowest it well! The last was when thou ledst her with thee to the house of yonder stern old Governor."

"And thou didst plead so bravely in her behalf and mine!" answered the mother. "I remember it; and so shall little Pearl. Fear nothing! She may be strange and shy at first, but will soon learn to love thee!"

By this time Pearl had reached the margin of the brook, and stood on the farther side, gazing silently at Hester and the clergyman, who still sat together on the mossy tree-trunk waiting to receive her. Just where she had paused the brook chanced to form a pool, so smooth and quiet that it reflected a perfect image of her little figure, with all the brilliant picturesqueness of her beauty, in its adornment of flowers and wreathed foliage, but more refined and spiritualized than the reality. This image, so nearly identical with the living Pearl, seemed to communicate somewhat of its own shadowy and intangible quality to the child herself. It was strange, the way in which Pearl stood, looking so steadfastly at them through the dim medium of the forest-gloom; herself, meanwhile, all glorified with a ray of sunshine, that was attracted thitherward as by a certain sympathy. In the brook beneath stood another child—another and the same—with likewise its ray of golden light. Hester felt herself, in some indistinct and tantalizing manner, estranged from Pearl; as if the child, in her lonely ramble through the forest, had strayed out of the sphere in which she and her mother dwelt together, and was now vainly seeking to return to it.

▶ *What feeling does Hester have as she looks at Pearl?*

▶ *According to the narrator, why are Hester and Pearl estranged?*

There were both truth and error in the impression; the child and mother were estranged, but through Hester's fault, not Pearl's. Since the latter rambled from her side, another inmate had been admitted within the circle of the mother's feelings, and so modified the aspect of them all, that Pearl, the returning wanderer, could not find her wonted place, and hardly knew where she was.

"I have a strange fancy," observed the sensitive minister, "that this brook is the boundary between two worlds, and that thou canst never meet thy Pearl again. Or is she an elfish spirit, who, as the legends of our childhood taught us, is forbidden to cross a running stream? Pray hasten her; for this delay has already imparted a tremor to my nerves."

"Come, dearest child!" said Hester encouragingly, and stretching out both her arms. "How slow thou art! When hast thou been so sluggish before now? Here is a friend of mine, who must be thy friend also. Thou wilt have twice as much love, henceforward, as thy mother alone could give thee! Leap across the brook and come to us. Thou canst leap like a young deer!"

Pearl, without responding in any manner to these honey-sweet expressions, remained on the other side of the brook. Now she fixed her bright, wild eyes on her mother, now on the minister, and now included them both in the same glance; as if to detect and explain to herself the relation which they bore to one another. For some unaccountable reason, as Arthur Dimmesdale felt the child's eyes upon himself, his hand—with that gesture so habitual as to have become involuntary—stole over his heart. At length, assuming a singular air of authority, Pearl stretched out her hand, with the small forefinger extended, and pointing evidently towards her mother's breast. And beneath, in the mirror of the brook, there was the flower-girdled and sunny image of little Pearl, pointing her small forefinger too.

◀ To what does Pearl point with authority?

"Thou strange child, why dost thou not come to me?" exclaimed Hester.

Pearl still pointed with her forefinger; and a frown gathered on her brow; the more impressive from the childish, the almost baby-like aspect of the features that conveyed it. As her mother still kept beckoning to her, and arraying her face in a holiday suit of unaccustomed smiles, the child stamped her foot with a yet more imperious look and gesture. In the brook, again, was the fantastic beauty of the image, with its reflected frown, its pointed finger, and imperious gesture, giving emphasis to the aspect of little Pearl.

"Hasten, Pearl; or I shall be angry with thee!" cried Hester Prynne, who, however, <u>inured</u> to such behavior on the elf-child's

Words For Everyday Use

in • ure (in yoor´) vt., make accustomed to

part at other seasons, was naturally anxious for a more seemly deportment now. "Leap across the brook, naughty child, and run hither! Else I must come to thee!"

But Pearl, not a whit startled at her mother's threats, any more than <u>mollified</u> by her entreaties, now suddenly burst into a fit of passion, <u>gesticulating</u> violently, and throwing her small figure into the most extravagant contortions. She accompanied this wild outbreak with piercing shrieks, which the woods reverberated on all sides; so that, alone as she was in her childish and unreasonable wrath, it seemed as if a hidden multitude were lending her their sympathy and encouragement. Seen in the brook, once more, was the shadowy wrath of Pearl's image, crowned and girdled with flowers, but stamping its foot, wildly gesticulating, and, in the midst of all, still pointing its small forefinger at Hester's bosom!

► *What does Hester realize?*

"I see what ails the child," whispered Hester to the clergyman, and turning pale in spite of a strong effort to conceal her trouble and annoyance, "Children will not abide any, the slightest, change in the accustomed aspect of things that are daily before their eyes. Pearl misses something which she has always seen me wear!"

"I pray you," answered the minister, "if thou hast any means of <u>pacifying</u> the child, do it forthwith! Save it were the cankered wrath of an old witch, like Mistress Hibbins," added he, attempting to smile, "I know nothing that I would not sooner encounter than this passion in a child. In Pearl's young beauty, as in the wrinkled witch, it has a preternatural effect. Pacify her, if thou lovest me!"

Hester turned again towards Pearl, with a crimson blush upon her cheek, a conscious glance aside at the clergyman, and then a heavy sigh; while, even before she had time to speak, the blush yielded to a deadly pallor.

"Pearl," said she sadly, "look down at thy feet! There!—before thee!—on the hither side of the brook!"

The child turned her eyes to the point indicated; and there lay the scarlet letter, so close upon the margin of the stream, that the gold embroidery was reflected in it.

"Bring it hither!" said Hester.

"Come thou and take it up!" answered Pearl.

"Was ever such a child!" observed Hester aside to the

Words For Everyday Use

mol • li • fy (mäl´ə fī´) *vt.*, soothe the temper of

ges • tic • u • late (jes tik´yōō lāt´) *vi.*, express through movement

pac • i • fy (pas´ə fī´) *vt.*, make calm

minister. "O, I have much to tell thee about her. But, in very truth, she is right as regards this hateful token. I must bear its torture yet a little longer—only a few days longer—until we shall have left this region, and look back hither as to a land which we have dreamed of. The forest cannot hide it! The mid-ocean shall take it from my hand, and swallow it up for ever!"

With these words, she advanced to the margin of the brook, took up the scarlet letter, and fastened it again into her bosom. Hopefully, but a moment ago, as Hester had spoken of drowning it in the deep sea, there was a sense of inevitable doom upon her, as she thus received back this deadly symbol from the hand of fate. She had flung it into infinite space!—she had drawn an hour's free breath!—and here again was the scarlet misery, glittering on the old spot! So it ever is, whether thus typified or no, that an evil deed invests itself with the character of doom. Hester next gathered up the heavy tresses of her hair, and confined them beneath her cap. As if there were a withering spell in the sad letter, her beauty, the warmth and richness of her womanhood, departed, like fading sunshine; and a gray shadow seemed to fall across her.

When the dreary change was wrought, she extended her hand to Pearl.

"Dost thou know thy mother now, child?" asked she, reproachfully, but with a <u>subdued</u> tone. "Wilt thou come across the brook, and own thy mother, now that she has her shame upon her—now that she is sad?"

"Yes; now I will!" answered the child, bounding across the brook, and clasping Hester in her arms. "Now thou art my mother indeed! And I am thy little Pearl!"

In a mood of tenderness that was not usual with her, she drew down her mother's head, and kissed her brow and both her cheeks. But then—by a kind of necessity that always impelled this child to alloy whatever comfort she might chance to give with a throb of anguish—Pearl put up her mouth, and kissed the scarlet letter too!

"That was not kind!" said Hester. "When thou hast shown me a little love, thou mockest me!"

"Why doth the minister sit yonder?" asked Pearl.

◄ *How does Hester feel when she puts on the scarlet letter again?*

| Words For Everyday Use | **sub • dued** (səb dōōd´) *adj.,* softened; diminished |

"He waits to welcome thee," replied her mother. "Come thou, and entreat his blessing! He loves thee, my little Pearl, and loves thy mother too. Wilt thou not love him? Come! he longs to greet thee!"

▶ What does Pearl ask immediately when told that the minister loves her and her mother?

"Doth he love us?" said Pearl, looking up with acute intelligence into her mother's face. "Will he go back with us, hand in hand, we three together, into the town?"

"Not now, my child," answered Hester. "But in days to come he will walk hand in hand with us. We will have a home and fireside of our own; and thou shalt sit upon his knee; and he will teach thee many things, and love thee dearly. Thou wilt love him; wilt thou not?"

"And will he always keep his hand over his heart?" inquired Pearl.

"Foolish child, what a question is that!" exclaimed her mother. "Come and ask his blessing!"

But, whether influenced by the jealousy that seems instinctive with every petted child towards a dangerous rival, or from whatever caprice of her freakish nature, Pearl would show no favor to the clergyman. It was only by an exertion of force that her mother brought her up to him, hanging back, and manifesting her reluctance by odd grimaces; of which, ever since her babyhood, she had possessed a singular variety, and could transform her mobile physiognomy into a series of different aspects, with a new mischief in them, each and all. The minister—painfully embarrassed, but hoping that a kiss might prove a talisman to admit him into the child's kindlier regards—bent forward, and impressed one on her brow. Hereupon, Pearl broke away from her mother, and, running to the brook, stooped over it, and bathed her forehead, until the unwelcome kiss was quite washed off, and diffused through a long lapse of the gliding water. She then remained apart, silently watching Hester and the clergyman; while they talked together, and made such arrangements as were suggested by their new position, and the purposes soon to be fulfilled.

▶ How does Pearl react to the minister's kiss?

And now this fateful interview had come to a close. The dell was to be left in solitude among its dark, old trees, which, with their multitudinous tongues, would whisper long of what had passed there, and no mortal be the wiser. And the melancholy brook would add this other tale to the mystery with which its little heart was already overburdened, and whereof it still kept up a murmuring babble, with not a whit more cheerfulness of tone than for ages heretofore.

XX

The Minister in a Maze

As the minister departed, in advance of Hester Prynne and little Pearl, he threw a backward glance; half expecting that he should discover only some faintly traced features or outline of the mother and the child, slowly fading into the twilight of the woods. So great a <u>vicissitude</u> in his life could not at once be received as real. But there was Hester, clad in her gray robe, still standing beside the tree-trunk, which some blast had overthrown a long antiquity ago, and which time had ever since been covering with moss, so that these two fated ones, with earth's heaviest burden on them, might there sit down together, and find a single hour's rest and solace. And there was Pearl, too, lightly dancing from the margin of the brook—now that the intrusive third person was gone—and taking her old place by her mother's side. So the minister had not fallen asleep and dreamed!

In order to free his mind from this indistinctness and <u>duplicity</u> of impression, which vexed it with a strange disquietude, he recalled and more thoroughly defined the plans which Hester and himself had sketched for their departure. It had been determined between them, that the Old World, with its crowds and cities, offered them a more eligible shelter and concealment than the wilds of New England, or all America, with its alternatives of an Indian wigwam, or the few settlements of Europeans, scattered thinly along the seaboard. Not to speak of the clergyman's health, so inadequate to sustain the hardships of a forest life, his native gifts, his culture, and his entire development would secure him a home only in the midst of civilization and refinement; the higher the state, the more delicately adapted to it the man. In furtherance of this choice, it so happened that a ship lay in the harbor; one of those unquestionable cruisers, frequent at that day, which, without being absolutely outlaws of the deep, yet roamed over its surface with a remarkable irresponsibility of character. This vessel had recently arrived from the Spanish Main, and,

◄ *Where have Hester and Dimmesdale decided to go?*

Words
For
Everyday
Use

vi • cis • si • tude (vi sis´ə tōōd´) *n.*, state of constant change
du • plic • i • ty (dōō plis´ə tē) *adj.*, deception; double-dealing

within three days' time, would sail for Bristol. Hester Prynne—whose vocation, as a self-enlisted Sister of Charity, had brought her acquainted with the captain and crew—could take upon herself to secure the passage of two individuals and a child, with all the secrecy which circumstances <u>rendered</u> more than desirable.

▶ Why is Dimmesdale happy that the boat isn't leaving for four days?

The minister had inquired of Hester, with no little interest, the precise time at which the vessel might be expected to depart. It would probably be on the fourth day from the present. "This is most fortunate!" he had then said to himself. Now, why the Reverend Mr. Dimmesdale considered it so very fortunate, we hesitate to reveal. Nevertheless—to hold nothing back from the reader—it was because, on the third day from the present, he was to preach the Election Sermon;[1] and, as such an occasion formed an honorable epoch in the life of a New England clergyman, he could not have chanced upon a more suitable mode and time of terminating his professional career. "At least, they shall say of me," thought this exemplary man, "that I leave no public duty unperformed, nor ill performed!" Sad, indeed, that an introspection so profound and acute as this poor minister's should be so miserably deceived! We have had, and may still have, worse things to tell of him; but none, we apprehend, so pitiably weak; no evidence, at once so slight and <u>irrefragable</u>, of a subtle disease, that had long since begun to eat into the real substance of his character. No man, for any considerable period, can wear one face to himself, and another to the multitude, without finally getting bewildered as to which may be the true.

▶ The narrator calls Dimmesdale an "exemplary man." Does the narrator mean this literally, or is the narrator being ironic? Explain.

▶ In what way has Dimmesdale's encounter with Hester affected him physically?

The excitement of Mr. Dimmesdale's feelings, as he returned from his interview with Hester, lent him unaccustomed physical energy, and hurried him townward at a rapid pace. The pathway among the woods seemed wilder, more uncouth with its rude natural obstacles, and less trodden by the foot of man, than he remembered it on his outward journey. But he leaped across the plashy places, thrust himself through the clinging underbush, climbed the ascent, plunged into the hollow, and overcame, in short, all

---

1. **Election Sermon.** Sermon preached on the inauguration day of the governor. Election Day was set fifty days after Easter.

Words For Everyday Use

ren • der (ren′dər) *vt.*, cause to become, make
ir • ref • ra • ga • ble (ir ref′rə gə bəl) *adj.*, indisputable

the difficulties of the track, with an unwearable activity that astonished him. He could not but recall how feebly, and with what frequent pauses for breath, he had toiled over the same ground only two days before. As he drew near the town, he took an impression of change from the series of familiar objects that presented themselves. It seemed not yesterday, not one, not two, but many days, or even years ago, since he had quitted them. There, indeed, was each former trace of the street, as he remembered it, and all the peculiarities of the houses, with the due multitude of gable-peaks, and a weathercock at every point where his memory suggested one. Not the less, however, came this <u>importunately</u> obtrusive sense of change. The same was true as regarded the acquaintances whom he met, and all the well-known shapes of human life, about the little town. They looked neither older nor younger, now; the beards of the aged were no whiter, nor could the creeping babe of yesterday walk on his feet to-day; it was impossible to describe in what respect they differed from the individuals on whom he had so recently bestowed a parting glance; and yet the minister's deepest sense seemed to inform him of their <u>mutability</u>. A similar impression struck him most remarkably, as he passed under the walls of his own church. The edifice had so very strange, and yet so familiar, an aspect, that Mr. Dimmesdale's mind vibrated between two ideas; either that he had seen it only in a dream hitherto, or that he was merely dreaming about it now.

◄ How does Dimmesdale feel about the town? Has the town changed, or has Dimmesdale?

This phenomenon, in the various shapes which it assumed, indicated no external change, but so sudden and important a change in the spectator of the familiar scene, that the intervening space of a single day had operated on his consciousness like the lapse of years. The minister's own will, and Hester's will, and the fate that grew between them, had wrought this transformation. It was the same town as heretofore; but the same minister returned not from the forest. He might have said to the friends who greeted him—"I am not the man for whom you take me! I left him yonder in the forest, withdrawn into a secret dell, by a mossy tree-trunk, and near a melancholy brook! Go, seek your minister, and see if his emaciated figure, his thin cheek, his white,

◄ Why does the town seem different to Dimmesdale?

Words For Everyday Use	**im • por • tu • nate • ly** (im pôr´tu nit lē) *adv.,* annoyingly urgent or persistent **mu • ta • bil • i •ty** (my$\overline{oo}$t´ə bil´ə tē) *n.,* change

heavy, pain-wrinkled brow, be not flung down there like a cast-off garment!" His friends, no doubt, would still have insisted with him—"Thou art thyself the man!"—but the error would have been their own, not his.

Before Mr. Dimmesdale reached home, his inner man gave him other evidences of a revolution in the sphere of thought and feeling. In truth, nothing short of a total change of dynasty and moral code, in that interior kingdom, was adequate to account for the impulses now communicated to the unfortunate and startled minister. At every step he was <u>incited</u> to do some strange, wild, wicked thing or other, with a sense that it would be at once involuntary and intentional; in spite of himself, yet growing out of a profounder self than that which opposed the impulse. For instance, he met one of his own deacons. The good old man addressed him with the paternal affection and patriarchal privilege, which his venerable age, his upright and holy character, and his station in the Church, entitled him to use; and, conjoined with this, the deep, almost worshipping respect, which the minister's professional and private claims alike demanded. Never was there a more beautiful example of how the majesty of age and wisdom may comport with the <u>obeisance</u> and respect enjoined upon it, as from a lower social rank, and inferior order of endowment, towards a higher. Now, during a conversation of some two or three moments between the Reverend Mr. Dimmesdale and this excellent and hoary-bearded deacon, it was only by the most careful self-control that the former could refrain from uttering certain blasphemous suggestions that rose into his mind, respecting the communion-supper. He absolutely trembled and turned pale as ashes, lest his tongue should wag itself, in utterance of these horrible matters, and plead his own consent for so doing, without his having fairly given it. And, even with this terror in his heart, he could hardly avoid laughing to imagine how the sanctified old patriarchal deacon would have been petrified by his minister's <u>impiety</u>!

Again, another incident of the same nature. Hurrying along the street, the Reverend Mr. Dimmesdale encountered the eldest female member of his church; a most pious and exemplary old dame; poor, widowed, lonely, and with a

▶ *What strange urge does Dimmesdale feel?*

Words For Everyday Use

in • cite (in sīt´) *vt.,* urge to action
o • bei • sance (ō bā´səns) *n.,* feelings of respect; homage
im • pi • e • ty (im pī´ə tē) *n.,* lack of respect

heart as full of reminiscences about her dead husband and children, and her dead friends of long ago, as a burial-ground is full of storied grave-stones. Yet all this, which would else have been such heavy sorrow, was made almost a solemn joy to her devout old soul by religious consolations and the truths of Scripture, wherewith she had fed herself continually for more than thirty years. And, since Mr. Dimmesdale had taken her in charge, the good grandam's chief earthly comfort—which, unless it had been likewise a heavenly comfort, could have been none at all—was to meet her pastor, whether casually, or of set purpose, and be refreshed with a word of warm, fragrant, heaven-breathing Gospel truth from his beloved lips into her dulled, but rapturously attentive ear.

◄ How does this older woman feel about her minister and about religion?

But, on this occasion, up to the moment of putting his lips to the old woman's ear, Mr. Dimmesdale, as the great enemy of souls would have it, could recall no text of Scripture, nor aught else, except a brief, <u>pithy</u>, and, as it then appeared to him, unanswerable argument against the immortality of the human soul. The instillment thereof into her mind would probably have caused this aged sister to drop down dead, at once, as by the effect of an intensely poisonous infusion. What he really did whisper, the minister could never afterwards recollect. There was, perhaps, a fortunate disorder in his utterance, which failed to impart any distinct idea to the good widow's comprehension, or which Providence interpreted after a method of its own. Assuredly, as the minister looked back, he beheld an expression of divine gratitude and ecstasy that seemed like the shine of the celestial city on her face, so wrinkled and ashy pale.

◄ What is the only thing the minister can think of to tell the elderly woman? What does he think would happen if he were to say such a thing to her?

Again, a third instance. After parting from the old church-member, he met the youngest sister of them all. It was a maiden newly-won—and won by the Reverend Mr. Dimmesdale's own sermon, on the Sabbath after his vigil—to barter the transitory pleasures of the world for the heavenly hope, that was to assume brighter substance as life grew dark around her, and which would gild the utter gloom with final glory. She was fair and pure as a lily that had bloomed in Paradise. The minister knew well that he was himself enshrined within the stainless sanctity of her heart, which hung its snowy curtains about his image,

Words For Everyday Use	**pith • y** (pith´ē) *adj.*, short and full of meaning

▶ In what way does the narrator describe Dimmesdale? Why might Dimmesdale be feeling this way?

▶ What does Dimmesdale want to do to the young woman's heart?

imparting to religion the warmth of love, and to love a religious purity. Satan, that afternoon, had surely led the poor young girl away from her mother's side, and thrown her into the pathway of this sorely tempted, or—shall we not rather say?—this lost and desperate man. As she drew nigh, the arch-fiend whispered him to condense into small compass and drop into her tender bosom a germ of evil that would be sure to blossom darkly soon, and bear black fruit betimes. Such was his sense of power over this virgin soul, trusting him as she did, that the minister felt potent to blight all the field of innocence with but one wicked look, and develop all its opposite with but a word. So—with a mightier struggle than he had yet sustained—he held his Geneva cloak before his face, and hurried onward, making no sign of recognition, and leaving the young sister to digest his rudeness as she might. She <u>ransacked</u> her conscience—which was full of harmless little matters, like her pocket or her work-bag—and took herself to task, poor thing, for a thousand imaginary faults; and went about her household duties with swollen eyelids the next morning.

Before the minister had time to celebrate his victory over this last temptation, he was conscious of another impulse, more ludicrous, and almost as horrible. It was—we blush to tell it—it was to stop short in the road, and teach some very wicked words to a knot of little Puritan children who were playing there, and had but just begun to talk. Denying himself this freak, as unworthy of his cloth, he met a drunken seaman, one of the ship's crew from the Spanish Main. And here, since he had so <u>valiantly</u> forborne all other wickedness, poor Mr. Dimmesdale longed, at least, to shake hands with the tarry blackguard, and recreate himself with a few improper jests, such as <u>dissolute</u> sailors so abound with, and a volley of good, round, solid, satisfactory, and heaven-defying oaths! It was not so much a better principle, as partly his natural good taste, and still more his buckramed[2] habit of clerical decorum, that carried him safely through the latter crisis.

---

2. **buckramed.** Made of a tough fabric stiffened with glue

Words
For
Everyday
Use

ran • sack (ran´sak´) *vt.,* examine thoroughly
val • iant • ly (val´yənt lē) *adv.,* with courage, resolutely
dis • so • lute (dis´ə lo͞ot´) *adj.,* immoral

"What is it that haunts and tempts me thus?" cried the minister to himself, at length, pausing in the street, and striking his hand against his forehead. "Am I mad? or am I given over utterly to the fiend? Did I make a contract with him in the forest, and sign it with my blood? And does he now summon me to its fulfillment, by suggesting the performance of every wickedness which his most foul imagination can conceive?"

At the moment when the Reverend Mr. Dimmesdale thus communed with himself, and struck his forehead with his hand, old Mistress Hibbins, the reputed witch-lady, is said to have been passing by. She made a very grand appearance; having on a high head-dress, a rich gown of velvet, and a ruff done up with the famous yellow starch, of which Anne Turner, her especial friend, had taught her the secret, before this last good lady had been hanged for Sir Thomas Overbury's murder. Whether the witch had read the minister's thoughts or no, she came to a full stop, looked shrewdly into his face, smiled craftily, and—though little given to converse with clergymen—began a conversation.

"So, reverend Sir, you have made a visit into the forest," observed the witch-lady, nodding her high head-dress at him. "The next time, I pray you to allow me only a fair warning, and I shall be proud to bear you company. Without taking overmuch upon myself, my good word will go far towards gaining any strange gentleman a fair reception from yonder <u>potentate</u> you wot of."

"I profess, madam," answered the clergyman, with a grave obeisance, such as the lady's rank demanded, and his own good-breeding made imperative—"I profess, on my conscience and character, that I am utterly bewildered as touching the purport of your words! I went not into the forest to seek a potentate, neither do I, at any future time, design a visit thither, with a view to gaining the favor of such personage. My one sufficient object was to greet that pious friend of mine, the Apostle Eliot, and rejoice with him over the many precious souls he hath won from heathendom!"

"Ha, ha, ha!" cackled the old witch-lady, still nodding her high head-dress at the minister. "Well, well, we must needs talk thus in the daytime! You carry it off like an old hand!

◄ What two explanations for his behavior does Dimmesdale consider?

◄ Who is the only person who notices a change in the minister? What does this person think has happened to the minister?

Words For Everyday Use

po • ten • tate (pōt″n tāt′) *n.*, monarch, ruler

But at midnight, and in the forest, we shall have other talk together!"

She passed on with her aged stateliness, but often turning back her head and smiling at him, like one willing to recognize a secret intimacy of connection.

"Have I then sold myself," thought the minister, "to the fiend whom, if men say true, this yellow-starched and velveted old hag has chosen for her prince and master!"

► Why does Dimmesdale consider his actions similar to a bargain with the devil?

The wretched minister! He had made a bargain very like it! Tempted by a dream of happiness, he had yielded himself with deliberate choice, as he had never done before, to what he knew was deadly sin. And the infectious poison of that sin had been thus rapidly diffused throughout his moral system. It had stupefied all blessed impulses, and awakened into vivid life the whole brotherhood of bad ones. Scorn, bitterness, unprovoked malignity, gratuitous desire of ill, ridicule of whatever was good and holy, all awoke, to tempt, even while they frightened him. And his encounter with old Mistress Hibbins, if it were a real incident, did but show its sympathy and fellowship with wicked mortals and the world of perverted spirits.

He had by this time reached his dwelling, on the edge of the burial-ground, and, hastening up the stairs, took refuge in his study. The minister was glad to have reached this shelter, without first betraying himself to the world by any of those strange and wicked eccentricities to which he had been continually impelled while passing through the streets. He entered the accustomed room, and looked around him on its books, its windows, its fireplace, and the tapestried comfort of the walls, with the same perception of strangeness that had haunted him throughout his walk from the forest-dell into the town, and thitherward. Here he had studied and written; here, gone through fast and vigil, and come forth half alive; here, striven to pray; here, borne a hundred thousand agonies! There was the Bible, in its rich old Hebrew, with Moses and the Prophets speaking to him, and God's voice through all! There, on the table, with the inky pen beside it, was an unfinished sermon, with a sentence broken in the midst, where his thoughts had ceased to gush out upon the page two days before. He knew that it was himself, the thin and white-cheeked minister, who had done and suffered these things, and written thus far into the Election Sermon! But he seemed to stand apart, and eye this former self with scornful, pitying, but half-envious curiosity. That self was gone! Another man had returned out of the forest; a wiser one; with a knowledge of hidden mysteries which the simplicity of the former never could have reached. A bitter kind of knowledge that!

While occupied with these reflections, a knock came at the door of the study, and the minister said, "Come in!"—not wholly devoid of an idea that he might behold an evil spirit. And so he did! It was old Roger Chillingworth that entered. The minister stood, white and speechless, with one hand on the Hebrew Scriptures, and the other spread upon his breast.

"Welcome home, reverend Sir," said the physician."And how found you that godly man, the Apostle Eliot? But methinks, dear Sir, you look pale; as if the travel through the wilderness had been too sore for you. Will not my aid be requisite to put you in heart and strength to preach your Election Sermon?"

"Nay, I think not so," rejoined the Reverend Mr. Dimmesdale. "My journey, and the sight of the holy Apostle yonder, and the free air which I have breathed, have done me good, after so long confinement in my study. I think to need no more of your drugs, my kind physician, good though they be, and administered by a friendly hand."

◄ Does Dimmesdale reveal that he knows Chillingworth's true identity, or does he pretend that Chillingworth is a good-intentioned doctor and friend? What does Dimmesdale refuse?

All this time, Roger Chillingworth was looking at the minister with the grave and intent regard of a physician towards his patient. But, in spite of this outward show, the latter was almost convinced of the old man's knowledge, or, at least, his confident suspicion, with respect to his own interview with Hester Prynne. The physician knew, then, that, in the minister's regard, he was no longer a trusted friend, but his bitterest enemy. So much being known, it would appear natural that a part of it should be expressed. It is singular, however, how long a time often passes before words embody things; and with what security two persons, who choose to avoid a certain subject, may approach its very verge, and retire without disturbing it. Thus, the minister felt no apprehension that Roger Chillingworth would touch, in express words, upon the real position which they sustained towards one another. Yet did the physician, in his dark way, creep frightfully near the secret.

◄ Of what is Dimmesdale convinced? What does Chillingworth know?

"Were it not better," said he, "that you use my poor skill to-night? Verily, dear Sir, we must take pains to make you strong and vigorous for this occasion of the Election discourse. The people look for great things from you; apprehending that another year may come about, and find their pastor gone."

"Yes, to another world," replied the minister, with pious resignation. "Heaven grant it be a better one; for, in good sooth, I hardly think to tarry with my flock through the flitting seasons of another year! But, touching your medicine, kind Sir, in my present frame of body I need it not."

"I joy to hear it," answered the physician. "It may be that my remedies, so long administered in vain, begin now to take due effect. Happy man were I, and well deserving of New England's gratitude, could I achieve this cure!"

"I thank you from my heart, most watchful friend," said the Reverend Mr. Dimmesdale, with a solemn smile. "I thank you, and can but requite your good deeds with my prayers."

"A good man's prayers are golden recompense!" rejoined old Roger Chillingworth, as he took his leave. "Yea, they are the current gold coin of the New Jerusalem, with the King's own mint-mark on them!"

► *What is Dimmesdale inspired to do?*

Left alone, the minister summoned a servant of the house, and requested food, which, being set before him, he ate with ravenous appetite. Then, flinging the already written pages of the Election Sermon into the fire, he forthwith began another, which he wrote with such an impulsive flow of thought and emotion, that he fancied himself inspired; and only wondered that Heaven should see fit to transmit the grand and solemn music of its oracles through so foul an organ-pipe as he. However, leaving that mystery to solve itself, or go unsolved for ever, he drove his task onward, with earnest haste and ecstasy. Thus the night fled away, as if it were a winged steed, and he careering on it; morning came, and peeped blushing through the curtains; and at last sunrise threw a golden beam into the study, and laid it right across the minister's bedazzled eyes. There he was, with the pen still between his fingers, and a vast, immeasurable tract of written space behind him!

Responding to the Selection

What do you think of Hester's and Dimmesdale's plan to escape? Do you agree with the minister that, in making this plan, he has given himself over to sin? Do you think that Hester and Dimmesdale's troubles will soon be over? Why, or why not?

Reviewing the Selection

Recalling and Interpreting

1. **R:** Why does Pearl at first refuse to cross the brook and go to her mother? What does she force her mother to do?

2. **I:** What is the significance of Pearl's demand? Do you think that Pearl fully understands the importance of this action, or, as Hester says, that she is simply acting like any young child who will not abide any change in her routine?

3. **R:** When Hester tells Pearl that Dimmesdale loves her, what two questions does Pearl ask? What does Pearl do when Dimmesdale kisses her?

4. **I:** Why might Pearl be willing to kiss her mother but not Dimmesdale? Why might Pearl be unwilling to accept Dimmesdale as someone who loves her?

5. **R:** How will Hester, Dimmesdale, and Pearl leave Boston? Where will they go? What will Dimmesdale be doing for the community right before they leave?

6. **I:** How is Dimmesdale feeling as he returns to town after making travel plans with Hester? Why might Dimmesdale be experiencing strange and corrupt impulses?

7. **R:** What does Dimmesdale suspect that Chillingworth knows? Is he correct in his suspicion?

8. **I:** How does Dimmesdale feel when he sees Chillingworth again? What two meanings can be given to Dimmesdale's assertion that he will soon be gone to another world?

Synthesizing

9. Why do Hester and Dimmesdale decide to leave Boston? What are their concerns as they prepare to do this? Do you think it is realistic to believe that both Hester and Dimmesdale can leave behind their troubles, particularly their feelings of guilt, and begin a new life? Why, or why not?

10. What opinion does Dimmesdale seem to have of himself in chapter 20? What does this opinion lead him to think and do?

Understanding Literature (QUESTIONS FOR DISCUSSION)

1. Personification. Personification is a figure of speech in which an idea, animal, or thing is described as if it were a person. List examples of personification appearing at the end of chapter 19. Why does Hawthorne try so hard to create a forest setting that seems detailed and alive? Why is this setting important to Hester, Pearl, and Dimmesdale?

2. Repetition. Repetition is the use, again, of a sound, word, phrase, sentence, or other element. Describe the appearance of Mistress Hibbins to Dimmesdale. At what point in the novel did she last appear to Hester? What does she know about Dimmesdale's meeting with Hester in the forest? What is the importance of her appearance? What does Dimmesdale believe that he has done after he sees her?

XXI

The New England Holiday

Betimes in the morning of the day on which the new Governor was to receive his office at the hands of the people, Hester Prynne and little Pearl came into the market-place. It was already thronged with the craftsmen and other plebeian inhabitants of the town, in considerable numbers; among whom, likewise, were many rough figures, whose attire of deer-skins marked them as belonging to some of the forest settlements, which surrounded the little metropolis of the colony.

On this public holiday, as on all other occasions, for seven years past, Hester was clad in a garment of coarse gray cloth. Not more by its hue than by some indescribable peculiarity in its fashion, it had the effect of making her fade personally out of sight and outline; while, again, the scarlet letter brought her back from this twilight indistinctness, and revealed her under the moral aspect of its own illumination. Her face, so long familiar to the townspeople, showed the marble quietude which they were accustomed to behold there. It was like a mask; or rather, like the frozen calmness of a dead woman's features; owing this dreary resemblance to the fact that Hester was actually dead, in respect to any claim of sympathy, and had departed out of the world with which she still seemed to mingle.

◄ How does Hester appear to the townspeople?

It might be, on this one day, that there was an expression unseen before, nor, indeed, vivid enough to be detected now; unless some preternaturally gifted observer should have first read the heart, and have afterwards sought a corresponding development in the countenance and mien. Such a spiritual seer might have conceived, that, after sustaining the gaze of the multitude through seven miserable years as a necessity, a penance, and something which it was a stern religion to endure, she now, for one last time more, encountered it freely and voluntarily, in order to convert what had so long been agony into a kind of triumph. "Look your last on the scarlet letter and its wearer!"—the people's victim and life-long bond-slave, as they fancied her, might say to them. "Yet a little while, and she will be beyond your reach! A few hours longer, and the deep, mysterious ocean will quench and hide for ever the symbol which ye have caused to burn on her bosom!" Nor were it an inconsistency too improbable to be

◄ What is Hester thinking as she goes among the townspeople?

assigned to human nature, should we suppose a feeling of regret in Hester's mind, at the moment when she was about to win her freedom from the pain which had been thus deeply <u>incorporated</u> with her being. Might there not be an irresistible desire to quaff a last, long, breathless draught of the cup of wormwood and aloes, with which nearly all her years of womanhood had been perpetually flavored? The wine of life, henceforth to be presented to her lips, must be indeed rich, delicious, and exhilarating, in its chased and golden beaker; or else leave an inevitable and weary <u>languor</u>, after the lees[1] of bitterness wherewith she had been drugged, as with a cordial of intensest potency.

Pearl was decked out with airy gaiety. It would have been impossible to guess that this bright and sunny apparition owed its existence to the shape of gloomy gray; or that a fancy, at once so gorgeous and so delicate as must have been requisite to contrive the child's apparel, was the same that had achieved a task perhaps more difficult, in imparting so distinct a peculiarity to Hester's simple robe. The dress, so proper was it to little Pearl, seemed an effluence, or inevitable development and outward manifestation of her character, no more to be separated from her than the many-hued brilliancy from a butterfly's wing, or the painted glory from the leaf of a bright flower. As with these, so with the child; her garb was all of one idea with her nature. On this eventful day, moreover, there was a certain singular inquietude and excitement in her mood, resembling nothing so much as the shimmer of a diamond, that sparkles and flashes with the varied throbbings of the breast on which it is displayed. Children have always a sympathy in the <u>agitations</u> of those connected with them; always, especially, a sense of any trouble or impending revolution, of whatever kind, in domestic circumstances; and therefore Pearl, who was the gem on her mother's unquiet bosom, betrayed, by the very dance of her spirits, the emotions which none could detect in the marble passiveness of Hester's brow.

This effervescence made her flit with a bird-like movement, rather than walk by her mother's side. She broke

▶ *What is the only way in which Hester's emotional state is betrayed?*

---

1. **lees.** Dregs; sediment remaining from a liquid

Words For Everyday Use

in • cor • po • rate (in kôr′pə rāt) *vt.,* make part of another thing

lan • guor (laŋ′gər) *n.,* lack of interest or spirit; indifference and sluggishness

ag • i • ta • tion (aj′ə tā′shən) *n.,* emotional disturbance

continually into shouts of a wild, inarticulate, and sometimes piercing music. When they reached the market-place,
she became still more restless, on perceiving the stir and bustle that enlivened the spot; for it was usually more like the
broad and lonesome green before a village meeting-house,
than the center of a town's business.

◄ In what way is the town different on Election Day?

"Why, what is this, mother?" cried she. "Wherefore have
all the people left their work to-day? Is it a play-day for the
whole world? See, there is the blacksmith! He has washed his
sooty face, and put on his Sabbath-day clothes, and looks as
if he would gladly be merry, if any kind body would only
teach him how! And there is Master Brackett, the old jailer,
nodding and smiling at me. Why does he do so, mother?"

"He remembers thee a little babe, my child," answered
Hester.

"He should not nod and smile at me, for all that—the
black, grim, ugly-eyed old man!" said Pearl. "He may nod at
thee if he will; for thou art clad in gray, and wearest the scarlet letter. But, see, mother, how many faces of strange people,
and Indians among them, and sailors! What have they all
come to do here in the market-place?"

"They wait to see the procession pass," said Hester. "For
the Governor and the magistrates are to go by, and the ministers, and all the great people and good people, with the
music, and the soldiers marching before them."

"And will the minister be there?" asked Pearl. "And will he
hold out both his hands to me, as when thou ledst me to
him from the brook-side?"

"He will be there, child," answered her mother. "But he
will not greet thee to-day, nor must thou greet him."

"What a strange, sad man is he!" said the child, as if
speaking partly to herself. "In the dark night-time, he calls us
to him, and holds thy hand and mine, as when we stood
with him on the scaffold yonder! And in the deep forest,
where only the old trees can hear, and the strip of sky see it,
he talks with thee, sitting on a heap of moss! And he kisses
my forehead, too, so that the little brook would hardly wash
it off! But here in the sunny day, and among all the people,
he knows us not; nor must we know him! A strange, sad man
is he, with his hand always over his heart!"

◄ What does Pearl note about the minister?

"Be quiet, Pearl! Thou understandest not these things,"
said her mother. "Think not now of the minister, but look
about thee, and see how cheery is every body's face to-day.
The children have come from their schools, and the grown
people from their workshops and their fields, on purpose to
be happy. For, to-day, a new man is beginning to rule over

them; and so—as has been the custom of mankind ever since a nation was first gathered—they make merry and rejoice; as if a good and golden year were at length to pass over the poor old world!"

It was as Hester said, in regard to the unwonted jollity that brightened the faces of the people. Into this festal season of the year—as it already was, and continued to be during the greater part of two centuries—the Puritans compressed whatever mirth and public joy they deemed allowable to human infirmity; thereby so far <u>dispelling</u> the customary cloud, that, for the space of a single holiday, they appeared scarcely more grave than most other communities at a period of general affliction.

► How mirthful do the Puritans appear on this holiday?

But we perhaps exaggerate the gray or sable tinge, which undoubtedly characterized the mood and manners of the age. The persons now in the market-place of Boston had not been born to an inheritance of Puritanic gloom. They were native Englishmen, whose fathers had lived in the sunny richness of the Elizabethan epoch; a time when the life of England, viewed as one great mass, would appear to have been as stately, magnificent, and joyous, as the world has ever witnessed. Had they followed their hereditary taste, the New England settlers would have illustrated all events of public importance by bonfires, banquets, pageantries, and processions. Nor would it have been impracticable, in the observance of majestic ceremonies, to combine mirthful recreation with solemnity, and give, as it were, a grotesque and brilliant embroidery to the great robe of state, which a nation, at such festivals, puts on. There was some shadow of an attempt of this kind in the mode of celebrating the day on which the political year of the colony commenced. The dim reflection of a remembered splendor, a colorless and manifold diluted repetition of what they had beheld in proud old London—we will not say at a royal coronation, but at a Lord Mayor's show—might be traced in the customs which our forefathers instituted, with reference to the annual installation of magistrates. The fathers and founders of the commonwealth—the statesman, the priest, and the soldier—deemed it a duty then to assume the outward state and majesty, which, in accordance with antique

► In what way were the Puritans' ancestors different from the Puritans?

Words For Everyday Use

dis • pel (di spel´) *vt.,* make vanish

style, was looked upon as the proper garb of public and social eminence. All came forth, to move in procession before the people's eye, and thus impart a needed dignity to the simple framework of a government so newly constructed.

Then, too, the people were <u>countenanced</u>, if not encouraged, in relaxing the severe and close application to their various modes of rugged industry, which at all other times, seemed of the same piece and material with their religion. Here, it is true, were none of the appliances which popular merriment would so readily have found in the England of Elizabeth's time, or that of James—no rude shows of a theatrical kind; no minstrel with his harp and legendary ballad, nor gleeman, with an ape dancing to his music; no juggler, with his tricks of mimic witchcraft; no Merry Andrew, to stir up the multitude with jests, perhaps hundreds of years old, but still effective, by their appeals to the very broadest sources of mirthful sympathy. All such professors of the several branches of <u>jocularity</u> would have been sternly repressed, not only by the rigid discipline of law, but by the general sentiment which gives law its vitality. Not the less, however, the great, honest face of the people smiled, grimly, perhaps, but widely too. Nor were sports wanting, such as the colonists had witnessed, and shared in, long ago, at the country fairs and on the village-greens of England; and which it was thought well to keep alive on this new soil, for the sake of the courage and manliness that were essential in them. Wrestling matches, in the different fashions of Cornwall and Devonshire, were seen here and there about the market-place; in one corner, there was a friendly bout at quarterstaff; and—what attracted most interest of all—on the platform of the pillory, already so noted in our pages, two masters of defense were commencing an exhibition with the buckler and broadsword. But, much to the disappointment of the crowd, this latter business was broken off by the interposition of the town beadle, who had no idea of permitting the majesty of the law to be violated by such an abuse of one of its consecrated places.

It may not be too much to affirm, on the whole, (the people being then in the first stages of joyless deportment, and the offspring of sires who had known how to be merry, in their day), that they would compare favorably, in point of holiday keeping, with their descendants, even at so long an interval as ourselves. Their immediate <u>posterity</u>, the generation next to the early emigrants, wore the blackest shade of Puritanism, and so darkened the national visage with it, that all the subsequent years have not sufficed to clear it up. We have yet to learn again the forgotten art of gaiety.

The picture of human life in the market-place, though its general tint was the sad gray, brown, or black of the English emigrants, was yet enlivened by some diversity of hue. A party of Indians—in their savage finery of curiously embroidered deerskin robes, wampum-belts,[2] red and yellow ochre, and feathers, and armed with the bow and arrow and stone-headed spear—stood apart, with countenances of inflexible gravity, beyond what even the Puritan aspect could attain. Nor, wild as were these painted barbarians, were they the wildest feature of the scene. This distinction could more justly be claimed by some mariners—a part of the crew of the vessel from the Spanish Main—who had come ashore to see the humors of Election Day. They were rough-looking desperadoes, with sun-blackened faces, and an immensity of beard; their wide, short trousers were confined about the waist by belts, often clasped with a rough plate of gold, and sustaining always a long knife, and, in some instances, a sword. From beneath their broad-brimmed hats of palm-leaf, gleamed eyes which, even in good nature and merriment, had a kind of animal <u>ferocity</u>. They transgressed, without fear or scruple, the rules of behavior that were binding on all others; smoking tobacco under the beadle's very nose, although each whiff would have cost a townsman a shilling; and quaffing, at their pleasure, draughts of wine or aqua-vitae[3] from pocket flasks, which they freely tendered to the gaping crowd around them. It remarkably characterized the incomplete morality of the age, rigid as we call it, that a license was allowed the seafaring class, not merely for their freaks on shore, but for far more desperate deeds on their proper element. The sailor of that day would go near to be arraigned as a pirate in our own. There could be little doubt, for instance, that this very ship's

> ► *What group of people freely violate the Puritan code of behavior and appearance?*

---

2. **wampum belts.** Belts made of beads of shell used by Native Americans as money

3. **aqua-vitae.** Brandy or other strong liquor

Words For Everyday Use

pos • ter • i • ty (päs ter´ə tē) *n.*, descendants
fe • roc • i • ty (fə räs´ə tē) *n.*, fierceness, savageness

crew, though no unfavorable specimens of the nautical brotherhood, had been guilty, as we should phrase it, of <u>depredations</u> on the Spanish commerce, such as would have periled all their necks in a modern court of justice.

But the sea, in those old times, heaved, swelled, and foamed very much at its own will, or subject only to the <u>tempestuous</u> wind, with hardly any attempts at regulation by human law. The buccaneer on the wave might relinquish his calling, and become at once, if he chose, a man of <u>probity</u> and piety on land; nor, even in the full career of his reckless life, was he regarded as a personage with whom it was <u>disreputable</u> to traffic, or casually associate. Thus, the Puritan elders, in their black cloaks, starched bands, and steeple-crowned hats, smiled not unbenignantly at the clamor and rude deportment of these jolly seafaring men; and it excited neither surprise nor animadversion[4] when so reputable a citizen as old Roger Chillingworth, the physician, was seen to enter the market-place in close and familiar talk with the commander of the questionable vessel.

◀ Who shows an interest in the captain of the vessel?

The latter was by far the most showy and gallant figure, so far as apparel went, anywhere to be seen among the multitude. He wore a profusion of ribbons on his garment, and gold lace on his hat, which was also encircled by a gold chain, and surmounted with a feather. There was a sword at his side and a sword-cut on his forehead, which, by the arrangement of his hair, he seemed anxious rather to display than hide. A landsman could hardly have worn this garb and shown this face, and worn and shown them both with such a galliard[5] air, without undergoing stern question before a magistrate, and probably incurring a fine or imprisonment, or perhaps an exhibition in the stocks. As regarded the shipmaster, however, all was looked upon as pertaining to the character, as to a fish his glistening scales.

After parting from the physician, the commander of the Bristol ship strolled idly through the market-place; until, happening to approach the spot where Hester Prynne was

---

4. **animadversion.** Sharp criticism
5. **galliard.** Quick, lively dance

Words For Everyday Use

dep • re • da • tion (dep´rə dā´shən) n., wicked act

tem • pes • tu • ous (tem pes´chō̅o̅ əs) adj., violent, stormy

pro • bi • ty (prō´bə tē) n., good character

dis • rep • u • ta • ble (dis rep´yo̅o̅ tə bəl) adj., causing a bad reputation standing, he appeared to recognize, and did not hesitate to address her. As was usually the case wherever Hester stood, a small vacant area—a sort of magic circle—had formed itself about her, into which, though the people were elbowing one another at a little distance, none ventured, or felt disposed to intrude. It was a forcible type of the moral solitude in which the scarlet letter enveloped its fated wearer; partly by her own reserve, and partly by the instinctive, though no longer so unkindly, withdrawal of her fellow-creatures. Now, if never before, it answered a good purpose, by enabling Hester and the seaman to speak together without risk of being overheard; and so changed was Hester Prynne's repute before the public, that the matron in town most eminent for rigid morality could not have held such intercourse with less result of scandal than herself.

► *What does the mariner reveal?*

"So, mistress," said the mariner, "I must bid the steward make ready one more berth than you bargained for! No fear of scurvy or ship-fever this voyage! What with the ship's surgeon and this other doctor, our only danger will be from drug or pill; more by token, as there is a lot of apothecary's stuff aboard, which I traded for with a Spanish vessel."

"What mean you?" inquired Hester, startled more than she permitted to appear. "Have you another passenger?"

"Why, know you not," cried the shipmaster, "that this physician here—Chillingworth, he calls himself—is minded to try my cabin-fare with you? Ay, ay, you must have known it; for he tells me he is of your party, and a close friend to the gentleman you spoke of—he that is in peril from these sour old Puritan rulers!"

"They know each other well, indeed," replied Hester, with a <u>mien</u> of calmness, though in the utmost <u>consternation</u>. "They have long dwelt together."

Nothing further passed between the mariner and Hester Prynne. But, at that instant, she beheld old Roger Chillingworth himself, standing in the remotest corner of the market-place, and smiling on her; a smile which—across the wide and bustling square, and through all the talk and laughter, and various thoughts, moods, and interests of the crowd—conveyed secret and fearful meaning.

Words For Everyday Use

mien (mēn) *n.*, manner
con • ster • na • tion (kä´stər nā´shən) *n.*, great fear that makes one feel helpless

XXII

The Procession

Before Hester Prynne could call together her thoughts, and consider what was practicable to be done in this new and startling aspect of affairs, the sound of military music was heard approaching along a <u>contiguous</u> street. It denoted the advance of the procession of magistrates and citizens, on its way towards the meeting-house; where, in compliance with a custom thus early established, and ever since observed, the Reverend Mr. Dimmesdale was to deliver an Election Sermon.

Soon the head of the procession showed itself, with a slow and stately march, turning a corner, and making its way across the market-place. First came the music. It comprised a variety of instruments, perhaps imperfectly adapted to one another, and played with no great skill, but yet attaining the great object for which the harmony of drum and clarion addresses itself to the multitude—that of imparting a higher and more heroic air to the scene of life that passes before the eye. Little Pearl at first clapped her hands, but then lost, for an instant, the restless agitation that had kept her in a continual <u>effervescence</u> throughout the morning; she gazed silently, and seemed to be borne upward, like a floating sea-bird on the long heaves and swells of sound. But she was brought back to her former mood by the shimmer of the sunshine on the weapons and bright armor of the military company, which followed after the music, and formed the honorary escort of the procession. This body of soldiery— which still sustains a corporate existence, and marches down from past ages with an ancient and honorable fame—was composed of no mercenary materials. Its ranks were filled with gentlemen, who felt the stirrings of martial impulse, and sought to establish a kind of College of Arms, where, as in an association of Knights Templars,[1] they might learn the

---

1. **Knights Templars.** Group of crusaders from the thirteenth century

Words For Everyday Use	con • tig • u • ous (kən tig′ yo͞o əs) *adj.*, near, adjacent
	ef • fer • ves • cence (ef′ər ves′əns) *n.*, lively, high-spirited state

science, and, so far as peaceful exercise would teach them, the practices of war. The high estimation then placed upon the military character might be seen in the lofty port of each individual member of the company. Some of them, indeed, by their services in the Low Countries and on other fields of European warfare, had fairly won their title to assume the name and pomp of soldiership. The entire array, moreover, clad in burnished steel, and with plumage nodding over their bright morions,[2] had a brilliancy of effect which no modern display can <u>aspire</u> to equal.

And yet the men of civil eminence, who came immediately behind the military escort, were better worth a thoughtful observer's eye. Even in outward demeanor they showed a stamp of majesty that made the warrior's haughty stride look vulgar, if not absurd. It was an age when what we call talent had far less consideration than now, but the massive materials which produce stability and dignity of character a great deal more. The people possessed, by hereditary right, the quality of reverence; which, in their descendants, if it survive at all, exists in smaller proportion, and with a vastly diminished force in the selection and estimate of public men. The change may be for good or ill, and is partly, perhaps, for both. In that old day, the English settler on these rude shores—having left king, nobles, and all degrees of awful rank behind, while still the faculty and necessity of reverence was strong in him—bestowed it on the white hair and venerable brow of age; on long-tried integrity; on solid wisdom and sad-colored experience; on endowments of that grave and weighty order, which gives the idea of permanence, and comes under the general definition of respectability. These primitive statesmen, therefore—Bradstreet, Endicott, Dudley, Bellingham, and their compeers—who were elevated to power by the early choice of the people,

▶ *What qualities were important in Puritan leaders?*

seem to have been not often brilliant, but distinguished by a ponderous sobriety, rather than activity of intellect. They had <u>fortitude</u> and self-reliance, and, in time of difficulty or peril, stood up for the welfare of the state like a line of cliffs against a tempestuous tide. The traits of character here

---

2. **morions.** Helmets

Words For Everyday Use	**as • pire** (ə spīr´) *vi.*, seek **for • ti • tude** (fôrt´ə tōōd´) *n.*, strength to bear pain and misfortune

indicated were well represented in the square cast of counte-nance and large physical development of the new colonial magistrates. So far as a demeanor of natural authority was concerned, the mother country need not have been ashamed to see these foremost men of an actual democracy adopted into the House of Peers, or made the Privy Council of the Sovereign.

Next in order to the magistrates came the young and emi-nently distinguished divine, from whose lips the religious discourse of the anniversary was expected. His was the pro-fession, at that era, in which intellectual ability displayed itself far more than in political life; for—leaving a higher motive out of the question—it offered inducements power-ful enough, in the almost worshipping respect of the com-munity, to win the most aspiring ambition into its service. Even political power—as in the case of Increase Mather[3] was within the grasp of a successful priest.

◄ What advantages were there to follow-ing the religious pro-fession in Puritan times?

It was the observation of those who beheld him now, that never, since Mr. Dimmesdale first set his foot on the New England shore, had he exhibited such energy as was seen in the gait and air with which he kept his pace in the proces-sion. There was no feebleness of step, as at other times; his frame was not bent; nor did his hand rest ominously upon his heart. Yet, if the clergyman were rightly viewed, his strength seemed not of the body. It might be spiritual, and imparted to him by angelical ministrations. It might be the exhilaration of that potent cordial, which is distilled only in the furnace-glow of earnest and long-continued thought. Or, perchance, his sensitive temperament was invigorated by the loud and piercing music, that swelled heavenward, and uplifted him on its ascending wave. Nevertheless, so abstracted was his look, it might be questioned whether Mr. Dimmesdale even heard the music. There was his body, mov-ing onward, and with an unaccustomed force. But where was his mind? Far and deep in its own region, busying itself, with preternatural activity, to marshal a procession of stately thoughts that were soon to issue thence; and so he saw noth-ing, heard nothing, knew nothing, of what was around him; but the spiritual element took up the feeble frame, and car-ried it along, unconscious of the burden, and converting it to spirit like itself. Men of uncommon intellect, who have grown morbid, possess this occasional power of mighty effort, into which they throw the life of many days, and then are lifeless for as many more.

◄ In what way does Dimmesdale appear different to the townspeople?

---

3. **Increase Mather.** (1639–1723) Influential Puritan minister of early New England who helped negotiate a new charter for the Massachusetts Bay Colony

► Why can Hester
scarcely forgive
Dimmesdale?

Hester Prynne, gazing steadfastly at the clergyman, felt a
dreary influence come over her, but wherefore or whence
she knew not; unless that he seemed so remote from her
own sphere, and utterly beyond her reach. One glance of
recognition, she had imagined, must needs pass between
them. She thought of the dim forest, with its little dell of
solitude, and love, and anguish, and the mossy tree-trunk,
where, sitting hand-in-hand, they had mingled their sad
and passionate talk with the melancholy murmur of the
brook. How deeply had they known each other then! And
was this the man? She hardly knew him now! He, moving
proudly past, enveloped, as it were, in the rich music, with
the procession of majestic and venerable fathers; he, so
unattainable in his worldly position, and still more so in
that far vista of his unsympathizing thoughts, through
which she now beheld him! Her spirit sank with the idea
that all must have been a delusion, and that, vividly as she
had dreamed it, there could be no real bond betwixt the
clergyman and herself. And thus much of woman was there
in Hester, that she could scarcely forgive him—least of all
now, when the heavy footstep of their approaching Fate
might be heard, nearer, nearer, nearer!—for being able so
completely to withdraw himself from their mutual world;
while she groped darkly, and stretched forth her cold hands,
and found him not.

Pearl either saw and responded to her mother's feelings, or
herself felt the remoteness and intangibility that had fallen
around the minister. While the procession passed, the child
was uneasy, fluttering up and down, like a bird on the point
of taking flight. When the whole had gone by, she looked up
into Hester's face.

"Mother," said she, "was that the same minister that
kissed me by the brook?"

"Hold thy peace, dear little Pearl!" whispered her mother.
"We must not always talk in the market-place of what happens to us in the forest."

► What would Pearl
have done if the min-
ister had not looked
so strange? What
does Pearl think the
minister would have
done?

"I could not be sure that it was he; so strange he looked,"
continued the child. "Else I would have run to him, and bid
him kiss me now, before all the people; even as he did yonder among the dark old trees. What would the minister have
said, mother? Would he have clapped his hand over his
heart, and scowled on me, and bid me begone?"

"What should he say, Pearl," answered Hester, "save that
it was no time to kiss, and that kisses are not to be given in
the market-place? Well for thee, foolish child, that thou didst
not speak to him!"

Another shade of the same sentiment, in reference to Mr. Dimmesdale, was expressed by a person whose <u>eccentricities</u>—or insanity, as we should term it—led her to do what few of the townspeople would have ventured on; to begin a conversation with the wearer of the scarlet letter, in public. It was Mistress Hibbins, who, arrayed in great magnificence, with a triple ruff, a broidered stomacher, a gown of rich velvet, and a gold-headed cane, had come forth to see the procession. As this ancient lady had the renown (which subsequently cost her no less a price than her life) of being a principal actor in all the works of necromancy[4] that were continually going forward, the crowd gave way before her, and seemed to fear the touch of her garment, as if it carried the plague among its gorgeous folds. Seen in conjunction with Hester Prynne—kindly as so many now felt towards the latter—the dread inspired by Mistress Hibbins was doubled, and caused a general movement from that part of the market-place in which the two women stood.

◄ What does Mistress Hibbins do that few townspeople would do?

"Now, what mortal imagination could conceive it!" whispered the old lady confidentially to Hester. "Yonder divine man! That saint on earth, as the people uphold him to be, and as—I must needs say—he really looks! Who, now, that saw him pass in the procession, would think how little while it is since he went forth out of his study—chewing a Hebrew text of Scripture in his mouth, I warrant—to take an airing in the forest! Aha! we know what that means, Hester Prynne! But, truly, forsooth, I find it hard to believe him the same man. Many a church-member saw I, walking behind the music, that has danced in the same measure with me, when Somebody was fiddler, and, it might be, an Indian powwow or a Lapland wizard changing hands with us! That is but a trifle, when a woman knows the world. But this minister! Couldst thou surely tell, Hester, whether he was the same man that encountered thee on the forest-path!"

"Madam, I know not of what you speak," answered Hester Prynne, feeling Mistress Hibbins to be of infirm mind; yet strangely startled and awe-stricken by the confidence with which she affirmed a personal connection between so many

---

4. **necromancy.** Black magic

Words For Everyday Use

ec • cen • tric • i • ty (ek´sən tris´ə tē) *n.*, oddity

persons (herself among them) and the Evil One. "It is not for me to talk lightly of a learned and pious minister of the Word, like the Reverend Mr. Dimmesdale!"

"Fie, woman, fie!" cried the old lady, shaking her finger at Hester. "Dost thou think I have been to the forest so many times, and have yet no skill to judge who else has been there? Yea; though no leaf of the wild garlands, which they wore while they danced, be left in their hair! I know thee, Hester; for I behold the token. We may all see it in the sunshine; and it glows like a red flame in the dark. Thou wearest it openly; so there need be no question about that. But this minister! Let me tell thee in thine ear! When the Black Man sees one of his own servants, signed and sealed, so shy of owning to the bond as is the Reverend Mr. Dimmesdale, he hath a way of ordering matters so that the mark shall be disclosed in open daylight to the eyes of all the world! What is that the minister seeks to hide, with his hand always over his heart? Ha, Hester Prynne!"

▶ What does Mistress Hibbins say about Dimmesdale?

"What is it, good Mistress Hibbins?" eagerly asked little Pearl. "Hast thou seen it?"

"No matter, darling!" responded Mistress Hibbins, making Pearl a profound reverence. "Thou thyself wilt see it, one time or another. They say, child, thou art of the lineage of the Prince of Air! Wilt thou ride with me, some fine night, to see thy father? Then thou shalt know wherefore the minister keeps his hand over his heart!"

Laughing so shrilly that all the market-place could hear her, the weird old gentlewoman took her departure.

By this time the preliminary prayer had been offered in the meeting-house, and the accents of the Reverend Mr. Dimmesdale were heard <u>commencing</u> his <u>discourse</u>. An irresistible feeling kept Hester near the spot. As the sacred edifice was too much thronged to admit another auditor, she took up her position close beside the scaffold of the pillory. It was in sufficient proximity to bring the whole sermon to her ears, in the shape of an indistinct, but varied, murmur and flow of the minister's very peculiar voice.

This vocal organ was in itself a rich endowment, insomuch that a listener, comprehending nothing of the language in which the preacher spoke, might still have been

---

Words
For
Everyday
Use

com • mence (kə mens´) vt., begin
dis • course (dis´kôrs´) n., lecture

---

swayed to and fro by the mere tone and cadence. Like all other music, it breathed passion and pathos, and emotions high or tender, in a tongue native to the human heart, wherever educated. Muffled as the sound was by its passage through the church walls, Hester Prynne listened with such intenseness, and sympathized so intimately, that the sermon had throughout a meaning for her, entirely apart from its indistinguishable words. These, perhaps, if more distinctly heard, might have been only a grosser medium, and have clogged the spiritual sense. Now she caught the low undertone, as of the wind sinking down to repose itself; then ascended with it, as it rose through progressive gradations of sweetness and power, until its volume seemed to envelop her with an atmosphere of awe and solemn grandeur. And yet, majestic as the voice sometimes became, there was for ever in it an essential character of plaintiveness. A loud or low expression of anguish—the whisper, or the shriek, as it might be conceived, of suffering humanity, that touched a sensibility in every bosom! At times this deep strain of pathos was all that could be heard, and scarcely heard, sighing amid a desolate silence. But even when the minister's voice grew high and commanding—when it gushed irrepressibly upward—when it assumed its utmost breadth and power, so overfilling the church as to burst its way through the solid walls, and diffuse itself in the open air—still, if the auditor listened intently, and for the purpose, he could detect the same cry of pain. What was it? The complaint of a human heart, sorrow-laden, perchance guilty, telling its secret, whether of guilt or sorrow, to the great heart of mankind; beseeching its sympathy or forgiveness—at every moment— in each accent—and never in vain! It was this profound and continual undertone that gave the clergyman his most appropriate power.

◄ Why does the sermon mean something different for Hester?

◄ What gives Dimmesdale's sermon its power?

During all this time, Hester stood, statue-like, at the foot of the scaffold. If the minister's voice had not kept her there, there would nevertheless have been an inevitable magnetism in that spot, whence she dated the first hour of her life of ignominy. There was a sense within her—too ill-defined to be made a thought, but weighing heavily on her mind—that her whole orb of life, both before and after, was connected with this spot, as with the one point that gave it unity.

Little Pearl, meanwhile, had quitted her mother's side, and was playing at her own will about the market-place. She made the somber crowd cheerful by her erratic and glistening ray; even as a bird of bright plumage illuminates a whole tree of dusky foliage by darting to and fro, half seen and half concealed, amid the twilight of the clustering leaves. She had an <u>undulating</u>, but oftentimes, a sharp and irregular movement. It indicated the restless vivacity of her spirit, which to-day was doubly indefatigable in its tiptoe dance, because it was played upon and vibrated with her mother's disquietude. Whenever Pearl saw any thing to excite her ever active and wandering curiosity, she flew thitherward, and, as we might say, seized upon that man or thing as her own property, so far as she desired it; but without yielding the minutest degree of control over her motions in requital. The Puritans looked on, and, if they smiled, were none the less inclined to pronounce the child a demon offspring, from the indescribable charm of beauty and eccentricity that shone through her little figure, and sparkled with its activity. She ran and looked the wild Indian in the face; and he grew conscious of a nature wilder than his own. Thence, with native <u>audacity</u>, but still with a reserve as characteristic, she flew into the midst of a group of mariners, the swarthy-cheeked wild men of the ocean, as the Indians were of the land; and they gazed wonderingly and admiringly at Pearl, as if a flake of the sea-foam had taken the shape of a little maid, and were gifted with a soul of the sea-fire, that flashes beneath the prow in the night-time.

One of these seafaring men—the shipmaster, indeed, who had spoken to Hester Prynne—was so smitten with Pearl's aspect, that he attempted to lay hands upon her, with purpose to snatch a kiss. Finding it as impossible to touch her as to catch a humming-bird in the air, he took from his hat the gold chain that was twisted about it, and threw it to the child. Pearl immediately twined it around her neck and waist, with such happy skill, that, once seen there, it became a part of her, and it was difficult to imagine her without it.

"Thy mother is yonder woman with the scarlet letter," said the seaman. "Wilt thou carry her a message from me?"

"If the message pleases me I will," answered Pearl.

"Then tell her," rejoined he, "that I spake again with the black-a-visaged, hump-shouldered old doctor, and he engages to bring his friend, the gentleman she wots of, aboard with him. So let thy mother take no thought, save for herself and thee. Wilt thou tell her this, thou witch-baby?"

▶ *What has Roger Chillingworth told the mariner?*

Words
For
Everyday
Use

un • du • lat • ing (un´dyo͞o lāt´ iŋ) *adj.*, wavy
au • dac • i • ty (ô das´ə tē) *n.*, shameless boldness; daring

"Mistress Hibbins says my father is the Prince of the Air!" cried Pearl, with her naughty smile. "If thou callest me that ill name, I shall tell him of thee; and he will chase thy ship with a tempest!"

Pursuing a zigzag course across the market-place, the child returned to her mother, and communicated what the mariner had said. Hester's strong, calm steadfastly enduring spirit almost sank, at last, on beholding this dark and grim countenance of an inevitable doom, which—at the moment when a passage seemed to open for the minister and herself out of their labyrinth of misery—showed itself, with an unrelenting smile, right in the midst of their path.

With her mind harassed by the terrible perplexity in which the shipmaster's intelligence involved her, she was also subjected to another trial. There were many people present, from the country roundabout, who had often heard of the scarlet letter, and to whom it had been made terrific by a hundred false or exaggerated rumors, but who had never beheld it with their own bodily eyes. These, after exhausting other modes of amusement, now thronged about Hester Prynne with rude and <u>boorish</u> intrusiveness. Unscrupulous as it was, however, it could not bring them nearer than a circuit of several yards. At that distance they accordingly stood, fixed there by the centrifugal[5] force of the repugnance which the mystic symbol inspired. The whole gang of sailors, likewise, observing the press of spectators, and learning the purport of the scarlet letter, came and thrust their sunburnt and desperado-looking faces into the ring. Even the Indians were affected by a sort of cold shadow of the white man's curiosity, and, gliding through the crowd, fastened their snake-like black eyes on Hester's bosom, conceiving, perhaps, that the wearer of this brilliantly embroidered badge must needs be a personage of high dignity among her people. Lastly, the inhabitants of the town (their own interest in this worn-out subject languidly reviving itself, by sympathy with what they saw others feel) lounged idly to the same quarter, and tormented Hester Prynne, perhaps more than all the rest, with their cool, well-

---

5. **centrifugal force.** Apparent force tending to pull a thing outward when it is rotating around a center

Words
For
Everyday
Use

boor • ish (bŏŏr´ish) *adj.*, rude, awkward

acquainted gaze at her familiar shame. Hester saw and recognized the self-same faces of that group of matrons, who had awaited her forthcoming from the prison-door, seven years ago; all save one, the youngest and only compassionate among them, whose burial-robe she had since made. At the final hour, when she was so soon to fling aside the burning letter, it had strangely become the center of more remark and excitement, and was thus made to sear her breast more painfully, than at any time since the first day she put it on.

While Hester stood in that magic circle of ignominy, where the cunning cruelty of her sentence seemed to have fixed her for ever, the admirable preacher was looking down from the sacred pulpit upon an audience, whose very inmost spirits had yielded to his control. The sainted minister in the church! The woman of the scarlet letter in the marketplace! What imagination would have been irreverent enough to surmise that the same scorching stigma was on them both?

► *What ironic event occurs "at the final hour"?*

► *What does the narrator's question imply?*

Responding to the Selection

"The sainted minister in the church! The woman of the scarlet letter in the market place! What imagination would have been irreverent enough to surmise that the same scorching stigma was on them both?" How must Hester feel as Dimmesdale walks by her without so much as a look, or as people look at Dimmesdale as if he were a saint? What were your feelings toward Hester, Dimmesdale, and the crowd as you read chapters 21 and 22?

Reviewing the Selection

Recalling and Interpreting

1. **R:** What is Hester's mood as she and Pearl arrive to celebrate Election Day? What instructions does she give Pearl for the time when Dimmesdale arrives?

2. **I:** What is the reason for Hester's mood as she arrives to celebrate Election Day? What does Pearl observe about Dimmesdale?

3. **R:** What news does the commander of the vessel give to Hester?

4. **I:** How does the commander's news affect Hester? What might Chillingworth's smile from across the public square mean?

5. **R:** When the Election Day procession begins, what does Hester expect from Dimmesdale as he walks by her? What does Pearl ask her mother about Dimmesdale?

6. **I:** How does Hester feel as Dimmesdale walks by her? Why does Pearl not recognize Dimmesdale?

7. **R:** What does Hester hear in Dimmesdale's speech? What does the captain of the ship tell Pearl?

8. **I:** What are Hester's feelings as she stands in the crowd listening to Dimmesdale and thinking about her plans? What happens to her spirits?

Synthesizing

9. What events on Election Day shake Hester's confidence in the future that she and Dimmesdale have planned? In what way has she lost control of the situation?

10. What acknowledgment does Pearl want Dimmesdale to make and before whom? What would be the practical consequences if Dimmesdale did such a thing? What would be the spiritual or moral consequences?

Understanding Literature (QUESTIONS FOR DISCUSSION)

1. Setting. The **setting** of a literary work is the time and place in which it occurs, together with all the details used to create a sense of a particular time and place. In the beginning of chapter 21, Hawthorne presents many details about Puritans as they gather for Election Day. What information does he give the reader about how Puritans dressed as opposed to how Native Americans and sailors dressed? What information does he give about a Puritan's willingness to show excitement, friendliness, or joy? Is Hawthorne critical of Puritan ways? Is he also sympathetic? Cite passages from the text as evidence to support your views.

2. Suspense. Suspense is a feeling of expectation, anxiousness, or curiosity created by questions raised in the mind of a reader or viewer. Chapters 21 and 22 contain many moments of suspense. These moments cause the reader to ask the following questions: Will Dimmesdale follow his heart and go to Europe with Hester? Will Chillingworth be on the ship with them, and if so, does he intend to terrorize the couple indefinitely? Will Pearl come to accept Dimmesdale as her father? What specific moments in the two chapters raise these questions? What other questions are raised in your mind?

3. Foreshadowing. Foreshadowing is the act of presenting materials that hint at events to occur later in a story. Discuss the final appearance of Mistress Hibbins. What does she tell Hester? What does Hester say in response? What might Mistress Hibbins be predicting?

XXIII

The Revelation of the Scarlet Letter

The eloquent voice, on which the souls of the listening audience had been borne aloft, as on the swelling waves of the sea, at length came to a pause. There was a momentary silence, profound as what should follow the utterance of oracles. Then ensued a murmur and half-hushed tumult; as if the auditors, released from the high spell that had transported them into the region of another's mind, were returning into themselves, with all their awe and wonder still heavy on them. In a moment more, the crowd began to gush forth from the doors of the church. Now that there was an end, they needed other breath, more fit to support the gross and earthly life into which they relapsed, than that atmosphere which the preacher had converted into words of flame, and had burdened with the rich fragrance of his thought.

In the open air their rapture broke into speech. The street and the market-place absolutely babbled, from side to side, with applauses of the minister. His hearers could not rest until they had told one another of what each knew better than he could tell or hear. According to their united testimony, never had man spoken in so wise, so high, and so holy a spirit, as he that spake this day; nor had inspiration ever breathed through mortal lips more evidently than it did through his. Its influence could be seen, as it were, descending upon him, and possessing him, and continually lifting him out of the written discourse that lay before him, and filling him with ideas that must have been as marvelous to himself as to his audience. His subject, it appeared, had been the relation between the Deity and the communities of mankind, with a special reference to the New England which they were here planting in the wilderness. And, as he drew towards the close, a spirit as of prophecy had come upon him, constraining him to its purpose as mightily as the old prophets of Israel were constrained; only with this difference, that, whereas the Jewish seers had denounced judgments and ruin on their country, it was his mission to foretell a high and glorious destiny for the newly gathered people of the Lord. But, throughout it all, and through the whole discourse, there had been a certain deep, sad undertone of pathos, which could not be interpreted otherwise than as the natural regret of one soon to pass away. Yes; their minister whom they so

◄ *What do the townspeople think of Dimmesdale's sermon?*

◄ *What do the townspeople think the sad undertone in Dimmesdale's sermon means?*

loved—and who so loved them all, that he could not depart heavenward without a sigh—had the foreboding of untimely death upon him, and would soon leave them in their tears! This idea of his transitory stay on earth gave the last emphasis to the effect which the preacher had produced; it was if an angel, in his passage to the skies, had shaken his bright wings over the people for an instant—at once a shadow and a splendor—and had shed down a shower of golden truths upon them.   .

Thus, there had come to the Reverend Mr. Dimmesdale—as to most men, in their various spheres, though seldom recognized until they see it far behind them—an epoch of life more brilliant and full of triumph than any previous one, or than any which could hereafter be. He stood, at this moment, on the very proudest eminence of superiority, to which the gifts of intellect, rich lore, prevailing eloquence, and a reputation of whitest sanctity, could exalt a clergyman in New England's earliest days, when the professional character was of itself a lofty pedestal. Such was the position which the minister occupied, as he bowed his head forward on the cushions of the pulpit, at the close of his Election Sermon. Meanwhile, Hester Prynne was standing beside the scaffold of the pillory, with the scarlet letter still burning on her breast!

▶ What is Dimmesdale's social position at this moment?

▶ How does Hester's position contrast with Dimmesdale's?

Now was heard again the clangor of the music, and the measured tramp of the military escort, issuing from the church-door. The procession was to be marshaled thence to the town-hall, where a solemn banquet would complete the ceremonies of the day.

Once more, therefore, the train of venerable and majestic fathers was seen moving through a broad pathway of the people, who drew back reverently, on either side, as the Governor and magistrates, the old and wise men, the holy ministers, and all that were eminent and renowned, advanced into the midst of them. When they were fairly in the market-place, their presence was greeted by a shout. This—though doubtless it might acquire additional force and volume from the childlike loyalty which the age awarded to its rulers—was felt to be an irrepressible outburst of enthusiasm kindled in the auditors by that high strain of eloquence which was yet reverberating in their ears. Each felt the impulse in himself, and, in the same breath, caught it from his neighbor. Within the church, it had hardly been kept down; beneath the sky, it pealed upward to the zenith. There were human beings enough, and enough of highly wrought and symphonious feeling, to produce that more impressive sound than the organ tones of the blast, or the thunder, or the roar of the sea; even that mighty swell of many voices, blended into one great voice by the universal impulse which makes likewise one vast heart out of the many. Never, from the soil of New England, had gone up such a shout! Never, on New England soil, had stood the man so honored by his mortal brethren as the preacher!

How fared it with him then? Were there not the brilliant particles of a halo in the air about his head? So etherealized by spirit as he was, and so apotheosized[1] by worshipping admirers, did his footsteps in the procession really tread upon the dust of earth?

As the ranks of military men and civil fathers moved onward, all eyes were turned towards the point where the minister was seen to approach among them. The shout died into a murmur, as one portion of the crowd after another obtained a glimpse of him. How feeble and pale he looked amid all his triumph! The energy—or say, rather, the inspiration which had held him up, until he should have delivered the sacred message that had brought its own strength along with it from heaven—was withdrawn, now that it had so faithfully performed its office. The glow, which they had just before beheld burning on his cheek, was extinguished, like a flame that sinks down hopelessly among the late-decaying embers. It seemed hardly the face of a man alive, with such a deathlike hue: it was hardly a man with life in him, that tottered on his path so nervously, yet tottered, and did not fall!

◄ *In what way has Dimmesdale's appearance changed once again?*

One of his clerical brethren—it was the venerable John Wilson—observing the state in which Mr. Dimmesdale was left by the retiring wave of intellect and sensibility, stepped forward hastily to offer his support. The minister tremulously, but decidedly, repelled the old man's arm. He still walked onward, if that movement could be so described, which rather resembled the wavering effort of an infant, with its mother's arms in view, outstretched to tempt him forward. And now, almost <u>imperceptible</u> as were the latter steps of his progress, he had come opposite the well-remembered and weather-darkened scaffold, where, long since, with all that dreary lapse of time between, Hester Prynne had encountered

◄ *Where does the minister pause?*

---

1. **apotheosized.** Glorified; idealized; deified

Words
For
Everyday
Use

im • per • cep • ti • ble (im´pər sep´tə bəl) *adj.*, not easily noticed the world's ignominious stare. There stood Hester, holding little Pearl by the hand! And there was the scarlet letter on her breast! The minister here made a pause; although the music still played the stately and rejoicing march to which the procession moved. It summoned him onward—onward to the festival!—but here he made a pause.

Bellingham, for the last few moments, had kept an anxious eye upon him. He now left his own place in the procession, and advanced to give assistance; judging from Mr. Dimmesdale's aspect that he must otherwise <u>inevitably</u> fall. But there was something in the latter's expression that warned back the magistrate, although a man not readily obeying the vague <u>intimations</u> that pass from one spirit to another. The crowd, meanwhile, looked on with awe and wonder. This earthly faintness was, in their view, only another phase of the minister's celestial strength; nor would it have seemed a miracle too high to be wrought for one so holy, had he ascended before their eyes, waxing dimmer and brighter, and fading at last into the light of heaven!

He turned towards the scaffold, and stretched forth his arms.

"Hester," said he, "come hither! Come, my little Pearl!"

It was a ghastly look with which he regarded them; but there was something at once tender and strangely triumphant in it. The child, with the bird-like motion which was one of her characteristics, flew to him, and clasped her arms about his knees. Hester Prynne—slowly, as if impelled by inevitable fate, and against her strongest will—likewise drew near, but paused before she reached him. At this instant old Roger Chillingworth thrust himself through the crowd—or, perhaps, so dark, disturbed, and evil was his look, he rose up out of some nether region—to snatch back his victim from what he sought to do! Be that as it might, the old man rushed forward, and caught the minister by the arm.

"Madman, hold! What is your purpose?" whispered he. "Wave back that woman! Cast off this child! All shall be well! Do not blacken your fame, and perish in dishonor! I can yet save you! Would you bring infamy on your sacred profession?"

"Ha, tempter! Methinks thou art too late!" answered the minister, encountering his eye, fearfully, but firmly. "Thy

> ► What does the crowd almost expect the minister to do?

> ► What does the minister do? How does the minister appear?

> ► What does Roger Chillingworth try to do? Why?

Words For Everyday Use

in • ev • i • ta • bly (in ev´i tə blē) *adv.*, unavoidably

in • ti • ma • tion (in´tə mā´shən) *n.*, hint; indirect suggestion power is not what it was! With God's help, I shall escape thee now!"

He again extended his hand to the woman of the scarlet letter.

"Hester Prynne," cried he, with a piercing earnestness, "in the name of Him, so terrible and so merciful, who gives me grace, at this last moment, to do what—for my own heavy sin and miserable agony—I withheld myself from doing seven years ago, come hither now, and twine thy strength about me! Thy strength, Hester; but let it be guided by the will which God hath granted me! This wretched and wronged old man is opposing it with all his might!—with all his own might and the fiend's! Come, Hester—come! Support me up yonder scaffold!"

◀ Where does Dimmesdale ask Hester to lead him?

The crowd was in a tumult. The men of rank and dignity, who stood more immediately around the clergyman, were so taken by surprise, and so perplexed as to the purport of what they saw—unable to receive the explanation which most readily presented itself, or to imagine any other—that they remained silent and inactive spectators of the judgement which Providence seemed about to work. They beheld the minister, leaning on Hester's shoulder, and supported by her arm around him, approach the scaffold, and ascend its steps; while still the little hand of the sin-born child was clasped in his. Old Roger Chillingworth followed, as one intimately connected with the drama of guilt and sorrow in which they had all been actors, and well entitled, therefore, to be present at its closing scene.

"Hadst thou sought the whole earth over," said he looking darkly at the clergyman, "there was no one place so secret— no high place nor lowly place, where thou couldst have escaped me—save on this very scaffold!"

◀ What does Chillingworth say about the scaffold?

"Thanks be to Him who hath led me hither!" answered the minister.

Yet he trembled, and turned to Hester with an expression of doubt and anxiety in his eyes, not the less evidently betrayed, that there was a feeble smile upon his lips.

"Is not this better," murmured he, "than what we dreamed of in the forest?"

◀ What does Dimmesdale ask Hester? Does she agree with him?

"I know not! I know not!" she hurriedly replied. "Better? Yea; so we may both die, and little Pearl die with us!"

"For thee and Pearl, be it as God shall order," said the minister; "and God is merciful! Let me now do the will which he hath made plain before my sight. For, Hester, I am a dying man. So let me make haste to take my shame upon me."

Partly supported by Hester Prynne, and holding one hand

of little Pearl's, the Reverend Mr. Dimmesdale turned to the dignified and venerable rulers; to the holy ministers, who were his brethren; to the people, whose great heart was thoroughly appalled, yet overflowing with tearful sympathy, as knowing that some deep life-matter—which, if full of sin, was full of anguish and repentance likewise—was now to be laid open to them. The sun, but little past its meridian, shone down upon the clergyman, and gave a distinctness to his figure, as he stood out from all the earth to put in his plea of guilty at the bar of Eternal Justice.

► What does Dimmesdale claim to be?

"People of New England!" cried he, with a voice that rose over them, high, solemn, and majestic—yet had always a tremor through it, and sometimes a shriek, struggling up out of a <u>fathomless</u> depth of remorse and woe—"ye, that have loved me!—ye, that have deemed me holy!—behold me here, the one sinner of the world! At last!—at last!—I stand upon the spot where, seven years since, I should have stood; here, with this woman, whose arm, more than the little strength wherewith I have crept hitherward, sustains me, at this dreadful moment, from groveling down upon my face! Lo, the scarlet letter which Hester wears! Ye have all shuddered at it! Wherever her walk hath been—wherever, so miserably burdened, she may have hoped to find repose—it hath cast a lurid gleam of awe and horrible repugnance roundabout her. But there stood one in the midst of you, at whose brand of sin and infamy ye have not shuddered!"

It seemed, at this point, as if the minister must leave the remainder of his secret undisclosed. But he fought back the bodily weakness—and, still more, the faintness of heart—that was striving for the mastery with him. He threw off all assistance, and stepped passionately forward a pace before the woman and the child.

"It was on him!" he continued, with a kind of fierceness; so determined was he to speak out the whole. "God's eye beheld it! The angels were for ever pointing at it! The Devil knew it well, and fretted it continually with the touch of his burning finger! But he hid it cunningly from men, and walked among you with the mien of a spirit, mournful, because so pure in a sinful world!—and sad, because he missed his heavenly kindred! Now, at the death-hour, he

Words For Everyday Use

fath • om • less (fath´əm lis) *adj.*, incomprehensible, very deep stands up before you! He bids you look again at Hester's scarlet letter! He tells you, that, with all its mysterious horror, it is but the shadow of what he bears on his own breast, and that even this, his own red stigma, is no more than the type of what has seared his inmost heart! Stand any here that question God's judgment on a sinner? Behold! Behold a dreadful witness of it!"

◄ What do you think Dimmesdale reveals?

With a convulsive motion, he tore away the ministerial band from before his breast. It was revealed! But it were irreverent to describe that revelation. For an instant the gaze of the horror-stricken multitude was concentrated on the ghastly miracle; while the minister stood with a flush of triumph in his face, as one who, in the crisis of acutest pain, had won a victory. Then, down he sank upon the scaffold! Hester partly raised him, and supported his head against her bosom. Old Roger Chillingworth knelt down beside him, with a blank, dull countenance, out of which the life seemed to have departed.

◄ How does Roger Chillingworth look once he knows the minister is dying?

"Thou hast escaped me!" he repeated more than once. "Thou hast escaped me!"

"May God forgive thee!" said the minister. "Thou, too, hast deeply sinned!"

He withdrew his dying eyes from the old man, and fixed them on the woman and the child.

"My little Pearl," said he feebly, and there was a sweet and gentle smile over his face, as of a spirit sinking into deep repose; nay, now that the burden was removed, it seemed almost as if he would be sportive with the child—"dear little Pearl, wilt thou kiss me now? Thou wouldst not, yonder, in the forest! But now thou wilt?"

◄ What does the minister ask Pearl?

Pearl kissed his lips. A spell was broken. The great scene of grief, in which the wild infant bore a part, had developed all her sympathies; and as her tears fell upon her father's cheek, they were the pledge that she would grow up amid human joy and sorrow, nor for ever do battle with the world, but be a woman in it. Towards her mother, too, Pearl's errand as a messenger of anguish was fulfilled.

◄ In what way does this scene affect Pearl?

"Hester," said the clergyman, "farewell!"

"Shall we not meet again?" whispered she, bending her face down close to his. "Shall we not spend our immortal life together? Surely, surely, we have ransomed one another, with all this woe! Thou lookest far into eternity, with those bright dying eyes! Then tell me what thou seest!"

"Hush, Hester, hush!" said he, with tremulous solemnity. "The law we broke!—the sin here awfully revealed!—let these alone be in thy thoughts! I fear! I fear! It may be, that, when

◄ What does Hester ask the minister? What is his response?

we forgot our God—when we violated our reverence each for the other's soul—it was thenceforth vain to hope that we could meet hereafter, in an everlasting and pure reunion. God knows; and He is merciful! He hath proved his mercy, most of all, in my afflictions. By giving me this burning torture to bear upon my breast! By sending yonder dark and terrible old man, to keep the torture always at red-heat! By bringing me hither, to die this death of triumphant ignominy before the people! Had either of these agonies been wanting, I had been lost for ever! Praised be his name! His will be done! Farewell!"

That final word came forth with the minister's expiring breath. The multitude, silent till then, broke out in a strange, deep voice of awe and wonder, which could not as yet find utterance, save in this murmur that rolled so heavily after the departed spirit.

XXIV

Conclusion

After many days, when time sufficed for the people to arrange their thoughts in reference to the foregoing scene, there was more than one account of what had been witnessed on the scaffold.

Most of the spectators testified to having seen, on the breast of the unhappy minister, a SCARLET LETTER—the very semblance of that worn by Hester Prynne—imprinted in the flesh. As regarded its origin, there were various explanations, all of which must necessarily have been conjectural. Some affirmed that the Reverend Mr. Dimmesdale, on the very day when Hester Prynne first wore her ignominious badge, had begun a course of penance—which he afterwards, in so many futile methods, followed out—by inflicting a hideous torture on himself. Others contended that the stigma had not been produced until a long time subsequent, when old Roger Chillingworth, being a potent necromancer, had caused it to appear, through the agency of magic and poisonous drugs. Others, again—and those best able to appreciate the minister's peculiar sensibility, and the wonderful operation of his spirit upon the body—whispered their belief, that the awful symbol was the effect of the ever active tooth of remorse, gnawing from the inmost heart outwardly, and at last manifesting Heaven's dreadful judgment by the visible presence of the letter. The reader may choose among these theories. We have thrown all the light we could acquire upon the portent, and would gladly, now that it has done its office, erase its deep print out of our own brain; where long meditation has fixed it in very undesirable distinctness.

It is singular, nevertheless, that certain persons, who were spectators of the whole scene, and professed never once to have removed their eyes from the Reverend Mr. Dimmesdale, denied that there was any mark whatever on his breast, more than on a new-born infant's. Neither, by their report, had his dying words acknowledged, nor even remotely implied, any, the slightest connection, on his part, with the guilt for which Hester Prynne had so long worn the scarlet letter. According to these highly respectable witnesses, the minister, conscious that he was dying—conscious, also, that the reverence of the multitude placed him already among saints and angels—had desired, by yielding up his breath in the

◄ *About what did most of the spectators agree?*

◄ *What different explanations for the letter do people consider?*

◄ *What do "certain persons" say about the scene?*

arms of that fallen woman, to express to the world how utterly <u>nugatory</u> is the choicest of man's own righteousness. After exhausting life in his efforts for mankind's spiritual good, he had made the manner of his death a parable, in order to impress on his admirers the mighty and mournful lesson, that, in the view of Infinite Purity, we are sinners all alike. It was to teach them, that the holiest among us has but attained so far above his fellows as to discern more clearly the Mercy which looks down, and repudiate more utterly the phantom of human merit, which would look aspiringly upward. Without disputing a truth so momentous, we must be allowed to consider this version of Mr. Dimmesdale's story as only an instance of that stubborn fidelity with which a man's friends—and especially a clergyman's—will sometimes uphold his character; when proofs, clear as the mid-day sunshine on the scarlet letter, establish him a false and sin-stained creature of the dust.

▶ *What explanation do these people provide for Dimmesdale's actions?*

▶ *In what way does the narrator view these friends of Dimmesdale?*

The authority which we have chiefly followed—a manuscript of old date, drawn up from the verbal testimony of individuals, some of whom had known Hester Prynne, while others had heard the tale from contemporary witnesses—fully confirms the view taken in the foregoing pages. Among many morals which press upon us from the poor minister's miserable experience, we put only this into a sentence:—"Be true! Be true! Be true! Show freely to the world, if not your worst, yet some trait whereby the worst may be inferred!"

▶ *What is the moral of the story, according to the narrator?*

Nothing was more remarkable than the change which took place, almost immediately after Mr. Dimmesdale's death, in the appearance and demeanor of the old man known as Roger Chillingworth. All his strength and energy—all his vital and intellectual force—seemed at once to desert him; insomuch that he positively withered up, shriveled away, and almost vanished from mortal sight, like an uprooted weed that lies wilting in the sun. This unhappy man had made the very principle of his life to consist in the pursuit and systematic exercise of revenge; and when, by its completest triumph and consummation, that evil principle was left with no further material to support it—when, in short, there was no more devil's work on earth for him to do, it only remained for the unhumanized mortal to betake himself whither his Master would find him tasks enough, and pay

▶ *Why does Roger Chillingworth die not long after Dimmesdale?*

Words For Everyday Use

nu • ga • to • ry (nōō´gə tôr´ē) *adj.,* worthless

him his wages duly. But, to all these shadowy beings, so long our near acquaintances—as well Roger Chillingworth as his companions—we would fain be merciful. It is a curious subject of observation and inquiry, whether hatred and love be not the same thing at bottom. Each, in its utmost development, supposes a high degree of intimacy and heart-knowledge; each renders one individual dependent for the food of his affections and spiritual life upon another; each leaves the passionate lover, or the no less passionate hater, forlorn and desolate by the withdrawal of his subject. Philosophically considered, therefore, the two passions seem essentially the same, except that one happens to be seen in a celestial radiance, and the other in a dusky and lurid glow. In the spiritual world, the old physician and the minister—mutual victims as they have been—may, unawares, have found their earthly stock of hatred and antipathy <u>transmuted</u> into golden love.

Leaving this discussion apart, we have a matter of business to communicate to the reader. At old Roger Chillingworth's decease (which took place within the year), and by his last will and testament, of which Governor Bellingham and the Reverend Mr. Wilson were executors, he bequeathed a very considerable amount of property, both here and in England to little Pearl, the daughter of Hester Prynne.

◄ *What does Chillingworth leave to Pearl? In what way does this change people's attitudes towards Pearl?*

So Pearl—the elf-child—the demon offspring, as some people, up to that epoch, persisted in considering her—became the richest heiress of her day, in the New World. Not improbably, this circumstance wrought a very material change in the public estimation; and had the mother and child remained here, little Pearl, at a marriageable period of life, might have mingled her wild blood with the lineage of the devoutest Puritan among them all. But, in no long time after the physician's death, the wearer of the scarlet letter disappeared, and Pearl along with her. For many years, though a vague report would now and then find its way across the sea—like a shapeless piece of driftwood tossed ashore, with the initials of a name upon it—yet no tidings of them unquestionably authentic were received. The story of the scarlet letter grew into a legend. Its spell, however, was still potent, and kept the scaffold awful where the poor minister had died, and likewise the cottage by the sea-shore, where

Words For Everyday Use   **trans • mute** (trans myōōt´) *vi.,* transform

► Who returns to the cottage many years later?

Hester Prynne had dwelt. Near this latter spot, one afternoon, some children were at play, when they beheld a tall woman, in a gray robe, approach the cottage-door. In all those years it had never once been opened; but either she unlocked it, or the decaying wood and iron yielded to her hand, or she glided shadow-like through these impediments—and, at all events, went in.

On the threshold she paused—turned partly round—for, perchance, the idea of entering, all alone, and all so changed, the home of so intense a former life, was more dreary and desolate than even she could bear. But her hesitation was only for an instant, though long enough to display a scarlet letter on her breast.

And Hester Prynne had returned, and taken up her long-forsaken shame. But where was little Pearl? If still alive, she must now have been in the flush and bloom of early womanhood. None knew—nor ever learned, with the fullness of perfect certainty—whether the elf-child had gone thus untimely to a maiden grave; or whether her wild, rich nature had been softened and subdued and made capable of a woman's gentle happiness. But, through the remainder of Hester's life, there were indications that the recluse of the scarlet letter was the object of love and interest with some inhabitant of another land. Letters came, with armorial seals upon them, though of bearings unknown to English heraldry. In the cottage there were articles of comfort and luxury, such as Hester never cared to use, but which only wealth could have purchased, and affection have imagined for her. There were trifles, too, little ornaments, beautiful tokens of a continual remembrance, that must have been wrought by delicate fingers, at the impulse of a fond heart. And, once, Hester was seen embroidering a baby-garment, with such a lavish richness of golden fancy as would have raised a public tumult, had any infant, thus apparelled, been shown to our somber-hued community.

► What probably has become of Pearl?

In fine, the gossips of that day believed—and Mr. Surveyor Pue, who made investigations a century later, believed—and one of his recent successors in office, moreover, faithfully believes—that Pearl was not only alive, but married, and happy, and mindful of her mother; and that she would most joyfully have entertained that sad and lonely mother at her fireside.

But there was a more real life for Hester Prynne, here, in New England, than in that unknown region where Pearl had found a home. Here had been her sin; here, her sorrow; and here was yet to be her penitence. She had returned, therefore, and resumed—of her own free will, for not the sternest magistrate of that iron period would have imposed it—resumed

► What does Hester do voluntarily?

the symbol of which we have related so dark a tale. Never afterwards did it quit her bosom. But, in the lapse of the toilsome, thoughtful, and self-devoted years that made up Hester's life, the scarlet letter ceased to be a stigma which attracted the world's scorn and bitterness, and became a type of something to be sorrowed over, and looked upon with awe, yet with reverence too. And, as Hester Prynne had no selfish ends, nor lived in any measure for her own profit and enjoyment, people brought all their sorrows and perplexities, and besought her counsel, as one who had herself gone through a mighty trouble. Women, more especially—in the continually recurring trials of wounded, wasted, wronged, misplaced, or erring and sinful passion—or with the dreary burden of a heart unyielded, because unvalued and unsought—came to Hester's cottage, demanding why they were so wretched, and what the remedy! Hester comforted and counseled them, as best she might. She assured them, too, of her firm belief, that, at some brighter period, when the world should have grown ripe for it, in Heaven's own time, a new truth would be revealed, in order to establish the whole relation between man and woman on a surer ground of mutual happiness. Earlier in life, Hester had vainly imagined that she herself might be the destined prophetess, but had long since recognized the impossibility that any mission of divine and mysterious truth should be confided to a woman stained with sin, bowed down with shame, or even burdened with a life-long sorrow. The angel and apostle of the coming revelation must be a woman, indeed, but lofty, pure, and beautiful; and wise, moreover, not through dusky grief, but the ethereal medium of joy; and showing how sacred love should make us happy, by the truest test of a life successful to such an end!

So said Hester Prynne, and glanced her sad eyes downward at the scarlet letter. And, after many, many years, a new grave was delved, near an old and sunken one, in that burial-ground beside which King's Chapel has since been built. It was near that old and sunken grave, yet with a space between, as if the dust of the two sleepers had no right to mingle. Yet one tombstone served for both. All around, there were monuments carved with armorial bearings; and on this simple slab of slate—as the curious investigator may still discern, and perplex himself with the purport—there appeared the semblance of an engraved escutcheon.[1] It bore a device, a herald's wording of which may serve for a motto and brief description of our now concluded legend; so somber is it, and relieved only by one ever-glowing point of light gloomier than the shadow:—

"ON A FIELD, SABLE, THE LETTER A, GULES."[2]

---

1. **escutcheon.** Shield
2. **"On a field . . . gules."** On a black background, the letter *A*, in red

◀ In what way do others now view the scarlet letter?

◀ What role does Hester now play in her society?

◀ What prophecy does Hester make?

◀ Near whom was Hester buried?

Responding to the Selection

"Among many morals that press upon us from the poor minister's miserable experience, we put only this into a sentence—'Be true! Be true! Be true! Show freely to the world, if not your worst, yet some trait whereby the worst may be inferred!'" Discuss this moral. Did you learn this lesson from the minister's experience? Can you think of any other lessons that might be derived from this story?

Reviewing the Selection

Recalling and Interpreting

1. **R:** What is the public's opinion of Dimmesdale after he gives his Election Day sermon?

2. **I:** What injustice is there in the crowd's reaction to Dimmesdale, given that Hester stands as an outcast by the scaffold, marked with the scarlet *A*?

3. **R:** What does Dimmesdale reveal to the crowd? What happens to him soon after this revelation? What does he ask of God?

4. **I:** Why does Dimmesdale fear that he and Hester will not spend eternity together? Why does Pearl finally kiss Dimmesdale? What has he at last proved to her?

5. **R:** What does Chillingworth say to Dimmesdale as the minister stands at the scaffold and calls for Hester and Pearl?

6. **I:** What has been Chillingworth's purpose in life since he first spoke with Hester in her jail cell? Why does Chillingworth so strongly oppose Dimmesdale's decision? What destroys Chillingworth in the end?

7. **R:** What becomes of Hester? In what way does she eventually render service to her community?

8. **I:** Why does Hester continue to wear the scarlet letter? What does it mean to her? What does it mean to the community?

Synthesizing

9. Why is Dimmesdale unable to escape with Hester and Pearl to the Old World? Why doesn't Dimmesdale trust the idea of following one's passion? What does he lose through his secret suffering? What does Hester, on the other hand, gain from her public suffering?

10. What role does Pearl play in the action of this novel? What influence does she exert? What does she want Dimmesdale to do? In what way does she help Dimmesdale to save himself? In what way, from the narrator's point of view, is Dimmesdale saved even though he dies?

Understanding Literature (QUESTIONS FOR DISCUSSION)

1. Symbol. A **symbol** is a thing that stands for or represents both itself and something else. When Dimmesdale makes his way to the scaffold, he rejects offers of assistance from Reverend Wilson and Governor Bellingham but turns to Hester for help in this final moment. When he reveals his secret to the crowd, he does not rely on anyone for assistance, but rather steps forward on his own. What is symbolic in these actions? Why did he need to reject officials of the church and state, turn to Hester, and finally stand alone before the crowd? What is symbolic about the final kiss he receives from Pearl? Why has she accepted him at last?

2. Theme. Theme is the central idea in a literary work. What does the reader learn from the actions of the three adult main characters—Hester, Chillingworth, and Dimmesdale? What would you say is Hawthorne's main theme? Despite Hawthorne's acknowledgment of Hester and Dimmesdale's suffering and of the couple's love for one another, does he completely approve of their actions? Does Hawthorne completely accept the idea of following one's passions, or does he himself hold some Puritan ideals? Explain, using examples from chapters 23 and 24.

3. Psychological Fiction. Psychological Fiction is imaginative prose that emphasizes the interior, subjective experiences of its characters, especially such prose when it deals with emotional or mental disturbances or anguish. Hawthorne is known for his sharp insights into the human mind. Using Dimmesdale as an example, discuss why *The Scarlet Letter* is a good example of psychological fiction. Are both Dimmesdale and Hester psychologically complex characters? Why, or why not?

Plot Analysis of *The Scarlet Letter*

The Parts of a Plot

A **plot** is a series of events related to a **central conflict**, or struggle. The following diagram, known as Freytag's Pyramid, illustrates the main parts of a plot.

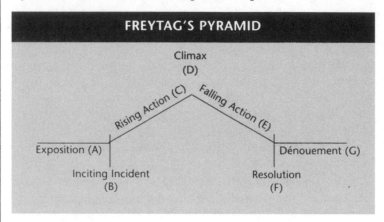

FREYTAG'S PYRAMID

The parts of a plot are as follows:

The **exposition** is the part of a plot that provides background information, often about the characters, setting, or conflict.

The **inciting incident** is the event that introduces the central conflict.

The **rising action**, or **complication**, develops the conflict to a high point of intensity.

The **climax** is the high point of interest or suspense in the plot.

The **falling action** is all the events that follow the climax.

The **resolution** is the point at which the central conflict is ended, or resolved.

The **dénouement** is any material that follows the resolution and that ties up loose ends.

Exposition (A)

Hester Prynne is charged with the sin of adultery after giving birth to an illegitimate child. As punishment, she is forced to stand on a public scaffold for three hours. In addition, she must forever wear a red letter *A* on her dress as a symbol of her sinfulness. Hester had come to the American colonies two years earlier. Her husband was supposed to join her, but he never arrived, and people assume that he was lost at sea. The father of Pearl, Hester's infant, is Hestor's pastor, the Reverend Arthur Dimmesdale. Hester refuses to reveal the father's identity.

Inciting Incident (B)

Hester's lawful husband, who has assumed the name Roger Chillingworth, suddenly appears on the day of Hester's public punishment. He tells Hester not to reveal his identity to anyone. Meanwhile, he vows to seek revenge on the person who ruined his marriage and disgraced his wife.

Rising Action (C)

Chillingworth, a physician, moves in with the ailing Reverend Dimmesdale. Having learned that Dimmesdale is Pearl's father, Chillingworth begins to destroy the minister by means of herbs and subtle psychological torment. Finally, Hester informs Dimmesdale about Chillingworth's true identity. Hester and Dimmesdale subsequently decide to escape with Pearl across the ocean.

Climax (D)

Tormented by a guilty conscience, Dimmesdale realizes that the only way to escape his torment is to go to the scaffold and to reveal his sin to the townspeople. On Election Day, after delivering an inspired sermon, Dimmesdale ascends the scaffold. Chillingworth shouts in protest because he does not want Dimmesdale to be relieved of his torment. Dimmesdale tells Hester that he is dying and then reveals to the crowd that he is Pearl's father.

Falling Action (E)

Dimmesdale collapses onto the scaffold. Hester cradles his head in her arms, while Chillingworth laments the fact that Dimmesdale has escaped him.

Resolution (F)

Dimmesdale asks Pearl for a kiss. She kisses him and cries. This kiss symbolizes the final union of the child with her father. Dimmesdale says good-bye to Hester, asking God to have mercy. Dimmesdale dies.

Dénouement (G)

With Dimmesdale's death, Chillingworth loses his life's purpose—revenge—and dies as well. Hester and Pearl move back to England. Pearl becomes wealthy from money Chillingworth has left her. Pearl marries, and Hester returns to Boston. She voluntarily wears the scarlet letter, and she becomes known as a person of great wisdom to whom many women turn for advice.

Creative Writing Activities

Creative Writing Activity A: Mood and Setting

Hawthorne carefully crafted the opening chapters of *The Scarlet Letter*, setting a particular mood for his story. Write a one-page descriptive piece of your own in which you create a setting and try to set a particular mood. To begin, focus on a setting that you feel you can describe well. Possible settings include a classroom, a family dinner, an office, a beach, or a forest. Then decide what mood you would like to create. What details would you use to describe a classroom filled with excitement? What details would you use to describe a classroom filled with sadness? Begin by making a list of concrete details—images of sight, sound, touch, taste, and smell—that will make your description vivid for a reader.

Creative Writing Activity B: Dialogue

Reread Chapter 4 of *The Scarlet Letter* and notice how Hawthorne carefully crafts the dialogue between Hester and Roger Chillingworth to reveal their attitudes and their relationship. Create your own one-page scene in which two characters reveal themselves through dialogue. Your characters can be based on real people, or they can be completely fictional. Just be sure that you know them well before you begin writing your dialogue. To learn more about your characters, write their names at the top of a sheet of paper. Then list each character's personality traits. Decide what topic your characters are going to discuss or what situation they are in. One way to create interesting dialogue is to imagine a conflict, or struggle, between the characters or a conflict that they face together. Begin creating conversation between your characters, allowing yourself to write freely. Then revise your dialogue, reading it aloud to make sure that each line sounds natural.

Creative Writing Activity C: Humorous Letter

Attitudes have changed dramatically, since Puritan times, toward events such as those that set in motion the plot of this novel. Choose a modern character with attitudes very different from those of Arthur Dimmesdale—a rap singer, for example, or a talk show host—and write a letter to Dimmesdale in that character's voice. See what humor you can derive from the juxtaposition of such opposed world views.

Creative Writing Activity D: Historical Fiction/Poetry

In addition to being a compelling story, *The Scarlet Letter* reflects an interesting and important time in American history by showing readers the values and beliefs of the early Puritans. Write a scene, poem, or story of your own that reflects some aspect of the time and place in which you live. For example, you might write a scene that takes place at a student council meeting, a story about two students in your school, or a poem about a current social issue. Be sure to use vivid details as you write—the kinds of details that will make a future reader truly understand your experience in your own time and place.

Critical Writing Activities

The following topics are suitable for short critical essays on *The Scarlet Letter*. An essay written on one of these topics should begin with an introductory paragraph that states the thesis, or main idea, of the essay. The introductory paragraph should be followed by several paragraphs that support the thesis using examples from the novel. The essay should conclude with a paragraph that summarizes the points made in the body of the essay and that restates the thesis in different words.

Critical Writing Activity A: The Scaffold Scenes as a Structural Device in *The Scarlet Letter*

The Scarlet Letter contains three important scenes that take place on the scaffold in the center of town—the opening scene of the novel, a scene in Chapter 12 (halfway through the book), and the final scene of the novel. Write an essay explaining how these three scaffold scenes represent the basic structure of the book. In your essay, briefly describe the events that occur in each scene and tell how each scene advances the action of the story.

Critical Writing Activity B: The Struggle for the Soul of Arthur Dimmesdale

The events of the opening of *The Scarlet Letter* place Arthur Dimmesdale in a precarious position in which, from the point of view of the narrator, Dimmesdale's soul is in jeopardy. One way to view the novel is as a description of the struggle that takes place between Chillingworth, on the one hand, and Pearl, on the other, for Dimmesdale's soul. Write an essay explaining what Dimmesdale's sin is, what Chillingworth and Pearl want Dimmesdale to do, and why, from the narrator's point of view, Chillingworth's path would lead to Dimmesdale's destruction, whereas Pearl's would lead to his salvation.

Critical Writing Activity C: Hawthorne's Conflicted Narrator in *The Scarlet Letter*

Critics have commented that Hawthorne's narrator seems to be of two minds. Sometimes this narrator seems to adopt a moralizing attitude, condemning Dimmesdale's and Hester's actions and supporting the notion that they must repent for and atone for what they have done. At other times, the narrator seems to adopt the opinion that Dimmesdale's and Hester's actions are understandable given the circumstances, and that love such as theirs represents something truly sacred—the capacity of people to love one another. Write an essay in which you present evidence from the novel to support the idea that the narrator is of two minds on this issue. In the conclusion of your essay, present where you stand on the issue, and why.

Critical Writing Activity D: Truth and Falsehood in *The Scarlet Letter*

In many ways, *The Scarlet Letter* is a story about the consequences of truth and falsehood. Write an essay on the theme of truthfulness in the novel. In your essay, discuss Hester and Dimmesdale's initial falsehood toward Hester's husband, Hester's falsehood toward Dimmesdale in concealing Chillingworth's identity, and Dimmesdale's falsehood toward everyone in concealing his sin. Explain how the conclusion of the novel resolves each of these falsehoods by revealing the truth.

Critical Writing Activity E: The Symbolism of The Black Man and the Forest in *The Scarlet Letter*

Woods, or forests, are traditional symbols of being lost morally or spiritually. Write an essay in which you explain the significance of the forest in *The Scarlet Letter*. Tell how the forest is related to The Black Man and to Dimmesdale's moral confusion. Explain why Hester and Dimmesdale feel free when they meet there, and tell how Chillingworth is associated with The Black Man and, through his medicinal herbs, the forest.

Projects

Project A: Insights into the Puritan Movement

In groups of various sizes, put together presentations about different people, places, and ideas associated with Puritanism in America. Your group should focus on a topic, research that topic, and then present your information to the rest of the class. In presenting a particular topic, you might use words, pictures, or props. Possible topics include Plymouth Colony, the Massachusetts Bay Colony, Pilgrims or Separatist Puritans, William Bradford, John Winthrop, John Calvin, Predestination and Elections, Roger Williams, Anne Hutchinson, the Half-Way Covenant, the Salem Witch Trials, Anne Bradstreet, Cotton Mather, and Jonathan Edwards.

Project B: Meeting of the Boston Magistrates

According to a townsperson in *The Scarlet Letter*, the official punishment for Hester Prynne's crime is death. The magistrates, however, take into account Hester's youth and her husband's lengthy disappearance and decide to treat her case with leniency. The scarlet *A* and three hours on the scaffold are alternatives to the death penalty. Form small groups and act out a scene in which the Boston magistrates discuss Hester's crime and possible punishments. In the scene, the magistrates should discuss the seriousness of the crime and what message they want to send to Hester and to the other people living in Puritan Boston. Draw upon what you've learned from this book's historical introduction and from *The Scarlet Letter* about the values and beliefs of the early Puritans.

Project C: Living Pictures

In theater, a tableau is a living picture created by actors. To create a tableau, an actor or a group of actors, standing motionless and silent, represents one dramatic picture or scene. In small groups, create tableaus, or living pictures, of some of the most striking, dramatic scenes in *The Scarlet Letter*. You might consider any of the three scaffold scenes, a moment between Hester and Pearl or Dimmesdale and Pearl, or a scene involving Chillingworth and Dimmesdale. In creating your living pictures, depict the drama of a particular scene with appropriate poses and facial expressions and without sound or motion. You might use costumes and props, but these are not completely necessary. The tableaus can be as simple or as elaborate as you would like. When one group creates a picture, the other members of the class should try to guess which scene is being depicted.

Project D: Panel Discussion

Assemble a panel of characters from the *Scarlet Letter*. Class members should take turns sitting on the panel playing the roles of Hester Prynne, Arthur Dimmesdale, Roger Chillingworth, Pearl, Governor Bellingham, John Wilson, Mistress Hibbins, and two average townspeople—a man and a woman. Students who are not sitting on the panel should ask the panel members questions related to the action and events of *The Scarlet Letter* and to Puritan society in general. Each person sitting on the panel should concentrate on truly becoming his or her character and responding to questions appropriately. Before beginning, you might want to brainstorm possible questions and discussion topics for the panel.

Glossary

a • bate (ə bāt´) *vt.*, lessen, diminish

ab • hor • rence (ab hôr´əns) *n.*, loathing, detestation

a • bode (ə bōd´) *n.*, home

a • bom • i • na • tion (ə bäm´ə nā´shən) *n.*, something hateful or disgusting

ab • struse (ab strōōs´) *adj.*, hard to understand

ac • crue (ə krōō´) *vi.*, come as a natural growth

ac • cu • mu • la • tion (ə kyōōm´yōō lā´shən) *n.*, collection or pile that has increased over time

ac • qui • esce (ak´wē es´) *vi.*, consent

a • cute • ness (ə kyōōt´nəs) *n.*, quickness of mind; sensitivity to impressions

ad • duce (ad´yōō s) *vt.*, give as reason or proof

ad • vent (ad´vent´) *n.*, coming or arrival

ad • verse (ad vʉrs´) *adj.*, unfavorable, harmful

af • fin • i • ty (ə fin´i tē) *n.*, close relationship; connection

ag • i • tate (aj´i tāt´) *vt.*, excite; stir up strong emotions

ag • i • ta • tion (aj´ə tā´shən) *n.*, emotional disturbance

a • lac • ri • ty (ə lak´rə tē) *n.*, eager willingess or readiness

a • me • na • ble (ə mē´nə bəl) *adj.*, obedient

a • nath • e • ma (ə nath´ə mə) *n.*, curse

an • ni • hi • late (ə nī´ə lāt´) *vt.*, destroy completely; kill

an • tip • a • thy (an tip´ə thē) *n.*, aversion; deep dislike

ap • palled (ə pôld´) *adj.*, filled with horror or dismay

ap • pre • hen • sive (ap´rē hen´siv) *adj.*, anxious or fearful

as • cet • ic (ə set´ik) *adj.*, severe; self-denying

as • per • i • ty (ə sper´ə tē) *n.*, harshness of temper

as • pi • ra • tion (as´pə rā´shən) *n.*, desire, ambition

as • pire (ə spīr´) *vi.*, seek

as • sim • i • late (ə sim´ə lāt´) *vt.*, make like

at • trib • ute (a trə byōōt´) *n.*, characteristic or quality

au • dac • i • ty (ô das´ə tē) *n.*, shameless boldness; daring

au • gur (ô´ger) *vt.*, foretell, prophesize

aus • ter • i • ty (ô ster´ə tē) *n.*, plainness

a • venge (ə venj´) *vt.*, get revenge

a • ver (ə vʉr´) *vt.*, affirm; declare to be true

a • wry (ə rī´) *adj.*, wrong; amiss

bane (bān) *n.*, cause of distress, death, or ruin

be • nev • o • lence (bə nev´ə ləns) *n.*, kindliness; tendency to be charitable

be • nev • o • lent (bə nev´ə lənt) *adj.*, kind

be • nign (bi nīn´) *adj.,* kind

boor • ish (bo͞or´ish) *adj.,* rude, awkward

ca • ba • lis • tic (kab´ə lis´tik) *adj.,* occult

ca • dence (kād´´ns) *n.,* rhythmic flow of sound

ca • lam • i • ty (kə lam´ə tē) *n.,* disaster

ca • price (kə prēs´) *n.,* whim

cha • os (kā´äs´) *n.,* extreme disorder and confusion

col • lo • quy (käl´ə kwē) *n.,* formal discussion

com • mence (kə mens´) *vt.,* begin

com • pel (kəm pel´) *vt,* force

com • pul • sion (kəm pul´shən) *n.,* force, coercion

con • cord (kän´kôrd´) *n.,* harmony; agreement

con • dem • na • tion (kän´dəm nā´shen´) *n.,* severe reproof or censure

con • de • scen • sion (kän´di sen´shən) *n.,* act of descending voluntarily to the level of another

con • ge • nial (kən jēn´yəl) *adj.,* compatible

con • jec • ture (kən jek´chər) *vi.,* guess

con • junc • tion (kən juŋk´shən) *n.,* combination

con • ju • ra • tion (kän´jo͞o ra´shən) *n.,* magic; sorcery

con • spic • u • ous (kən spik´ yo͞o əs) *adj.,* noticeable

con • ster • na • tion (kän´stər nā´shən) *n.,* great fear that makes one feel helpless

con • sti • tute (kän´stə to͞o t´) *vt.,* form

con • strain (kən strān´) *vt.,* force, compel; restrain

con • strained (kən strānd´) *adj.,* forced

con • temp • tu • ous (kə temp´cho͞o əs) *adj.,* scornful, disdainful

con • ti • gu • i • ty (kän´tə gyo͞o´ə tē) *n.,* nearness or contact

con • tig • u • ous (kən tig´ yo͞o əs) *adj.,* near, adjacent

con • trive (kən trīv´) *vt.,* scheme, plan

con • tu • ma • cious • ly (kän´ tyo͞o mā´shəs lē) *adv.,* rebelliously

con • vert (kən vʉrt´) *vt.,* transform

con • vul • sive (kən vul´ siv) *adj.,* having the nature of violent, involuntary spasms

coun • te • nance (koun´tə nəns) *n.,* face

coun • te • nance (koun´tə nəns) *vt.,* give support or permission to

cred • i • bil • i • ty (kred´ə bil´i tē) *n.,* believability

daunt • less (dônt´ les) *adj.,* fearless

dearth (dʉrth) *n.,* scarcity, lack

dec • o • rous • ly (dek´ə rəs lē) *adv.,* showing good behavior

de • crep • it (dē krep´it) *adj.,* broken down or worn out by age de • file (dē fīl´) *vt.,* corrupt, make impure

del • e • te • ri • ous (del´ə tir´ē əs) *adj.,* harmful to health or well-being

de • mean • or (di mēn´ər) *n.,* conduct

de • prav • i • ty (dē prav´ə tē) *n.,* corruption, wickedness

dep • re • da • tion (dep´rə dā´shən) *n.,* wicked act

de • ri • sive • ly (di rī´siv lē) *adv.,* in a ridiculing manner

de • rive (di rīv´) *vt.,* get or receive

de • spond • en • cy (di spän´dən sē) *n.,* dejection; loss of hope

des • pot • ic (des pät´ik) *adj.,* autocratic, tyrannical

det • ri • ment (de´trə mənt) *n.,* damage, injury, harm

de • void (di void´) *adj.,* completely without

dex • ter • i • ty (deks ter´ə tē) *n.,* skill in using hands

di • lap • i • dat • ed (də lap´ə dāt´id) *adj.,* shabby, neglected, and broken down

dis • cern (di zʉrń) *vt.,* recognize

dis • course (dis´kôrś) *n.,* lecture

dis • in • clined (dis´in klīnd´) *adj.,* unwilling, reluctant

dis • pel (di spel´) *vt.,* make vanish

dis • rep • u • ta • ble (dis rep´yo͞o tə bəl) *adj.,* causing a bad reputation

dis • so • lute (dis´ə lo͞ot´) *adj.,* immoral

dis • tort • ing (di stôrt´iŋ) *adj.,* shape-changing; modifying

di • verge (dī vʉrj´) *vi.,* go or move in different directions

dole • ful • ly (dōl´fəl lē) *adv.,* mournfully

du • plic • i • ty (do͞o plis´ə tē) *n.,* deception; double-dealing

ear • nest • ly (ʉr´ nist lē) *adv.,* seriously and sincerely

ec • cen • tric • i • ty (ek ´sən tris´ə tē) *n.,* oddity

ed • i • fice (ed´i fis) *n.,* large, imposing building

ef • fer • ves • cence (ef´ər ves´əns) *n.,* lively, high-spirited state

ef • fi • ca • cy (ef´i kə sē) *n.,* effectiveness

ef • flu • ence (ef´lo͞o əns) *n.,* flowing forth; emanation

ef • fu • sion (e fyo͞o´zhən) *n.,* emotional expression

e • ma • ci • at • ed (ē mā´ shē āt´ əd) *adj.,* abnormally thin

e • man • ci • pate (ē man´sə pāt´) *vt.,* make free

em • i • nence (em´i nəns) *n.,* high place

em • i • nent (em´ə nent) *adj.,* famous; distinguished

e • mol • u • ment (ē mäl ´yo͞o ment) *n.,* payment for work

en • cum • brance (en kum´brəns) *n.,* hindrance, burden

en • dow (en dou´) *vt.,* provide with a quality

en • er • vat • ing (en´ər vāt´iŋ) *adj.,* debilitating, weakening

en • fee • ble (en fē´bəl) *vt.,* make weak or frail

en • gross (en grōs´) *vt.,* express formally

e • nig • ma (i nig´mə) *n.,* mystery

en • mi • ty (en´mə tē) *n.,* hostility

en • tice (en tīs´) *vt.,* tempt, lure

en • treat • y (en trēt´ē) *n.,* earnest request

er • u • dite (er´yo͞o dīt) *adj.,* scholarly; learned

er • u • di • tion (er´yo͞o dish´ən) *n.,* learning acquired by study

es • teem (e stēm´) *vt.,* regard highly

e • vade (ē vād´) *vi.,* escape

ev • a • nes • cent (ev´ə nes´ənt) *adj.,* ephemeral; short-lived; likely to vanish or disappear

ex • em • pla • ry (eg zem´plə rē) *adj.,* serving as a model or example; worth imitating

ex • hort (eg zôrt´) *vt.,* urge strongly

ex • hor • ta • tion (eg´zôr tā´shən) *n.,* plea; warning

ex • i • gen • cy (eks´ə jen sē) *n.,* pressing need; demand; requirement

ex • pa • ti • ate (eks pā´she at´) *vi.,* speak in great detail; elaborate

ex • pi • a • tion (eks´ pē ā´ shən) *n.,* act of making amends; reparation

ex • pos • tu • la • tion (eks päs´ chə lā´ shən) *n.,* objection

ex • tant (eks´tənt) *adj.,* existing

ex • ten • u • a • tion (ek sten´yo͞o ā´shən) *n.,* partial excuse

ex • tort (eks tôrt´) *vt.,* get something through violence or threats

fath • om • less (fath´əm lis) *adj.,* incomprehensible, very deep

feign (fān) *vt.,* make a false show of; pretend

fe • roc • i • ty (fə räs´ə tē) *n.,* fierceness, savageness

fer • vent (fur´vənt) *adj.,* passionate; emotional

fer • vor (fur´vər) *n.,* zeal, passion

fla • grant (flā´grənt) *adj.,* outrageous

flor • id (flôr´id) *adj.,* ruddy, red

for • lorn (fôr lôrn´) *adj.,* wretched; miserable

for • ti • tude (fôrt´ə to͞od´) *n.,* strength to bear pain and misfortune

gal • ling (gôl´ in) *adj.,* annoying; bitter

ge • ni • al (jēn´yəl) *adj.,* friendly and sympathetic

ges • tic • u • late (jes tik´yo͞o lāt´) *vi.,* express through movement

ges • tic • u • la • tion (jes tik´yo͞o lā´shən) *n.,* energetic motion

glean (glēn) *vi.,* collect or gather

grave (grāv) *adj.,* serious; grievous

gris • ly (griz´lē) *adj.,* ghastly; terrifying

hag • gard (hag´ərd) *adj.,* having a wild, worn look

har • row (har´ō) *vt.,* cause mental distress

haugh • ty (hôt´ ē) *adj.,* proud, scornful

heed • ful (hēd´ fəl) *adj.*, careful

het • er • o • ge • ne • ous (het´ər ō´jē´nē əs) *adj.*, varied; made up of unlike parts

ig • no • min • i • ous • ly (ig´nə min´ē əs lē) *adv.*, shamefully; despicably

ig • no • min • y (ig´nə min´ē) *n.*, shame, dishonor

im • bibe (im bīb´) *vi.*, drink

im • bue (im byo͞o ´) *vt.*, fill or permeate

im • pal • pa • ble (im pal´ pə bəl) *adj.*, lacking substance; not perceivable through touch

im • pede (im pēd´) *vt.*, hinder

im • ped • i • ment (im ped´ə mənt) *n.*, obstacle

im • pel (im pel´) *vt.*, force, urge

im • per • a • tive • ly (im per´ə tiv lē) *adv.*, commandingly; urgently

im • per • cep • ti • ble (im´pər sep´tə bəl) *adj.*, not easily noticed

im • pe • ri • ous (im pir´ē əs) *adj.*, commanding

im • pi • e • ty (im pī´ə tē) *n.*, lack of respect

im • pli • cate (im´pli kāt´) *vt.*, show to be connected to a crime

im • plic • it • ly (im plis´it lē) *adv.*, absolutely, unquestionably

im • por • tu • nate • ly (im pôr´tu nit lē) *adv.*, annoyingly urgent or persistent

im • pu • ni • ty (im pyo͞o´ni tē) *n.*, exemption

im • pute (im pyo͞ot´) *vt.*, attribute; charge with

in • aus • pi • cious (in´ô spish´əs) *adj.*, unfavorable, unlucky

in • cite (in sīt´) *vt.*, urge to action

in • co • her • ent (in´kō hir´ənt) *adj.*, not clearly articulated; not logically connected

in • con • ceiv • a • ble (in´kən sēv´ə bəl) *adj.*, that cannot be thought of, understood, or believed

in • con • gru • i • ty (in´kän gro͞o´i tē) *n.*, lack of agreement or appropriateness

in • cor • po • rate (in kôr´pə rāt) *vt.*, make part of another thing

in • cre • du • li • ty (in´krə do͞o´lə tē) *n.*, unwillingness to believe; doubt

in • cum • ben • cy (in kum´bən sē) *n.*, term of office

in • cur (in kʉr´) *vt.*, bring upon oneself

in • de • fat • i • ga • ble (in´di fat´i gə bəl) *adj.*, untiring; not yielding to fatigue

in • de • fea • si • ble (in´dē fē´zə bəl) *adj.*, not capable of being undone

in • dif • fer • ent • ly (in dif´ər ənt lē) *adv.*, apathetically; without interest

in • do • lent (in´də lənt) *adj.*, lazy; idle

in • du • bi • ta • bly (in do͞o´bi tə blē) *adv.*, unquestionably

in • ev • i • ta • ble (in ev´i tə bəl) *adj.*, unavoidable

in • ev • i • ta • bly (in ev´i tə blē) *adv.*, unavoidably

in • ex • tri • ca • ble (in eks´tri kə bəl) *adj.*, incapable of being untangled or untied

in • fa • my (in´ fə mē) *n.*, dishonor, disgrace

in • fer • ence (in´fər əns) *n.*, conclusion

in • fir • mi • ty (in fʉr´mə tē) *n.*, weakness

in • ge • nu • i • ty (in´jə no͞o´ə tē) *n.*, cleverness

i • nim • i • cal (i nim´i kəl) *adj.,* in opposition; hostile

in • iq • ui • ty (i nik´wi tē) *n.,* wickedness

in • nate (in´nāt´) *adj.,* naturally existing from birth

in • op • por • tune (in äp´ər to͞on´) *adj.,* inappropriate

in • op • por • tune • ness (in äp´ər to͞on´nəs) *n.,* inappropriateness; poor timing

in • quis • i • to • ri • al (in kwiz´ə tôr´ē əl) *adj.,* questioning; prying

in • scru • ta • ble (in skro͞ot´ə bəl) *adj.,* mysterious

in • sid • i • ous (in sid´ē əs) *adj.,* sly, crafty

in • sub • or • di • na • tion (in´ sə bor´də nā´shən) *n.,* disobedience

in • teg • ri • ty (in teg´rə tē) *n.,* wholeness; soundness characterized by adherence to moral principles

in • ter • po • si • tion (in´tər pə zish´ən) *n.,* interruption or intervention

in • ter • ven • ing (in´tər vēn´ iŋ) *adj.,* coming between

in • ti • ma • tion (in´tə mā´shən) *n.,* hint; indirect suggestion

in • tri • cate (in´tri kit) *adj.,* complex

in • trin • sic (in trin´sik) *adj.,* not dependent on exterior forces; inherent

in • tu • i • tion (in to͞o ish´ən) *n.,* ability to know without conscious reasoning

in • ure (in yo͞or´) *vt.,* make accustomed to

in • vet • er • ate • ly (in vet´ər it lē) *adv.,* firmly; habitually

in • vi • o • la • ble (in vī´ō lə bəl) *adj.,* safe or secure against envy or violation; sacred

irk • some (ʉrk´səm) *adj.,* annoying

ir • ref • ra • ga • ble (ir ref´rə gə bəl) *adj.,* indisputable

ir • re • press • i • bly (ir´ri pres´ə blē) *adv.,* unrestrainably

ir • rev • er • ent (ir rev´ər ənt) *adj.,* disrespectful

ir • rev • o • ca • bly (ir´rəv´ə kə blē) *adv.,* unchangeably

joc • u • lar • i • ty (jäk´yo͞o lar´ə tē) *n.,* humor

lam • en • ta • tion (lam´ən tā´shən) *n.,* expression of grief

la • tent (lāt´´nt) *adj.,* present but not visible

lan • guid (laŋ´gwid) *adj.,* indifferent; dull

lan • guor (laŋ´gər) *n.,* lack of interest or spirit; indifference and sluggishness

lat • i • tude (lat´ə to͞od´) *n.,* freedom of opinion and action

lo • quac • i • ty (lō kwas´ə tē) *n.,* talkativeness

lu • di • crous (lo͞o´di krəs) *adj.,* absurd, ridiculous

lu • rid (lo͞or´ id) *adj.,* shocking, sensational

mach • i • na • tions (mak´ə nā´shəns) *n.,* evil plans and plotting

ma • lev • o • lence (mə lev´ə ləns) *n.,* malice, ill will

mal • ice (mal´is) *n.,* ill will; spite

ma • lig • nant (mə lig´nənt) *adj.,* harmful, dangerous

man • i • fest (man ´ə fest´) *adj.,* apparent to the senses

mel • an • chol • y (mel´ən käl´ē) *adj.,* sad; gloomy

mien (mēn) *n.,* manner, bearing

mis • an • thro • py (mis an´thrə pē) *n.*, hatred or distrust of all people

mol • li • fy (mäl´ə fī´) *vt.*, soothe the temper of

mu • ta • bil • i • ty (myo͞ot´ə bil´ə tē) *n.*, ability to change

non • en • ti • ty (nän´en´tə tē) *n.*, person of little or no importance

nuc • le • us (no͞o´ klē əs) *n.*, center

nu • ga • to • ry (no͞o´gə tôr´ē) *adj.*, worthless

o • bei • sance (ō bā´səns) *n.*, feelings of respect; homage

ob • scure • ly (əb skyo͞or´lē) *adv.*, indistinctly

ob • sti • na • cy (äb´stə nə sē) *n.*, stubbornness

ob • tuse • ness (äb to͞os´nəs) *n.*, slowness of understanding

o • di • ous (ō´dē əs) *adj.*, repugnant, detestable

om • i • nous (äm´ə nəs) *adj.*, threatening

out • land • ish (out´lan ´dish) *adj.*, very odd, bizarre

pac • i • fy (pas´ə fī´) *vt.*, make calm

per • emp • to • ry (pər emp´tə rē) *adj.*, unable to be delayed

per • pe • trate (pʉr´pe trāt´) *vt.*, commit; do something wrong

per • vade (pər vād´) *vt.*, be prevalent throughout

per • verse (pər vʉrś) *adj.*, stubbornly contrary; wicked

per • vers • i • ty (pər vʉr´sə tē) *n.*, wickedness; stubborn contrariness

pes • ti • lence (pes´tə ləns) *n.*, fatal, contagious disease

pet • u • lant (pech´ə lənt) *adj.*, impatient or irritable

pith • y (pith´ē) *adj.*, short and full of meaning

pla • cid • i • ty (plə sid´ə tē) *n.*, calmness, tranquility

plain • tive (plān´tiv) *adj.*, mournful; sad

pon • der • ous (pän´dər əs) *adj.*, labored; heavy

pos • ter • i • ty (päs ter´ə tē) *n.*, descendants

po • tent (pōt´ ´nt´) *adj.*, powerful

po • ten • tate (pōt´´n tāt´) *n.*, monarch, ruler

prec • i • pice (pres´i pis) *n.*, steep cliff

pred • i • lec • tion (pred´´l ek´shən) *n.*, preference; preconceived liking

pre • coc • i • ty (pri käs´ə tē) *n.*, premature development

pre • ter • nat • u • ral • ly (prē´tər nach´ər əl lē) *adv.*, abnormally, supernaturally

pre • vail (prē vāl´) *vi.*, triumph

pris • tine (pris´tēn) *adj.*, pure, uncorrupted

pro • bi • ty (prō´bə tē) *n.*, good character

pro • cure (prō kyo͞or´) *vt.*, obtain

pro • found (prō found´) *adj.*, very deep

pro • lif • ic (prō lif´ik) *adj.*, fertile; abounding

prom • i • nence (präm´ə nəns) *n.*, conspicuous position or state

prop • a • gate (präp´ə gāt´) *vt.*, reproduce

pro • pen • si • ty (prə pen´sə tē) *n.*, inclination

pro • pin • qui • ty (prō piŋ´kwə tē) *n.*, nearness of relationship

pro • voke (prō vōk´) *vt.*, excite to some feeling

prox • im • i • ty (präks im´ə tē) *n.*, nearness

ran • sack (ran´sak´) *vt.*, examine thoroughly

re • buke (ri byo͞ok´) *n.*, sharp reprimand

re • cip • ro • cate (ri sip´rə kāt´) *vt.*, give or do in return

re • du • pli • cate (ri do͞o´plə kāt´) *vt.*, to double, or repeat

ref • u • ta • tion (ref´yə ta´shən) *n.*, disproof

re • lin • quish (ri liŋ´kwish) *vt.*, give up, abandon

rem • i • nis • cence (rem´ə nis´ əns) *n.*, memory, recollection

re • mon • strance (ri män´strəns) *n.*, act of protesting or objecting

ren • der (ren´dər) *vt.*, cause to become, make

re • pose (ri pōz´) *n.*, rest; peace of mind

re • pu • di • ate (ri pyo͞o ´dē at´) *vt.*, cast off publicly

re • pug • nance (ri pug´nəns) *n.*, extreme dislike; aversion

res • ig • na • tion (re´zig nā´shən) *n.*, passive acceptance

ret • ri • bu • tion (re´trə byo͞o´shən) *n.*, punishment

re • ver • ber • ate (ri vur´bə rāt´) *vi.*, echo

sa • ga • cious • ly (sə gā´shəs lē) *adv.*, in a manner that shows keen perception or sound judgment

sa • gac • i • ty (sə gas´ə tē) *n.*, shrewdness; intelligence and sound judgment

sanc • ti • ty (sank´tə tē) *n.*, sacredness

scant • ly (skant´lē) *adv.*, scarcely, barely

scru • pu • lous (skro͞o´pyə ləs) *adj.*, extremely careful

scru • ti • ny (skro͞ot´ nē) *n.*, close examination

scur • ri • lous (skur´ə ləs) *adj.*, vulgar; indecent

sed • u • lous (sej´o͞o ləs) *adj.*, diligent; working hard and steadily

se • ver • i • ty (sə ver´ə tē) *n.*, strictness

si • mil • i • tude (sə mil´ə to͞od´) *n.*, likeness

so • journ (sō´ jurn) *n.*, brief or temporary stay

sol • ace (säl´is) *n.*, consolation; easing of grief or discomfort

som • nif • er • ous (säm nif´ər əs) *adj.*, inducing sleep

stealth • i • ly (stel´thə lē) *adv.*, slyly; in a secretive manner

sub • dued (səb do͞od´) *adj.*, softened; diminished

sub • ju • gate (sub´jə gāt´) *vt.*, make subservient

suc • cor (suk´ər) *vt.*, assist

suf • fice (sə fīs´) *vi.*, be sufficient; be enough

sun • der (sun´dər) *vt.*, break apart, separate

su • per • flu • ous (sə pur´flo͞o əs) *adj.*, excessive; not needed

sup • pos • i • tion (sup´ə zish´ ən) *n.*, assumption, hypothesis

sus • tain (sə stān´) *vt.*, support, buoy up

taint (tānt) *n.*, corruption or evil; a moral defect considered as a stain or spot

te • di • ous (tē´dē əs) *adj.*, tiresome, boring

tem • pes • tu • ous (tem pes´ cho͞o əs) *adj.*, violent, turbulent

tem • po • ral (tem´pə rəl) *adj.*, existing in time; worldly; not spiritual

te • na • cious • ly (tə nā´shəs lē) *adv.*, stubbornly; persistently

te • nac • i • ty (tə nas´ə tē) *n.*, stubborn persistance

thwart (thwôrt) *vt.*, hinder, obstruct

tor • pid (tôr´pid) *adj.*, dormant, sluggish

trans • gress (trans gres´) *vi.*, break a law or commandment; commit a sin

tran • si • to • ry (tran´sə tôr´ē) *adj.*, temporary, fleeting

trans • mute (trans myo͞ot´) *vi.*, transform

trem • u • lous (trem´yo͞o ləs) *adj.*, trembling, quivering

tri • fling (trī´fliŋ) *adj.*, trivial, of little value

truc • u • len • cy (truk´yo͞o lən cē) *n.*, meanness, ferocity

tu • mult (to͞o´mult´) *n.*, commotion, confusion

ul • te • ri • or (ul tir´ē ər) *adj.*, undisclosed; lying beyond what is evident or of immediate interest

unc • tion (uŋk´shən) *n.*, earnestness

un • du • lat • ing (un´dyo͞o lāt´ iŋ) *adj.*, wavy

un • feign • ed • ly (un fān´id le) *adv.*, genuinely, sincerely

un • in • tel • li • gi • ble (un´in tel´i jə bəl) *adj.*, incomprehensible; not understandable

un • mal • le • a • ble (un mal´ē ə bəl) *adj.*, not pliable, not adaptable

un • wont • ed (un wän´tid) *adj.*, unusual; rare

val • iant • ly (val´yənt lē) *adv.*, with courage, resolutely

ve • he • ment • ly (vē´ə mənt lē) *adv.*, passionately; violently

ven • er • a • ble (ven´ər ə bəl) *adj.*, impressive; worthy of respect

ven • er • a • tion (ven´ər ā´shən) *n.*, feeling of deep respect

ven • ture (ven´chər) *vi.*, go or do at some risk

ves • tige (ves´tij) *n.*, trace of something that once existed

vi • cis • si • tude (vi sis´ə to͞od´) *n.*, change

vie (vī) *vi.*, compete

vil • i • fy (vil´ə fī´) *vt.*, put down; slander

vile • ness (vīl´nəs) *n.*, evilness, offensiveness

vi • vac • i • ty (vī vas´ə tē) *n.*, liveliness of spirit

vo • lu • mi • nous (və lo͞om´ə nəs) *adj.*, having a large capacity or interior area

vogue (vōg) *n.*, popularity

writh • ing (rīth´ iŋ) *adj.*, twisting, distressing

zeal • ous • ly (zel´əs lē) *adv.*, enthusiastically, fervently

Handbook of Literary Terms

Characterization. Characterization is the use of literary techniques to create a character. Writers use three major techniques to create characters: direct description, portrayal of characters' behavior, and representations of characters' internal states. When using direct description, the writer, through a speaker, a narrator, or another character, simply comments on the character, telling the reader about such matters as the character's appearance, habits, dress, background, personality, motivations, and so on. When using portrayal of a character's behavior, the writer presents the actions and speech of the character, allowing the reader to draw his or her own conclusions from what the character says or does. When using representations of internal states, the writer reveals directly the character's private thoughts and emotions.

Dialogue. Dialogue is conversation involving two or more people or characters. Plays are made up of dialogue and stage directions. Fictional works are made up of dialogue, narration, and description.

Foreshadowing. Foreshadowing is the act of presenting materials that hint at events to occur later in a story.

Image. An **image** is a word or phrase that names something that can be seen, heard, touched, tasted, or smelled. The images in a literary work are referred to, collectively, as the work's imagery.

Imagery. See image.

Irony. Irony is a difference between appearance and reality. Types of irony include the following: *dramatic irony,* in which something is known by the reader or audience but unknown to the characters; *verbal irony,* in which a statement is made that implies its opposite; and *irony of situation,* in which an event occurs that violates the expectations of the characters, the reader, or the audience.

Mood. Mood, or atmosphere, is the emotion created in the reader by part or all of a literary work. A writer creates a mood through judicious use of concrete details.

Motivation. A **motivation** is a force that moves a character to think, feel, or behave in a certain way.

Personification. **Personification** is a figure of speech in which an idea, animal, or thing is described as if it were a person.

Psychological Fiction. **Psychological fiction** is fiction that emphasizes the interior, subjective experiences of its characters, and especially fiction that deals with emotional or mental disturbance or anguish.

Repetition. **Repetition** is the use, again, of a sound, word, phrase, sentence, or other element

Satire. **Satire** is humorous writing or speech intended to point out errors, falsehoods, foibles, or failings. It is written for the purpose of reforming human behavior or human institutions.

Setting. The **setting** of a literary work is the time and place in which it occurs, together with all the details used to create a sense of a particular time and place. Writers create setting by various means. In fiction, setting is most often revealed by means of description of such elements as landscape, scenery, buildings, furniture, clothing, the weather, and the season. It can also be revealed by how characters talk and behave. In its widest sense, setting includes the general social, political, moral, and psychological conditions in which characters find themselves.

Suspense. **Suspense** is a feeling of expectation, anxiousness, or curiosity created by questions raised in the mind of a reader or viewer.

Symbol. A **symbol** is a thing that stands for or represents both itself and something else. Writers use two types of symbols—conventional and personal, or idiosyncratic. A *conventional symbol* is one with traditional, widely recognized associations. Such symbols include doves for peace; laurel wreaths for heroism or poetic excellence; the color green for jealousy; the color purple for royalty; the color red for anger;

morning or spring for youth; winter, evening, or night for old age; wind for change or inspiration; rainbows for hope; roses for beauty; the moon for fickleness or inconstancy; roads or paths for the journey through life; woods or darkness for moral or spiritual confusion; thorns for troubles or pain; stars for unchangeableness or constancy; mirrors for vanity or introspection; snakes for evil or duplicity; and owls for wisdom. A *personal* or *idiosyncratic symbol* is one that assumes its secondary meaning because of the special use to which it is put by a writer.

Theme. A **theme** is a central idea in a literary work.

Tone. **Tone** is the emotional attitude toward the reader or toward the subject implied by a literary work. Examples of the different tones that a work may have include familiar, ironic, playful, sarcastic, serious, and sincere.

Transcendentalism. As a variation of European Romanticism, **Transcendentalism** advocated a belief in spiritual, or transcendent, truths beyond sense perception and material existence. Placing oneself in natural environs would increase one's ability to attain transcendent thought. In contrast to the materialism valued by the Puritans and Benjamin Franklin, Transcendentalists exalted the spiritual and the individual.